THE THREE SISTERS

May Sinclair

THE THREE SISTERS

With a new Introduction by
Jean Radford

The Dial Press
DOUBLEDAY & COMPANY, INC.
GARDEN CITY, NEW YORK
1985

Published by The Dial Press

First published in Great Britain by The Macmillan Co., 1914

Copyright © Mrs. H. L. Sinclair 1946
Introduction copyright © Jean Radford 1982

Manufactured in the United States of America
All rights reserved

10 9 8 7 6 5 4 3 2 1

Library of Congress Cataloging in Publication Data
Sinclair, May.
The three sisters.
I. Title.
PR6037.I73T5   1985   823'.912   84-23266
ISBN 0-385-19703-9

INTRODUCTION

The Three Sisters was first published in October 1914, barely two months after the outbreak of the First World War and shortly after May Sinclair's visit to an ambulance unit serving in Belgium. So despite Ezra Pound's view that the novel was "the best she has done", it was somewhat submerged by subsequent events. Yet if the war marked the end of an era and, particularly for women, the start of·something new, this novel, May Sinclair's tenth, has a special historical significance.

For *The Three Sisters* (like D. H. Lawrence's story 'The Daughters of the Vicar' published in the same year) examines the situation of many middle-class women of the Victorian and Edwardian periods. It focuses not on 'the New Woman' – the Sue Bridesheads or Ann Veronicas – but on the sexual and emotional lives of their predecessors. The three Cartaret sisters and their clergyman father are modelled partly on the early Victorian Brontës, but are portraits in a 20th-century retrospective – illuminated by the insights of the contemporary feminist movement and the "new psychology" of Freud, Jung and Havelock Ellis.

The parallel with the Brontës' situation and setting is both striking and deliberate. May Sinclair (1863–1946), a novelist, poet and translator whose first works were published in the 1890s, had just written a series of introductions to the Brontë novels re-issued by Dent between 1907–1914, and in 1912 published *The Three Brontës* – of which the novel's title is a strategic echo. In this early feminist study of the Brontë sisters'

work, Sinclair suggests that a particular tradition of women's
writing begins here. As she says in an introductory comment
to *Villette*:

> The book is flung, as it were, from Lucy's beating heart;
> it is one profound protracted cry of longing and frustra-
> tion. This was a new voice in literature. *Villette* was the
> unsealing of the sacred secret springs, the revelation of
> all that proud, decorous mid-Victorian reticence most
> sedulously sought to hide. There is less overt, audacious
> passion than in *Jane Eyre*, but there is a surer, a subtler
> and more intimate psychology.

The 'sacred secret springs' of sexual feeling that in *Jane Eyre*
are presented in image and symbol, are in *The Three Sisters*
treated more analytically. Sinclair uses her knowledge of
psychoanalytic theory to dramatise the tension between conscious and unconscious motives in her characters, between the
social rationalisations and the irrational forces of their sexual
drives. In this she was undoubtedly influenced by the new
developments in psychology: Freud's *Three Contributions to a
Theory of Sexuality* first appeared in English in 1910, and
Havelock Ellis' *Studies in the Psychology of Sex* was published
between 1897–1910.

May Sinclair did not in fact need Freud or Jung to convince
her of the centrality of sexuality. In an earlier novel *The
Helpmate* (1907) she had already made a major assault on the
Victorian stereotype of the sexless angel in the house, suggesting that the asexual, spiritual woman, was an abnormal and
destructive idealisation. This novel is a very early study of the
power and importance of women's sexuality. What May
Sinclair liked about the new psychoanalytic ideas was that they
confirmed and theorised her own beliefs not only in the
importance of sexual drives and the harmful effects of
repression, but also in the personal and social value of sexual

development and expression. As she stated in her 1916 essay 'Symbolism and Sublimation', in the psychoanalysts she found support for her view that organised religion and the family were the enemies of women's (and men's) development.

> Jung's quarrel with Christian religion is that besides being a first-class engine of repression it has fostered an infantile dependence on God as the father to which man is already too much prone. Parents and man's childish passion for them are the backward forces that retard his development as an individual . . . the conflict with parents must be fought to the finish and the child must win it or remain forever immature.

It was from these liberating aspects of psychoanalysis that Sinclair attempted to develop the 'intimate psychology' of *Villette*.

The element of social protest in Charlotte Brontë's novels is also developed and extended in *The Three Sisters*. There is a sharp critique of Victorian forms of marriage and the family, which was informed by May Sinclair's involvement in the feminist debates of the period. The role of men as well as institutions is subjected to a more careful scrutiny than in *Jane Eyre*. Gwenda Cartaret is as much in revolt against a life of "making puddings and knitting stockings" as was Jane Eyre, but unlike Charlotte Brontë's heroine there is no Byronic hero to come to the rescue – only a tyrannical father and a local doctor uselessly sacrificed to her younger sister's health and happiness.

The Vicar of Garth is used as the embodiment of patriarchal power, and the claustrophobia and petty tyrannies of clerical ménage are vividly presented. Sensual, without self-knowledge and to himself "the image of rectitude", he is an unwilling celibate who gets his satisfaction by keeping his daughters from theirs. When finally deprived of this by their revolt, he suffers a stroke and defence amnesia which, in effect enable him to retain the services of his only unmarried daughter. Steven Rowcliffe, the only "eligible" male in the district, is also critically presented. Though an able and socially responsible physician, trained in one of the teaching hospitals in Leeds and an enlightened reader of Pierre Janet's work on hysteria, the 'spots of commonness' in his character emerge in his relations with women. It is his male vanity which is antagonised by the independence of the sister he loves, and his love of masculine comforts which ensnares him into marriage with the "womanly" Mary. Sinclair analyses with great acuity the process whereby these conventional attitudes to women undermine Rowcliffe's own self-development and lead to his personal and professional degeneration. In this portrait she draws on both Lydgate in George Eliot's *Middlemarch* and Dr John in *Villette*, but as a character he is individual enough to be both substantial and convincing.

The third male character in the novel has some resemblance to Branwell Brontë in his uncontrolled drinking habits, and Sinclair develops him as a contrast to both Cartaret and Rowcliffe. He represents a more primitive instinctual type of maleness, the "natural" rebel against the forces of repression. Unlike Gwenda, whose mystical appreciation of the natural world he shares, he is able to realise his own nature and to enable Alice to realise her sexual and maternal impulses. In. many ways a Lawrentian figure, Jim Greatorex is an image of the same values as the heroine but in this novel, as in so many by May Sinclair, it is the woman who pays.

All three Cartaret women, then, face the same social conditions in their struggle for self-development; the restrictions of their father's house, the difficulty of earning a living outside, marriage as the sole channel for their sexual and child-bearing potential, and the lack of marriageable men. Each, according to her psychological type, responds differently to these same conditions: Alice in neurotic illness, Gwenda in sublimation and Mary by manipulating reality to achieve her ends. In earlier novels, Sinclair concentrates on the external restraints of women's lives: here in the first of her three psychological novels (*The Three Sisters* (1914), *Mary Olivier* (1919) and *The Life and Death of Harriett Frean* (1922)) she explores the inner world of motive and behaviour.

To do this her method shifts from the external realism of Wells and Arnold Bennett toward a more experimental presentation of character. She had not at this stage adopted the stream-of-consciousness technique which she discovered in the first volume of Dorothy Richardson's *Pilgrimage* (1915) and which she used so successfully in *Mary Olivier* and the later novels. Some of the difficulties of representing unconscious life are evident in *The Three Sisters* – in the parenthetic authorial interventions to *tell* the reader where there is a discrepancy between conscious and unconscious mind, for example. May Sinclair was not alone in these technical problems; Lawrence's struggle to represent the unconscious in the rhythms of his prose and Joyce and Richardson's experimentation with syntax are all part of the modernist revolution in fiction.

Despite these problems, the characterisation of the three sisters is perhaps the most radical feature of the book. Sinclair has chosen fairly well-established literary and social types – the steady, womanly elder sister, the independent "tomboy", the frail younger girl (almost the Meg, Jo and Beth-Amy of Louisa May Alcott's *Little Women*) – and grafted on an exposure of their unconscious sexuality which clashes with all the traditional attributes associated with these stereotypes. Thus the virginal figure on the Victorian sofa is also shown to be a woman of strong desires, the image of innocent girlhood is used in this novel to represent the power of the Id. The

"Sweet Woman" with her home-making skills here is dramat-
ised as the strongest ego of the three, best able to negotiate
conventional male expectations of women. Even Gwendolyn,
who early in the novel is linked with Artemis – the goddess of
unmarried women – recognises her own and her sisters'
sexuality but is dominated by her over-developed conscience
or super-ego. She is shown as caught and crushed between her
instinctive needs and the code of "decency" imposed by the
narrow "morality" of women of her class.

Apart from the general interest of her material, May Sinclair's narrative skills and the brilliant evocation of the north
Yorkshire moors, one of the great strengths of this novel is the
precision with which May Sinclair explodes, authoritatively
and finally, Victorian stereotypes of women – in that most
appropriate of years, 1914.

Jean Radford, London, 1981

THE THREE SISTERS

I

NORTH of east, in the bottom, where the road drops from the High Moor, is the village of Garth in Garthdale.

It crouches there with a crook of the dale behind and before it, between half-shut doors of the west and south. Under the mystery and terror of its solitude it crouches, like a beaten thing, cowering from its topmost roof to the bowed back of its stone bridge.

It is the last village up Garthdale; a handful of gray houses, old and small and humble. The high road casts them off and they turn their backs to it in their fear and huddle together, humbly, down by the beck. Their stone roofs and walls are naked and blackened by wind and rain as if fire had passed over them.

They have the silence, the darkness and the secrecy of all ultimate habitations.

North, where the high road begins to rise again, the Vicarage stands all alone. It turns its face toward the village, old and gray and humble as any house there, and looks on the road sideways, through the small shy window of its gable end. It has a strip of garden in front and on its farther side and a strip of orchard at the back. The garden slopes down to the churchyard, and a lane, leading to the pastures, runs between.

And all these things of stone, the village, the Vicarage, the church, the churchyard and the gravestones of the dead

1

are alike naked and black, blackened as if fire had passed
over them.   And in their grayness and their desolation
they are one with each other and with the network of low
walls that links them to the last solitary farm on the High
Moor.   And on the breast of the earth they show, one moment, solid as if hewn out of her heart, and another, slender and wind-blown as a tangle of gray thread on her
green gown.

II

THROUGH four of its five front windows the house gave
back darkness to the dark. One, on the ground floor,
showed a golden oblong, skirted with watery gray where
the lamp-light thinned the solid blackness of the wall.

The three sisters, Mary, Gwendolen and Alice, daughters
of James Cartaret, the Vicar of Garth, were sitting there
in the dining-room behind the yellow blind, doing nothing.
In their supine, motionless attitudes they seemed to be
waiting for something to happen, to happen so soon that,
if there had been anything to do, it was not worth their
while doing it.

All three were alike in the small, broad faces that
brooded, half sullen and half sad; in the wide eyes that
watched vaguely; in the little tender noses, and in the
mouths, tender and sullen, too; in the arch and sweep of
the upper lips, the delicate fulness of the lower; in the
way of the thick hair, parted and turned back over the
brows in two wide and shallow waves.

Mary, the eldest, sat in a low chair by the fireside.
Her hands were clasped loosely on the black woolen socks
she had ceased to darn.

She was staring into the fire with her gray eyes, the
thick gray eyes that never let you know what she was
thinking. The firelight woke the flame in her reddish-
tawny hair. The red of her lips was turned back and
crushed against the white. Mary was shorter than her
sisters, but she was the one that had the color. And with

3

it she had a stillness that was not theirs. Mary's face brooded more deeply than their faces, but it was untroubled in its brooding.

She had learned to darn socks for her own amusement on her eleventh birthday, and she was twenty-seven now.

Alice, the youngest girl (she was twenty-three) lay stretched out on the sofa.

She departed in no way from her sister's type but that her body was slender and small boned, that her face was lightly finished, that her gray eyes were clear and her lips pale against the honey-white of her face, and that her hair was colorless as dust except where the edge of the wave showed a dull gold.

Alice had spent the whole evening lying on the sofa. And now she raised her arms and bent them, pressing the backs of her hands against her eyes. And now she lowered them and lifted one sleeve of her thin blouse, and turned up the milk-white under surface of her arm and lay staring at it and feeling its smooth texture with her fingers.

Gwendolen, the second sister, sat leaning over the table with her arms flung out on it as they had tossed from her the book she had been reading.

She was the tallest and the darkest of the three. Her face followed the type obscurely; and vividly and emphatically it left it. There was dusk in her honey-whiteness, and dark blue in the gray of her eyes. The bridge of her nose and the arch of her upper lip were higher, lifted as it were in a decided and defiant manner of their own. About Gwenda there was something alert and impatient. Her very supineness was alive. It had distinction, the savage grace of a creature utterly abandoned to a sane fatigue.

Gwenda had gone fifteen miles over the moors that

evening. She had run and walked and run again in the riotous energy of her youth.

Now she was too tired to read.

Gwenda was the first to speak.

"Is it ten yet?"

"No." Mary smiled, but the word shuddered in her throat like a weary moan.

"How long?"

"Forty-three minutes."

"Oh, Lord——" Gwenda laughed the laugh of brave nerves tortured.

From her sofa beyond the table Alice sighed.

At ten o'clock Essy Gale, the maid-servant, would come in from the kitchen and the Vicar from the inner room. And Essy would put the Bible and Prayer-book on the table, and the Vicar would read Prayers.

That was all they were waiting for. It was all that could happen. It happened every night at ten o'clock.

III

ALICE spoke next.

"What day of the month is it?"

"The thirtieth." Mary answered.

"Then we've been here exactly five months to-day."

"That's nothing," said Mary, "to the months and years we shall be here."

"I can't think what possessed Papa to come and bury us all in this rotten place."

"Can't you?" Mary's eyes turned from their brooding. Her voice was very quiet, barely perceptible the significant stress.

"Oh, if you mean it's *me* he wants to bury——. You needn't rub that in."

"I'm not rubbing it in."

"You are. You're rubbing it in every time you look like that. That's the beastly part of it. Supposing he does want to get back on me, why should he go and punish you two?"

"If he thinks he's punishing me he's sold," said Gwenda.

"He couldn't have stuck you in a rottener hole."

Gwenda raised her head.

"A hole? Why, there's no end to it. You can go for miles and miles without meeting anybody, unless some darling mountain sheep gets up and looks at you. It's—it's a divine place, Ally."

6

"Wait till you've been another five months in it. You'll
be as sick as I am."

"I don't think so. You haven't seen the moon get up
over Greffington Edge. If you had—if you knew what
this place was like, you wouldn't lie there grizzling. You
wouldn't talk about punishing. You'd wonder what you'd
done to be allowed to look at it—to live in it a day. Of
course I'm not going to let on to Papa that I'm in love
with it."

Mary smiled again.

"It's all very well for you," she said. "As long as
you've got a moor to walk on *you're* all right."

"Yes. I'm all right," Gwenda said.

Her head had sunk again and rested in the hollow of her
arms. Her voice, muffled in her sleeve, came soft and
thick. It died for drowsiness.

In the extreme immobility and stillness of the three
the still house stirred and became audible to them, as if it
breathed. They heard the delicate fall of the ashes on the
hearth, and the flame of the lamp jerking as the oil sput-
tered in the burnt wick. Their nerves shook to the creeping, crackling sounds that came from the wainscot, infinitely minute. A tongue of fire shot hissing from the
coal. It seemed to them a violent and terrifying thing.
The breath of the house passed over them in thick smells
of earth and must, as the fire's heat sucked at its damp.

The church clock struck the half hour. Once, twice;
two dolorous notes that beat on the still house and died.

Somewhere out at the back a door opened and shut, and
it was as if the house drew in its breath at the shock of
the sound.

Presently a tremor crept through Gwenda's young body
as her heart shook it.

She rose and went to the window.

IV

She was slow and rapt in her going like one walking in her sleep, moved by some impulse profounder than her sleep.

She pulled up the blind. The darkness was up against the house, thick and close to the pane. She threw open the window, and the night entered palpably like slow water, black and sweet and cool.

From the unseen road came the noise of wheels and of a horse that in trotting clanked forever one shoe against another.

It was young Rowcliffe, the new doctor, driving over from Morthe to Upthorne on the Moor, where John Greatorex lay dying.

The pale light of his lamps swept over the low garden wall.

Suddenly the four hoofs screamed, grinding together in the slide of their halt. The doctor had jerked his horse up by the Vicarage gate.

The door at the back opened and shut again, suddenly, sharply, as if in fear.

A voice swung out like a mournful bell into the night. A dalesman's voice; such a voice as the lonely land fashions sometimes for its own delight, drawling and tender, hushed by the hills and charged with the infinite, mysterious sadness of their beauty.

It belonged to young Greatorex and it came from the doorway of the Vicarage yard.

8

"That yo, Dr. Rawcliffe? I wuss joost gawn oop t'road
t' see ef yo wuss coomin'."

"Of course I was coming."

The new doctor was short and stern with young Greatorex.

The two voices, the soft and the stern, spoke together
for a moment, low, inaudible. Then young Greatorex's
voice was heard again, and in its softness there was the
furtive note of shame.

"I joost looked in to Vicarage to leave woord with
Paason."

The noise of the wheels and hoofs began again, the iron
shoes clanked together and struck out the rhythm that the
sisters knew.

And with the first beat of it, and with the sound of the
two voices in the road, life, secret and silent, stirred in
their blood and nerves. It quivered like a hunting thing
held on the leash.

V

Their stillness, their immobility were now intense. And not one spoke a word to the other.

All three of them were thinking.

Mary thought, "Wednesday is his day. On Wednesday I will go into the village and see all my sick people. Then I shall see him. And he will see me. He will see that I am kind and sweet and womanly." She thought, "That is the sort of woman that a man wants." But she did not know what she was thinking.

Gwenda thought, "I will go out on to the moor again. I don't care if I *am* late for Prayers. He will see me when he drives back and he will wonder who is that wild, strong girl who walks by herself on the moor at night and isn't afraid. He has seen me three times, and every time he has looked at me as if he wondered. In five minutes I shall go." She thought (for she knew what she was thinking), "I shall do nothing of the sort. I don't care whether he sees me or not. I don't care if I never see him again. I don't care."

Alice thought, "I will make myself ill. So ill that they'll *have* to send for him. I shall see him that way."

VI

ALICE sat up. She was thinking another thought.

"If Mr. Greatorex is dead, Dr. Rowcliffe won't stay long at Upthorne. He will come back soon. And he will have to call and leave word. He will come in and I shall see him."

But if Mr. Greatorex wasn't dead? If Mr. Greatorex were a long time over his dying? Then he might be kept at Upthorne, perhaps till midnight, perhaps till morning. Then, even if he called to leave word, she would not see him. When she looked deep she found herself wondering how long Mr. Greatorex would be over his dying. If she had looked a little deeper she would have found herself hoping that Mr. Greatorex was already dead.

If Mr. Greatorex was dead before he got to Upthorne he would come very soon, perhaps before prayer-time.

And he would be shown into the drawing-room.

Would he? Would Essy have the sense? No. Not unless the lamp was lit there. Essy wouldn't show him into a dark room. And Essy was stupid. She might have *no* sense. She might take him straight into the study and Papa would keep him there. Trust Papa.

Alice got up from her sofa and left the room; moving with her weary grace and a little air of boredom and of unconcern. She was always most unconcerned when she was most intent.

Outside in the passage she stood a moment, listening. All the ways of the house gave upon the passage in a space so narrow that by stretching out one arm she could have touched both walls.

With a door open anywhere the passage became a gully for the north wind. Now, with all doors shut, it was as if the breath of the house was being squeezed out there, between closing walls. The passage, instead of dividing the house, drew it together tight. And this tightness was intolerable to Alice.

She hated it. She hated the whole house. It was so built that there wasn't a corner in it where you could get away from Papa. His study had one door opening into the passage and one into the dining-room. The window where he sat raked the garden on the far side. The window of his bedroom raked the front; its door commanded the stairhead. He was aware of everything you did, of everything you didn't do. He could hear you in the dining-room; he could hear you overhead; he could hear you going up and downstairs. He could positively hear you breathe, and he always knew whether you were in bed or not. She drew in her breath lest he should hear it now.

At the far end of the passage, on the wall-space between the staircase and the kitchen door, raised on a small bracket, a small tin lamp showed a thrifty flame. Under it, on a mahogany table-flap, was a row of bedroom candlesticks with their match-boxes.

Her progress to the table-flap was stealthy. She exalted this business of lighting the drawing-room lamp to a desperate, perilous adventure. The stone floor deadened her footsteps as she went.

Her pale eyes, half sullen, half afraid, slewed round to the door of the study on her right. With a noiseless hand she secured her matches and her candle. With noiseless feet she slid into the darkness of the drawing-room. She dared not light her candle out there in the passage. For the Vicar was full of gloom and of suspicion in the half hour before prayer-time, and at the spurt of the match he might come out blustering and insist on knowing what she was doing and where she was going, whereas presently he would know, and he might be quiet as long as he was satisfied that she wasn't shirking Prayers.

Stealthily, with her air of desperate adventure, she lit the drawing-room lamp. She shook out the puffs and frills of its yellow paper shade. Under its gaudy skirts the light was cruel to the cramped and shabby room, to the huddled furniture, to the tarnished gilt, the perishing tones of gray and amber.

Alice set the lamp on the top of the cottage piano that stood slantwise in a side window beyond the fireplace. She had pulled back the muslin curtains and opened both windows wide so that the room was now bared to the south and west. Then, with the abrupt and passionate gesture of desire deferred, she sat down at the little worn-out Erard and began to play.

Sitting there, with the open window behind her, she could be seen, and she knew that she could be seen from over the wall by anybody driving past in a high dog-cart.

And she played. She played the Chopin Grande Polonaise, or as much of it as her fingers, tempestuous and inexpert, could clutch and reach. She played, neither with her hands nor with her brain, but with her temperament, febrile and frustrate, seeking its outlet in exultant and violent sound. She fell upon the Erard like some fierce and hungry thing, tearing from the forlorn, humble instrument a strange and savage food. She played—with incredible omissions, discords and distortions, but she played. She flung out her music through the windows into the night as a signal and an appeal. She played (on the little worn-out Erard) in ecstasy and expectation, as if something momentous hung upon her playing. There was joy and triumph and splendor in the Grande Polonaise; she felt them in her heart and nerves as a delicate, dangerous tremor, the almost intolerable on coming of splendor, of triumph and of joy.

And as she played the excitement gathered; it swung in more and more vehement vibrations; it went warm and flooding through her brain like wine. All the life of her bloodless body swam there, poised and thinned, but urgent, aspiring to some great climax of the soul.

VII

THE whole house was full of the Chopin Grande Polonaise.

It raged there like a demon. Tortured out of all knowledge, the Grande Polonaise screamed and writhed in its agony. It writhed through the windows, seeking its natural attenuation in the open air. It writhed through the shut house and was beaten back, pitilessly, by the roof and walls. To let it loose thus was Alice's defiance of the house and her revenge.

Mary and Gwenda heard it in the dining-room, and set their mouths and braced themselves to bear it. The Vicar in his study behind the dining-room heard it and scowled. Essy, the maid-servant, heard it, she heard it worse than anybody, in her kitchen on the other side of the wall. Now and then, when the Polonaise screamed louder, Mary drew a hissing breath of pain through her locked teeth, and Gwenda grinned. Not that to Gwenda there was anything funny in the writhing and screaming of the Grande Polonaise. It was that she alone appreciated its vindictive quality; she admired the completeness, the audacity of Alice's revenge.

But Essy in her kitchen made no effort to stand up to the Grande Polonaise. When it began she sat down and laid her arms on the kitchen table, and her head, muffled in her apron, on her arms, and cried. She couldn't have told you what the Polonaise was like or what it did to her; all that she could have said was that it went through and

through her. She didn't know, Essy didn't, what had
come over her; for whatever noise Miss Alice made, she
hadn't taken any notice, not at first. It was in the last
three weeks that the Polonaise had found her out and had
begun to go through and through her, till it was more than
she could bear. But Essy, crying into her apron, wouldn't
have lifted a finger to stop Miss Alice.

"Poor laass," Essy said to herself, "she looves to plaay.
And Vicar, he'll not hold out mooch longer. He'll put
foot down fore she gets trow."

Through the screaming of the Polonaise Essy listened
for the opening of the study door.

VIII

The study door did not open all at once.

"Wisdom and patience, wisdom and patience——" The Vicar kept on muttering as he scowled. Those were his watchwords in his dealings with his womenkind.

The Vicar was making a prodigious effort to maintain what seemed to him his god-like serenity. He was unaware that he was trying to control at one and the same time his temper and his temperament.

He was a man of middle height and squarish build, dark, pale-skinned and blue-eyed like his daughter Gwendolen. The Vicar's body stretched tight the seams of his black coat and kept up, at fifty-seven, a false show of muscular energy. The Vicar's face had a subtle quality of deception. The austere nose, the lean cheek-bones, the square-cut moustache and close-clipped, pointed beard (black, slightly grizzled) made it appear, at a little distance, the face of an ascetic. It approached, and the blue of the eyes, and the black of their dilated pupils, the stare of the nostrils and the half hidden lines of the red mouth revealed its profound and secret sensuality.

The interior that contained him was no less deceptive. Its book-lined walls advertised him as the scholarly recluse that he was not. He had had an eye to this effect. He had placed in prominent positions the books that he had inherited from his father, who had been a schoolmaster. You were caught at the very door by the thick red line of The Tudor Classics; by the eleven volumes of The Bek-

ker's Plato, with Notes, bound in Russia leather, side by
side with Jowett's Translations in cloth; by Sophocles and
Dean Plumptre, the Odyssey and Butcher and Lang; by
Æschylus and Robert Browning. The Vicar had carried
the illusion of scholarship so far as to hide his Aris-
tophanes behind a little curtain, as if it contained for him
an iniquitous temptation. Of his own accord and with a
deliberate intention to deceive, he had added the Early
Fathers, Tillotsen's *Sermons* and Farrar's *Life of Christ.*

On another shelf, rather less conspicuous, were some
bound volumes of *The Record,* with the novels of Mrs.
Henry Wood and Miss Marie Corelli. On the ledge of
his bureau *Blackwood's Magazine,* uncut, lay ready to his
hand. The *Spectator,* in process of skimming, was on his
knees. The *Standard,* fairly gutted, was on the floor.
There was no room for it anywhere else.

For the Vicar's study was much too small for him. Sitting there, in an arm-chair and with his legs in the fender,
he looked as if he had taken flight before the awful invasion of his furniture. His bookcases hemmed him in on
three sides. His roll-top desk, advancing on him from the
window, had driven and squeezed him into the arm-chair.
His bureau, armed to the teeth, leaning from its ambush
in the recess of the fireplace, threatened both the retreat
and the left flank movement of the chair. The Vicar was
neither tall nor powerful, but his study made him look like
a giant imprisoned in a cell.

The room was full of the smell of tobacco, of a smolder-
ing coal fire, of old warm leather and damp walls, and of
the heavy, virile odor of the Vicar.

A brown felt carpet and thick serge curtains shut out
the draft of the northeast window.

On a September evening the Vicar was snug enough in

his cell; and before the Grande Polonaise had burst in upon him he had been at peace with God and man.

But when he heard those first exultant, challenging bars he scowled inimically.

Not that he acknowledged them as a challenge. He was inclined rather to the manly course of ignoring the Grande Polonaise altogether. And not for a moment would he have admitted that there had been anything in his behavior that could be challenged or defied, least of all by his daughter Alice. To himself in his study Mr. Cartaret appeared as the image of righteousness established in an impregnable place. Whereas his daughter Alice was not at all in a position to challenge and defy.

She had made a fool of herself.

She knew it; he knew it; everybody knew it in the parish they had left five months ago. It had been the talk of the little southern seaside town. He thanked God that nobody knew it, or was ever likely to know it, here.

For Alice's folly was not any ordinary folly. It was the kind that made the parish which was so aware of it uninhabitable to a sensitive vicar.

He reflected that she would be clever if she made a fool of herself here. By his decisive action in removing her from that southern seaside town he had saved her from continuing her work. In order to do it he had ruined his prospects. He had thrown up a good living for a poor one; a living that might (but for Alice it certainly would) have led to preferment for a living that could lead to nothing at all; a living where he could make himself felt for a living where there was nobody to feel him.

And, having done it, he was profoundly sorry for himself.

So far as Mr. Cartaret could see there had been nothing

else to do. If it had all to be done over again, he told
himself that he would do it.

But there Mr. Cartaret was wrong. He couldn't have
done it or anything like it twice. It was one of those
deeds, supremeful sacrificial, that strain a man's moral
energies to breaking point and render him incapable of
further sacrifice; if, indeed, it did not render further
sacrifice superfluous. Mr. Cartaret honestly felt that even
an exacting deity could require no more of him.

And it wasn't the first time either, nor his daughter
Alice the first woman who had come between the Vicar and
his prospects. Looking back he saw himself driven from
pillar to post, from parish to parish, by the folly or incom-
petence of his womankind.

Strictly speaking, it was his first wife, Mary Gwendolen, the one the children called Mother, who had begun it.
She had made his first parish unendurable to him by dying
in it. This she had done when Alice was born, thereby
making Alice unendurable to him, too. Poor Mamie! He
always thought of her as having, inscrutably, failed him.

All three of them had failed him.

His second wife, Frances, the one the children called
Mamma (the Vicar had made himself believe that
he had married her solely on their account), had turned
into a nervous invalid on his hands before she died of that
obscure internal trouble which he had so wisely and patiently ignored.

His third wife, Robina (the one they called Mummy),
had run away from him in the fifth year of their marriage.
When she implored him to divorce her he said that, whatever her conduct had been, that course was impossible to
him as a churchman, as she well knew; but that he forgave
her. He had made himself believe it.

And all the time he was aware, without admitting it,

that, if the thing came into court, Robina's evidence might be a little damaging to the appearances of wisdom and patience, of austerity and dignity, which he had preserved so well. He had had an unacknowledged vision of Robina standing in the witness box, very small and shy, with her eyes fluttering while she explained to the gentlemen of the jury that she ran away from her husband because she was afraid of him. He could hear the question, "Why were you afraid?" and Robina's answer—but at that point he always reminded himself that it was as a churchman that he objected to divorce.

For his profession had commited him to a pose. He had posed for more than thirty years to his parish, to his three wives, to his three children, and to himself, till he had become unconscious of his real thoughts, his real motives, his real likings and dislikings. So that when he told himself that it would have been better if his third wife had died, he thought he meant that it would have been better for her and for his opinion of her, whereas what he really did mean was that it would have been better for himself.

For if Robina had died he could have married again. As it was, her infidelity condemned him to a celibacy for which, as she knew, he was utterly unsuited.

Therefore he thought of her as a cruel and unscrupulous woman. And when he thought of her he became more sorry for himself than ever.

Now, oddly enough, the Grande Polonaise had set Mr. Cartaret thinking of Robina. It was not that Robina had ever played it. Robina did not play. It was not the discords introduced into it by Alice, though Robina had been a thing of discords. It was that something in him, obscurely but intimately associated with Robina, responded to that sensual and infernal tremor that Alice was wringing

out of the Polonaise. So that, without clearly knowing
why it was abominable, Mr. Cartaret said to himself that
the tune Alice was playing was an abominable tune and
must be stopped at once.

He went into the drawing-room to stop it.

And Essy, in the kitchen, raised her head and dried her
eyes on her apron.

"If you must make a noise," said Mr. Cartaret, "be
good enough to make one that is less—disturbing."

He stood in the doorway staring at his daughter Alice.

Her excitement had missed by a hairsbreadth the spiritual climax. It had held itself in for one unspeakable
moment, then surged, crowding the courses of her nerves.
Beaten back by the frenzy of the Polonaise, it made a
violent return; it rose, quivering, at her eyelids and her
mouth; it broke, and, with a shudder of all her body, split
itself and fell.

The Vicar stared. He opened his mouth to say something, and said nothing; finally he went out, muttering.

"Wisdom and patience. Wisdom and patience."

It was a prayer.

Alice trailed to the window and leaned out, listening
for the sound of hoofs and wheels. Nothing there but the
darkness and stillness of the moors. She trailed back to
the Erard and began to play again.

This time it was Beethoven, the Pathetic Sonata.

IX

Mr. Cartaret sat in his study, manfully enduring the Pathetic Sonata.

He was no musician and he did not certainly know when Alice went wrong; therefore, except that it had some nasty loud moments, he could not honestly say that the First Movement was disturbing. Besides, he had scored. He had made Alice change her tune.

Wisdom and patience required that he should be satisfied, so far. And, being satisfied, in the sense that he no longer had a grievance, meant that he was very badly bored.

He began to fidget. He took his legs out of the fender and put them back again. He shifted his weight from one leg to the other, but without relief. He turned over his *Spectator* to see what it had to say about the Deceased Wife's Sister Bill, and found that he was not interested in what it had to say. He looked at his watch and compared it with the clock in the faint hope that the clock might be behindhand.

The watch and clock both agreed that it was not a minute later than fifteen minutes to ten. A whole quarter of an hour before Prayer-time.

There was nothing but Prayer-time to look forward to.

He began to fidget again. He filled his pipe and thought better about smoking it. Then he rang the bell for his glass of water.

After more delay than was at all necessary Essy appeared, bringing the glass of water on a plate.

She came in, soft-footed, almost furtive, she who used to enter so suddenly and unabashed. She put the plate down on the roll-top desk and turned softly, furtively, away.

The Vicar looked up. His eyes were large and blue as suspicion drew in the black of their pupils.

"Put it down here," he said, and he indicated the ledge of the bureau.

Essy stood still and stared like a half-wild creature in doubt as to its way. She decided to make for the bureau by rounding the roll-top desk on the far side, thus approaching her master from behind.

"What are you doing?" said the Vicar. "I said, Put it down here."

Essy turned again and came forward, tilting the plate a little in her nervousness. The large blue eyes, the stern voice, fascinated her, frightened her.

The Vicar looked at her steadily, remorselessly, as she came.

Essy's lowered eyelids had kept the stain of her tears. Her thick brown hair was loose and rumpled under her white cap. But she had put on a clean, starched apron. It stood out stiffly, billowing, from her waist. Essy had not always been so careless about her hair or so fastidious as to her aprons. There was a little strained droop at the corners of her tender mouth, as if they had been tied with string. Her dark eyes still kept their young largeness and their light, but they looked as if they had been drawn tight with string at their corners too.

All these signs the Vicar noted as he stared. And he hated Essy. He hated her for what he saw in her, and for her buxom comeliness, and for the softness of her youth.

"Did I hear young Greatorex round at the back door this evening?" he said.

Essy started, slanting her plate a little more.

"I doan knaw ef I knaw, sir."

"Either you know or you don't know," said the Vicar.

"I doan know, I'm sure, sir," said Essy.

The Vicar was holding out his hand for his glass of water, and Essy pushed the plate toward him, so blindly and at such a perilous slant that the glass slid and toppled over and broke itself against the Vicar's chair.

Essy gave a little frightened cry.

"Clever girl. She did that on purpose," said the Vicar to himself.

Essy was on her knees beside him, picking up the bits of glass and gathering them in her apron. She was murmuring, "I'll mop it oop. I'll mop it oop."

"That'll do," he said roughly. "That'll do, I tell you. You can go."

Essy tried to go. But it was as if her knees had weights on them that fixed her to the floor. Holding up her apron with one hand, she clutched the arm of her master's chair with the other and dragged herself to her feet.

"I'll mop it oop," she repeated, shamefast.

"I told you to go," said the Vicar.

"I'll fetch yo anoother glass?" she whispered. Her voice was hoarse with the spasm in her throat.

"No," said the Vicar.

Essy slunk back into her kitchen with terror in her heart.

X

"Attacca subito l'Allegro."

Alice had fallen on it suddenly.

"I suppose," said Mary, "it's a relief to her to make that row."

"It isn't," said Gwenda. "It's torture. That's how she works herself up. She's playing on her own nerves all the time. If she really *could* play—— If she cared about the music—— If she cared about anything on earth except——"

She paused.

"Molly, it must be awful to be made like that."

"Nothing could be worse for her than being shut up here."

"I know. Papa's been a frightful fool about her. After all, Molly, what did she do?"

"She did what you and I wouldn't have done."

"How do you know what you wouldn't have done? How do I know? If we'd been in her place——"

"If *I'd* been in her place I'd have died rather."

"How do you know Ally wouldn't have rather died if she could have chosen? She didn't want to fall in love with that young ass, Rickards. And I don't see what she did that was so very awful."

"She managed to let everybody else see, anyhow."

"What if she did? At least she was honest. She went straight for what she wanted. She didn't sneak and scheme to get him from any other girl. And she hadn't

26

a mother to sneak and scheme *for* her. That's fifty times worse, yet it's done every day and nobody thinks anything of it."

She went on. "Nobody would have thought anything as it was, if Papa hadn't been such a frantic fool about it. It he'd had the pluck to stand by her, if he'd kept his head and laughed in their silly faces, instead of grizzling and growling and stampeding out of the parish as if poor Ally had disgraced him."

"Well—it isn't a very pleasant thing for the Vicar of the parish——"

"It wasn't a very pleasant thing for any of us. But it was beastly of him to go back on her like that. And the silliness of it! Caring so frightfully about what people think, and then going on so as to make them think it."

"Think what?"

"That she really *had* done something."

"Do you suppose they did?"

"Yes. You can't blame them. He couldn't have piled it on more if she *had*. It's enough to make her."

"Oh Gwenda!"

"It would be his own fault. Just as it's his own fault that he hates her."

"He doesn't hate her. He's fond of all of us, in his way."

"Not of Ally. Don't you know why? He can't look at her without thinking of how awful *he* is."

"And if he *is*—a little—— You forget what he's had to go through."

"You mean Mummy running away from him?"

"Yes. And Mamma's dying. And before that—there was Mother."

Gwenda raised her head.

"He killed Mother."

"What do you mean?"

"He did. He was told that Mother would die or go mad if she had another baby. And he let her have Ally. No wonder Mummy ran away from him."

"Who told you that story?"

"Mummy."

"It was horrid of her."

"Everything poor Mummy did was horrid. It was horrid of her to run away from him, I suppose."

"Why did you tell me that? I didn't know it. I'd rather not have known."

"Well, now you do know, perhaps you'll be sorrier for Ally."

"I am sorry for Ally. But I'm sorry for Papa, too. You're not."

"I'd be sorry for him right enough if he wasn't so sorry for himself."

"Gwenda, *you're* awful."

"Because I won't waste my pity? Ally's got nothing— He's got everything."

"Not what he cares most for."

"He cares most for what people think of him. Everybody thought him a good kind husband. Everybody thinks him a good kind father."

The music suddenly ceased. A sound of voices came instead of it.

"There," said Gwenda. "He's gone in and stopped her."

He had, that time.

And in the sudden ceasing of the Pathetic Sonata the three sisters heard the sound of wheels and the clank of horseshoes striking together.

Mr. Greatorex was not yet dead of his pneumonia.   The doctor had passed the Vicarage gate.

And as he passed he had said to himslf.   "How execrably she plays."

The three sisters waited without a word for the striking of the church clock.

XI

THE church clock struck ten.

At the sound of the study bell Essy came into the dining-room. Essy was the acolyte of Family Prayers. Though a Wesleyan she could not shirk the appointed ceremonial. It was Essy who took the Bible and Prayer-book from their place on the sideboard under the tea-urn and put them on the table, opening them where the Vicar had left a marker the night before. It was Essy who drew back the Vicar's chair from the table and set it ready for him. It was Essy whom he relied on for responses that *were* responses and not mere mumblings and mutterings. She was Wesleyan, the one faithful, the one devout person in his household.

To-night there was nothing but a mumbling and a muttering. And that was Mary. She was the only one who was joining in the Lord's Prayer.

Essy had failed him.

Prayers over, there was nothing to sit up for. All the same, it was Mr. Cartaret's rule to go back into the study and to bore himself again for a whole hour till it was bed-time. He liked to be sure that the doors were all bolted and that everybody else was in bed before he went himself.

But to-night he had bored himself so badly that the thought of his study was distasteful to him. So he stayed where he was with his family. He believed that he was doing this solely on his family's account. He told himself

30

that it was not right that he should leave the three girls too much to themselves. It did not occur to him that as long as he had had a wife to sit with, he hadn't cared how much he had left them. He knew that he had rather liked Mary and Gwendolen when they were little, and though he had found himself liking them less and less as they grew into their teens he had never troubled to enquire whose fault that was, so certain was he that it couldn't be his. Still less was it his fault if they were savage and inaccessible in their twenties. Of course he didn't mean that Mary was savage and inaccessible. It was Gwendolen that he meant.

So, since he couldn't sit there much longer without saying something, he presently addressed himself to Mary.

"Any news of Greatorex to-day?"

"I haven't heard. Shall I ask Essy?"

"No," said Mr. Cartaret, so abruptly that Mary looked at him.

"He was worse yesterday," said Gwenda.

They all looked at Gwenda.

"Who told you that?" said Mr. Cartaret by way of saying something.

"Mrs. Gale."

"When did she tell you?"

"Yesterday, when I was up at the farm."

"What were you doing at the farm?"

"Nothing. I went to see if I could do anything." She said to herself, "Why does he go on at us like this?" Aloud she said, "It was time some of us went."

She had him there. She was always having him.

"I shall have to go myself to-morrow," he said.

"I would if I were you," said Gwenda.

"I wonder what Jim Greatorex will do if his father dies."

It was Mary who wondered.

"He'll get married, like a shot," said Alice.

"Who to?" said Gwenda. "He can't marry *all* the girls——"

She stopped herself. Essy Gale was in the room. Three months ago Essy had been a servant at the Farm where her mother worked once a fortnight.

She had come in so quietly that none of them had noticed her. She brought a tray with a fresh glass of water for the Vicar and a glass of milk for Alice. She put it down quietly and slipped out of the room without her customary "Anything more, Miss?" and "Good-night."

"What's the matter with Essy?" Gwenda said.

Nobody spoke but Alice who was saying that she didn't want her milk.

More than a year ago Alice had been ordered milk for her anæmia. She had milk at eleven, milk at her midday dinner, milk for supper, and milk last thing at night. She did not like milk, but she liked being ordered it. Generally she would sit and drink it, in the face of her family, pathetically, with little struggling gulps. She took a half-voluptuous, half-vindictive pleasure in her anæmia. She knew that it made her sisters sorry for her, and that it annoyed her father.

Now she declared that she wasn't feeling well, and that she didn't want her milk.

"In that case," said Mr. Cartaret, "you had better go to bed."

Alice went, raising her white arms and rubbing her eyes along the backs of her hands, like a child dropping with sleep.

One after another, they rose and followed her.

At the half-landing five steep steps in a recess of the

wall led aside to the door of Essy's bedroom. There Gwenda stopped and listened.

A sound of stifled crying came from the room. Gwenda went up to the door and knocked.

"Essy, are you in bed?"

A pause. "Yes, miss."

"What is it? Are you ill?"

No answer.

"Is there anything wrong?"

A longer pause. "I've got th' faace-ache."

"Oh, poor thing! Can I do anything for you?"

"Naw, Miss Gwenda, thank yo."

"Well, call me if I can."

But somehow she knew that Essy wouldn't call.

She went on, passing her father's door at the stair head. It was shut. She could hear him moving heavily within the room. On the other side of the landing was the room over the study that she shared with Alice.

The door stood wide. Alice in her thin nightgown could be seen sitting by the open window.

The nightgown, the small, slender body showing through, the hair, platted for the night, in two pig-tails that hung forward, one over each small breast, the tired face between the parted hair made Alice look childlike and pathetic.

Gwendolen had a pang of compassion.

"Dear lamb," she said. "*That* isn't any good. Fresh air won't do it. You'd much better wait till Papa gets a cold. Then you can catch it."

"It'll be his fault anyway," said Alice. "Serve him jolly well right if I get pneumonia."

"Pneumonia doesn't come to those who want it. I wonder what's wrong with Essy."

Alice was tired and sullen. "You'd better ask Jim Greatorex," she said.

"What do you mean, Ally?"

But Ally had set her small face hard.

"Can't you be sorry for her?" said Gwenda.

"Why should I be sorry for her? *She's* all right."

She had sorrow enough, but none to waste on Essy. Essy's way was easy. Essy had only to slink out to the back door and she could have her will. *She* didn't have to get pneumonia.

XII

John Greatorex did not die that night. He had no mind to die: he was a man of stubborn pugnacity and he fought his pneumonia.

The long gray house at Upthorne looks over the marshes of the high land above Garth. It stands alone, cut off by the marshes from the network of gray walls that links the village to the hill farms.

The light in its upper window burned till dawn, a sign to the brooding and solitary land. Up there, in the low room with its sunken ceiling, John Greatorex lay in the big bed and rallied a little as the clean air from the moors lapped him like water. For the doctor had thrown open all the windows of the house before he left. Presently Mrs. Gale, the untrained village nurse, would come and shut them in terror, and John Greatorex's pneumonia would get the upper hand. That was how the fight went on, with Steven Rowcliffe on John Greatorex's side and Mrs. Gale for the pneumonia. It was ten to one against John Greatorex and the doctor, for John Greatorex was most of the time unconscious and the doctor called but once or twice a day, while Mrs. Gale was always there to shut the windows as fast as he opened them. In the length and breadth of the Dale there wasn't another woman who would not have done the same. She was secure from criticism. If she didn't know how to nurse pneumonia, who did? Seeing that her own husband had died of it.

35

Young Rowcliffe was a dalesman and he knew his people. In six months his face had grown stiff in the struggle with them. It was making his voice stern and his eyes hard, so that they could see nothing round him but stupidity and distrust and an obstinacy even greater than his own.

Nothing in his previous experience had prepared him for it. In his big provincial hospital he had had it practically his own way. He had faced a thousand horrible and intractable diseases with a thousand appliances and with an army of assistants and trained nurses under him. And if in his five years' private practice in Leeds he had come to grips with human nature, it had been at any rate a fair fight. If his work was harder his responsibility was less. He still had trained nurses under him; and if a case was beyond him there were specialists with whom he could consult.

Here he was single-handed. He was physician and surgeon and specialist and nurse in one. He had few appliances and no assistant beside naked and primeval nature, the vast high spaces, the clean waters and clean air of the moors.

Yet it was precisely these things that his romantic youth had cried for—that solitary combat and communion, that holy and solitary aid.

At thirty Rowcliffe was still in his romantic youth.

He had all its appearances about him. A life of continual labor and discomfort had kept his body slender; and all the edges of his face—clean-shaven except for its little dark moustache—were incomparably firm and clear. His skin was bronzed and reddened by sun and wind. The fine hard mouth under the little dark moustache was not so hard that it could not, sometimes, be tender. His irreproachable nose escaped the too high curve that would have made it arrogant. And his eyes, keen and hard in movement, by simply keeping quiet under lowered brows, became charged with a curious and engaging pathos.

Their pathos had appealed to the little red-haired, pink-skinned, green-eyed nurse who had worked under him in Leeds. She was clever and kind—much too kind, it was supposed—to Rowcliffe. There had been one or two others before the little red-haired nurse, so that, though he was growing hard, he had not grown bitter.

He was not in the least afraid of growing bitter; for he knew that his eyes, as long as he could keep them quiet, would preserve him from all necessity for bitterness.

Rowcliffe had always trusted a great deal to his eyes. Because of them he had left several young ladies, his patients, quite heart-broken in Leeds. The young ladies knew nothing about the little red-haired nurse and had never ceased to wonder why Dr. Rowcliffe did not want to marry them.

And Steven Rowcliffe's eyes, so disastrous to the young ladies in Leeds, saw nobody in Morfe whom he could possibly want to marry. The village of Morfe is built in a square round its green. The doctor's house stands on a plot of rising ground on the north side of the square, and from its front windows young Rowcliffe could see the inhabitants of Morfe coming and going before him as on a stage, and he kept count of them all. There were the three middle-aged maiden ladies in the long house on the west side of whom all he knew was that they ate far too many pikelets and griddle cakes for tea. There were the two old ladies in the white house next door who were always worrying him to sound their chests, one for her lungs and the other for her arteries. In spite of lungs and arteries they were very gay old ladies. The tubes of Rowcliffe's queer, new-fangled stethescope, appearing out

of his coat pocket, sent them into ecstacies of mirth.   They
always made the same little joke about it; they called the
stethescope his telephone.   But of course he didn't want
to marry them.   There was the very old lady on the east
side, who had had one stroke and was expecting another
every day.   There were the two unmarried daughters of
a retired manufacturer on the far side of the Green.
They were plump and had red cheeks, if he had cared for
plumpness and red cheeks; but they had no conversation.
The only pretty girl whose prettiness appealed to Rowcliffe had an "adenoid" mouth which he held to be a drawback.   There was the daughter of his predecessor, but
she again was well over forty, rigid and melancholy and
dry.

All these people became visibly excited when they saw
young Rowcliffe starting off in his trap and returning;
but young Rowcliffe was never excited, never even interested when he saw them.   There was nothing about them
that appealed to his romantic youth.

As for Morfe Manor, and Garth Manor and Greffington
Hall, they were nearly always empty, so that he had not
very much chance of improving his acquaintance there.

And he had nothing to hope for from the summer visitors, girls with queer clothes and queer manners and queer
accents; bouncing, convivial girls who spread themselves
four abreast on the high roads; fat, lazy girls who sat
about on the Green; blowsed, slouching girls who tramped
the dales with knapsacks and no hats.   The hard eyes of
young Rowcliffe never softened as he looked at the summer visitors.   Their behavior irritated him.   It reminded
him that there were women in the world and that he
missed, quite unbearably at moments, the little red-haired
nurse who had been so clever and so kind.   Moreover it
offended his romantic youth.   The little publicans and

shop-keepers of Morfe did not offend it; neither did the
peasants and the farmers; they were part of the place;
generations of them had been born in those gray houses,
built from the gaunt ribs of the hills; whereas the presence of the summer visitors was an outrage to the silent
and solitary country that his instincts inscrutably adored.
No wonder that he didn't care to look at them.

But one night in September, when the moon was high
in the south, as he was driving toward Garth on his way
to Upthorne, the eyes of young Rowcliffe were startled out
of their aversion by the sudden and incredible appearance
of a girl.

It was at the bend of the road where Karva lowers its
head and sinks back on the moor; and she came swinging
up the hill as Rowcliffe's horse scraped his way slowly
down it. She was in white (he couldn't have missed her)
and she carried herself like a huntress; slender and quick,
with high, sharp-pointed breasts. She looked at him as
she passed and her face was wide-eyed and luminous under
the moon. Her lips were parted with her speed, so that,
instinctively, his hands tightened on the reins as if he
had thought that she was going to speak to him. But of
course she did not speak.

He looked back and saw her swing off the high road
and go up Karva. A flock of mountain sheep started
from their couches on the heather and looked at her, and
she went driving them before her. They trailed up Karva
slowly, in a long line, gray in the moonlight. Their
mournful, musical voices came to him from the hill.

He saw her again late—incredibly late—that night as
the moon swept from the south toward Karva. She was
a long way off, coming down from her hill, a white speck
on the gray moor. He pulled up his horse and waited

below the point where the track she followed struck the
high road; he even got out of his trap and examined,
deliberately, his horse's hoofs in turn, spinning out the
time. When he heard her he drew himself upright and
looked straight at her as she passed him. She flashed by
like a huntress, like Artemis carrying the young moon
on her forehead. From the turn of her head and the even
falling of her feet he felt her unconscious of his existence.
And her unconsciousness was hateful to him. It wiped
him clean out of the universe of noticeable things.

The apparition fairly cried to his romantic youth. And
he said to himself. "Who is the strange girl who walks
on the moor by herself at night and isn't afraid?"

He saw her three times after that; once in the broad
daylight, on the high road near Morfe, when she passed
him with a still more perfect and inimical unconsciousness; once in the distance on the moor, when he caught
her, short-skirted and wild, jumping the wide water
courses as they came, evidently under the impression that
she was unobserved. And he smiled and said to himself,
"She's doing it for fun, pure fun."

The third time he came upon her at dawn with the
dew on her skirts and on her hair. She darted away at
the clank of his horse's hoofs, half-savage, divinely shy.
And he said to himself that time, "I'm getting on. She's
aware of me all right."

She had come down from Karva, and he was on his way
to Morfe from Upthorne. He had sat up all night with
John Greatorex who had died at dawn.

The smell of the sick man, and of the bed and of the
low close room was still in his nostrils, and in his ears the
sounds of dying and of mourning, and at his heart the

oppression (he was still young enough to feel it) of the secret and abominable things he knew.   And in his eyes the unknown girl and her behavior became suddenly adorable.   She was the darting joy and the poignant sweetness, and the sheer extravagant ardor and energy of life.   His tempestuously romantic youth rose up and was troubled at the sight of her.   And his eyes, that had stared at her in wonder and amusement and inquisitive interest, followed her now with that queer pathos that they had. It was the look that he relied on to move desire in women's eyes; and now it traveled, forlorn and ineffectual, abject almost in its futility, over the gray moor-grass where she went.

That was on Wednesday the fourteenth.   On Friday the sixteenth he saw her again at nightfall, in the doorway of John Greatorex's house.

He had overtaken the cart that was carrying John Greatorex's coffin to Upthorne.   Low lighted, the long gray house brooded over the marshes, waiting to be disencumbered of its dead.

In the east the broken shoulders of the hills receded, winding with the dale like a coast line of gray cliffs above the mist that was their sea.   Tortured, mutilated by the jagged cloud that held her, the moon struggled and tore her way, she lifted and freed herself high and struck the marshes white.   Defaced and sinister, above her battlements, she looked at the house and made it terrible, moon-haunted.   Its door, low lighted, stood open to the night.

Rowcliffe drew back from the threshold to let a woman pass out.   Looking up, he was aware that he had seen her again.   He supposed it was the light of that detestable moon that gave her face its queer morbid whiteness.

She went by without seeing him, clenching her hands and carrying her young head high; and he saw that her eyes still held the tears that she was afraid to spill.

Mrs. Gale stood behind her with a lamp, lighting her passage.

"Who is that young lady?" he asked.

"T' Vicar's laass, Gwanda."

The woman leaned to him and whispered, "She's seen t' body."

And in the girl's fear and blindness and defiance he saw the pride of her youth beaten and offended by that which it had seen.

Out there, in the bridle path leading from the high road to the farm, the cart had stopped. The men were lifting the coffin out, shouldering it, carrying it along. He saw Gwenda Cartaret swerve out of their way. Presently he heard her running down the road.

Then he remembered what he had been sent for.

He turned his attention to Mrs. Gale. She was a square-set, blunt-featured woman of forty-five or so, who had once been comely like her daughter Essy. Now her soft chin had sagged; in her cheeks the stagnant blood crawled through a network of little veins, and the gloss had gone from her dark hair. Her brown eyes showed a dull defiance and deprecation of the human destiny.

"Where is he?" he said.

"Oop there, in t' room wi' 's feyther."

"Been drinking again, or what?"

"Naw, Dr. Rawcliffe, 'e 'assn't. I suddn' a sent for yo all this road for nowt."

She drew him into the house place, and whispered.

"I'm feared 'e'll goa queer in 'is 'head, like. 'E's sot there by t' body sence yesterda noon. 'E's not takken off

'is breeches for tree daas. 'E caaun't sleap; 'e wunna eat
and 'e wunna drink. There's work to be doon and 'e
wunna lay haand to it. Wull yo goa oop t' 'im, Dr.
Rawcliffe?"

Rowcliffe went up.

XIII

In the low lighted room the thing that Gwenda Cartaret had seen lay stretched in the middle of the great bed, covered with a sheet. The bed, with its white mound, was so much too big for the four walls that held it, the white plaster of the ceiling bulging above it stooped so low, that the body of John Greatorex lay as if already closed up in its tomb.

Jim Greatorex, his son, sat on a wooden chair at the head of the bed. His young, handsome face was loose and flushed as if he had been drinking. His eyes—the queer, blue, wide-open eyes that had hitherto looked out at you from their lodging in that ruddy, sensuous face, incongruously spiritual, high and above your head, like the eyes of a dreamer and a mystic—Jim's eyes were sunken now and darkened in their red and swollen lids. They stared at the rug laid down beside the bed, while Jim's mind set itself to count, stupidly and obstinately, the snippets of gray and scarlet cloth that made the pattern on the black. Every now and then he would recognise a snippet as belonging to some suit his father had worn years ago, and then Jim's brain would receive a shock and would stagger and have to begin its counting all over again.

The door opened to let Rowcliffe in. And at the sound of the door, as if a spring had been suddenly released in his spine, Jim Greatorex shot up and started to his feet.

"Well, Greatorex——"

44

"Good evening, Dr. Rawcliffe." He came forward awkwardly, hanging his head as if detected in an act of shame.

There was a silence while the two men turned their backs upon the bed, determined to ignore what was on it. They stood together by the window, pretending to stare at things out there in the night; and so they became aware of the men carrying the coffin.

They could no longer ignore it.

"Wull yo look at 'Im, doctor?"

"Better not——." Rowcliffe would have laid his hand on the young man's arm, muttering a refusal, but Greatorex had moved to the bed and drawn back the sheet.

What Gwenda Cartaret had seen was revealed.

The dead man's face, upturned with a slight tilt to the ceiling that bulged so brutally above it, the stiff dark beard accentuating the tilt, the eyes, also upturned, white under their unclosing lids, the nostrils, the half-open mouth preserved their wonder and their terror before a thing so incredible—that the walls and roof of a man's room should close round him and suffocate him. On this horrified face there were the marks of dissolution, and, at the corners of the grim beard and moustache, a stain.

It left nothing to be said. It was the face of the man who had drunk hard and had told his son that he had never been the worse for drink.

Jim Greatorex stood and looked at it as if he knew what Rowcliffe was thinking of it and defied him to think.

Rowcliffe drew up the sheet and covered it. "You'd better come out of this. It isn't good for you," he said.

"I knaw what's good for me, Dr. Rawcliffe."

Jim stuck his hands in his breeches and gazed stubbornly at the sheeted mound.

"Come," Rowcliffe said, "don't give way like this. Buck up and be a man."

"A ma-an? You wait till yor turn cooms, doctor."

"My turn came ten years ago, and it may come again."

"And yo'll knaw then what good it doos ta-alkin'." He paused, listening. "They've coom," he said.

There was a sound of scuffling on the stone floor below and on the stairs. Mrs. Gale's voice was heard out on the landing, calling to the men.

"Easy with un—easy. Mind t' lamp. Eh—yo'll never get un oop that road. Yo mun coax un round corner."

A swinging thud on the stone wall. Then more and more desperate scuffling with muttering. Then silence.

Mrs. Gale put her head in at the door.

"Jimmy, yo mun coom and gie a haand wi' t' coffin. They've got un faasst in t' turn o' t' stair."

Through the open doorway Rowcliffe could see the broad shoulders of the coffin jammed in the stairway.

Jim, flushed with resentment, strode out; and the struggling and scuffling began again, subdued, this time, and respectful. Rowcliffe went out to help.

Mrs. Gale on the landing went on talking to herself. "They sud 'ave browt trestles oop first. There's naw place to stond un in. Eh dear! It's job enoof gettin' un oop. What'll it be gettin' un down again wit' 'E layin' in un? 'Ere—yo get oonder un, Jimmy, and 'eave un oop."

Jim crouched and went backward down the stair under the coffin. His flushed face, with its mournful, mystic eyes, looked out at Rowcliffe for a moment under the coffin head. Then, with a heave of his great back and pushing with his powerful arms against the wall and stair rail, he loosened the shoulders of the coffin and bore it, steadied by Rowcliffe and the men, up the stair and into the room.

They set it on its feet beside the bed, propped against the wall. And Jim Greatorex stood and stared at it.

Rowcliffe went down into the kitchen, followed by Mrs. Gale.

"What d'yo think o' Jimmy, Dr. Rawcliffe?"

"He oughtn't to be left alone. Isn't there any sister or anybody who could come to him?"

"Naw; 'e's got naw sisters, Jimmy 'assn't."

"Well, you must get him to lie down and eat."

"Get 'im? Yo can do nowt wi' Jimmy. 'E'll goa 'is own road. 'Is feyther an' 'e they wuss always quar'ling, yo med say. Yet when t' owd gentleman was taaken bad, Jimmy, 'e couldn' do too mooch for 'im. 'E was set on pullin' 's feyther round. And when 'e found 'e couldn't keep t' owd gentleman, 'e gets it on 'is mind like —broodin'. And 'e's got nowt to coomfort 'im."

She sat down to it now.

"Yo see, Dr. Rawcliffe, Jim's feyther and 'is gran-feyther before 'im, they wuss good Wesleyans. It's in t' blood. But Jim's moother that died, she wuss Choorch. And that slip of a laass, when John Greatorex coom courtin', she turned 'im. 'E was that soft wi' laasses. 'Er feyther 'e was steward to lord o' t' Manor and 'e was Choorch and all t' family saame as t' folk oop at Manor. Yo med say, Jim Greatorex, 'e's got naw religion. Neither Choorch nor Chapel 'e is. Nowt to coomfort 'im."

Upstairs the scuffling and the struggling became frightful. Jim's feet and Jim's voice were heard above the muttering of the undertaker's men.

Mrs. Gale whispered. "They're gettin' 'im in. 'E's gien a haand wi' t' body. Thot's soomthin'."

She brooded ponderously. A sound of stamping and scraping at the back door roused her.

"Eh—oo's there now?" she asked irritably.

Willie, the farm lad, appeared on the threshold. His face was flushed and scared.

"Where's Jim?" he said in a thick voice.

"Ooosh-sh! Doan't yo' knaw t' coffin's coom? 'E's oopstairs w' t' owd maaster."

"Well—'e mun coom down. T' mare's taaken baad again in 'er insi-ide."

"T' mare, Daasy?"

"Yes."

"Eh dear, there's naw end to trooble. Yo go oop and fatch Jimmy."

Willie hesitated. His flush deepened.

"I daarss'nt," he whispered hoarsely.

"Poor laad, 'e 's freetened o' t' body," she explained. "Yo stay there, Wullie. I'll goa. T' body's nowt to me. I've seen too many o' they," she muttered as she went.

They heard her crying excitedly overhead. "Jimmy! Yo coom to t' ma-are! Yo coom to t' ma-are!"

The sounds in the room ceased instantly. Jim Greatorex, alert and in violent possession of all his faculties, dashed down the stairs and out into the yard.

Rowcliffe followed into the darkness where his horse and trap stood waiting for him.

He was lighting his lamps when Jim Greatorex appeared beside him with a lantern.

"Dr. Rawcliffe, will yo joost coom an' taak a look at lil maare?"

Jim's sullenness was gone. His voice revealed him humble and profoundly agitated.

Rowcliffe sighed, smiled, pulled himself together and turned with Greatorex into the stable.

In the sodden straw of her stall, Daisy, the mare, lay, heaving and snorting after her agony. From time to time she turned her head toward her tense and swollen flank, seeking with eyes of anguish the mysterious source of pain. The feed of oats with which Willie had tried to tempt her lay untouched in the skip beside her head.

"I give 'er they oats an hour ago," said Willie. 'An' she 'assn't so mooch as nosed 'em."

"Nawbody but a domned gawpie would have doon thot with 'er stoomach raw. Yo med 'ave killed t' mare."

Willie, appalled by his own deed and depressed, stooped down and fondled the mare's face, to show that it was not affection that he lacked.

"Heer—clear out o' thot and let doctor have a look in."

Willie slunk aside as Rowcliffe knelt with Greatorex in the straw and examined the sick mare.

"Can yo tell at all what's amiss, doctor?"

"Colic, I should say. Has the vet seen her?"

"Ye-es. He sent oop soomthing—"

"Well, have you given it her?"

Jim's voice thickened. "I sud have given it her yesterda."

"And why on earth didn't you?"

"The domned thing went clane out o' my head."

He turned to the window ledge by the stable door where, among a confusion of cobwebs and dusty bottles and tin cans, the drench of turpentine and linseed oil, the little phial of chlorodyne, and the clean tin pannikin with its wide protruding mouth, stood ready, all gleaming in the lantern light, forgotten since the day before.

"Thot's the stoof. Will yo halp me give it 'er, doctor?"

"All right. Can you hold her?"

"That I can. Coom oop, Daasy. Coom oop. There, my beauty. Gently, gently, owd laass."

Rowcliffe took off his coat and shook up the drench and poured it into the pannikin, while Greatorex got the struggling mare on to her feet.

Together, with gentleness and dexterity they cajoled her. Then Jim laid his hands upon her mouth and opened it, drawing up her head against his breast. Willie, suddenly competent, held the lantern while Rowcliffe poured the drench down her throat.

Daisy, coughing and dribbling, stood and gazed at them with sad and terrified eyes. And while the undertaker's men screwed down the lid upon John Greatorex in his coffin, Jim Greatorex, his son, watched with Daisy in her stall.

And Steven Rowcliffe watched with him, nursing the sick mare, making up a fresh, clean bed for her, rubbing and fomenting her swollen and tortured belly. When Daisy rolled in another agony, Rowcliffe gave her chlorodyne and waited till suddenly she lay still.

In Jim's face, as he looked down at her, there was an infinite tenderness and pity and compunction.

Rowcliffe, wriggling into his coat, regarded him with curiosity and wonder, till Jim drew himself up and fixed him with his queer, unhappy eyes.

"Shall I saave her, doctor?"

"I can't tell you yet. I'd better send the vet up to-morrow hadn't I?"

"Ay——" Jim's voice was strangled in the spasm of his throat. But he took Rowcliffe's hand and wrung it, discharging many emotions in that one excruciating grip.

Rowcliffe pointed to the little phial of chlorodyne lying in the straw. "If I were you," he said, "I shouldn't leave that lying about."

Through his long last night in the gray house haunted by the moon, John Greatorex lay alone, screwed down under a coffin lid, and his son, Jim, wrapped in a horse-blanket and with his head on a hay sack, lay in the straw of the stable, beside Daisy his mare. From time to time, as his mood took him, he turned and laid his hand on her in a poignant caress. As if she had been his first-born, or his bride, he spoke to her in the thick, soft voice of passion, with pitiful, broken words and mutterings.

"What is it, Daasy—what is it? There, did they, then, did they? My beauty—my lil laass. I—I wuss a domned brute to forget tha, a domned brute."

All that night and the next night he lay beside her. The funeral passed like a fantastic interlude between the long acts of his passion. His great sorrow made him humble to Mrs. Gale so that he allowed her to sustain him with food and drink. And on the third day it was known throughout Garthdale that young Greatorex, who had lost his father, had saved his mare.

Only Steven Rowcliffe knew that the mare had saved young Greatorex.

And the little phial of chlorodyne was put back among the cobwebs and forgotten.

XIV

Down at the Vicarage the Vicar was wrangling with his youngest daughter. For the third time Alice declared that she was not well and that she didn't want her milk.

"Whether you want it or not you've got to drink it," said the Vicar.

Alice took the glass in her lap and looked at it.

"Am I to stand over you till you drink it?"

Alice put the rim of the glass to her mouth and shuddered.

"I can't," she said. "It'll make me sick."

"Leave the poor child alone, Papa," said Gwenda.

But the Vicar ignored Gwenda.

"You'll drink it, if I stand here all night," he said.

Alice struggled with a spasm in her throat. He held the glass for her while she groped piteously.

"Oh, where's my hanky?"

With superhuman clemency he produced his own.

"It'll serve you right if I'm ill," said Alice.

"Come," said the Vicar in his wisdom and his patience. "Come."

He proffered the disgusting cup again.

"I'd drink it and have done with it, if I were you," said Mary in her soft voice.

Mary's soft voice was too much for Alice.

"Why c-can't you leave me alone? You—you—beast, Mary," she sobbed.

And Mr. Cartaret began again, "Am, I to stand here——"

Alice got up, she broke loose from them and left the room.

"You might have known she wasn't going to drink it," Gwenda said.

But the Vicar never knew when he was beaten.

"She would have drunk it," he said, "if Mary hadn't interfered.

Alice had not got the pneumonia that had killed John Greatorex. Such happiness, she reflected, was not for her. She had desired it too much.

But she was doing very well with her anæmia.

Bloodless and slender and inert, she dragged herself about the village. She could not get away from it because of the steep hills she would have had to climb. A small, unhappy ghost, she haunted the fields in the bottom and the path along the beck that led past Mrs. Gale's cottage.

The sight of Alice was more than ever annoying to the Vicar. Only you wouldn't have known it. As she grew whiter and weaker he braced himself, and became more hearty and robust. When he caught her lying on the sofa he spoke to her in a robust and hearty tone.

"Don't lie there all day, my girl. Get up and go out. What you want is a good blow on the moor."

"Yes. If I didn't die before I got there," Alice would say, while she thought, "Serve him right, too, if I did."

And the Vicar would turn from her in disgust. He knew what was the matter with his daughter Alice.

At dinner time he would pull himself together again, for, after all, he was her father. He was robust and hearty over the sirloin and the leg of mutton. He would call for a glass and press into it the red juice of the meat.

"Don't peak and pine, girl. Drink that. It'll put some blood into you."

And Alice would refuse to drink it.

Next she refused to drink her milk at eleven. She carried it out to Essy in the scullery.

"I wish you'd drink my milk for me, Essy. It makes me sick," she said.

"I don't want your milk," said Essy.

"Please—" she implored her.

But Essy was angry. Her face flamed and she banged down the dishes she was drying. "I sall not drink it. What should I want your milk for? You can pour it in t' pig's bucket."

And the milk would be left by the scullery window till it turned sour and Essy poured it into the pig's bucket that stood under the sink.

Three weeks passed, and with every week Alice grew more bloodless, more slender, and more inert, and more and more like an unhappy ghost. Her small face was smaller; there was a tinge of green in its honey-whiteness, and of mauve in the dull rose of her mouth. And under her shallow breast her heart seemed to rise up and grow large, while the rest of Alice shrank and grew small. It was as if her fragile little body carried an enormous engine, an engine of infernal and terrifying power. When she lay down and when she got up and with every sudden movement its throbbing shook her savagely.

Night and morning she called to her sister: "Oh Gwenda, come and feel my heart. I do believe it's growing. It's getting too big for my body. It frightens me when it jumps about like that."

It frightened Gwenda.

But it did not really frighten Alice. She rejoiced in

it, rather, and exulted.   After all, it was a good thing that
she had not got pneumonia, which might have killed her
as it had killed John Greatorex.   She had got what served
her purpose better.   It served all her purposes.   If she
had tried she could not have hit on anything that would
have annoyed her father more or put him more conspicu-
ously in the wrong.   To begin with, it was his doing.   He
had worried her into it.   And he had brought her to a
place which was the worst place conceivable for anybody
with a diseased heart, since you couldn't stir out of doors
without going up hill.

Night and morning Alice stood before the looking-glass
and turned out the lining of her lips and eyelids and saw
with pleasure the pale rose growing paler.   Every other
hour she laid her hand on her heart and took again the
full thrill of its dangerous throbbing, or felt her pulse to
assure herself of the halt, the jerk, the hurrying of the
beat.   Night and morning and every other hour she
thought of Rowcliffe.

"If it goes on like this, they'll *have* to send for him,"
she said.

But it had gone on, the three weeks had passed, and
yet they had not sent.   The Vicar had put his foot down.
He wouldn't have the doctor.   He knew better than a
dozen doctors what was the matter with his daughter
Alice.

Alice said nothing.   She simply waited.   As if some
profound and dead-sure instinct had sustained her, she
waited, sickening.

And on the last night of the third week she fainted.
She had dragged herself upstairs to bed, staggered across
the little landing and fallen on the threshold of her room.

They kept her in bed next day.   At one o'clock she refused her chicken-broth. She would neither eat nor drink. And a little before three Gwenda went for the doctor.

She had not told Alice she was going. She had not told anybody.

XV

She had to walk, for Mary had taken her bicycle. Nobody knew where Mary had gone or when she had started or when she would be back.

But the four miles between Garth and Morfe were nothing to Gwenda, who would walk twenty for her own amusement. She would have stretched the way out indefinitely if she could; she would have piled Garthdale Moor on Greffington Edge and Karva on the top of them and put them between Garth and Morfe, so violent was her fear of Steven Rowcliffe.

She had no longer any desire to see him or to be seen by him. He had seen her twice too often, and too early and too late. After being caught on the moor at dawn, it was preposterous that she should show herself in the doorway of Upthorne at night.

How was he to know that she hadn't done it on purpose? Girls did these things. Poor little Ally had done them. And it was because Ally had done them that she had been taken and hidden away here where she couldn't do them any more.

But—couldn't she? Gwenda stood still, staring in her horror as the frightful thought struck her that Ally could, and that she would, the very minute she realised young Rowcliffe. And he would think—not that it mattered in the least what he thought—he would think that there were two of them.

If only, she said to herself, if only young Rowcliffe were a married man. Then even Ally couldn't——

Not that she blamed poor little Ally. She looked on little Ally as the victim of a malign and tragic tendency, the fragile vehicle of an alien and overpowering impulse. Little Ally was doomed. It wasn't her fault if she was made like that.

And this time it wouldn't be her fault at all. Their father would have driven her. Gwenda hated him for his persecution and exposure of the helpless creature.

She walked on thinking.

It wouldn't end with Ally. They were all three exposed and persecuted. For supposing—it wasn't likely, but supposing—that this Rowcliffe man was the sort of man she liked, supposing—what was still more unlikely—that he was the sort of man who would like her, where would be the good of it? Her father would spoil it all. He spoiled everything.

Well, no, to be perfectly accurate, not everything. There was one thing he had not spoiled, because he had never suspected its existence—her singular passion for the place. Of course, if he had suspected it, he would have stamped on it. It was his business to stamp on other people's passions. Luckily, it wasn't in him to conceive a passion for a place.

It had come upon her at first sight as they drove between twilight and night from Reyburn through Rathdale into Garthdale. It was when they had left the wooded land behind them and the moors lifted up their naked shoulders, one after another, darker than dark, into a sky already whitening above the hidden moon. And she saw Morfe, gray as iron, on its hill, bearing the square crown and the triple pendants of its lights; she saw the long straight line of Greffington Edge, hiding the secret

moon, and Karva with the ashen west behind it. There
was something in their form and in their gesture that
called to her as if they knew her, as if they waited for
her; they struck her with the shock of recognition, as if
she had known them and had waited too.

And close beside her own wonder and excitement
she had felt the deep and sullen repulsion of her com-
panions. The Vicar sat huddled in his overcoat. His
nostrils, pinched with repugnance, sniffed as they drank
in the cold, clean air. From time to time he shuddered,
and a hoarse muttering came from under the gray woolen
scarf he had wound round his mouth and beard. He was
the righteous man, sent into uttermost abominable exile
for his daughter's sin. Behind him, on the back seat of
the trap, Alice and Mary cowed under their capes and
rugs. They had turned their shoulders to each other,
hostile in their misery. Gwenda was sorry for them.

The gray road dipped and turned and plunged them to
the bottom of Garthdale. The small, scattering lights of
the village waited for her in the hollow, with something
humble and sad and familiar in their setting. They too
stung her with that poignant and secret sense of
recognition.

"This is the place," the Vicar had said. He had addressed himself to Alice; and it had been as if he had
said, This the place, the infernal, the damnable place,
you've brought us to with your behavior.

Their hatred of it had made Gwenda love it. "You can
have your old Garthdale all to yourself," Alice had said.
"Nobody else wants it."

That, to Gwenda, was the charm of it. The adorable
place was her own. Nobody else wanted it. She loved
it for itself. It had nothing but itself to offer her. And
that was enough. It was almost, as she had said, too

much. Her questing youth conceived no more rapturous adventure than to follow the sheep over Karva, to set out at twilight and see the immense night come down on the high moors above Upthorne; to get up when Alice was asleep and slip out and watch the dawn turning from gray to rose, and from rose to gold above Greffington Edge.

As it happened you saw sunrise and moonrise best from the platform of Morfe Green. There Greffington Edge breaks and falls away, and lets slip the dawn like a rosy scarf from its shoulder, and sets the moon free of her earth and gives her to the open sky.

But, just as the Vicar had spoiled Rowcliffe, so Rowcliffe had spoiled Morfe for Gwenda. Therefore her fear of him was mingled with resentment. It was as if he had had no business to be living there, in that house of his looking over the Green.

Incredible that she should have wanted to see and to know this person. But now, that she didn't want to, of course she was going to see him.

At the bend of the road, within a mile of Morfe, Mary came riding on Gwenda's bicycle. Large parcels were slung from her handle bars. She had been shopping in the village.

Mary, bowed forward as she struggled with an upward slope, was not aware of Gwenda. But Gwenda was aware of Mary, and, not being in the mood for her, she struck off the road on to the moor and descended upon Morfe by the steep lane that leads from Karva into Rathdale.

It never occurred to her to wonder what Mary had been doing in Morfe, so evident was it that she had been shopping.

XVI

THE doctor was at home, but he was engaged, at the moment, in the surgery.

The maid-servant asked if she would wait.

She waited in the little cold and formal dining-room that looked through two windows on to the Green. So formal and so cold, so utterly impersonal was the air of the doctor's mahogany furniture that her fear left her. It was as if the furniture assured her that she would not really *see* Rowcliffe; as for knowing him, she needn't worry.

She had sent in her card, printed for convenience with the names of the three sisters:

> Miss Cartaret.
> Miss Gwendolen Cartaret.
> Miss Alice Cartaret.

She felt somehow that it protected her. She said to herself, "He won't know which of us it is."

Rowcliffe was washing his hands in the surgery when the card was brought to him. He frowned at the card,

"But—— You've brought this before," he said. "I've seen the lady."

"No, sir. It's another lady."

"Another? Are you certain?"

"Yes, sir. Quite certain."

"Did she come on a bicycle?"

"No, sir, that was the lady you've seen.   I think this'll
be her sister."

Rowcliffe was still frowning as he dried his hands with
fastidious care.

"She's different, sir.   Taller like."

"Taller ?"

"Yes, sir."

Rowcliffe turned to the table and picked up a probe
and a lancet and dropped them into a sterilising solution.

The maid waited. Rowcliffe's absorption was complete.

"Shall I ask her to call again, sir ?"

"No.   I'll see her.   Where is she ?"

"In the dining-room, sir."

"Show her into the study."

Nothing could have been more distant and reserved than
Rowcliffe's dining-room.   But, to a young woman who had
made up her mind that she didn't want to know anything
about him, Rowcliffe's study said too much.   It told her
that he was a ferocious and solitary reader; for in the
long rows of book shelves the books leaned slantwise
across the gaps where his hands had rummaged and ran-
sacked.   It told her that his gods were masculine and
many—Darwin and Spencer and Haeckel, Pasteur, Curie
and Lord Lister, Thomas Hardy, Walt Whitman and Ber-
nard Shaw.   Their photogravure portraits hung above the
bookcase.   He was indifferent to mere visible luxury, or
how could he have endured the shabby drugget, the
cheap, country wall-paper with its design of dreadful roses
on a white watered ground ?   But the fire in the grate and
the deep arm-chair drawn close to it showed that he loved
warmth and comfort.   That his tastes made him solitary
she gathered from the chair's comparatively unused and

unworn companion, lurking and sulking in the corner
where it had been thrust aside.

The one window of this room looked to the west upon
a little orchard, gray trunks of apple trees and plum trees
against green grass, green branches against gray stone,
gray that was softened in the liquid autumn air, green that
was subtle, exquisite, charmingly austere.

He could see his little orchard as he sat by his fire.
She thought she rather liked him for keeping his window
so wide open.

She was standing by it looking at the orchard as he
came in.

He was so quiet in his coming that she did not see or
hear him till he stood before her.

And in his eyes, intensely quiet, there was a look of
wonder and of incredulity, almost of concern.

Greetings and introductions over, the unused arm-chair
was brought out from its lair in the corner. Rowcliffe, in
his own arm-chair, sat in shadow, facing her. What light
there was fell full on her.

"I'm sorry you should have had to come to me," he said,
"your sister was here a minute or two ago."

"My sister?"

"I think it *must* have been your sister. She said it
was *her* sister I was to go and see."

"I didn't know she was coming. She never told me."

"Pity. I was coming out to see you first thing to-
morrow morning."

"Then you know? She told you?"

"She told me something." He smiled. "She must
have been a little overanxious. You don't look as if there
was very much the matter with you."

"But there isn't. It isn't me."

"Who is it then?"

"My other sister."

"Oh. I seem to have got a little mixed."

"You see, there are three of us."

He laughed.

"Three! Let me get it right. I've seen Miss Cartaret. You are Miss Gwendolen Cartaret. And the lady I am to see is—— ?

"My youngest sister, Alice."

"Now I understand. I wondered how you managed those four miles. Tell me about her."

She began. She was vivid and terse. He saw that she made short cuts to the root of the matter. He showed himself keen and shrewd. Once or twice he said "I know, I know," and she checked herself.

"My sister has told you all that."

"No, she hasn't. Nothing like it. Please go on."

She went on till he interrupted her. "How old is she?"

"Just twenty-three."

"I see. Yes." He looked so keen now that she was frightened.

"Does that make it more dangerous?" she said.

He laughed. "No. It makes it less so. I don't suppose it's dangerous at all. But I can't tell till I've seen her. I say, you must be tired after that long walk."

"I'm never tired."

"That's good."

He rang the bell. The maid appeared.

"Tell Acroyd I want the trap. And bring tea—at once."

"For two, sir?"

"For two."

Gwenda rose. "Thanks very much, I must be going."

"Please stay. It won't take five minutes. Then I can drive you back."

"I can walk."

"I know you can. But—you see——" His keenness and shrewdness went from him. He was almost embarrassed. "I *was* going round to see your sister in the morning. But—I think I'd rather see her to-night. And——" He was improvising freely now—"I ought, perhaps, to see you after, as you understand the case. So, if you don't *mind* coming back with me——"

She didn't mind. Why should she?

She stayed. She sat in Rowcliffe's chair before his fire and drank his tea and ate his hot griddle-cakes (she had a healthy appetite, being young and strong). She talked to him as if she had known him a long time. All these things he made her do, and when he talked to her he made her forget what had brought her there; he made her forget Alice and Mary and her father.

When he left her for a moment she got up, restless and eager to be gone. And when he came back to her she was standing by the open window again, looking at the orchard.

Rowcliffe looked at *her,* taking in her tallness, her slenderness, the lithe and beautiful line of her body, curved slightly backward as she leaned against the window wall.

Never before and never again, afterwards, never, that was to say, for any other woman, did Rowcliffe feel what he felt then. Looking back on it (afterward) he could only describe it as a sense of certainty. It lacked, surprisingly, the element of surprise.

"You like my north-country orchard? (He was certain that she did.)

She turned, smiling. "I like it very much."

They had been a long time over tea.   It was half-past
five before they started.   He brought an overcoat and put
it on her.   He wrapped a rug round her knees and feet
and tucked it well in.

"You don't like rugs," he said (he knew she didn't),
"but you've got to have it."

She did like it.   She liked his rug and his overcoat, and
his little brown horse with the clanking hoofs.   And she
liked him, most decidedly she liked him, too.   He was the
sort of man you could like.

They were soon out on the moor.

Rowcliffe's youth rose in him and put words into his
mouth.

"Ripping country, this."

She said it was ripping.

For the life of them they couldn't have said more about
it.   There were no words for the inscrutable ecstasy it
gave them.

As they passed Karva Rowcliffe smiled.

"It's all right," he said, "my driving you.   Of course
you don't remember, but we've met—several times before."

"Where?"

"I'll show you where. Anyhow, that's your hill, isn't it?"

"How did you know it was?"

"Because I've seen you there.   The first time I ever saw
you—— No, *that* was a bit farther on.   At the bend of
the road.   We're coming to it."

They came.

"Just here," he said.

And now they were in sight of Garthdale.

"Funny I should have thought it was you who were ill."

"I'm never ill."

"You won't be as long as you can walk like that.   And
run.   And jump——"

A horrid pause.

"You did it very nicely."

Another pause, not quite so horrid.

And then—— "Do you *always* walk after dark and before sunrise?"

And it was as if he had said, "Why am I always meeting you? What do you do it for? It's queer, isn't it?"

But he had given her her chance. She rose to it.

"I've done it ever since we came here." (It was as if she had said "Long before *you* came.") "I do it because I like it. That's the best of this place. You can do what you like in it. There's nobody to see you."

("Counting me," he thought, "as nobody.")

"I should like to do it, too," he said—"to go out before sunrise—if I hadn't got to. If I did it for fun—like you."

He knew he would not really have liked it. But his romantic youth persuaded him in that moment that he would.

XVII

Mary was up in the attic, the west attic that looked on to the road through its shy gable window.

She moved quietly there, her whole being suffused exquisitely with a sense of peace, of profound, indwelling goodness. Every act of hers for the last three days had been incomparably good, had been, indeed, perfect. She had waited on Alice hand and foot. She had made the chicken broth refused by Alice. There was nothing that she would not do for poor little Ally. When little Ally was petulant and sullen, Mary was gentle and serene. She felt toward little Ally, lying there so little and so white, a poignant, yearning tenderneess. To-day she had visited all the sick people in the village, though it was not Wednesday, Dr. Rowcliffe's day. (Only by visiting them on other days could Mary justify and make blameless her habit of visiting them on Wednesdays.) She had put the house in order. She had done her shopping in Morfe to such good purpose that she had concealed even from herself the fact that she had gone into Morfe, surreptitiously, to fetch the doctor.

Of course Mary was aware that she had fetched him. She had been driven to that step by sheer terror. All the way home she kept on saying to herself, "I've saved Ally." "I've saved Ally." That thought, splendid and exciting, rushed to the lighted front of Mary's mind; if the thought of Rowcliffe followed its shining trail, it thrust him back, it spread its luminous wings to hide him, it substituted its heavenly form for his.

So effectually did it cover him that Mary herself never dreamed that he was there.

Neither did the Vicar, when he saw her arrive, laden with parcels, wholesomely cheerful and reddened by her ride. He had said to her "You're a good girl, Mary," and the sadness of his tone implied that he wished her sister Gwendolen and her sister Alice were more like her. And he had smiled at her under his austere moustache, and carried in the biggest parcels for her.

The Vicar was pleased with his daughter Mary. Mary had never given him an hour's anxiety. Mary had never put him in the wrong, never made him feel uncomfortable. He honestly believed that he was fond of her. She was like her poor mother. Goodness, he said to himself, was in her face.

There had been goodness in Mary's face when she went into Alice's room to see what she could do for her. There was goodness in it now, up in the attic, where there was nobody but God to see it; goodness at peace with itself, and utterly content.

She had been back more than an hour. And ever since teatime she had been up in the attic, putting away her summer gowns. She shook them and held them out and looked at them, the poor pretty things that she had hardly ever worn. They hung all limp, all abashed and broken in her hands, as if aware of their futility. She said to herself, "They were no good, no good at all. And next year they'll all be old-fashioned. I shall be ashamed to be seen in them." And she folded them and laid them by for their winter's rest in the black trunk. And when she saw them lying there she had a moment of remorse. After all, they had been part of herself, part of her throbbing, sensuous womanhood, warmed once by her body. It wasn't their fault, poor things, any more than hers, if they had been futile and unfit. She shut the lid down on them gently, and it was as if she buried them gently out of her sight. She could afford to forgive them, for she knew that there was no futility nor unfitness in her. Deep down in her heart she knew it.

She sat on the trunk in the attitude of one waiting, waiting in the utter stillness of assurance. She could afford to wait. All her being was still, all its secret impulses appeased by the slow and orderly movements of her hands.

Suddenly she started up and listened. She heard out on the road the sound of wheels, and of hoofs that struck together. And she frowned. She thought, He might as well have called to-day, if he's passing.

The clanking ceased, the wheels slowed down, and Mary's peaceful heart moved violently in her breast. The trap drew up at the Vicarage gate.

She went over to the window, the small, shy gable window that looked on to the road. She saw her sister standing in the trap and Rowcliffe beneath her, standing in the road and holding out his hand. She saw the two faces, the man's face looking up, the woman's face looking down, both smiling.

And Mary's heart drew itself together in her breast. Through her shut lips her sister's name forced itself almost audibly.

"*Gwen*-da!"

Suddenly she shivered. A cold wind blew through the open window. Yet she did not move to shut it out. To have interfered with the attic window would have been a breach of compact, an unholy invasion of her sister's rights. For the attic, the smallest, the coldest, the darkest and most thoroughly uncomfortable room in the whole house, was Gwenda's, made over to her in the Vicar's magnanimity, by way of compensation for the necessity that forced her to share her room with Alice. As the attic was used for storing trunks and lumber, only two square yards of floor could be spared for Gwenda. But the two square yards, cleared, and covered with a strip of old carpet, and furnished with a little table and one chair; the wall-space by the window with its hanging bookcase; the window itself and the corner fireplace near it were hers beyond division and dispute. Nobody wanted them.

And as Mary from among the boxes looked toward her sister's territory, her small, brooding face took on such sadness as good women feel in contemplating a character inscrutable and unlike their own. Mary was sorry for Gwenda because of her inscrutability and unlikeness.

Then, thinking of Gwenda, Mary smiled. The smile began in pity for her sister and ended in a nameless, secret satisfaction. Not for a moment did Mary suspect its source. It seemed to her one with her sense of her own goodness.

When she smiled it was as if the spirit of her small brooding face took wings and fluttered, lifting delicately the rather heavy corners of her mouth and eyes.

Then, quietly, and with no indecorous haste, she went down into the drawing-room to receive Rowcliffe. She was the eldest and it was her duty.

By the mercy of Heaven the Vicar had gone out.

Gwenda left Rowcliffe with Mary and went upstairs to prepare Alice for his visit. She had brushed out her sister's long pale hair and platted it, and had arranged the plats, tied with knots of white ribbon, one over each low breast, and she had helped her to put on a little white flannel jacket with a broad lace collar. Thus arrayed and decorated, Alice sat up in her bed, her small slender body supported by huge pillows, white against white, with no color about her but the dull gold of her hair.

Gwenda was still in the room, tidying it, when Mary brought Rowcliffe there.

It was a Rowcliffe whom she had not yet seen. She had her back to him as he paused in the doorway to let Mary pass through. Ally's bed faced the door, and the look in Ally's eyes made her aware of the change in him. All of a sudden he had become taller (much taller than he really was) and rigid and austere. His youth and its charm dropped clean away from him. He looked ten years older than he had been ten minutes ago. Compared with him, as he stood beside her bed, Ally looked more than ever like a small child, a child vibrating with shyness and fear, a child that implacable adult authority has found out in foolishness and naughtiness; so evident was it to Ally that to Rowcliffe nothing was hidden, nothing veiled.

It was as a child that he treated her, a child who can conceal nothing, from whom most things—all the serious and important things—must be concealed. And Ally knew the terrible advantage that he took of her.

It was bad enough when he asked her questions and took no more notice of her answers than if she had been a born fool. That might have been his north-country manners and probably he couldn't help them. But there was no necessity that Ally could see for his brutal abruptness, and the callous and repellent look he had when she bared her breast to the stethescope that sent all her poor secrets flying through the long tubes that attached her heart to his abominable ears. Neither (when he had disentangled

himself from the stethescope) could she understand why
he should scowl appallingly as he took hold of her poor
wrist to feel her pulse.

She said to herself, "He knows everything about me
and he thinks I'm awful."

It was anguish to Ally that he should think her awful.

And (to make it worse, if anything could make it)
there was Mary standing at the foot of the bed and staring
at her. Mary knew perfectly well that he was thinking
how awful she was. It was what Mary thought herself.

If only Gwenda had stayed with her! But Gwenda had
left the room when she saw Rowcliffe take out his
stethescope.

And as it flashed on Ally what Rowcliffe was thinking
of her, her heart stopped as if it was never going on
again, then staggered, then gave a terrifying jump.

Rowcliffe had done with Ally's little wrist. He laid it
down on the counterpane, not brutally at all, but gently,
almost tenderly, as if it had been a thing exquisitely fragile and precious.

He rose to his feet and looked at her, and then, all of
a sudden, as he looked, Rowcliffe became young again;
charmingly young, almost boyish. And, as if faintly
amused at her youth, faintly touched by her fragility, he
smiled. With a mouth and with eyes from which all
austerity had departed he smiled at Alice.

(It was all over. He had done with her. He could
afford to be kind to her as he would have been kind to a
little, frightened child.)

And Alice smiled back at him with her white face between the pale gold, serious bands of platted hair.

She was no longer frightened. She forgot his austerity

as if it had never been. She saw that he hadn't thought her awful in the least. He couldn't have looked at her like that if he had.

A sense of warmth, of stillness, of soft happiness flooded her body and her brain, as if the stream of life had ceased troubling and ran with an even rhythm. As she lay back, her tormented heart seemed suddenly to sink into it and rest, to be part of it, poised on the stream.

Then, still looking down at her, he spoke.

"It's pretty evident," he said, "what's the matter with you."

"*Is* it?"

Her eyes were all wide. He had frightened her again.

"It is," he said. "You've been starved."

"Oh," said little Ally, is *that* all?"

And Rowcliffe smiled again, a little differently.

Mary said nothing. She had found out long ago that silence was her strength. Her small face brooded. Impossible to tell what she was thinking.

"What has become of the other one, I wonder?" he said to himself.

He wanted to see her. She was the intelligent one of the three sisters, and she was honest. He had said to her quite plainly that he would want her. Why, on earth, he wondered, had she gone away and left him with this sweet and good, this quite exasperatingly sweet and good woman who had told him nothing but lies?

He was aware that Mary Cartaret was sweet and good. But he had found that sweet and good women were not invariably intelligent. As for honesty, if they were always honest they would not always be sweet and good.

Through the door he opened for the eldest sister to pass out the other slipped in. She had been waiting on the landing.

He stopped her. He made a sign to her to come out with him. He closed the door behind them.

"Can I see you for two minutes?"

"Yes."

They whispered rapidly.

At the head of the stairs Mary waited. He turned. His smile acknowledged and paid deference to her sweetness and goodness, for Rowcliffe was sufficiently accomplished.

But not more so than Mary Cartaret. Her face, wide and candid, quivered with subdued interrogation. Her lips parted as if they said, "I am only waiting to know what I am to do. I will do what you like, only tell me."

Rowcliffe stood by the bedroom door, which he had opened for her to pass through again. His eyes, summoning their powerful pathos, implored forgiveness.

Mary, utterly submissive, passed through.

He followed Gwendolen Cartaret downstairs to the dining-room.

He knew what he was going to say, but what he did say was unexpected.

For, as she stood there in the small and old and shabby room, what struck him was her youth.

"Is your father in?" he said.

He surprised her as he had surprised himself.

"No," she said. "Why? Do you want to see him?"

He hesitated. "I almost think I'd better."

"He won't be a bit of good, you know. He never is. He doesn't even know we sent for you."

"Well, then——"

"You'd better tell me straight out. You'll have to, in the end. Is it serious?"

"No. But it will be if we don't stop it. How long has it been going on?"

"Ever since we came to this place."

"Six months, you said. And she's been worse than this last month?"

"Much worse."

"If it was only the anæmia——"

"Isn't it?"

"Yes—among other things."

"Not—her heart?"

"No—her heart's all right." He corrected himself. "I mean there's no disease in it. You see, she ought to have got well up here in this air. It's the sort of place you send anæmic people to to cure them."

"The dreadful thing is that she doesn't like the place."

"Ah—that's what I want to get at. She isn't happy in it?"

"No. She isn't happy."

He meditated. "Your sister didn't tell me that.'

"She couldn't."

"I mean your other sister—Miss Cartaret."

"*She* wouldn't. She'd think it rather awful."

He laughed. "Heaps of people think it awful to tell the truth. Do you happen to know *why* she doesn't like the place?"

She was silent. Evidently there was some "awfulness" she shrank from.

"Too lonely for her, I suppose?"

"Much too lonely."

"Where were you before you came here?"

She told him.

"Why did you leave it?"

She hesitated again. "We couldn't help it."

"Well—it seems a pity. But I suppose clergymen can't choose where they'll live."

She looked away from him. Then, as if she were trying to divert her from the trail he followed, "You forget —she's been starving herself. Isn't that enough?"

"Not in her case. You see, she isn't ill because she's been starving herself. She's been starving herself because she's ill. It's a symptom. The trouble is not that she starves herself—but that she's been starved."

"I know. I know."

"If you could get her back to that place where she was happy——"

"I can't. She can never go back there. Besides, it wouldn't be any good if she did."

He smiled. "Are you quite sure?"

"Certain."

"Does she know it?"

"No. She never knew it. But she *would* know it if she went back."

"That's why you took her away?"

She hesitated again. "Yes."

Rowcliffe looked grave.

"I see. That's rather unfortunate."

He said to himself: "She doesn't take it in *yet*. I don't see how I'm to tell her."

To her he said: "Well, I'll send the medicine along to-night."

As the door closed behind Rowcliffe, Mary appeared on the stairs.

"Gwenda," she said, "Ally wants you. She wants to know what he said."

"He said nothing."

"You look as if he'd said a great deal."

"He said nothing that she doesn't know."

"He told her there was nothing the matter with her except that she'd been starving herself."

"He told me she'd been starved."

"I don't see the difference."

"Well," said Gwenda. *"He* did."

That night the Vicar scowled over his supper. And before it was ended he broke loose.

"Which of you two sent for Dr. Rowcliffe?"

"I did," said Gwenda.

Mary said nothing.

"And what—do you—mean by doing such a thing without consulting me?"

"I mean," said Gwenda quietly, "that he should see Alice."

"And *I* meant—most particularly—that he shouldn't see her. If I'd wanted him to see her I'd have gone for him myself."

"When it was a bit too late," said Gwenda.

His blue eyes dilated as he looked at her.

"Do you suppose I don't know what's the matter with her as well as he does?"

As he spoke the stiff, straight moustache that guarded his mouth lifted, showing the sensual redness and fulness of the lips.

And of this expression on her father's face Gwenda understood nothing, divined nothing, knew nothing but that she loathed it.

"You may know what's the matter with her," she said, "but can you cure it?"

"Can he?" said the Vicar.

XVIII

THE next day, which was a Tuesday, Alice was up and about again. Rowcliffe saw her on Wednesday and on Saturday, when he declared himself satisfied with her progress and a little surprised.

So surprised was he that he said he would not come again unless he was sent for.

And then in three days Alice slid back.

But they were not to worry about her, she said. There was nothing the matter with her except that she was tired. She was so tired that she lay all Tuesday on the drawing-room sofa and on Wednesday morning she was too tired to get up and dress.

And on Wednesday afternoon Dr. Rowcliffe found a note waiting at the blacksmith's cottage in Garth village, where he had a room with a brown gauze blind in the window and the legend in gilt letters:

SURGERY

Dr. S. Rowcliffe, M.D., F.R.C.S.

Hours of Attendance
Wednesday, 2.30-4.30.

The note ran:

"DEAR DR. ROWCLIFFE: Can you come and see me this afternoon? I think I'm rather worse. But I don't

79

want to frighten my people—so perhaps, if you just looked
in about teatime, as if you'd called?

"Yours truly,

"ALICE CARTARET."

Essy Gale had left the note that morning.

Rowcliffe looked at it dubiously. He was honest and
he had the large views of a man used to a large practice.
His patients couldn't complain that he lengthened his
bills by paying unnecessary visits. If he wanted to add
to his income in that way, he wasn't going to begin with
a poor parson's hysterical daughter. But as the Vicar of
Garth had called on him and left his card on Monday,
there was no reason why he shouldn't look in on Wednesday about teatime. Especially as he knew that the Vicar
was in the habit of visiting Upthorne and the outlying
portions of his parish on Wednesday afternoons.

All day Alice lay in her little bed like a happy child
and waited. Propped on her pillows, with her slender
arms stretched out before her on the counterpane, she
waited.

Her sullenness was gone. She had nothing but sweetness for Mary and for Essy. Even to her father she was
sweet. She could afford it. Her instinct was now sure.
From time to time a smile flickered on her small face like
a light almost of triumph.

The Vicar and Miss Cartaret were out when Rowcliffe
called at the Vicarage, but Miss Gwendolen was in if he
would like to see her.

He waited in the crowded shabby gray and amber
drawing-room with the Erard in the corner, and it was
there that she came to him.

He said he had only called to ask after her sister, as he had heard in the village that she was not so well.

"I'm afraid she isn't."

"May I see her? I don't mean professionally—just for a talk."

The formula came easily. He had used it hundreds of times in the houses of parsons and of clerks and of little shopkeepers, to whom bills were nightmares.

She took him upstairs.

On the landing she turned to him.

"She doesn't *look* worse. She looks better."

"All right. She won't deceive me."

She did look better, better than he could have believed. There was a faint opaline dawn of color in her face.

Heaven only knew what he talked about, but he talked; for over a quarter of an hour he kept it up.

And when he rose to go he said, "You're not worse. You're better. You'll be perfectly well if you'll only get up and go out. Why waste all this glorious air?"

"If I could live on air!" said Alice.

"You can—you do to a very large extent. You certainly can't live without it."

Downstairs he lingered. But he refused the tea that Gwenda offered him. He said he hadn't time. Patients were waiting for him.

"But I'll look in next Wednesday, if I may."

"At teatime?"

"Very well—at teatime."

"How's Alice?" said the Vicar when he returned from Upthorne.

"She's better."

"Has that fellow Rowcliffe been here again?"

"He called—on you, I think."

(Rowcliffe's cards lay on the table flap in the passage, proving plainly that his visit was not professional.)

"And you made him see her ?" he insisted.

"He saw her."

"Well ?"

"He says she's all right. She'll be well if only she'll go out in the open air."

"It's what I've been dinning into her for the last three months. She doesn't want a doctor to tell her that."

He drew her into the study and closed the door. He was not angry. He had more than ever his air of wisdom and of patience.

"Look here, Gwenda," he said gravely. "I know what I'm doing. There's nothing in the world the matter with her. But she'll never be well as long as you keep on sending for young Rowcliffe."

But his daughter Gwendolen was not impressed. She knew what it meant—that air of wisdom and of patience.

Her unsubmissive silence roused his temper.

"I won't have him sent for—do you hear ?"

And he made up his mind that he would go over to Morfe again and give young Rowcliffe a hint. It was to give him a hint that he had called on Monday.

But the Vicar did not call again in Morfe. For before he could brace himself to the effort Alice was well again.

Though the Vicar did not know it, Rowcliffe had looked in at teatime the next Wednesday and the next after that.

Alice was no longer compelled to be ill in order to see him.

XIX

"'Oh Gawd, our halp in a-ages paasst,
    Our 'awp in yeears ter coom,
  Our shal-ter from ther storm-ee blaasst,
    And our ee-tarnal 'oam!'"

"'Ark at 'im! That's Jimmy arl over. T' think that
'is poor feyther's not in 'is graave aboove a moonth, an' 'e
singin' fit t' eave barn roof off! They should tak' an'
shoot 'im oop in t' owd powder magazine," said Mrs.
Gale.

"Well—but it's a wonderful voice," said Gwenda Cartaret.

"I've never heard another like it, and I know something
about voices," Alice said.

They had gone up to Upthorne to ask Mrs. Gale to look
in at the Vicarage on her way home, for Essy wasn't very
well.

But Mrs. Gale had shied off from the subject of Essy.
She had done it with the laughter of deep wisdom and a
shake of her head. You couldn't teach Mrs. Gale anything about illness, nor about Essy.

"I knaw Assy," she had said. "There's nowt amiss
with her. Doan't you woorry."

And then Jim Greatorex, though unseen, had burst out
at them with his big voice. It came booming from the
mistal at the back.

Alice told the truth when she said she had never heard
anything like it; and even in the dale, so critical of

83

strangers, it was admitted that she knew. The village
had a new schoolmaster who was no musician, and hope-
less with the choir. Alice, as the musical one of the family, had been trained to play the organ, and she played
it, not with passion, for it was her duty, but with mechani-
cal and perfunctory correctness, as she had been taught.
She was also fairly successful with the village choir.

"Mebbe yo 'aven't 'eard anoother," said Mrs. Gale.
"It's rackoned there isn't anoother woon like it in t'
daale."

"But it's just what we want for our choir—a big barytone voice. Do you think he'd sing for us, Mrs. Gale?"

Alice said it light-heartedly, for she did not know what
she was asking. She knew nothing of the story of Jim
Greatorex and his big voice. It had been carefully kept
from her.

"I doan knaw," said Mrs. Gale. "Jim, look yo, 'e
useter sing in t' Choorch choir."

"Why ever did he leave it?"

Mrs. Gale looked dark and tightened up her face. She
knew perfectly well why Jim Greatorex had left. It was
because he wasn't going to have that little milk-faced lass
learning *him* to sing. His pride wouldn't stomach it.
But not for worlds would Mrs. Gale have been the one
to let Miss Alice know that.

Her eyes sought for inspiration in a crack on the stone
floor.

"I can't rightly tall yo', Miss Olice. 'E sang fer t' owd
schoolmaaster, look yo, an' wann schoolmaaster gaave it
oop, Jimmy, 'e said 'e'd give it oop too."

"But don't you think he'd sing for *me,* if I were to ask
him?"

"Yo' may aask 'im, Miss Olice, but I doan' knaw. Wann
Jim Greatorex is sat, 'e's sat."

"There's no harm in asking him."

"Naw. Naw 'aarm there isn't," said Mrs. Gale doubtfully.

"I think I'll ask him now," said Alice.

"I wouldn', look yo, nat ef I wuss yo, Miss Olice. I wouldn' gaw to 'im in t' mistal all amoong t' doong. Yo'll sha-ame 'im, and yo'll do nowt wi' Jimmy ef 'e's sha-amed."

"Leave it, Ally. We can come another day," said Gwenda.

"Thot's it," said Mrs. Gale. "Coom another daay."

And as they turned away Jim's voice thundered after them from his stronghold in the mistal.

"From av-ver-lasstin'—THOU ART GAWD!
    To andless ye-ears ther sa-ame!"

The sisters stood listening. They looked at each other.

"I say!" said Gwenda.

"Isn't he gorgeous? We'll *have* to come again. It would be a sin to waste him."

"It would."

"When shall we come?"

"There's heaps of time. That voice won't run away."

"No. But he might get pneumonia. He might die."

"Not he."

But Alice couldn't leave it alone.

"How about Sunday? Just after dinner? He'll be clean then."

"All right. Sunday."

But it was not till they had passed the schoolhouse outside Garth village that Alice's great idea came to her.

"Gwenda! The Concert! Wouldn't he be ripping for the Concert!"

XX

But the concert was not till the first week in December; and it was in November that Rowcliffe began to form the habit that made him remarkable in Garth, of looking in at the Vicarage toward teatime every Wednesday afternoon.

Mrs. Gale, informed by Essy, was the first to condole with Mrs. Blenkiron, the blacksmith's wife, who had arranged to provide tea for Rowcliffe every Wednesday in the Surgery.

"Wall, Mrs. Blenkiron," she said, "yo' 'aven't got to mak' tae for yore doctor now?"

"Naw. I 'aven't," said Mrs. Blenkiron. "And it's sexpence clane gone out o' me packet av'ry week."

Mrs. Blenkiron was a distant cousin of the Greatorexs. She had what was called a superior manner and was handsome, in the slender, high-nosed, florid fashion of the Dale.

"But there," she went on. "I doan't groodge it. 'E's yoong and you caann't blaame him. They's coompany for him oop at Vicarage."

" 'E's coompany fer they, I rackon. And well yo' med saay yo' doan't groodge it ef yo knawed arl we knaw, Mrs. Blenkiron. It's no life fer yoong things oop there, long o' t' Vicar. Mind yo"—Mrs. Gale lowered her voice and looked up and down the street for possible eavesdroppers—"ef 'e was to 'ear on it, thot yoong Rawcliffe wouldn't be 'lowed t' putt 's nawse in at door agen. But

86

theer—there's nawbody'd be thot crool an' spittiful fer
to goa an' tall 'im. Our Assy wouldn't. She'd coot 'er
toong out foorst, Assy would."

"Nawbody'll get it out of *mae,* Mrs. Gale, though it's
wae as 'as to sooffer for 't."

"Eh, but Dr. Rawcliffe's a good maan, and 'e'll mak' it
oop to yo', naw feear, Mrs. Blenkiron."

"And which of 'em will it bae, Mrs. Gaale, think you?"

"I caann't saay. But it woonna bae t' eldest. Nor t'
yoongest—joodgin'."

"Well—the lil' laass isn' breaaking 'er 'eart fer him, t'
joodge by the looks of 'er. I naver saw sech a chaange in
anybody in a moonth."

" 'T assn' takken mooch to maake 'er 'appy," said Mrs.
Gale. For Essy, who had informed her, was not subtle.

But of Ally's happiness there could be no doubt. It
lapped her, soaked into her like water and air. Her
small head flowered under it and put out its secret colors;
the dull gold of her hair began to shine again, her face
showed a shallow flush under its pallor; her gray eyes
were clear as if they had been dipped in water. Two
slender golden arches shone above them. They hadn't
been seen there for five years.

"Who would have believed," said Mary, "that Ally
could have looked so pretty?"

Ally's prettiness (when she gazed at it in the glass) was
delicious, intoxicating joy to Ally. She was never tired
of looking at it, of turning round and round to get new
views of it, of dressing her hair in new ways to set it off.

"Whatever have you done your hair like that for?" said
Mary on a Wednesday when Ally came down in the afternoon with her gold spread out above her ears and twisted
in a shining coil on the top of her head.

"To make it grow better," said Ally.

"Don't let Papa catch you at it," said Gwenda, "if you want it to grow any more."

Gwenda was going out. She had her hat on, and was taking her walking-stick from the stand. Ally stared.

"You're *not* going out?"

"I am," said Gwenda.

And she laughed as she went. *She* wasn't going to stay at home for Rowcliffe every Wednesday.

As for Ally, the Vicar did catch her at it. He caught her the very next Wednesday afternoon. She thought he had started for Upthorne when he hadn't. He was bound to catch her.

For the best looking-glass in the house was in the Vicar's bedroom. It went the whole length and width of the wardrobe door, and Ally could see herself in it from head to foot. And on the Vicar's dressing-table there lay a large and perfect hand-glass that had belonged to Ally's mother. Only by opening the wardrobe door and with the aid of the hand-glass could Ally obtain a satisfactory three-quarters view of her face and figure.

Now, by the Vicar's magnanimity, his daughters were allowed to use his bedroom twice in every two years, in the spring and in the autumn, for the purpose of trying on their new gowns; but this year they were wearing out last winter's gowns, and Ally had no business in the Vicar's bedroom at four o'clock in the afternoon.

She was turning slowly round and round, with her head tilted back over her left shoulder; she had just caught sight of her little white nose as it appeared in a vanishing profile and was adjusting her head at another and still more interesting angle when the Vicar caught her.

He was well in the middle of the room, and staring at her, before she was aware of him. The wardrobe door, flung wide open, had concealed his entrance, but if Ally had not been blinded and intoxicated with her own beauty she would have seen him before she began smiling, full-face first, then three-quarters, then sideways, a little tilted.

Then she shut to the door of the wardrobe (for the back view that was to reassure her as to the utter prettiness of her shoulders and the nape of her neck), and it was at that moment that she saw him, reflected behind her in the long looking-glass.

She screamed and dropped the hand-glass. She heard it break itself at her feet.

"Papa," she cried, "how you frightened me!"

It was not so much that he had caught her smiling at her own face, it was that *his* face, seen in the looking-glass, was awful. And besides being awful it was evil. Even to Ally's innocence it was evil. If it had been any other man Ally's instinct would have said that he looked horrid without Ally knowing or caring to know what her instinct meant. But the look on her father's face was awful because it was mysterious. Neither she nor her instinct had a word for it. There was cruelty in it, and, besides cruelty, some quality nameless and unrecognisable, subtle and secret, and yet crude somehow and vivid. The horror of it made her forget that he had caught her in one of the most deplorably humiliating situations in which a young girl can be caught—deliberately manufacturing smiles for her own amusement.

"You've no business to be here," said the Vicar.

He picked up the broken hand-glass, and as he looked at it the cruelty and the nameless quality passed out of his face as if a hand had smoothed it, and it became suddenly weak and pathetic, the face of a child whose precious magic thing another child has played with and broken.

Then Alice remembered that the hand-glass had been her mother's.

"I'm sorry I've broken it, Papa, if you liked it."

Her voice recalled him to himself.

"Ally," he said, "what am I to think of you? Are you a fool—or what?"

The sting of it lashed Ally's brain to a retort. (All that she had needed hitherto to be effective was a little red blood in her veins, and she had got it now.)

"I'd be a fool," she said, "if I cared two straws what you think of me, since you can't see what I am. I'm sorry if I've broken your old hand-glass, though I didn't break it. You broke it yourself."

Carrying her golden top-knot like a crown, she left the room.

The Vicar took the broken hand-glass and hid it in a drawer. He was sorry for himself. The only impression left on his mind was that his daughter Ally had been cruel to him.

But Ally didn't care a rap what he thought of her, or what impression she had left on his mind. She was much too happy. Besides, if you once began caring what Papa thought there would be no peace for anybody. He was so impossible that he didn't count. He wasn't even an effective serpent in her Paradise. He might crawl all over it (as indeed he did crawl), but he left no trail. The thought of how he had caught her at the looking-glass might be disagreeable, but it couldn't slime those holy lawns. Neither could it break the ecstasy of Wednesday, that heavenly day. Nothing could break it as long as Dr.

Rowcliffe continued to look in at tea-time and her father to explore the furthest borders of his parish.

The peace of Paradise came down on the Vicarage every Wednesday the very minute the garden gate had swung back behind the Vicar. He started so early and he was back so late that there was never any chance of his encountering young Rowcliffe.

To be sure, young Rowcliffe hardly ever said a word to her. He always talked to Mary or to Gwenda. But there was nothing in his reticence to disturb Ally's ecstasy. It was bliss to sit and look at Rowcliffe and to hear him talk. When she tried to talk to him herself her brain swam and she became unhappy and confused. Intellectual effort was destructive to the blessed state, which was pure passivity, untroubled contemplation in its early stages, before the oncoming of rapture.

The fact that Mary and Gwenda could talk to him and talk intelligently showed how little they cared for him or were likely to care, and how immeasurably far they were from the supreme act of adoration. Similarly, the fact that Rowcliffe could talk to Mary and to Gwenda showed how little *he* cared. If he had cared, if he were ever going to care as Ally understood caring, his brain would have swum like hers and his intellect would have abandoned him.

Whereas, it was when he turned to Ally that he hadn't a word to say, any more than she had, and that he became entangled in his talk, and that the intellect he tried to summon to him tottered and vanished at his call.

Another thing—when he caught her looking at him (and though Ally was careful he did catch her now and then) he always either lowered his eyelids or looked away. He was afraid to look at her; and *that,* as everybody knew, was an infallible sign. Why, Ally was afraid to look at *him,* only she couldn't help it. Her eyes were dragged to the terror and the danger.

So Ally reasoned in her Paradise.

For when Rowcliffe was once gone her brain was frantically busy. It never gave her any rest. From the one stuff of its dreams it span an endless shining thread; from the one thread it wove an endless web of visions. From nothing at all it built up drama after drama. It was all beautiful what Ally's brain did, all noble, all marvelously pure. (The Vicar would have been astonished if he had known how pure.) There was no sullen and selfish Ally in Ally's dreams. They were all of sacrifice, of self-immolation, of beautiful and noble things done for Rowcliffe, of suffering for Rowcliffe, of dying for him. All without Rowcliffe being very palpably and positively there.

It was only at night, when Ally's brain slept among its dreams, that Rowcliffe's face leaned near to hers without ever touching it, and his arms made as if they clasped her and never met. Even then, always at the first intangible approach of him, she woke, terrified because dreams go by contraries.

"Is your sister always so silent?" Rowcliffe asked that Wednesday (the Wednesday when Ally had been caught).

He was alone with Mary.

"Who? Ally? No. She isn't silent at all. What do you think of her?"

"I think," said Rowcliffe, "she looks extraordinarily well."

"That's owing to you," said Mary. "I never saw her pull round so fast before."

"No? I assure you," said Rowcliffe, "I haven't anything to do with it." He was very stiff and cold and stern.

Rowcliffe was annoyed because it was two Wednesdays running that he had found himself alone with the eldest and the youngest Miss Cartaret. The second one had gone off heaven knew where.

XXI

THE Vicar of Garth considered himself unhappy (to say the least of it) in his three children, but he had never asked himself what, after all, would he have done without them? After all (as they had frequently reminded themselves), without them he could never have lived comfortably on his income. They did the work and saved him the expenses of a second servant, a housekeeper, an under-gardener, an organist and two curates.

The three divided the work of the Vicarage and parish, according to the tastes and abilities of each. At home Mary kept the house and did the sewing. Gwenda looked after the gray and barren garden, she trimmed the narrow paths and the one flower-bed and mowed the small square of grass between. Alice trailed through the lower rooms, dusting furniture feebly; she gathered and arranged the flowers when there were any in the bed. Outside, Mary, being sweet and good, taught in the boys' Sunday-school; Alice, because she was fond of children, had the infants. For the rest, Mary, who was lazy, had taken over that small portion of the village that was not Baptist or Wesleyan or Congregational. Gwenda, for her own amusement, and regardless of sect and creed, the hopelessly distant hamlets and the farms scattered on the long, raking hillsides and the moors. Alice declared herself satisfied with her dominion over the organ and the village choir.

Alice was behaving like an angel in her Paradise. No

longer listless and sullen, she swept through the house with an angel's energy. A benign, untiring angel sat at the organ and controlled the violent voices of the choir.

The choir looked upon Ally's innocent art with pride and admiration and amusement. It tickled them to see those little milk-white hands grappling with organ pieces that had beaten the old schoolmaster.

Ally enjoyed the pride and admiration of the choir and was unaware of its amusement. She enjoyed the importance of her office. She enjoyed the massive, voluptuous vibrations that made her body a vehicle for the organ's surging and tremendous soul. Ally's body had become a more and more tremulous, a more sensitive and perfect medium for vibrations. She would not have missed one choir practice or one service.

And she said to herself, "I may be a fool, but Papa or the parish would have to pay an organist at least forty pounds a year. It costs less to keep me. So he needn't talk."

Then in November came the preparations for the village concert.

They were stupendous.

All morning the little Erad piano shook with the Grande Valse and the Grande Polonaise of Chopin. The diabolic thing raged through the shut house, knowing that it went unchallenged, that its utmost violence was licensed until the day after the concert.

Rowcliffe heard it whenever he drove past the Vicarage on his way over the moors.

XXII

Rowcliffe was now beginning to form that other habit (which was to make him even more remarkable than he was already), the hunting down of Gwendolen Cartaret in the open.

He was annoyed with Gwendolen Cartaret. When she had all the rest of the week to walk in she would set out on Wednesdays before teatime and continue until long after dark. He had missed her twice now. And on the third Wednesday he saw her swinging up the hill toward Upthorne as he, leaving his surgery, came round the corner of the village by the bridge.

"I believe," he thought, "she's doing it on purpose. To avoid me."

He was determined not to be avoided.

"The doctor's very late this afternoon," said Mary. "I suppose he's been sent for somewhere."

Alice said nothing. She couldn't trust herself to speak. She lived in sickening fear that on some Wednesday afternoon he would be sent for. It had never happened yet, but that made it all the more likely that it had happened now.

They waited till five; till a quarter-past.

"I really can't wait any longer," said Mary, "for a man who doesn't come."

By that time Rowcliffe and Gwenda were far on the road to Upthorne.

He had overtaken her about a hundred yards above the schoolhouse, before the road turned to Upthorne Moor.

"I say, how you do sprint up these hills!"

She turned.

"Is that you, Dr. Rowcliffe?"

"Of course it's me. Where are you off to?"

"Upthorne. Anywhere."

"May I come too?"

"If you want to."

"Of course I want to."

"Have you had any tea?"

"No."

"Weren't they in?"

"I didn't stop to ask."

"Why not?"

"Because I saw you stampeding on in front of me, and I swore I'd overtake you before you got round that corner. And I have overtaken you."

"Shall we go back? We've time."

He frowned. "No. I never turn back. Let's get on. Get on."

They went on at a terrific pace. And as she persisted in walking about half a foot in front of him he saw the movement of her fine long limbs and the little ripple of her shoulders under the gray tweed.

Presently he spoke.

"It wasn't you I heard playing the other night?"

"No. It must have been my youngest sister."

"I knew it wasn't you."

"It might have been for all you knew."

"It couldn't possibly. If you played you wouldn't play that way."

"What way?"

"Your sister's way. Whatever you wanted to do you'd do it beautifully or not at all."

She made no response. She did not even seem to have heard him.

"I don't mean to say," he said, "that your sister doesn't play beautifully."

She turned malignly. He liked her when she turned.

"You mean that she plays abominably."

"I didn't mean to *say* it."

"Why shouldn't you say it?"

"Because you don't say those things. It isn't polite."

"But I know Alice doesn't play well—not those big things. The wonder is she can play them at all."

"Why does she attempt—the big things?"

"Why does anybody? Because she loves them. She's never heard them properly played. So she doesn't know. She just trusts to her feeling."

"Is there anything else, after all, you *can* trust?"

"I don't know. You see, Alice's feeling tells her it's all right to play like that, and *my* feeling tells me it's all wrong."

"You can trust *your* feelings."

"Why mine more than hers?"

"Because *your* feelings are the feelings of a beautifully sane and perfectly balanced person."

"How can you possibly tell? You don't know me."

"I know your type."

"My type isn't me. You can't tell by that."

"You can if you're a physiologist."

"Being a physiologist won't tell you anything about *me*."

"Oh, won't it?"

"It can't."

"Why not?"

"How can it?"

"You think it can't tell me anything about your soul?"

"Oh—my soul——" Her shoulders expressed disdain for it.

"Do you dislike my mentioning it? Would you rather we didn't talk about it? Perhaps you're tired of having it talked about?"

"No; my poor soul has never done anything to get itself talked about."

"I only thought that as your father, perhaps, specialises in souls——"

"He doesn't specialise in mine. He knows nothing about it."

"The specialist never does. To know anything—the least little thing—about the soul, you must know everything—everything you *can* know—about the body. So that you're wrong even about your soul. Being a physiologist tells me that your sort of body—a transparently clean and strong and utterly unconscious body—goes with a transparently clean and strong and utterly unconscious soul."

"Utterly unconscious?"

He was silent a moment and then answered:

"Utterly unconscious."

They walked on in silence till they came in sight of the marshes and the long gray line of Upthorne Farm.

"That's where I met you once," he said. "Do you remember? You were coming out of the door as I went in."

"You seem to have been always meeting me."

"Always meeting you. And then—always missing you. Just when I expected most to find you."

"If we go much farther in this direction," said Gwenda, "we shall meet Papa."

"Well—I suppose some day I shall have to meet him. Do you realise that I've never met him yet?"

"Haven't you?"

"No. Always I've been on the point of meeting him, and always some malignant fate has interfered."

She smiled. He loved her smile.

"Why are you smiling?"

"I was only wondering whether the fate was really so malignant."

"You mean that if he met me he'd dislike me?"

"He always *has* disliked anybody we like. You see, he's a very funny father."

"All fathers," said Rowcliffe, "are more or less funny."

She laughed. Her laughter enchanted him.

"Yes. But *my* father doesn't mean to be as funny as he is."

"I see. He wouldn't really mean to dislike me. Then, perhaps, if I regularly laid myself out for it, by years of tender and untiring devotion I might win him over?"

She laughed again; she laughed as youth laughs, for the pure joy of laughter. She looked on her father as a persistent, delightful jest. He adored her laughter.

It proved how strong and sane she was—if she could take him like that. Rowcliffe had seen women made bitter, made morbid, driven into lunatic asylums by fathers who were as funny as Mr. Cartaret.

"You wouldn't, you wouldn't," she said. "He's funnier than you've any idea of."

"Is he ever ill?"

"Never."

"That of course makes it difficult."

"Except colds in his head. But he wouldn't have you for a cold in his head. He wouldn't have you for anything if he could help it."

"Well—perhaps—if he's as funny as all that, we'd better turn."

They turned.

They were walking so fast now that they couldn't talk. Presently they slackened and he spoke.

"I say, shall you ever get away from this place?"

"Never, I think."

"Do you never want to get away?"

"No. Never. You see, I love it."

"I know you do." He said it savagely, as if he were jealous of the place.

"So do you," she answered.

"If I didn't I suppose I should have to."

"Yes, it's better, if you've got to live in it."

"That wasn't what I meant."

After that they were silent for a long time. She was wondering what he did mean.

When they reached the Vicarage gate he sheered off the path and held out his hand.

"Oh—aren't you coming in for tea?" she said.

"Thanks. No. It's a little late. I don't think I want any."

He paused. "I've got what I wanted."

He stepped backward, facing her, raising his cap, then he turned and hurried down the hill.

Gwenda walked slowly up the flagged path to the house door. She stood there, thinking.

"He's got what he wanted. He only wanted to see what I was like."

XXIII

Rowcliffe had ten minutes on his hands while they were bringing his trap round from the Red Lion.

He was warming his hands at the surgery fire when he heard voices in the parlor on the other side of the narrow passage. One voice pleaded, the other reserved judgment.

"Do you think he'd do it if I were to go up and ask him?" It was Alice Cartaret's voice.

"I caann't say, Miss Cartaret, I'm sure."

"Could you persuade him yourself, Mrs. Blenkiron?"

"It wouldn't be a bit of good me persuadin' him. Jim Greatorex wouldn' boodge *that* mooch for me."

A pause. Alice was wavering, aware, no doubt, of the folly of her errand. Rowcliffe had only to lie low and she would go."

"Could Mr. Blenkiron?"

No. Rowcliffe in the surgery smiled all to himself as he warmed his hands. Alice was holding her ground. She was spinning out the time.

"Not he. Mr. Blenkiron's got soomat alse to do without trapseing after Jim Greatorex."

"Oh."

Alice's voice was distant and defensive. He was sorry for Alice. She was not yet broken in to the north country manner, and her softness winced under these blows. There was nobody to tell her that Mrs. Blenkiron's manner was a criticism of her young kinsman, Jim Greatorex.

Mrs. Blenkiron presently made this apparent.

"Jim's sat oop enoof as it is. You'd think there was nawbody in this village good enoof to kape coompany wi' Jimmy, the road he goas. Ef I was you, Miss Olice, I should let him be."

"I would, but it's his voice we want. I'm thinking of the concert, Mrs. Blenkiron. It's the only voice we've got that'll fill the room."

Mrs. Blenkiron laughed.

"Eh—he'll fill it fer you, right enoof. You'll have all the yoong laads and laasses in the Daale toomblin' in to hear Jimmy."

"We want them. We want everybody. You Wesleyans and all."

Another pause. Rowcliffe was interested. Alice was really displaying considerable intelligence. Almost she persuaded him that her errand was genuine.

"Do you think Essy Gale could get him to come?"

In the surgery Rowcliffe whistled inaudibly. *That* was indeed a desperate shift.

Rowcliffe had turned and was now standing with his back to the fire. He was intensely interested.

"Assy Gaale? He would n' coom for Assy's asskin', a man like Greatorex."

Mrs. Blenkiron's blood, the blood of the Greatorexs, was up.

"Naw," said Jim Greatorex's kinswoman, "if you want Greatorex to sing for you as bad as all that, Miss Cartaret, you'd better speak to the doctor."

Rowcliffe became suddenly grave. He watched the door.

"He'd mebbe do it for him. He sats soom store by Dr. Rawcliffe."

"But"—Ally's voice sounded nearer—"he's gone, hasn't he?"

(The minx, the little, little minx!)

"Naw. But he's joost goin'. Shall I catch him?"

"You might."

Mrs. Blenkiron caught him on the threshold of the surgery.

"Will you speak to Miss Cartaret a minute, Dr. Rawcliffe?"

"Certainly."

Mrs. Blenkiron withdrew. The kitchen door closed on her flight. For the first time in their acquaintance Rowcliffe was alone with Alice Cartaret, and though he was interested he didn't like it.

"I thought I heard your voice," said he with reckless geniality.

They stood on their thresholds looking at each other across the narrow passage. It was as if Alice Cartaret's feet were fixed there by an invisible force that held her fascinated and yet frightened.

Rowcliffe had paused too, as at a post of vantage, the better to observe her.

A moment ago, warming his hands in the surgery, he could have sworn that she, the little maneuvering minx, had laid a trap for him. She had come on her fool's errand, knowing that it was a fool's errand, for nothing on earth but that she might catch him, alone and defenseless, in the surgery. It was the sort of thing she did, the sort of thing she always would do. She didn't want to know (not she!) whether Jim Greatorex would sing or not, she wanted to know, and she meant to know, why he, Steven Rowcliffe, hadn't turned up that afternoon, and where he had gone, and what he had been doing, and the rest of it. There were windows at the back of the Vicarage. Possibly she had seen him charging up the

hill in pursuit of her sister, and she was desperate. All
this he had believed and did still believe.

But, as he looked across at the little hesitating figure
and the scared face framed in the doorway, he had compassion on her. Poor little trapper, so pitifully trapped;
so ignorant of the first rules and principles of trapping
that she had run hot-foot after her prey when she should
have lain low and lured it silently into her snare. She
was no more than a poor little frightened minx, caught
in his trap, peering at him from it in terror. God knew
he hadn't meant to set it for her, and God only knew
how he was going to get her out of it.

"Poor things," he thought, "if they only knew how
horribly they embarrass me!"

For of course she wasn't the first. The situation had
repeated itself, monotonously, scores of times in his experience. It would have been a nuisance even if Alice
Cartaret had not been Gwendolen Cartaret's sister. That
made it intolerable.

All this complex pity and repugnance was latent in his
one sense of horrible embarrassment.

Then their hands met.

"You want to see me?"

"I *did*——" She was writhing piteously in the trap.

"You'd better come into the surgery. There's a fire
there."

He wasn't going to keep her out there in the cold; and
he wasn't going to walk back with her to the Vicarage.
He didn't want to meet the Vicar and have the door shut
in his face. Rowcliffe, informed by Mrs. Blenkiron, was
aware, long before Gwenda had warned him, that he ran
this risk. The Vicar's funniness was a byword in the
parish.

But he left the door ajar.

"Well," he said gently, "what is it?"

"Shall you be seeing Jim Greatorex soon?"

"I might. Why?"

She told her tale again; she told it in little bursts of excitement punctuated with shy hesitations. She told it with all sorts of twists and turns, winding and entangling herself in it and coming out again breathless and frightened, like a lost creature that has been dragged through the brake. And there were long pauses when Alice put her head on one side, considering, as if she held her tale in her hands and were looking at it and wondering whether she really could go on.

"And what is it you want me to do?" said Rowcliffe finally.

"To ask him."

"Hadn't you better ask him yourself?"

"Would he do it for me?"

"Of course he would."

"I wonder. Perhaps—if I asked him prettily——"

"Oh, then—he couldn't help himself."

There was a pause. Rowcliffe, a little ashamed of himself, looked at the floor, and Alice looked at Rowcliffe and tried to fathom the full depth of his meaning from his face. That there was a depth and that there was a meaning she never doubted. This time Rowcliffe missed the pathos of her gray eyes.

An idea had come to him.

"Look here—Miss Cartaret—if you can get Jim Greatorex to sing for you, if you can get him to take an interest in the concert or in any mortal thing besides beer and whisky, you'll be doing the best day's work you ever did in your life."

"Do you think I *could?*" she said.

"I think you could probably do anything with him if you gave your mind to it."

He meant it. He meant it. That was really his opinion of her. Her lifted face was radiant as she drank bliss at one draught from the cup he held to her. But she was not yet satisfied.

"You'd *like* me to do it?"

"I should very much."

His voice was firm, but his eyes looked uneasy and ashamed.

"Would you like me to get him back in the choir?"

"I'd like you to get him back into anything that'll keep him out of mischief."

She raised her chin. There was a more determined look on her small, her rather insignificant face than he would have thought to see there.

She rose.

"Very well," she said superbly. "I'll do it."

He held out his hand.

"I don't say, Miss Cartaret, that you'll reclaim him."

"Nor I. But—if you want me to, I'll try."

They parted on it.

Rowcliffe smiled as he closed the surgery door behind him.

"That'll give her something else to think about," he said to himself. "And it'll take her all her time."

XXIV

THE next Sunday, early in the afternoon, Alice went, all by herself, to Upthorne.

Hitherto she had disliked going to Upthorne by herself. She had no very subtle feeling for the aspects of things; but there was something about the road to Upthorne that repelled her. A hundred yards or so above the schoolhouse it turned, leaving behind it the wide green bottom and winding up toward the naked moor. To the north, on her right, it narrowed and twisted; the bed of the beck lay hidden. A thin scrub of low thorn trees covered the lower slopes of the further hillside. Here and there was a clearing and a cottage or a farm. On her left she had to pass the dead mining station, the roofless walls, the black window gaps, the melancholy haunted colonnades, the three chimneys of the dead furnaces, square cornered, shooting straight and high as the bell-towers of some hill city of the South, beautiful and sinister, guarding that place of ashes and of ruin. Then the sallow winter marshes. South of the marshes were the high moors. Their flanks showed black where they have been flayed by the cuttings of old mines. At intervals, along the line of the hillside, masses of rubble rose in hummocks or hung like avalanches, black as if they had been discharged by blasting. Beyond, in the turn of the Dale, the village of Upthorne lay unseen.

And hitherto, in all that immense and inhuman desolation nothing (to Alice) had been more melancholy, more

sinister, more haunted than the house where John Greatorex had died. With its gray, unsleeping face, its lidless
eyes, staring out over the marshes, it had lost (for Alice)
all likeness to a human habitation. It repudiated the living; it remembered; it kept a grim watch with its dead.

But Alice's mind, acutely sensitive in one direction, had
become callous in every other.

Greatorex was in the kitchen, smoking his Sunday afternoon pipe in the chimney corner, screened from the open
doorway by the three-foot thickness of the house wall.

Maggie, his servant, planted firmly on the threshold,
jerked her head over her shoulder to call to him.

"There's a yoong laady wants to see yo, Mr. Greatorex!"

There was no response but a sharp tapping on the hob,
as Greatorex knocked the ashes out of his pipe.

Maggie stood looking at Alice a little mournfully with
her deep-set, blue, pathetic eyes. Maggie had once been
pretty in spite of her drab hair and flat features, but
where her high color remained it had hardened with her
thirty-five years.

"Well yo' coom?"

Maggie called again and waited. Courageous in her
bright blue Sunday gown, she waited while her master
rose, then, shame-faced as if driven by some sharp sign
from him, she slunk into the scullery.

Jim Greatorex appeared on his threshold.

On his threshold, utterly sober, carrying himself with
the assurance of the master in his own house, he would
not have suffered by comparison with any man. Instead
of the black broadcloth that Alice had expected, he wore
a loose brown shooting jacket, drab corduroy breeches, a
drab cloth waistcoat and brown leather leggings, and he

wore them with a distinction that Rowcliffe might have envied. His face, his whole body, alert and upright, had the charm of some shy, half-savage animal. When he stood at ease his whole face, with all its features, sensed you and took you in; the quivering eyebrows were aware of you; the nose, with its short, high bridge, its fine, wide nostrils, repeated the sensitive stare of the wide eyes; his mouth, under its golden brown moustache, was somber with a sort of sullen apprehension, till in a sudden, child-like confidence it smiled. His whole face and all its features smiled.

He was smiling at Alice now, as if struck all of a sudden by her smallness.

"I've come to ask a favor, Mr. Greatorex," said Alice.

"Ay," said Greatorex. He said it as if ladies called every day to ask him favors. "Will you coom in, Miss Cartaret?" It was the mournful and musical voice that she had heard sometimes last summer on the road outside the back door of the Vicarage.

She came in, pausing on the threshold and looking about her, as if she stood poised on the edge of an adventure. Her smallness, and the delicious, exploring air of her melted Jim's heart and made him smile at her.

"It's a roough plaace fer a laady," he said.

"It's a beautiful place, Mr. Greatorex," said Alice.

And she did actually think it was beautiful with its stone floor, its white-washed walls, its black oak dresser and chest and settle; not because of these things but because it was on the border of her Paradise. Rowcliffe had sent her there. Jim Greatorex had glamour for her, less on his own account than as a man in whom Rowcliffe was interested.

"You'd think it a bit loansoom, wouldn' yo', ef yo' staayed in it yeear in and yeear out?"

"I don't know," said Alice doubtfully. "Perhaps—a little," she ventured, encouraged by Greatorex's indulgent smile.

"An' loansoom it is," said Greatorex dismally.

Alice explored, penetrating into the interior.

"Oh—but aren't you glad you've got such a lovely fireplace?"

"I doan' knaw as I've thought mooch about it. We get used to our own."

"What are those hooks for in the chimney?"

"They? They're fer 'angin' the haams on—to smoak 'em."

"I see."

She would have sat there on the oak settle but that Greatorex was holding open the door of an inner room.

"Yo'd better coom into t' parlor, Miss Cartaret. It'll be more coomfortable for you."

She rose and followed him. She had been long enough in Garth to know that if you are asked to go into the parlor you must go. Otherwise you risk offending the kind gods of the hearth and threshold.

The parlor was a long low room that continued the line of the house to its southern end. One wide mullioned window looked east over the marsh, the other south to the hillside across a little orchard of dwarfed and twisted trees.

To Alice they were the trees of her Paradise and the hillside was its boundary.

Greatorex drew close to the hearth the horsehair and mahogany armchair with the white antimacassar.

"Sit yo' down and I'll putt a light to the fire."

"Not for me," she protested.

But Greatorex was on his knees before her, lighting the fire.

"You'll 'ave wet feet coomin' over t' moor. Cauld, too, yo'll be."

She sat and watched him. He was deft with his great hands, like a woman, over his fire-lighting.

"There—she's burning fine." He rose, turning triumphantly on his hearth as the flame leaped in the grate.

"Yo'll let me mak' yo' a coop of tae, Miss Cartaret."

There was an interrogative lilt at the end of all his sentences, even when, as now, he was making statements that admitted of no denial. But his guest missed the incontrovertible and final quality of what was said.

"Please don't trouble."

"It's naw trooble—naw trooble at all. Maaggie'll 'ave got kettle on."

He strode out of his parlor into his kitchen. "Maaggie! Maaggie!" he called. "Are yo' there? Putt kettle on and bring tae into t' parlor."

Alice looked about her while she waited.

Though she didn't know it, Jim Greatorex's parlor was a more tolerable place than the Vicarage drawing-room. Brown cocoanut matting covered its stone floor. In front of the wide hearth on the inner wall was a rug of dyed sheepskin bordered with a strip of scarlet snippets. The wooden chimney-piece, the hearth-place, the black hobs, the straight barred grate with its frame of fine fluted iron, belonged to a period of simplicity. The oblong mahogany table in the center of the room, the sofa and chairs, upholstered in horsehair, were of a style austere enough to be almost beautiful. Down the white ground of the wall-paper an endless succession of pink nosegays ascended and descended between parallel stripes of blue.

There were no ornaments to speak of in Greatorex's parlor but the grocer's tea-caddies on the mantelshelf and the little china figures, the spotted cows, the curly dogs, the boy in blue, the girl in pink; and the lustre ware and the tea-sets, the white and gold, the blue and white, crowded behind the diamond panes of the two black oak cupboards. Of these one was set in the most conspicuous corner, the other in the middle of the long wall facing the east window, bare save for the framed photographs of Greatorex's family, the groups, the portraits of father and mother and of grandparents, enlarged from vignettes taken in the seventies and eighties—faces defiant, stolid and pathetic; yearning, mournful, tender faces, slightly blurred.

All these objects impressed themselves on Ally's brain, adhering to its obsession and receiving from it an immense significance and importance.

She heard Maggie's running feet, and the great leisurely steps of Greatorex, and his voice, soft and kind, encouraging Maggie.

"Theer—that's t' road. Gently, laass—moor' 'aaste, less spead. Now t' tray—an' a clane cloth—t' woon wi' laace on 't. Thot's t' road."

Maggie whispered, awestruck by these preparations:

"Which coops will yo' 'ave, Mr. Greatorex?"

"T' best coops, Maaggie."

Maggie had to fetch them from the corner cupboard (they were the white and gold). At Greatorex's command she brought the little round oak table from its place in the front window and set it by the hearth before the visitor. Humbly, under her master's eye, yet with a sort of happy pride about her, she set out the tea-things and the glass dishes of jam and honey and tea-cakes.

Greatorex waited, silent and awkward, till his servant had left the room. Then he came forward.

"Theer's caake," he said. "Maaggie baaked un yester-da'. An' theer's hooney."

He made no servile apologies for what he set before her. He was giving her nothing that was not good, and he knew it.

And he sat down facing her and watched her pour out her tea and help herself with her little delicate hands. If he had been a common man, a peasant, his idea of courtesy would have been to leave her to herself, to turn away his eyes from her in that intimate and sacred act of eating and drinking. But Greatorex was a farmer, the descendant of yeomen, and by courtesy a yeoman still, and courtesy bade him watch and see that his guest wanted for nothing.

That he did not sit down at the little table and drink tea with her himself showed that his courtesy knew where to draw the dividing line.

"But why aren't you having anything yourself?" said Alice. She really wondered.

He smiled. "It's a bit too early for me, thank yo'. Maaggie'll mak' me a coop by and bye."

And she said to herself, "How beautifully he did it."

He was indeed doing it beautifully all through. He watched her little fingers, and the very instant they had disposed of a morsel he offered her another. It was a deep and exquisite pleasure to him to observe her in that act of eating and drinking. He had never seen anything like the prettiness, the dainty precision that she brought to it. He had never seen anything so pretty as Ally her-self, in the rough gray tweed that exaggerated her fineness and fragility; never anything so distracting and at the same time so heartrending as the gray muff and collar of squirrel fur, and the little gray fur hat with the bit of blue peacock's breast laid on one side of it like a folded wing.

As he watched her he thought, "If I was to touch her I should break her."

Then the conversation began.

"I was sorry," he said, "to hear yo was so poorly, Miss Cartaret."

"I'm all right now. You can see I'm all right."

He shook his head. "I saw yo' a moonth ago, and I didn't think then I sud aver see yo' at Oopthorne again."

He paused.

"'E's a woonderful maan, Dr. Rawcliffe."

"He is," said Alice.

Her voice was very soft, inaudible as a breath. All the blood in her body seemed to rush into her face and flood it and spread up her forehead to the roots of the gold hair that the east wind had crisped round the edges of her hat. She thought, "It'll be awful if he guesses, and if he talks." But when she looked at Greatorex his face reassured her, it was so utterly innocent of divination. And the next moment he went straight to the matter in hand.

"An' what's this thing you've coom to aassk me, Miss Cartaret?"

"Well"—she looked at him and her gray eyes were soft and charmingly candid—"it *was* if you'd be kind enough to sing at our concert. You've heard about it?"

"Ay, I've heard about it, right enoof."

"Well—*won't* you? You *have* sung, you know."

"Yes. I've soong. But thot was in t' owd school-maaster's time. Yo' wouldn't care to hear my singin' now. I've got out of the way of it, like."

"You haven't, Mr. Greatorex. I've heard you. You've

got a magnificent voice. There isn't one like it in the choir."

"Ay, there's not mooch wrong with my voice, I rackon. But it's like this, look yo. I joost soong fer t' school-maaster. He was a friend—a personal friend of mine. And he's gone. And I'm sure I doan' knaw——"

"I know, Mr. Greatorex. I know exactly how you feel about it. You sang to please your friend. He's gone and you don't like the idea of singing for anybody else—for a set of people you don't know."

She had said it. It was the naked truth and he wasn't going to deny it.

She went on. "We're strangers and perhaps you don't like us very much, and you feel that singing for us would be like singing the Lord's song in a strange country; you feel as if it would be profanation—a kind of disloyalty."

"Thot's it. Thot's it." Never had he been so well interpreted.

"It's that—and it's because you miss him so awfully."

"Wall——" He seemed inclined, in sheer honesty, to deprecate the extreme and passionate emotion she suggested. I would n' saay—— O' course, I sort o' miss him. I caann't afford to lose a friend—I 'aven't so many of 'em."

"I know. It's the waters of Babylon, and you're hanging up your voice in the willow tree." She could be gay and fluent enough with Greatorex, who was nothing to her. "But it's an awful pity. A willow tree can't do anything with a big barytone voice hung up in it."

He laughed then. And afterward, whenever he thought of it, he laughed.

She saw that he had adopted his attitude first of all in resentment, that he had continued it as a passionate, melancholy pose, and that he was only keeping it up through sheer obstinacy. He would be glad of a decent excuse to abandon it, if he could find one.

"And your friend must have been proud of your voice, wasn't he?"

"He sat more store by it than what I do. It was he, look yo, who trained me so as I could sing proper."

"Well, then, he must have taken some trouble over it. Do you think he'd like you to go and hang it up in a willow tree?"

Greatorex looked up, showing a shamefaced smile. The little lass had beaten him.

"Coom to think of it, I doan' knaw as he would like it mooch."

"Of course he wouldn't like it. It would be wasting what he'd done."

"So 't would. I naver thought of it like thot."

She rose. She knew the moment of surrender, and she knew, woman-like, that it must not be overpassed. She stood before him, drawing on her gloves, fastening her squirrel collar and settling her chin in the warm fur with the movement of a small burrowing animal, a movement that captivated Greatorex. Then, deliberately and finally, she held out her hand.

"Good-bye, Mr. Greatorex. It's all right, isn't it? You're coming to sing for *him,* you know, not for *us.*"

"I'm coomin'," said Greatorex.

She settled her chin again, tucked her hands away in the squirrel muff and went quickly toward the door. He followed.

"Let me putt Daasy in t' trap, Miss Cartaret, and drive yo' home."

"I wouldn't think of it. Thank you all the same."

She was in the kitchen now, on the outer threshold. He followed her there.

"Miss Cartaret——"

She turned. "Well?"

His face was flushed to the eyes. He struggled visibly for expression. "Yo' moosn' saay I doan' like yo'. Fer it's nat the truth."

"I'm glad it isn't," she said.

He walked with her down the bridle path to the gate. He was dumb after his apocalypse.

They parted at the gate.

With long, slow, thoughtful strides Greatorex returned along the bridle path to his house.

Alice went gaily down the hill to Garth. It was the hill of Paradise. And if she thought of Greatorex and of how she had cajoled him into singing, and of how through singing she would reclaim him, it was because Greatorex and his song and his redemption were a small, hardly significant part of the immense thought of Rowcliffe.

"How pleased he'll be when he knows what I've done!"

And her pure joy had a strain in it that was not so pure. It pleased her to please Rowcliffe, but it pleased her also that he should realise her as a woman who could cajole men into doing for her what they didn't want to do.

"I've got him! I've got him!" she cried as she came, triumphant, into the dining-room where her father and her sisters still sat round the table. "No, thanks. I've had tea."

"Where did you get it?" the Vicar asked with his customary suspicion.

"At Upthorne. Jim Greatorex gave it me."

The Vicar was appeased. He thought nothing of it that Greatorex should have given his daughter tea. Greatorex was part of the parish.

XXV

Rowcliffe was coming to the concert. Neither floods
nor tempests, he declared, would keep him away from it.

For hours, night after night, of the week before the
concert, Jim Greatorex had been down at Garth, in the
schoolhouse, practicing with Alice Cartaret until she assured him he was perfect.

Night after night the schoolhouse, gray in its still yard,
had a door kept open for them and a light in the solemn
lancet windows. The tall gray ash tree that stood back
in the angle of the porch knew of their coming and their
going. The ash tree was friendly. When the north wind
tossed its branches it beckoned to the two, it summoned
them from up and down the hill.

And now the tables and blackboards had been cleared
out of the big schoolroom. The matchboarding of white
pine that lined the lower half of its walls had been hung
with red twill, with garlands of ivy and bunches of holly.
Oil lamps swung from the pine rafters of the ceiling and
were set on brackets at intervals along the walls. A few
boards raised on joists made an admirable platform. One
broad strip of red felt was laid along the platform, another hid the wooden steps that led to it. On the right
a cottage piano was set slantwise. In the front were chairs
for the principal performers. On the left, already in
their places, were the glee-singers chosen from the village
choir. Behind, on benches, the rest of the choir.

Over the whole scene, on the chalk white of the dado, the blond yellow of varnished pinewood, the blazing scarlet of the hangings, the dark glitter of the ivy and the holly; on the faces, ruddy and sallow, polished with cleanliness, on the sleek hair, on the pale frocks of the girls, the bright neckties of the men, the lamplight rioted and exulted; it rippled and flowed; it darted; it lay suave and smooth as still water; it flaunted; it veiled itself. Stately and tall and in a measured order, the lancet windows shot up out of the gray walls, the leaded framework of their lozenges gray on the black and solemn night behind them.

A smell of dust, of pine wood, of pomade, of burning oil, of an iron stove fiercely heated, a thin, bitter smell of ivy and holly; that wonderful, that overpowering, inspiring and revolting smell, of elements strangely fused, of flying vapors, of breathing, burning, palpitating things.

Greatorex, conspicuous in his front seat on the platform, drew it in with great heavings of his chest. He loved that smell. It fairly intoxicated him every time. It soared singing through his nostrils into his brain, like gin. There could be no more violent and voluptuous contrast of sensations than to come straight from the cold, biting air of Upthorne and to step into that perfect smell. It was a thick, a sweet, a fiery and sustaining smell. It helped him to face without too intolerable an agony the line of alien (he deemed them alien) faces in the front row of the audience: Mr. Cartaret and Miss Cartaret (utter strangers; he had never got, he never would get used to them) and Dr. Rowcliffe (not altogether a stranger, after what he had done one night for Greatorex's mare Daisy); then Miss Gwendolen (not a stranger either after what she had done, and yet formidably strange, the strangest, when he came to think of it, and the queerest of them all). Rowcliffe, he observed, sat between her and her sister.

Divided from them by a gap, more strangers, three girls whom Rowcliffe had driven over from Morfe and afterward (Greatorex observed that also, for he kept his eye on him) had shamelessly abandoned.

If Greatorex had his eye on Rowcliffe, Rowcliffe had his eye, though less continuously, on him. He did not know very much about Greatorex, after all, and he could not be sure that his man would turn up entirely sober. He was unaware of Greatorex's capacity for substituting one intoxication for another. He had no conception of what the smell of that lighted and decorated room meant for this man who lived so simply and profoundly by his senses and his soul. It was interfused and tangled with Greatorex's sublimest feelings. It was the draw-net of submerged memories, of secret, unsuspected passions. It held in its impalpable web his dreams, the divine and delicate things that his grosser self let slip. He would forget, forget for ages, until, in the schoolroom at concert time, at the first caress of the magical smell, those delicate and divine, those secret, submerged, and forgotten things arose, and with the undying poignancy and subtlety of odors they entered into him again. And besides these qualities which were indefinable, the smell was vividly symbolic. It was entwined with and it stood for his experience of art and ambition and the power to move men and women; for song and for the sensuous thrill and spiritual ecstasy of singing and for the subsequent applause. It was the only form of intoxication known to him that did not end in headache and in shame.

Suddenly the charm that had sustained him ceased to work.

Under it he had been sitting in suspense, waiting for something, knowing and not daring to own to himself what it was he waited for. The suspense and the waiting seemed all part of the original excitement.

Then Alice Cartaret came up the room.

Her passage had been obscured and obstructed by the crowd of villagers at the door. But they had cleared a way for her and she came.

She carried herself like a crowned princess. The cords of her cloak (it was of dove color, lined with blue) had loosened in her passage, and the cloak had slipped, showing her naked shoulders. She wore a little dove-gray gown with some blue about it and a necklace of pale amber. Her white arms hung slender as a child's from the immense puffs of the sleeves. Her fair hair was piled in front of a high amber comb.

As she appeared before the platform Rowcliffe rose and took her cloak from her (Greatorex saw him take it, but he didn't care; he knew more about the doctor than the doctor knew himself). He handed her up the steps on to the platform and then turned, like a man who has done all that chivalry requires of him, to his place between her sisters. The hand that Rowcliffe had let go went suddenly to her throat, seizing her necklace and loosening it as if it choked her. Rowcliffe was not looking at her.

Still with her hand at her throat, she smiled and bowed to the audience, to the choir, to Greatorex, to the schoolmaster who came forward (Greatorex cursed him) and led her to the piano.

She sat down, wiped her hands on her handkerchief, and waited, enduring like an angel the voices of the villagers and the shuffling of their feet.

Then somebody (it was the Vicar) said, "Hush!" and she began to play.

In her passion for the unattainable she had selected Chopin's Grande Valse in A Flat, beginning with the long shake of eight bars.

Greatorex did not know whether she played well or badly. He only knew it looked and sounded wonderful. He could have watched forever her little hands that were like white birds. He had never seen anything more delicious and more amusing than their fluttering in the long shake and their flying with spread wings all over the piano.

Then the jumping and the thumping began; and queer noises, the like of which Greatorex had never heard, came out of the piano. It jarred him; but it made him smile. The little hands were marvelous the way they flew, the way they leaped across great spaces of piano.

Alice herself was satisfied. She had brought out the air; she had made it sing above the confusion of the bass and treble that evidently had had no clear understanding when they started; as for the bad bits, the tremendous crescendo chords that your hands must take at a flying leap or miss altogether, Rowcliffe had already assured her that they were impracticable anyhow; and Rowcliffe knew.

Flushed and softened with the applause (Rowcliffe had joined in it), she took her place between Greatorex and the schoolmaster. The glee-singers, two men and two women, came forward and sang their glees, turning and bowing to each other like mummers. The schoolmaster recited the "Pied Piper of Hamelin." A young lady who had come over from Morfe expressly for that purpose sang the everlasting song about the miller.

Leaning stiffly forward, her thin neck outstretched, her brows bent toward Rowcliffe, summoning all that she knew of archness to her eyes, she sang.

"Oh miller, miller, miller, miller, miller, let me go!"

sang the young lady from Morfe. Alice could see that she sang for Rowcliffe and at Rowcliffe; she sang into his face until he turned it away, and then, utterly unabashed, she sang into his left ear.

The presence and the song of the young lady from Morfe would have been torture to Alice, but that her eyelids and her face were red as if perpetually smitten by the east wind and scarified with weeping. To Alice, at the piano, it was terrible to be associated with the song of the young lady from Morfe. She felt that Rowcliffe was looking at her (he wasn't) and she strove by look and manner to detach herself. As the young lady flung herself into it and became more and more intolerably arch, Alice became more and more severe. She purified the accompaniment from all taint of the young lady's intentions. It grew graver and graver. It was a hymn, a solemn chant, a dirge. The dirge of the last hope of the young lady from Morfe.

When it ceased there rose from the piano that was its grave the Grande Polonaise of Chopin. It rose in splendor and defiance; Alice's defiance of the young lady from Morfe. It brought down the schoolhouse in a storm of clapping and thumping, of "Bravos" and "Encores." Even Rowcliffe said, "Bravo!"

But Alice, still seated at the piano, smiled and signaled. And Jim Greatorex stood up to sing.

He stood facing the room, but beside her, so that she could sign to him if anything went wrong.

> " 'Oh, that we two-oo were May-ing
>   Down the stream of the so-oft spring breeze,
>   Like children with vi-olets pla-aying.' "

Greatorex's voice was a voice of awful volume and it ranged somewhere from fairly deep barytone almost to tenor. It was at moments unmanageable, being untrained, yet he seemed to do as much with it as if it had been bass and barytone and tenor all in one. It had grown a little thick in the last year, but he brought out of its very thickness a brooding, yearning passion and an intolerable pathos.

The song, overladen with emotion, appealed to him; it expressed as nothing else could have expressed the passions that were within him at that moment. It swept the whole range of his experiences, there were sheep in it and a churchyard and children (his lady could never be anything more to him than a child).

> " 'Oh, that we two-oo were ly-ing
>   In our nest in the chu-urch-yard sod,
>   With our limbs at rest on the quiet earth's breast,
>   And our souls—at home—with God!' "

That finished it. There was no other end.

And as he sang it, looking nobly if a little heavily over the heads of his audience, he saw Essy Gale hidden away, and trying to hide herself more, beside her mother in the farthest corner of the room.

He had forgotten Essy.

And at the sight of her his nobility went from him and only his heaviness remained.

It didn't matter that they shouted for him to sing again, that they stamped and bellowed, and that he did sing, again and again, taking the roof off at the last with "John Peel."

Nothing mattered. Nothing mattered. Nothing could matter now.

And then something bigger than his heart, bigger than his voice, something immense and brutal and defiant, as-

serted itself and said that Come to that Essy didn't matter. She had put herself in his way. And Maggie had
been before and after her. And Maggie didn't matter
either.

For the magical smell had wrapped itself round Alice
Cartaret, and her dove-gray gown and dove-gray eyes, and
round the thought of her. It twined and tangled her in
the subtle mesh. She was held and embalmed in it forever.

XXVI

It was Wednesday, the day after the concert.

Mr. Cartaret was standing before the fire in his study. He had just rung the bell and now he waited in an attitude of wisdom and of patience. It was only ten o'clock in the morning and wisdom and patience should not be required of any man at such an hour. But the Vicar had a disagreeable duty to perform.

Whenever the Vicar had a disagreeable duty to perform he performed it as early as possible in the morning, so that none of its disagreeableness was lost. The whole day was poisoned by it.

He waited a little longer. And as he waited his patience began to suffer imperceptibly, though his wisdom remained intact.

He rang again. The bell sounded through the quiet house, angry and terrifying.

In another moment Essy came in. She had on a clean apron.

She stood by the roll-top desk. It offered her a certain cover and support. Her brown eyes, liquid and gentle, gazed at him. But for all her gentleness there was a touch of defiance in her bearing.

"Did you not hear me ring?" said the Vicar.

"Naw, sir."

Nothing more clear and pure than the candor of Essy's eyes. They disconcerted him.

"I have nothing to say to you, Essy. You know why I sent for you."

"Naw, sir." She thought it was a question.

He underlined it.

"You—know—why."

"Naw. I doan' knaw, sir."

"Then, if you don't know, you must find out. You will go down to the surgery this afternoon and see Dr. Rowcliffe, and he will report on your case."

She started and the red blood rose in her face.

"I s'all not goa and see him, Mr. Cartaret."

She was very quiet.

"Very good. Then I shall pay you a month's wages and you will go on Saturday."

It was then that her mouth trembled so that her eyes shone large through her tears.

"I wasn't gawn to staay, sir—to be a trooble. I sud a gien yo' nawtice in anoother moonth."

She paused. There was a spasm in her throat as if she swallowed with difficulty her bitter pride. Her voice came thick and hoarse.

"Woan't yo' kape me till th' and o' t' moonth, sir?" Her voice cleared suddenly. "Than I can see yo' trow Christmas."

The Vicar opened his mouth to speak; but instead of speaking he stared. His open mouth stared with a supreme astonishment. Up till now, in his wisdom and his patience, he had borne with Essy, the Essy who had come before him one evening in September, dejected and afraid. He hated Essy and he hated her sin, but he had borne with her then because of her sorrow and her shame.

And here was Essy with not a sign of sorrow or of shame about her, offering (in the teeth of her deserved dismissal), actually offering as a favor to stay over Christmas and to see them through. The naked impudence of it was what staggered him.

"I have no intention of keeping you over Christmas. You will take your notice and your wages from to-day, and you will go on Saturday."

"Yes, sir."

In her going Essy turned.

"Will yo' taake me back, sir, when it's all over?"

"No. No. I shouldn't think of taking you back."

The Vicar hid his hands in his pockets and leaned forward, thrusting his face toward Essy as he spoke.

"I'm afraid, my girl, it never will be all over, as long as you regard your sin as lightly as you do."

Essy did not see the Vicar's face thrust toward her. She was sidling to the door. She had her hand on the doorknob.

"Come back," said the Vicar. "I have something else to say to you."

Essy came no nearer. She remained standing by the door.

"Who is the man, Essy?"

At that Essy's face began to shake piteously. Standing by the door, she cried quietly, with soft sobs, neither hiding her face nor drying her tears as they came.

"You had better tell me," said the Vicar.

"I s'all nat tall yo'," said Essy, with passionate determination, between the sobs.

"You must."

"I s'all nat—I s'all nat."

"Hiding it won't help you," said the Vicar.

Essy raised her head.

"I doan' keer. I doan' keer what 'appens to mae. What wae did—what wae did—lies between him and mae."

"Did he tell you he'd marry you, Essy?"

Essy sobbed for answer.

"He didn't? Is he going to marry you?"

" 'Tisn' likely 'e'll marry mae. An' I'll not force him."

"You think, perhaps, it doesn't matter?"

She shook her head in utter helplessness.

"Come, make a clean breast of it."

Then the storm burst. She turned her tormented face to him.

"A clane breast, yo' call it? I s'all mak' naw clane breasts, Mr. Cartaret, to yo' or anybody. I'll 'ave nawbody meddlin' between him an' mae!"

"Then," said the Vicar, "I wash my hands of you."

But he said it to an empty room. Essy had left him.

In the outer room the three sisters sat silent and motionless. Their faces were turned toward the closed door of the study. They were listening to the sounds that went on behind it. The burden of Essy hung heavy over them.

The study door opened and shut. Then the kitchen door.

"Poor Essy," said Gwenda.

"Poor Essy," said Alice. She was sorry for Essy now. She could afford to be sorry for her.

Mary said nothing, and from her silence you could not tell what she was thinking.

The long day dragged on to prayer time.

The burden of Essy hung heavy over the whole house.

That night, at a quarter to ten, fifteen minutes before prayer time, Gwenda came to her father in his study.

"Papa," she said, "is it true that you've sacked Essy at three days' notice?"

"I have dismissed Essy," said the Vicar, "for a sufficient reason."

"There's no reason to turn her out before Christmas."

"There is," said the Vicar, "a very grave reason. We needn't go into it."

He knew that his daughter knew his reason. But he ignored her knowledge as he ignored all things that were unpleasant to him.

"We must go into it," said Gwenda. "It's a sin to turn her out at three days' notice."

"I know what I'm doing, Gwenda, and why I'm doing it."

"So do I. We all do. None of us want her to go—yet. You could easily have kept her another two months. She'd have given notice herself."

"I am not going to discuss it with you."

The Vicar put his head under the roll top of his desk and pretended to be looking for papers. Gwenda seated herself familiarly on the arm of the chair he had left.

"You'll have to, I'm afraid," she said. "Please take your head out of the desk, Papa. There's no use behaving like an ostrich. I can see you all the time. The trouble is, you know, that you won't *think*. And you *must* think. How's Essy going to do without those two months' wages she might have had? She'll want every shilling she can lay her hands on for the baby."

"She should have thought of that before."

The Vicar was answering himself. He did not acknowledge his daughter's right to discuss Essy.

"She'll think of it presently," said Gwenda in her unblushing calm. "Look here, Papa, while you're trying how you can make this awful thing more awful for her, what do you think poor Essy's bothering about? She's not bothering about her sin, nor about her baby. She's bothering about how she's landed *us*."

The Vicar closed his eyes. His patience was exhausted. So was his wisdom.

"I am not arguing with you, Gwenda."

"You can't. You know perfectly well what a beastly shame it is."

That roused him.

"You seem to think no more of Essy's sin than Essy does."

"How do you know what Essy thinks? How do I know? It isn't any business of ours what Essy thinks. It's what we do. I'd rather do what Essy's done, any day, than do mean or cruel things. Wouldn't you?"

The Vicar raised his eyebrows and his shoulders. It was the gesture of a man helpless before the unspeakable.

He took refuge in his pathos.

"I am very tired, Gwenda; and it's ten minutes to ten."

It may have been because the Vicar was tired that his mind wandered somewhat that night during family prayers.

Foremost among the many things that the Vicar's mind refused to consider was the question of the status, of the very existence, of family prayers in his household.

But for Essy, though the Vicar did not know it, it was doubtful whether family prayers would have survived what he called his daughters' godlessness. Mary, to be sure, conformed outwardly. She was not easily irritated, and, as she put it, she did not really *mind* prayers. But to Alice and Gwendolen prayers were a weariness and an exasperation. Alice would evade them under any pretext. By her father's action in transporting her to Gardale, she considered that she was absolved from her filial allegiance. But Gwendolen was loyal. In the matter of prayers, which—she made it perfectly clear to Alice and

Mary—could not possibly annoy them more than they did her, she was going to see Papa through. It would be beastly, she said, not to. They couldn't give him away before Essy.

But of the clemency and generosity of Gwendolen's attitude Mr. Cartaret was not aware. He believed that the custom of prayers was maintained in his household by his inflexible authority and will. He gloried in them as an expression of his power. They were a form of coercion which it seemed he could apply quite successfully to his womenkind, those creatures of his flesh and blood, yet so alien and intractable. Family prayers gave him a keener spiritual satisfaction than the church services in which, outwardly, he cut a far more imposing figure. In a countryside peopled mainly by abominable Wesleyans and impure Baptists (Mr. Cartaret spoke and thought of Wesleyans and Baptists as if they were abominable and impure) he had some difficulty in procuring a congregation. The few who came to the parish church came because it was respectable and therefore profitable, or because they had got into the habit and couldn't well get out of it, or because they liked it, not at all because his will and his authority compelled them. But to emerge from his study inevitably at ten o'clock, an hour when the souls of Mary and Gwendolen and Alice were most reluctant and most hostile to the thought of prayers, and by sheer worrying to round up the fugitives, whatever they happened to be doing and wherever they happened to be, this (though he said it was no pleasure to him) was more agreeable to Mr. Cartaret than he knew. The very fact that Essy was a Wesleyan and so far an unwilling conformist gave a peculiar zest to the performance.

It was always the same. It started with a look through his glasses, leveled at each member of his household in turn, as if he desired to satisfy himself as to the expression of their faces while at the same time he defied them to protest. For the rest, his rule was that of his father, the schoolmaster, before him. First, a chapter from the Bible, the Old Testament in the morning, the New Testament in the evening, working straight through from Genesis to Revelation (omitting Leviticus as somewhat unsuitable for family reading). Then prayers proper, beginning with what his daughter Gwendolen, seventeen years ago, had called "fancy prayers," otherwise prayers not lifted from the Liturgy, but compiled and composed in accordance with the freer Evangelical taste in prayers. Then (for both Mr. Cartaret and the schoolmaster, his father, held that the Church must not be ignored) there followed last Sunday's Collect, the Collect for Grace, the Benediction, and the Lord's Prayer.

Now, as his rule would have it, that evening of the fifth of December brought him to the Eighth chapter of St. John, in the one concerning the woman taken in adultery, which was the very last chapter which Mr. Cartaret that evening could have desired to read. He had always considered that to some minds it might be open to misinterpretation as a defense of laxity.

" 'Woman, where are those thine accusers? hath no man condemned thee?'

"She said, 'No man, Lord.' And Jesus said unto her, 'Neither do I condemn thee.' "

Mr. Cartaret lowered his voice and his eyes as he read, for he felt Gwendolen's eyes upon him.

But he recovered himself on the final charge.

" 'Go' "——now he came to think of it, that was what he had said to Essy——" 'and sin no more.' "

(After all, he was supported.)

Casting another and more decidedly uneasy glance at

his family, he knelt down. He felt better when they were all kneeling, for now he had their backs toward him instead of their faces.

He then prayed. On behalf of himself and Essy and his family he prayed to a God who (so he assumed his Godhead) was ever more ready to hear than they to pray, a God whom he congratulated on His ability to perform for them far more than they either desired or deserved; he thanked him for having mercifully preserved them to the close of another blessed day (as in the morning he would thank him for having spared them to see the light of another blessed day); he besought him to pardon anything which that day they had done amiss; to deliver them from disobedience and self-will, from pride and waywardness (he had inserted this clause ten years ago for Gwendolen's benefit) as well as from the sins that did most easily beset them, for the temptations to which they were especially prone. This clause covered all the things he couldn't mention. It covered his wife, Robina's case; it covered Essy's; he had dragged Alice's case as it were from under it; he had a secret fear that one day it might cover Gwendolen's.

Gwendolen was the child who, he declared and believed, had always given him most trouble. He recalled (perversely) a certain thing that (at thirteen) she had said about this prayer.

"It oughtn't to be prayed," she had said. "You don't really think you can fool God that way, Papa? If I had a servant who groveled to me like that I'd tell him he must learn to keep his chin up or go."

She had said it before Robina who had laughed. And Mr. Cartaret's answer to it had been to turn his back on both of them and leave the room. At least he thought it was his answer. Gwendolen had thought that in a flash of intellectual honesty he agreed with her, only that he hadn't quite enough honesty to say so before Mummy.

All this he recalled, and the question she had pursued him with about that time. "*What* are the sins that do most easily beset us? *What* are the temptations to which we are especially prone? And his own evasive answer. "Ask yourself, my child."

Another year and she had left off asking him questions. She drew back into herself and became every day more self-willed, more solitary, more inaccessible.

And now, if he could have seen things as they really were, Mr. Cartaret would have perceived that he was afraid of Gwenda. As it was, he thought he was only afraid of what Gwenda might do.

Alice was capable of some things; but Gwenda was capable of anything.

Suddenly, to Gwenda's surprise, her father sighed; a dislocating sigh. It came between the Benediction and the Lord's Prayer.

For, even as he invoked the blessing Mr. Cartaret suddenly felt sorry for himself again. His children were no good to him.

By which he meant that his third wife, Robina, was no good.

But he did not know that he visited his wife's shortcomings on their heads, any more than he knew that he hated Essy and her sin because he himself was an enforced, reluctant celibate.

XXVII

The next day at dusk, Essy Gale slipped out to her mother's cottage down by the beck.

Mrs. Gale had just cleared the table after her tea, had washed up the tea-things and was putting them away in the cupboard when Essy entered. She looked round sharply, inimically.

Essy stood by the doorway, shamefaced.

"Moother," she said softly, "I want to speaak to yo."

Mrs. Gale struck an attitude of astonishment and fear, although she had expected Essy to come at such an hour and with such a look, and only wondered that she had not come four months ago.

"Yo're nat goain' t' saay as yo've got yoresel into trooble?"

For four months Mrs. Gale had preserved an innocent face before her neighbors and she desired to preserve it to the last possible moment. And up to the last possible moment, even to her daughter, she was determined to ignore what had happened.

But she knew and Essy knew that she knew.

"Doan yo saay it, Assy. Doan yo saay it."

Essy said nothing.

"D'yo 'ear mae speaakin' to yo? Caann't yo aanswer? Is it thot, Assy? Is it thot?"

"Yas, moother, yo knaw 'tis thot."

"An' yo dare to coom 'ear and tell mae! Yo dirty 'oossy! Toorn an' lat's 'ave a look at yo."

Now that the innocence of her face was gone, Mrs. Gale had a stern duty to perform by Essy.

"They've gien yo t' saack?"

"T' Vicar give it mae."

"Troost 'im! Whan did 'e gie it yo?"

"Yasterda'."

"T' moonth's nawtice?"

"Naw. I aassked 'im t' kape me anoother two moonths an' 'e woonna. I aassked 'im t' kape me over Christmas an' 'e woonna. I'm to leaave Saturda'."

"Did yo expact 'im t' kape yo, yo gawpie? Did yo think you'd nowt to do but t' laay oop at t' Vicarage an' 'ave th' yoong laadies t' do yore wark for yo, an' t' waait on yo 'and an' foot? Miss Gwanda t' mak' yore bafe-tae an' chicken jally and t' Vicar t' daandle t' baaby?"

" ''Oo's goan t' kape yo? Mae? I woonna kape yo an' I canna' kape yo. Yo ain' t' baaby! I doan' waant naw squeechin', squallin' brats mookin' oop t' plaace as faast as I clanes it, An' 'E woonna kape yo—ef yo're raakonin' on 'im. Yo need na tall mae oo t' maan is. I knaw."

" ''Tis'n 'im, Moother. 'Tis'n 'im."

"Yo lil blaack liar! 'Tis 'im. Ooo alse could it bae? Yo selly! Whatten arth possessed yo t' goa an' tak oop wi' Jim Greatorex? Ef yo mun get into trooble yo medda chawsen battern Jim. What for did I tak' yo from t' Farm an' put yo into t' Vicarage ef 't wasn't t' get yo out o' Jimmy's road? 'E'll naver maarry yo. Nat 'e! Did 'e saay as 'e'd maarry yo? Naw, I warrant yo did na waat fer thot. Yo was mad t' roon affter 'im afore 'e called yo. Yo dirty cat!"

That last taunt drew blood. Essy spoke up.

"Naw, naw. 'E looved mae. 'E wanted mae bad."

" ''E wanted yo? Coorse 'e wanted yo. Yo sud na 'ave gien in to 'im, yo softie. D'yo think yo're the only

woon thot's tampted? Look at mae. I could 'a got into trooble saven times to yore woonce, ef I 'ad'n kaped my 'ead an' respected mysel. Yore Jim Greatorex! Ef a maan like Jim 'ad laaid a 'and on mae, 'e'd a got soomthin' t' remamber afore I'd 'a gien in to 'im. An' yo've naw 'scuse for disgracin' yoresel. Yo was brought oop ralegious an' respactable. Did yo aver 'ear saw mooch as a bad woord?"

"It's doon, Moother, it's doon. There's naw good taalkin'."

"Eh! Yo saay it's doon, it's doon, an' yo think nowt o' 't. An' nowt yo think o' t' trooble yo're brengin' on mae. I sooppawse yo'll be tallin' mae naxt yo looved 'im! Yo looved 'im!"

At that Essy began to cry, softly, in her manner.

"Doan' yo tall mae *thot* taale."

Mrs. Gale suddenly paused in her tirade and began to poke the fire with fury.

"It's enoof t' sicken t' cat!"

She snatched the kettle that stood upon the hob; she stamped out to the scullery and re-filled it at the tap. She returned, stamping, and set it with violence upon the fire.

She tore out of the cupboard a teapot, a cup and a saucer, a loaf on a plate and a jar of dripping. Still with violence (slightly modulated to spare the comparative fragility of the objects she was handling) she dashed them one by one upon the table where Essy, with elbows planted, propped her head upon her hands and wept.

Mrs. Gale sat down herself in the chair facing her, and kept one eye on the kettle and the other on her daughter. From time to time mutterings came from her, breaking the sad rhythm of Essy's sobs.

"Eh dear! I'd like t' knaw what I've doon t' ave *this* trooble !——

——" 'Tis enoof t' raaise yore pore feyther clane out of 'is graave !——

——" 'E'd sooner 'ave seed yo in yore coffin, Assy."——

She rose and took down the tea-caddy from the chimney-piece and flung a reckless measure into the tea-pot.

"Ef 'e'd 'a been a-livin', 'e'd a *killed* yo. Thot's what 'e'd 'a doon."

As she said it she grasped the kettle and poured the boiling water into the tea-pot.

She set the tea-pot before Essy.

"There's a coop of tae. An' there's bread an' drippin'. Yo'll drink it oop."

But Essy, desolated, shook her head.

"Wall," said Mrs. Gale. "I doan' want ter look at yo. 'T mak's mae seck."

As if utterly revolted by the sight of her daughter, she turned from her and left the kitchen by the staircase door.

Her ponderous stamping could be heard going up the staircase and on the floor overhead. There was a sound as of drawers opening and shutting and of a heavy box being dragged from under the bed.

Essy poured herself out a cup of tea, tried to drink it, choked and pushed it from her.

She was still weeping when her mother came to her.

Mrs. Gale came softly.

All alone in the room overhead she had evidently been doing something that had pleased her. The ghost of a smile still haunted her bleak face. She carried on her arm tenderly a pile of little garments.

These she began to spread out on the table before Essy, having first removed the tea-things.

"There !" she said. " 'Tis the lil cleathes fer t' baaby.

Look, Assy, my deear—there's t' lil rawb, wi' t' lil slaves,
so pretty—an' t' flanny petticut—an' t' lil vasst—see.
'Tis t' lil things I maade fer 'ee afore tha was born."

But Essy pushed them from her. She was weeping
violently now.

"Taake 'em away!" she cried. "I doan' want t' look
at 'em."

Mrs. Gale sat and stared at her.

"Coom," she said, "tha moos'n' taake it saw 'ard, like."

Between the sobs Essy looked up with her shining eyes.
She whispered.

"Will yo kape mae, Moother?"

"I sall 'ave t' kape yo. There's nawbody 'll keer
mooch fer thot job but yore moother."

But Essy still wept. Once started on the way of weeping, she couldn't stop.

Then, all of a sudden, Mrs. Gale's face became distorted.

She got up and put her hand heavily on her daughter's
shoulder.

"There, there, Assy, loove," she said. "Doan' tha taake
on thot road. It's doon, an' it caann't be oondoon."

She stood there in a heavy silence. Now and again she
patted the heaving shoulder, marking time to Essy's sobs.
Then she spoke.

"Tha'll feel batter whan t' lil baaby cooms."

Profoundly disturbed and resentful of her own emotion
Mrs. Gale seized upon the tea-pot as a pretext and shut
herself up with it in the scullery.

Essy, staggering, rose and dried her eyes. For a moment or so she stared idly at the square window with the
blue-black night behind it.

Then she looked down. She smiled faintly. One by one she took the little garments spread out in front of her. She folded them in a pile.

Her face was still and dreamy.

She opened the scullery door and looked in.

"Good-night, Moother."

"Good-night, Assy."

It was striking seven as she passed the church.

Above the strokes of the hour she heard through the half-open door a sound of organ playing and of a big voice singing.

And she began to weep again. She knew the singer, and the player too.

XXVIII

CHRISTMAS was over and gone.

It was the last week in January.

All through December Rowcliffe's visits to the Vicarage had continued. But in January they ceased. That was not to be wondered at. Even Ally couldn't wonder. There was influenza in every other house in the Dale.

Then, one day, Gwenda, walking past Upthorne, heard wheels behind her and the clanking hoofs of the doctor's horse. She knew what would happen. Rowcliffe would pull up a yard or two in front of her. He would ask her where she was going and he would make her drive with him over the moor. And she knew that she would go with him. She would not be able to refuse him.

But the clanking hoofs went by and never stopped. There were two men in the trap. Acroyd, Rowcliffe's groom, sat in Rowcliffe's place, driving. He touched his hat to her as he passed her.

Beside him there was a strange man.

She said to herself, "He's away then. I think he might have told me."

And Ally, passing through the village, had seen the strange man too.

"Dr. Rowcliffe must be away," she said at tea-time. "I wonder if he'll be back by Wednesday."

Wednesday, the last day in January, came, but Rowcliffe did not come. The strange man took his place in the surgery.

143

Mrs. Gale brought the news into the Vicarage dining-room at four o'clock.

She had taken her daughter's place for the time being. She was a just woman and she bore no grudge against the Vicar on Essy's account. He had done no more than he was obliged to do. Essy had given trouble enough in the Vicarage, and she had received a month's wages that she hadn't worked for. Mrs. Gale was working double to make up for it. And the innocence of her face being gone, she went lowly and humbly, paying for Essy Essy's debt of shame. That was her view.

"Sall I set the tae here, Miss Gwanda," she enquired. "Sence doctor isn't coomin'?"

"How do you know he isn't coming?" Alice asked.

Mrs. Gale's face was solemn and oppressed. She turned to Gwenda, ignoring Alice. (Mary was upstairs in her room.)

" 'Aven't yo 'eerd, Miss Gwanda?"

Gwenda looked up from her book.

"No," she said. "He's away, isn't he?"

"Away? 'El'll nat get away fer long enoof. 'E's too ill."

"Ill?" Alice sent the word out on a terrified breath. Nobody took any notice of her.

"T' poastman tell mae," said Mrs. Gale. "From what 'e's 'eerd, 'twas all along o' Nad Alderson's lil baaby up to Morfe. It was took wi' the diptheery a while back. An' doctor, 'e sat oop wi' 't tree nights roonin', 'e did. 'E didn' so mooch as taak 's cleathes off. Nad Alderson, 'e said, 'e'd navver seen anything like what doctor 'e doon for t' lil' thing.' "

Mrs. Gale's face reddened and she sniffed.

" 'E's saaved Nad's baaby for 'm, right enoof, Dr. Raw-cliffe 'as. But 'e's down wi't hissel, t' poastman says."

It was at Gwenda that she gazed. And as Gwenda made no sign, Mrs. Gale, still more oppressed by that extraordinary silence, gave her own feelings way.

"Mebbe wae sall navver see 'im in t' Daale again. It'll goa 'ard, look yo, wi' a girt man like 'im, what's navver saaved 'isself. Naw, 'e's navver saaved 'issel."

She ceased. She gazed upon both the sisters now. Alice, her face white and averted, shrank back in the corner of the sofa. Gwenda's face was still. Neither of them had spoken.

Mary had tea alone that afternoon.

Alice had dragged herself upstairs to her bedroom and locked herself in. She had flung herself face downward on her bed. She lay there while the room grew gray and darkened. Suddenly she passed from a violent fit of writhing and of weeping into blank and motionless collapses. From time to time she hiccoughed helplessly.

But in the moment before Mary came downstairs Gwenda had slipped on the rough coat that hung on its peg in the passage. Her hat was lying about somewhere in the room where Alice had locked herself in. She went out bareheaded.

There was a movement in the little group of villagers gathered on the bridge before the surgery door. They slunk together and turned their backs on her as she passed. They knew where she was going as well as she did. And she didn't care.

She was doing the sort of thing that Alice had done, and had suffered for doing. She knew it and she didn't care. It didn't matter what Alice had done or ever would do. It didn't matter what she did herself. It was quite simple. Nothing mattered to her so long as Rowcliffe lived. And if he died nothing would ever matter to her again.

For she knew now what it was that had happened to her. She could no longer humbug herself into insisting that it hadn't happened. The thing had been secret and treacherous with her, and she had been secret and treacherous with it. She had refused to acknowledge it, not because she had been ashamed of it but because, with the dreadful instance of Alice before her eyes, she had been afraid. She had been afraid of how it would appear to Rowcliffe. He might see in it something morbid and perverted, something horribly like Ally. She went in terror of the taint. Where it should have held its head up defiantly and beautifully, it had been beaten back; it cowered and skulked in the dark places and waited for its hour.

And now that it showed itself naked, unveiled, unarmed, superbly defenseless, her terror of it ceased.

It had received a sanction that had been withheld from it before.

Until half an hour ago (she was aware of it) there had been something lacking in her feeling. Mary and Ally (this she was not aware of) got more "out of" Rowcliffe, so to speak, than she did. Gwenda had known nothing approaching to Mary's serene and brooding satisfaction or Ally's ecstasy. She dreaded the secret gates, the dreamy labyrinths, the poisonous air of the Paradise of Fools. In Rowcliffe's presence she had not felt altogether safe or altogether happy. But, if she stood on the edge of an abyss, at least she *stood* there, firm on the solid earth. She could balance herself; she could even lean forward a little and look over, without losing her head, thrilled with the uncertainty and peril of the adventure. And of course it wasn't as if Rowcliffe had left her standing. He

hadn't.   He had held out his hand to her, as it were, and
said, "Let's get on—get on!" which was as good as saying
that, as long as it lasted, it was *their* adventure, not hers.
He had drawn her after him at an exciting pace, along
the edge of the abyss, never losing *his* head for a minute,
so that she ought to have felt safe with him.   Only she
hadn't.   She had said to herself, "If I knew him better,
if I saw what was in him, perhaps I should feel safe."

There was something she wanted to see in him; something that her innermost secret self, fastidious and exacting, demanded from him before it would loosen the grip
that held her back.

And now she knew that it *was* there.   It had been told
her in four words: "He never saved himself."

She might have known it.   For she remembered things
now; how he had nursed old Greatorex like a woman; how
he had sat up half the night with Jim Greatorex's mare
Daisy; how he kept Jim Greatorex from drinking; and
how he had been kind to poor Essy when she had the face
ache; and gentle to little Ally.

And now Ned Alderson's ridiculous baby would live
and Rowcliffe would die.   Was *that* what she had required of him?   She felt as if somehow *she* had done it;
as if her innermost secret self, iniquitously exacting, had
thrown down the gage into the arena and that he had
picked it up.

"He saved others.   Himself he"—never saved.

He had become god-like to her.

And the passion she had trampled on lifted itself and
passed into the phase of adoration.   It had received the
dangerous sanction of the soul.

She turned off the high road at the point where, three
months ago, she had seen Mary cycling up the hill from

Morfe.   Now, as then, she descended upon Morfe by the
stony lane from the moor below Karva.

It came over her that she was too late, that she would
see rows of yellow blinds drawn down in the long front
of Rowcliffe's house.

The blinds were up.   The windows looked open-eyed
upon the Green.   She noticed that one of them on the
first floor was half open, and she said to herself, "He is
up there, in that room, dying of diphtheria."

The sound of the bell, muffled funereally, at the back of
the house, fulfilled her premonition.

The door opened wide.   The maid stood back from it
to let her pass in.

"How is Dr. Rowcliffe?"

Her voice sounded abrupt and brutal, as it tore its way
from her tense throat.

The maid raised her eyebrows.   She held the door
wider.

"Would you like to see him, miss?"

"Yes."

Her throat closed on the word and choked it.

Down at the end of the passage, where it was dark, a
door opened, the door of the surgery, and a man came out,
went in as if to look for something, and came out again.

As he moved there in the darkness she thought it was
the strange doctor and that he had come out to forbid her
seeing Rowcliffe.   He would say that she mustn't risk the
infection.   As if she cared about the risk.

Perhaps he wouldn't see her.   He, too, might say she
mustn't risk it.

While the surgery door opened and shut, opened and
shut again, she saw that her seeing him was of all things
the most unlikely.   She remembered the house at Up-

thorne, and she knew that Rowcliffe was lying dead in
the room upstairs.

And the man there was coming out to stop her.

Only—in that case—why hadn't they drawn the blinds
down?

XXIX

She was still thinking of the blinds when she saw that the man who came towards her was Rowcliffe.

He was wearing his rough tweed suit and his thick boots, and he had the look of the open air about him.

"Is that you, Miss Cartaret? Good!"

He grasped her hand. He behaved exactly as if he had expected her. He never even wondered what she had come for. She might have come to say that her father or one of her sisters was dying, and would he go at once; but none of these possibilities occurred to him.

He didn't want to account for her coming to him. It was natural and beautiful that she should come.

Then, as she stepped into the lighted passage, he saw that she was bareheaded and that her eyelashes were parted and gathered into little wet points.

He took her arm gently and led her into his study and shut the door. They faced each other there.

"I say—is anything wrong?"

"I thought you were ill."

She hadn't grasped the absurdity of it yet. She was still under the spell of the illusion.

"I? Ill? Good heavens, no!"

"They told me in the village you'd got diphtheria. And I came to know if it was true. It *isn't* true?"

He smiled; an odd little embarrassed smile; almost as if he were owning that it was or had been true.

"*Is* it?" she persisted as he went on smiling.

"Of course it isn't."

She frowned as if she were annoyed with him for not being ill.

"Then what was that other man here for?"

"Harker? Oh, he just took my place for a day or two while I had a sore throat."

"You *had* a throat then?"

Thus she accused him.

"And you *did* sit up for three nights with Ned Alderson's baby?"

She defied him to deny it.

"That's nothing. Anybody would. I had to."

"And—you saved the baby?"

He shrugged his shoulders. "*I* don't know. Something or other pulled the little beggar through."

"And you might have got it?"

"I might but I didn't."

"You *did* get a throat. And it *might* have been diphtheria."

Thus by accusing him she endeavored to justify herself.

"It might," he said, "but it wasn't. I had to knock off work till I was sure."

"And you're sure now?"

"I can tell you *you* wouldn't be here if I wasn't."

"And they told me you were dying."

(She was utterly disgusted.)

At that he laughed aloud. An irresistible, extravagantly delighted laugh. When he stopped he choked and began all over again; the idea of his dying was so funny; so was her disgust.

"That," she said, "was why I came."

"Then I'm glad they told you."

"I'm not," said she.

He laughed again at her sudden funny dignity. **Then,** as suddenly, he was grave.

"I say—it *was* nice of you."

She held out her hand.

"And now—as you're not dead—I'm off."

"Oh no, you're not. You're going to stay and have tea and I'm going to walk back with you."

She stayed.

They walked over the moor by Karva. And as they went he talked to her as he hadn't talked before. It was all about himself and his tone was very serious. He talked about his work and (with considerable reservations and omissions) about his life in Leeds, and about his ambition. He told her what he had done and why he had done it and what he was going to do. He wasn't going to stay in Garthdale all his life. Not he. Presently he would want to get to the center of things. (He forgot to mention that this was the first time he had thought of it.) Nothing would satisfy him but a big London practice and a name. He might—ultimately—specialise. If he did he rather thought it would be gynæcology. He was interested in women's cases. Or it might be nervous diseases. He wasn't sure. Anyhow, it must be something big.

For under Gwenda Cartaret's eyes his romantic youth became fiery and turbulent inside him. It not only urged him to tremendous heights, it made him actually feel that he would reach them. For a solid three-quarters of an hour, walking over the moor by Karva, he had ceased to be one of the obscurest of obscure little country doctors. He was Sir Steven Rowcliffe, the great gynæcologist, or the great neurologist (as the case might be) with a row of letters after his name and a whole column under it in the Medical Directory.

And Gwenda Cartaret's eyes never for a moment contradicted him. They agreed with every one of his preposterous statements.

She didn't know that it was only his romantic youth and that he never had been and never would be more youthful than he was for that three-quarters of an hour. On the contrary, to *her* youth he seemed to have left youth behind him, and to have grown suddenly serious and clear-sighted and mature.

And then he stopped, right on the moor, as if he were suddenly aware of his absurdity.

"I say," he said, "what must you think of me? Gassing about myself like that."

"I think," she said, "it's awfully nice of you."

"I don't suppose I shall do anything really big. Do you?"

She was silent.

"Honestly now, do you think I shall?"

"I think the things you've done already, the things that'll never be heard of, are really big."

His silence said, "They are not enough for me," and hers, "For me they are enough."

"But the other things," he insisted—"the things I want to do——   Do you think I'll do them?"

"I think"—she said slowly—"in fact I'm certain that you'll do them, if you really mean to."

"That's what you think of me?"

"That's what I think of you."

"Then it's all right," he said. "For what I think of *you* is that you'd never say a thing you didn't really mean."

They parted at the turn of the road, where, as he again reminded her, he had seen her first.

Going home by himself over the moor, Rowcliffe wondered whether he hadn't missed his opportunity.

He might have told her that he cared for her. He might have asked her if she cared. If he hadn't, it was only because there was no need to be precipitate. He felt rather than knew that she was sure of him.

Plenty of time. Plenty of time. He was so sure of *her*.

XXX

PLENTY of time. The last week of January passed. Through the first weeks of February Rowcliffe was kept busy, for sickness was still in the Dale.

Whether he required it or not, Rowcliffe had a respite from decision. No opportunity arose. If he looked in at the Vicarage on Wednesdays it was to drink a cup of tea in a hurry while his man put his horse in the trap. He took his man with him now on his longer rounds to save time and trouble. Once in a while he would meet Gwenda Cartaret or overtake her on some road miles from Garth, and he would make her get up and drive on with him, or he would give her a lift home.

It pleased her to be taken up and driven. She liked the rapid motion and the ways of the little brown horse. She even loved the noise he made with his clanking hoofs. Rowcliffe said it was a beastly trick. He made up his mind about once a week that he'd get rid of him. But somehow he couldn't. He was fond of the little brown horse. He'd had him so long.

And she said to herself. "He's faithful then. Of course. He would be."

It was almost as if he had wanted her to know it.

Then April came and the long spring twilights. The sick people had got well. Rowcliffe had whole hours on his hands that he could have spent with Gwenda now, if he had known.

And as yet he did not altogether know.

155

There was something about Gwenda Cartaret for which
Rowcliffe with all his sureness and all his experience was
unprepared. Their whole communion rested and pro-
ceeded on undeclared, unacknowledged, unrealised assump-
tions, and it was somehow its very secrecy that made it
so secure. Rather than put it to the test he was content
to leave their meetings to luck and his own imperfect in-
genuity. He knew where and at what times he would
have the best chance of finding her. Sometimes, returning from his northerly rounds, he would send the trap on,
and walk back to Morfe by Karva, on the chance. Once,
when the moon was up, he sighted her on the farther
moors beyond Upthorne, when he got down and walked
with her for miles, while his man and the trap waited for
him in Garth.

Once, and only once, driving by himself on the Rathdale moors beyond Morfe, he overtook her, picked her up
and drove her through Morfe (to the consternation of its
inhabitants) all the way to Garth and to the very gate of
the Vicarage.

But that was reckless.

And in all those hours, for his opportunities counted by
hours now, he had never found his moment. There was
plenty of time, and their isolation (his and hers) in Garthdale left him dangerously secure. All the same, by April
Rowcliffe was definitely looking for the moment, the one
shining moment, that must sooner or later come.

It was, indeed, always coming. Over and over again he
had caught sight of it; it signaled, shining; he had been
ready to seize it, when something happened, something obscured it, something put him off.

He never knew what it was at the time, but when he
looked back on these happenings he discovered that it

was always something that Gwenda Cartaret did. You would have said that no scene on earth could have been more favorable to a lover's enterprise than these long, deserted roads and the vast, twilit moors; and that a young woman could have found nothing to distract her from her lover there.

But it was not so. On the open moors, as often as not, they had to go single file through the heather, along a narrow sheep track, Rowcliffe leading; and it is difficult, not to say impossible, to command the attention of a young woman walking in your rear. And a thousand things distracted Gwenda: the cry of a mountain sheep, the sound and sight of a stream, the whirr of dark wings and the sudden "Krenk-er-renk-errenk!" of the grouse shooting up from the heather. And on the high roads where they went abreast she was apt to be carried away by the pageant of earth and sky; the solid darkness that came up from the moor; the gray, aerial abysses of the dale; the awful, blank withdrawal of Greffington Edge into the night. She was off, Heaven knew where, at the lighting of a star in the thin blue; the movement of a cloud excited her; or she was held enchanted by the pale aura of moonrise along the rampart of Greffington Edge. She shared the earth's silence and the throbbing passion of the earth as the orbed moon swung free.

And in her absorption, her estranging ecstasy, Rowcliffe at last found something inimical.

He told himself that it was an affectation in her, or a lure to draw him after her, as it would have been in any other woman. The little red-haired nurse would have known how to turn the earth and the moon to her own purposes and his. But all the time he knew that it was not so. There was no purpose in it at all, and it was unaware of him and of his purposes. Gwenda's joy was pure and profound and sufficient to itself. He gathered that it had been with her before he came and that it would remain with her after he had gone.

He hated to think that she should know any joy that had not its beginning and its end in him. It took her from him. As long as it lasted he was faced with an incomprehensible and monstrous rivalry.

And as a man might leave a woman to his uninteresting rival in the certainty that she will be bored and presently return to him, Rowcliffe left Gwenda to the earth and moon. He sulked and was silent.

Then, suddenly, he made up his mind.

XXXI

It was one night in April. He had met her at the cross-roads on Morfe Green, and walked home with her by the edge of the moor. It had blown hard all day, and now the wind had dropped, but it had left darkness and commotion in the sky. The west was a solid mass of cloud that drifted slowly in the wake of the departing storm, its hindmost part shredded to mist before the path of the hidden moon.

For, mercifully, the moon was hidden. Rowcliffe knew his moment.

He meditated—the fraction of a second too long.

"I wonder——" he began.

Just then the rear of the cloud opened and cast out the moon, sheeted in the white mist that she had torn from it.

And then, before he knew where he was, he was quarreling with Gwenda.

"Oh, look at the moon!" she cried. "All bowed forward with the cloud wrapped round her head. Something's calling her across the sky, but the mist holds her and the wind beats her back—look how she staggers and charges head-downward. She's fighting the wind. And she goes—she goes!"

"She doesn't go," said Rowcliffe. "At least you can't see her going, and the cloud isn't wrapped round her head, it's nowhere near her. And the wind isn't driving her, it's driving the cloud on. It's the cloud that's going. Why can't you see things as they are?"

She was detestable to him in that moment.

"Because nobody sees them as they are. And you're spoiling the idea."

"The idea being so much more valuable than the truth."

He longed to say cruel and biting things to her.

"It isn't valuable to anybody but me, so you might have left it to me."

"Oh, I'll leave it to you, if you're in love with it."

"I'm not in love with it because it's mine. Anyhow, if I *am* in love I'm in love with the moon and not with my idea of the moon."

"You don't know how to be in love with anything— even the moon. But I suppose it's all right as long as you're happy."

"Of course I'm happy. Why shouldn't I be?"

"Because you haven't got anything to make you happy."

"Oh, haven't I?"

"You might have. But you haven't. You're too obstinate to be happy."

"But I've just told you that I *am* happy."

"What have you *got?*" he persisted.

"I've got heaps of things. I've got my two hands and my two feet. I've got my brain——"

"So have I. And yet——"

"It's absurd to say I've 'got' these things. They're me. Happiness isn't in the things you've got. It's either in you or it isn't."

"It generally isn't. Go on. What else? You've got the moon and your idea of the moon. I don't see that you've got much more."

"Anyhow, I've got my liberty."

"Your liberty—if that's all you want!"

"It's pretty nearly all. It covers most things."

"It does if you're an incurable egoist."

"You think I'm an egoist? And incurable?"

"It doesn't matter what I think."

"Not much. If you think that."

Silence. And then Rowcliffe burst out again.

"There are two things that I can't stand—a woman nursing a dog and a woman in love with the moon. They mean the same thing. And it's horrible."

"Why?"

"Because if it's humbug she's a hypocrite, and if it's genuine she's a monster."

"And if I'm in love with the moon—and you said I was——"

"I didn't. You said it yourself."

"Not at all. I said *if* I was in love with the moon, I'd be in love with *it* and not with my idea of it. I want reality."

"So do I. We're not likely to get it if we can't see it."

"No. If you're only in love with what you see."

"Oh, you're too clever. Too clever for me."

"Am I too clever for myself?"

"Probably."

He laughed abominably.

"I don't see the joke."

"If you don't see it this minute you'll see it in another ten years."

"Now," she said, "you're too clever for *me*."

They walked on in silence again. The mist gathered and dripped about them.

Abruptly she spoke.

"Has anything happened?"

"No, it hasn't."

"I mean—anything horrid?"

Her voice sounded such genuine distress that he dropped his hostile and contemptuous tone.

"No," he said, "why should it?"

"Because I've noticed that, when people are unusually horrid, it always means that something horrid's happened to them."

"Really?"

"Papa, for instance, is only horrid to us because Mummy—my stepmother, you know—was horrid to him."

"What did Mummy do to him?"

"She ran away from him. It's always that way. People aren't horrid on purpose. At least I'm sure *you* wouldn't be."

"*Was* I horrid?"

"Well—for the last half-hour——"

"You see, I find you a little exasperating at times."

"Not always?"

"No. Not by any means always."

"Can I tell when I am? Or when I'm going to be?"

He laughed (not at all abominably). "No. I don't think you can. That's rather what I resent in you."

"I wish I could tell. Then perhaps I might avoid it. You might just give me warning when you think I'm going to be it."

"I did give you warning."

"When?"

"When it began."

"There you are. I don't know when it did begin. What were we talking about?"

"I wasn't talking about anything. You were talking about the moon."

"It was the moon that did it."

"I suppose it was the moon."

"I see. I bored you. How awful."

"I didn't say you bored me. You never have bored me. You couldn't bore me."

"No—I just irritate you and drive you mad."

"You just irritate me and drive me mad."

The words were brutal but the voice caressed her. He took her by the arm and steered her amicably round a hidden boulder.

"Do you know many women?" she asked.

The question was startling by reason of its context. The better to consider it Rowcliffe withdrew his protecting arm.

"No," he said, "not very many."

"But those you do know you get on with? You get on all right with Mary?"

"Yes. I get on all right with 'Mary.'"

"You'd be horrid if you didn't. Mary's a dear."

"Well—I know where I am with *her*."

"And you get on all right—really—with Papa, as long as I'm not there."

"As long as you're not there, yes."

"So that," she pursued, *"I'm* the horrid thing that's happened to you? It looks like it."

"It feels like it. Let's say you're the horrid thing that's happened to me, and leave it at that."

They left it.

Rowcliffe had a sort of impression that he had said all that he had had to say.

XXXII

THE Vicar had called Gwenda into his study one day.

"What's this I hear," he said, "of you and young Rowcliffe scampering about all over the country?"

The Vicar had drawn a bow at a venture. He had not really heard anything, but he had seen something; two forms scrambling hand in hand up Karva; not too distant to be recognisable as young Rowcliffe and his daughter Gwenda, yet too distant to be pleasing to the Vicar. It was their distance that made them so improper.

"I don't know, Papa," said Gwenda.

"Perhaps you know what was said about your sister Alice? Do you want the same thing to be said about you?"

"It won't be, Papa. Unless you say it yourself."

She had him there; for what was said about Alice had been said first of all by him.

"What do you mean, Gwenda?"

"I mean that I'm a little different from Alice."

"Are you? *Are* you? When you're doing the same thing?"

"Let me see. What *was* the dreadful thing that Ally did? She ran after young Rickards, didn't she? Well—if you'd really seen us scampering you'd know that I'm generally running away from young Rowcliffe and that young Rowcliffe is generally running after me. He says it's as much as he can do to keep up with me."

"Gwenda," said the Vicar solemnly. "I won't have it."

"How do you propose to stop it, Papa?"

"You'll see how."

(It was thus that his god lured the Vicar to destruction. For he had no plan. He knew that he couldn't move into another parish.)

"It's no good locking me up in my room," said Gwenda, "for I can get out at the window. And you can't very well lock young Rowcliffe up in his surgery."

"I can forbid him the house."

"That's no good either so long as he doesn't forbid me his."

"You can't go to him there, my girl."

"I can do anything when I'm driven."

The Vicar groaned.

"You're right," he said. "You *are* different from Alice. You're worse than she is—ten times worse. *You*'d stick at nothing. I've always known it."

"So have I."

The Vicar leaned against the chimney-piece and hid his face in his hands to shut out the shame of her.

And then Gwenda had pity on him.

"It's all right, Papa. I'm not going to Dr. Rowcliffe, because there's no need. You're not going to lock him up in his surgery and you're not going to forbid him the house. You're not going to do anything. You're going to listen to me. It's not a bit of good trying to bully me. You'll be beaten every time. You can bully Alice as much as you like. You can bully her till she's ill. You can shut her up in her bedroom and lock the door and I daresay she won't get out at the window. But even Alice will beat you in the end. Of course there's Mary. But I shouldn't try it on with Mary either. She's really more dangerous than I am, because she looks so meek and mild. But she'll beat you, too, if you begin bullying her."

The Vicar raised his stricken head.

"Gwenda," he said, "you're terrible."

"No, Papa, I'm not terrible. I'm really awfully kind.
I'm telling you these things for your good. Don't you
worry. I shan't run very far after young Rowcliffe."

XXXIII

LEFT to himself, the Vicar fairly wallowed in his gloom. He pressed his hands tightly to his face, crushing into darkness the image of his daughter Gwenda that remained with him after the door had shut between them.

It came over him with the very shutting of the door not only that there never was a man so cursed in his children (that thought had occurred to him before) but that, of the three, Gwenda was the one in whom the curse was, so to speak, most active, through whom it was most likely to fall on him at any moment. In Alice it could be averted. He knew, he had always known, how to deal with Alice. And it would be hard to say exactly where it lurked in Mary. Therefore, in his times of profoundest self-commiseration, the Vicar overlooked the existence of his daughter Mary. He was an artist in gloom and Mary's sweetness and goodness spoiled the picture. But in Gwenda the curse was imminent and at the same time incalculable. Alice's behavior could be fairly predicted and provided for. There was no knowing what Gwenda would do next. The fear of what she might do hung forever over his head, and it made him jumpy.

And yet in this sense of cursedness the Vicar had found shelter for his self-esteem.

And now his fear, his noble and righteous fear of what Gwenda might do, his conviction that she would do something, disguised more than ever his humiliating fear of Gwenda. She was, as he had said, terrible. There was

no dealing with Gwenda; there never had been. Patience
failed before her will and wisdom before the deadly thrust
of her intelligence. She had stabbed him in several places
before she had left the room.

The outcome of his brooding (it would have shocked the
Vicar if he could have traced its genesis) was an extraordinary revulsion in Rowcliffe's favor. So far from
shutting the Vicarage door in the young man's face, the
Vicar was, positively he was, inclined to open it. He
couldn't stand the idea of other people marrying since he
wasn't really married himself, and couldn't be as long as
Robina persisted in being alive (thus cruelly was he held
up by that unscrupulous and pitiless woman, and the idea
of any of his daughters marrying was peculiarly disagreeable to him. He didn't know why it was disagreeable, and
it would have shocked him unspeakably if you had told
him why. And if you had asked him he would have had
half a dozen noble and righteous reasons ready for you at
his finger-ends. But the Vicar with his eyes shut could
see clearly that if Gwenda married Rowcliffe the unpleasant event would have its compensation. He would be rid
of an everlasting source of unpleasantness at home. He
didn't say to himself that his egoism would be rid of an
everlasting fear. He said that if Rowcliffe married
Gwenda he would keep her straight.

And then another consoling thought struck him.

He could deal with Alice more effectually than ever.
Neither Mary nor Alice knew what he knew. They
hadn't dreamed that it was Gwenda that young Rowcliffe
wanted. He would use his knowledge to bring Alice to her
senses.

It was on a Wednesday that he dealt with her.

He was coming in some hours earlier than usual from his rounds when she delivered herself into his hands by appearing at the foot of the staircase with her hair extravagantly dressed, and wearing what he took, rightly, to be a new blue gown.

He opened the study door, and, with a treacherous smile, invited her to enter. Then he looked at her.

"Is that another new dress you've got on?" he inquired, still with his bland treachery.

"Yes, Papa," said Alice. "Do you like it?"

The Vicar drew himself up, squared his shoulders and smiled again, not quite so blandly. His attitude gave him a sensation of exquisite and powerful virility.

"Do I like it? I should, perhaps, if I were a millionaire."

"It didn't cost so much as all that," said Alice.

"I'm not asking you what it cost. But I think you must have anticipated your next allowance."

Alice stared with wide eyes of innocence.

"What if I did? It won't make any difference in the long run."

The Vicar, with his hands plunged in his trousers pockets, jerked forward at her from the waist. It was his gesture when he thrust.

"For all the difference it'll make to *you,* my dear child, you might have spared yourself the trouble and expense."

He paused.

"Has young Rowcliffe been here to-day?"

"No," said Alice defiantly, "he hasn't."

"You expected him?"

"I daresay Mary did."

"I'm not asking what Mary did. Did you expect him or did you not?"

"He *said* he might turn up."

"He said he might turn up. You expected him. And he hasn't turned up. And you can't think why. Isn't that so?"

"I don't know what you mean, Papa."

"I mean, my child, that you're living in a fool's paradise."

"I haven't a notion what you mean by *that*."

"Perhaps Gwenda can enlighten you."

The color died in Ally's scared face.

"I can't see," she said, "what Gwenda's got to do with it."

"She's got something to do with young Rowcliffe's not turning up, I think. I met the two of them half way between Upthorne and Bar Hill at half past four."

He took out his watch.

"And it's ten past six now."

He sat down, turning his chair so as not to see her face. He did not, at the moment, care to look at her.

"You might go and ask Mrs. Gale to send me in a cup of tea."

Alice went out.

XXXIV

"It's a quarter past six now," she said to herself. "They must come back from Bar Hill by Upthorne. I shall meet them at Upthorne if I start now."

She slipped her rough coat over the new gown and started.

Her fear drove her, and she went up the hill at an impossible pace. She trembled, staggered, stood still and went on again.

The twilight of the unborn moon was like the horrible twilight of dreams. She walked as she had walked in nightmares, with knees, weak as water, that sank under her at every step.

She passed the schoolhouse with its beckoning ash-tree. The schoolhouse stirred the pain under her heart. She remembered the shining night when she had shown herself there and triumphed.

The pain then was so intolerable that her mind revolted from it as from a thing that simply could not be. The idea by which she lived asserted itself against the menace of destruction. It was not so much an idea as an instinct, blind, obstinate, immovable. It had behind it the wisdom and the persistence of life. It refused to believe where belief meant death to it.

She said to herself, "He's lying. He's lying. He's made it all up. He never met them."

She had passed the turn of the hill. She had come to

the high towers, sinister and indistinct, to the hollow walls
and haunted arcades of the dead mining station.   Upthorne was hidden by the shoulder of the hill.

She stopped suddenly, there where the road skirted the
arcades.   She was struck by a shock of premonition, an
instinct older and profounder than that wisdom of the
blood.   She had the sense that what was happening now,
her coming, like this, to the towers and the arcades, had
happened before, and was so related to what was about to
happen that she knew this also and with the same shock
of recognition.

It would happen when she had come to the last arch of
the colonnade.

It was happening now.   She had come to the last arch.

That instant she was aware of Rowcliffe and Gwenda
coming toward her down the hill.

Their figures were almost indiscernible in the twilight.
It was by their voices that she knew them.

Before they could see her she had slipped out of their
path behind the shelter of the arch.

She knew them by their voices.   Yet their voices had
something in them that she did not know, something that
told her that they had been with each other many times
before; that they understood each other; that they were
happy in each other and absorbed.

The pain was no longer inside her heart but under it.
It was dull rather than sharp, yet it moved there like a
sharp sickle, a sickle that gathered and ground the live
flesh it turned in and twisted.   A sensation of deadly sickness made her draw farther yet into the corner of the
arcade, feeling her way in the darkness with her hand on
the wall.   She stumbled on a block of stone, sank on it
and cowered there, sobbing and shivering.

Down in Garth village the church clock struck the half hour and the quarter and the hour.

At the half hour Blenkiron, the blacksmith, put Rowcliffe's horse into the trap. The sound of the clanking hoofs came up the hill. Rowcliffe heard them first.

"There's something wrong down there," he said. "They're coming for me."

In his heart he cursed them. For it was there, at the turn of the road, below the arches, that he had meant to say what he had not said the other night. There was no moon. The moment was propitious. And there (just like his cursed luck) was Blenkiron with the trap.

They met above the schoolhouse as the clock struck the quarter.

"You're wanted, sir," said the blacksmith, "at Mrs. Gale's."

"Is it Essy?"

"Ay, it's Assy."

In the cottage down by the beck Essy groaned and cried in her agony.

And on the road to Upthorne, under the arches by the sinister towers, Alice Cartaret, crouching on her stone, sobbed and shivered.

Not long after seven Essy's child was born.

Just before ten the three sisters sat waiting, as they had always waited, bored and motionless, for the imminent catastrophe of Prayers.

"I wonder how Essy's getting on," said Gwenda.

"Poor little Essy!" Mary said.

"She's as pleased as Punch," said Gwenda. "It's a boy. Ally—did you know that Essy's had a baby?"

"I don't care if she has," said Ally violently. "It's got nothing to do with me. I wish you wouldn't talk about her beastly baby."

As the Vicar came out of his study into the dining-room, he fixed his eyes upon his youngest daughter.

"What's the matter with you ?" he said.

"Nothing's the matter," said Alice defiantly. "Why ?"

"You look," he said, "as if somebody was murdering you."

XXXV

ALLY was ill; so ill this time that even the Vicar softened to her. He led her upstairs himself and made her go to bed and stay there. He would have sent for Rowcliffe but that Ally refused to see him.

Her mortal apathy passed for submission. She took her milk from her father's hand without a murmur. "There's a good girl," he said, as she drank it down.

But it didn't do her any good. Nothing did. The illness itself was no good to her, considering that she didn't want to be ill this time. She wanted to die. And of course she couldn't die. It would have been too much happiness and they wouldn't let her have it.

At first she resented what she called their interference. She declared, as she had declared before, that there was nothing the matter with her. She was only tired. Couldn't they see that she was tired? That *they* tired her?

"Why can't you leave me alone? If only you'd go away," she moaned, "—all of you—and leave me alone."

But very soon she was too tired even to be irritable. She lay quiet, sunk in the hollow of her bed, and kept her eyes shut, so that she never knew, she said, whether they were there or not. And it didn't matter. Nothing mattered so long as she could just lie there.

It was only when they talked of sending for Rowcliffe that they roused her. Then she sat up and became, first vehement, then violent.

"You shan't send for him," she cried. "I won't see him. If he comes into the house I'll crawl out of it."

One day (it was the last Wednesday in April) Gwenda came to her and told her that Rowcliffe was there and had asked to see her.

Ally's pale eyes lightened and grew large. They were transparent as glass in her white face.

"Did *you* send for him?"

"No."

"Who did then?"

"Papa."

She closed her eyes. The old sense of ecstasy came over her, of triumph too, of solemn triumph, as if she, whom they thought so insignificant, had vindicated her tragic dignity at last.

For if her father had sent for Rowcliffe it could only mean that she was really dying. Nothing else—nothing short of that—would have made him send.

And of course that was what she wanted, that Rowcliffe should see her die. He wouldn't forget her then. He would be compelled to think of her.

"You *will* see him, won't you, Ally?"

Ally smiled her little triumphant and mysterious smile.

"Oh yes, I'll see him."

The Vicar did not go on his rounds that afternoon. He stayed at home to talk to Rowcliffe. The two were shut up together in his study for more than half an hour.

As they entered the drawing-room at tea-time it could be seen from their manner and their faces that something had gone wrong. The Vicar bore himself like a man profoundly aggrieved, not to say outraged, in his own house, who nevertheless was observing a punctilious courtesy towards the offending guest. Rowcliffe's shoulders and his jaw were still squared in the antagonism that had closed their interview. He too observed the most perfect courtesy. Only by the consummate restraint of his manner did he show how impossible he had found the Vicar, while his face betrayed a grave preoccupation in which the Vicar counted not at all.

Mary began to talk to him about the weather. Neither she nor Gwenda dared ask him what he thought of Alice.

And in ten minutes he was gone. The Vicar went with him to the gate.

Still standing as they had stood to take leave of Rowcliffe, the sisters looked at each other. Mary spoke first.

"Whatever *can* Papa have said to him?"

This time Gwenda knew what Mary was thinking.

"It isn't that," she said. "It's something he's said to Papa."

XXXVI

Tʜᴀᴛ night, about nine o'clock, Gwenda came for the third time to Rowcliffe at his house.

She was shown into his study, where Rowcliffe was reading.

Though the servant had prepared him for her, he showed signs of agitation.

Gwenda's eyes were ominously somber and she had the white face of a ghost, a face that to Rowcliffe, as he looked at it, recalled the white face of Alice. He disliked Alice's face, he always had disliked it, he disliked it more than ever at that moment; yet the sight of this face that was so like it carried him away in an ecstasy of tenderness. He adored it because of that likeness, because of all that the likeness revealed to him and signified. And it increased, quite unendurably, his agitation.

Gwenda was supernaturally calm.

In another instant the illusion that her presence had given him passed. He saw what she had come for.

"Has anything gone wrong?" he asked.

She drew in her breath sharply.

"It's Alice."

"Yes, I know it's Alice. *Is* anything wrong?" he said. "What is it?"

"I don't know. I want you to tell me. That's what I've come for. I'm frightened."

"D'you mean, is she worse?"

She did not answer him. She looked at him as if she

178

were trying to read in his eyes something that he was trying not to tell her.

"Yes," he said, "she *is* worse."

"I know that," she said impatiently. "I can see it. You've got to tell me more."

"But I *have* told you. You *know* I have," he pleaded.

"I know you tried to tell me."

"Didn't I succeed?"

"You told me why she was ill—I know all that——"

"Do sit down." He turned from her and dragged the armchair forward. "There." He put a cushion at her back. "That's better."

As she obeyed him she kept her eyes on him. The book he had been reading lay where he had put it down, on the hearthrug at her feet. Its title, *"État mental des hystériques,"* Janet, stared at him. He picked it up and flung it out of sight as if it had offended him. With all his movements her head lifted and turned so that her eyes followed him.

He sat down and gazed at her quietly.

"Well," he said, "and what didn't I tell you?"

"You didn't tell me how it would end."

He was silent.

"Is that what you told father?"

"Hasn't he said anything?"

"He hasn't said a word. And you went away without saying anything."

"There isn't much to say that you don't know——"

"I know why she was ill. You told me. But I don't know why she's worse. She *was* better. She was quite well. She was running about doing things and looking so pretty—only the other day. And look at her now."

"It's like that," said Rowcliffe. "It comes and goes."

He said it quietly. But the blood rose into his face and forehead in a painful flush.

"But why? Why?" she persisted. "It's so horribly sudden."

"It's like that, too," said Rowcliffe.

"If it's like that now what is it going to be? How is it going to end? That's what you *won't* tell me."

"It's difficult——" he began.

"I don't care how difficult it is or how you hate it. You've got to."

All he said to that was "You're very fond of her?"

Her upper lip trembled. "Yes. But I don't think I knew it until now."

"That's what makes it difficult."

"My not knowing it?"

"No. Your being so fond of her."

"Isn't that just the reason why I ought to know?"

"Yes. I think it is. Only——"

She held him to it.

"Is she going to die?"

"I don't say she's *going* to die. But—in the state she's in—she *might* get anything and die of it if something isn't done to make her happy."

"Happy——"

"I mean of course—to get her married. After all, you know, you've got to face the facts."

"You think she's dying now, and you're afraid to tell me."

"No—I'm afraid I think—she's not so likely to die as to go out of her mind."

"Did you tell my father that?"

"Yes."

"What did he say?"

"He said she was out of her mind already."

"She isn't!"

"Of course she isn't. No more than you and I. He talks about putting the poor child under restraint——"

"Oh——"

"It's preposterous. But he'll make it necessary if he continues his present system. What I tried to impress on him is that she *will* go out of her mind if she's kept shut up in that old Vicarage much longer. And that she'd be all right—perfectly all right—if she was married. As far as I can make out he seems to be doing his best to prevent it. Well—in her case—that's simply criminal. The worse of it is I can't make him see it. He's annoyed with me."

"He never will see anything he doesn't like."

"There's no reason why he should dislike it so much—I mean her illness. There's nothing awful about it."

"There's nothing awful about Ally. She's as good as gold."

"I know she's as good as gold. And she'd be as strong as iron if she was married and had children. I've seen no end of women like that, and I'm not sure they don't make the best wives and mothers. I told your father that. But it's no good trying to tell him the truth."

"No. It's the one thing he can't stand."

"He seems," said Rowcliffe, "to have such an extraordinary distaste for the subject. He approaches it from an impossible point of view—as if it was sin or crime or something. He talks about her controlling herself, as if she could help it. Why, she's no more responsible for being like that than I am for the shape of my nose. I'm afraid I told him that if anybody was responsible *he* was, for bringing her to the worst place imaginable."

"He did that on purpose."

"I know. And I told him he might as well have put her in a lunatic asylum at once."

He meditated.

"It's not as if he hadn't anybody but himself to think of."

"That's no good. He never does think of anybody but himself. And yet he'd be awfully sorry, you know, if Ally died."

They sat silent, not looking at each other, until Gwenda spoke again.

"Dr. Rowcliffe——"

He smiled as if it amused him to be addressed so formally.

"Do you *really* mean it, or are you frightening us? Will Ally really die—or go mad—if she isn't—happy?"

He was grave again.

"I really mean it. It's a rather serious case. But it's only 'if.' As I told you, there are scores of women——"

But she waived them all away.

"I only wanted to know."

Her voice stopped suddenly, and he thought that she was going to break down.

"You mustn't take it so hard," he said. "It's not as if it wasn't absolutely curable. You must take her away."

Suddenly he remembered that he didn't particularly want Gwenda to go away. He couldn't, in fact, bear the thought of it.

"Better still," he said, "send her away. Is there anybody you could send her to?"

"Only Mummy—my stepmother." She smiled through her tears. "Papa would never let Ally go to *her*."

"Why not?"

"Because she ran away from him."

He tried not to laugh.

"She's really quite decent, though you mightn't think it." Rowcliffe smiled. "And she's fond of Ally. She's fond of all of us—except Papa. And," she added, "she knows a lot of people."

He smiled again. He pictured the third Mrs. Cartaret as a woman of affectionate gaiety and a pleasing worldliness, so well surrounded by adorers of his own sex that she could probably furnish forth her three stepdaughters from the numbers of those she had no use for. He was more than ever disgusted with the Vicar who had driven from him a woman so admirably fitted to play a mother's part.

"She sounds," he said, "as if she'd be the very one."

"She would be. It's an awful pity."

"Well," he said, "we won't talk any more about it now. We'll think of something. We simply *must* get her away."

He was thinking that he knew of somebody—a doctor's widow—who also would be fitted. If they could afford to pay her. And if they couldn't, he would very soon have the right——

That was what his "we" meant.

Presently he excused himself and went out to see, he said, about getting her some tea. He judged that if she were left alone for a moment she would pull herself together and be as ready as ever for their walk back to Garthdale.

It was in that moment when he left her that she made her choice. Not that when her idea had come to her she had known a second's hesitation. She didn't know when it had come. It seemed to her that it had been with her all through their awful interview.

It was she and not Ally who would have to go away.

She could see it now.

It had been approaching her, her idea, from the very instant that she had come into the room and had begun to speak to him. And with every word that *he* had said it had come closer. But not until her final appeal to him had she really faced it. Then it became clear. It crystallised. There was no escaping from the facts.

Ally would die or go mad if she didn't marry.

Ally (though Rowcliffe didn't know it) was in love with him.

And, even if she hadn't been, as long as they stayed in Garthdale there was nobody but Rowcliffe whom she could marry. It was her one chance.

And there were three of them there. Three women to one man.

And since *she* was the one—she knew it—who stood between him and Ally, it was she who would have to go away.

It seemed to her that long ago—all the time, in fact, ever since she had known Rowcliffe—she had known that this was what she would have to face.

She faced it now with a strange courage and a sort of spiritual exaltation, as she would have faced any terrible truth that Rowcliffe had told her, if, for instance, he had told her that she was going to die.

That, of course, was what it felt like. She had known that it would feel like that.

And, as sometimes happens to people who are going to die and know it, there came to her a peculiar vivid and poignant sense of her surroundings. Of Rowcliffe's room and the things in it,—the chair he had sat in, the pipe he had laid aside, the book he had been reading and that he had flung away. Outside the open window the trees

of the little orchard, whitened by the moonlight, stood
as if fixed in a tender, pure and supernatural beauty. She
could see the flags on the path and the stones in the gray
walls. They stood out with a strange significance and
importance. As if near and yet horribly far away, she
could hear Rowcliffe's footsteps in the passage.

It came over her that she was sitting in Rowcliffe's room
—like this—for the last time.

Then her heart dragged and tore at her, as if it fought
against her will to die. But it never occurred to her that
this dying of hers was willed by her. It seemed foredoomed, inevitable.

And now she was looking up in Rowcliffe's face and
smiling at him as he brought her her tea.

"That's right," he said.

He was entirely reassured by her appearance.

"Look here, shall I drive you back or do you feel like
another four-mile walk?"

She hesitated.

"It's late," he said. "But no matter. Let's be reckless."

"There's no need. I've got my bicycle."

"Then I'll get mine."

She rose. "Don't. I'm going back alone."

"You're not. I'm coming with you. I want to come."

"If you don't mind, I'd rather you didn't—to-night."

"I'll drive you, then. I can't let you go alone."

"But I *want*," she said, "to be alone."

He stood looking at her with a sort of sullen tenderness.

"You're not going to worry about what I told you?"

"You didn't tell me. I knew."

"Then——"

But she persisted.

"No. I shall be all right," she said. "There's a moon."

In the end he let her have her way.

Moon or no moon he saw that it was not his moment.

XXXVII

WHAT Gwenda had to do she did quickly.

She wrote to the third Mrs. Cartaret that night. She told her nothing except that she wanted to get something to do in London and to get it as soon as possible, and she asked her stepmother if she could put her up for a week or two until she got it. And would Mummy mind wiring Yes or No on Saturday morning?

It was then Thursday night.

She slipped out into the village about midnight to post the letter, though she knew that it couldn't go one minute before three o'clock on Friday afternoon.

She had no conscious fear that her will would fail her, but her instinct was appeased by action.

On Saturday morning Mrs. Cartaret wired: "Delighted. Expect you Friday. Mummy."

Five intolerable days. They were not more intolerable than the days that would come after, when the thing she was doing would be every bit as hard. Only her instinct was afraid of something happening within those five days that would make the hard thing harder.

On Sunday Mrs. Cartaret's letter came. Her house, she said, was crammed with fiends till Friday. There was a beast of a woman in Gwenda's room who simply wouldn't go. But on Friday Gwenda's room would be ready. It had been waiting for her all the time. Hadn't they settled it that Gwenda was to come and live with her if things became impossible at home? Robina supposed they *were* impossible? She sent her love to Alice and Mary, and she was always Gwenda's loving Mummy. And she enclosed a five-pound note; for she was a generous soul.

On Monday Gwenda told Peacock the carrier to bring her a Bradshaw from Reyburn.

She then considered how she was to account to her family for her departure.

She decided that she would tell Mary first. And she might as well tell her the truth while she was about it, since, if she didn't, Mary would be sure to find it out. She was sweet and good. Not so sweet and good that she couldn't hold her own against Papa if she was driven to it, but sweet enough and good enough to stand by Ally and to see her through.

It would be easy for Mary. It wasn't as if she had ever even begun to care for Rowcliffe. It wasn't as if Rowcliffe had ever cared for her.

And she could be trusted. A secret was always safe with Mary. She was positively uncanny in her silence, and quite superhumanly discreet.

Mary, then, should be told the whole truth and nothing but the truth. Her father should be told as much of it as he was likely to believe. Ally, of course, mustn't have an inkling.

Mary herself had an inkling already when she appeared that evening in the attic where Gwenda was packing a trunk. She had a new Bradshaw in her hand.

"Peacock gave me this," said Mary. "He said you ordered it."

"So I did," said Gwenda.

"What on earth for?"

"To look up trains in."

"Why—is anybody coming?"

"Does anybody *ever* come?"

Mary's face admitted her absurdity.

"Then"—she made it out almost with difficulty—"somebody must be going away."

"How clever you are. Somebody *is* going away."

Mary twisted her brows in her perplexity. She was evidently thinking things.

"Do you mean—Steven Rowcliffe?"

"No, dear lamb." (What on earth had put Steven Rowcliffe into Mary's head?) "It's not as bad as all that. It's only a woman. In fact, it's only me."

Mary's face emptied itself of all expression; it became a blank screen suddenly put up before the disarray of hurrying, eager things, unclothed and unexpressed.

"I'm going to stay with Mummy."

Gwenda closed the lid of the trunk and sat on it.

(Perturbation was now in Mary's face.)

"You can't, Gwenda. Papa'll never let you go."

"He can't stop me."

"What on earth are you going for?"

"Not for my own amusement, though it sounds amusing."

"Does Mummy want you?"

"Whether she wants me or not, she's got to have me."

"For how long?"

(Mary's face was heavy with thought now.)

"I don't know. I'm going to get something to do."

"To *do*?"

(Mary said to herself, then certainly it was not amusing. She pondered it.)

"Is it," she brought out, "because of Steven Rowcliffe?"

"No. It's because of Ally."

"Ally?"

"Yes.   Didn't Papa tell you about her?"

"Not he.   Did he tell you?"

"No.   It was Steven Rowcliffe."

And she told Mary what Rowcliffe had said to her.

She had made room for her on her trunk and they sat there, their bodies touching, their heads drawn back, each sister staring with eyes that gave and took the other's horror.

"Don't, Molly, don't——"

Mary was crying now.

"Does Papa know—that she'll die—or go mad?"

"Yes."

"But"—Mary lifted her stained face—"that's what they said about Mother."

"If she had children.   It's if Ally hasn't any."

"And Papa knew it *then*.   And he knows it now—how awful."

"It isn't as awful as Steven Rowcliffe thinks.   He doesn't really know what's wrong with her.   He doesn't know she's in love with *him*."

"Poor Ally.   What's the good?   He isn't in love with her."

"He isn't now," said Gwenda.   "But he will be."

"Not he.   It's you he cares for—if he cares for anybody."

"I know.   That's why I'm going."

"Oh, Gwenda——"

Mary's face was somber as she took it in.

"That won't do Ally any good.   If you *know* he cares."

"I don't absolutely know it.   And if I did it wouldn't make any difference."

"And if—you care for him?"

"That doesn't make any difference either.   I've got to

clear out. It's her one chance, Molly. I've got to give it her. How *can* I let her die, poor darling, or go mad? She'll be all right if he marries her."

"And if he doesn't?"

"He may, Molly, he may, if I clear out in time. Anyhow, there isn't anybody else."

"If only," Mary said, "Papa had kept a curate."

"But he hasn't kept a curate. He never will keep a curate. And if he does he'll choose a man with a wife and seven children—no, he'll choose no children. The wife mustn't have a chance of dying."

"Gwenda—do you think anybody *knows?* They did, you know—before, and it was awful."

"Nobody knows this time, except Papa and Steven Rowcliffe and you and me."

"I wish I didn't. I wish you hadn't told me."

"You *had* to know or I wouldn't have told you. Do you think Steven Rowcliffe would have told *me*——"

"How could he? It was awful of him."

"He could because he isn't a coward or a fool and he knew that I'm not a coward or a fool either. He thought Ally had nobody but me. She'll have nobody but you when I'm gone. You mustn't let her see you think her awful. You mustn't *think* it. She isn't. She's as good as gold. Steven Rowcliffe said so. If she wasn't, Molly, I wouldn't ask you to help her—with him."

"Gwenda, you mustn't put it all on me. I'd do anything for poor Ally, but I *can't* make him marry her if he doesn't want to."

"I think Ally can make him want to, if she gets a chance. You've only got to stick to her and see her through. You'll have to ask him here, you know. *She* can't. And you'll have to keep Papa off her. If you're not very careful, he'll go and put her under **restraint or** something."

"Oh—would it come to that?"

"Yes. Papa'd do it like a shot. I believe he'd do it just to stop her marrying him. You mustn't tell Papa what I've told you. You mustn't tell Ally. And you mustn't tell him. Do you hear, Molly? You must never tell him."

"Of course I won't tell him. But it's no use thinking we can do things."

Gwenda stood up.

"We haven't got to *do* things. That's his business. We've only got to sit tight and play the game."

Gwenda went on with her packing.

"It will be time enough," she thought, "to tell Ally to-morrow."

Ally was in her room. She never came downstairs now; and this week she was worse and had stayed all day in bed. They couldn't rouse her.

But something had roused her this evening.

A sort of scratching on the door made Gwenda look up from her packing.

Ally stood on the threshold. She had dressed herself completely in her tweed skirt, white blouse and knitted tie. Her strength had failed her only in the struggle with her hair. The coil had fallen and hung in a loose pigtail down her back. Slowly, in the weakness of her apathy, she trailed across the floor.

"Ally, what is it? Why didn't you send for me?"

"It's all right. I wanted to get up. I'm coming down to supper. You can leave off packing that old trunk. You haven't got to go."

"Who told you I was going?"

"Nobody. I knew it." She answered Gwenda's eyes. "I don't know how I knew it, but I did. And I know why you're going and it's all rot. You're going because you know that if you stay Steven Rowcliffe'll marry you, and you think that if you go he'll marry me."

"Whatever put that idea into your head?"

"Nothing put it. It came. It shows how awful you must think me if you think I'd go and do a beastly thing like that."

"Like what?"

"Why—sneaking him away from you behind your back when I know you like him. You needn't lie about it. You *do* like him.

"I may be awful," she went on. "In fact I know I'm awful. But I'm decent. I couldn't do a caddish thing like that—I couldn't really. And, if I couldn't, there's no need for you to go."

She was sitting on the trunk where Mary had sat, and when she began to speak she had looked down at her small hands that grasped the edge of the lid, their fingers picking nervously at the ragged flap. They ceased and she looked up.

And in her look, a look that for the moment was divinely lucid, Gwenda saw Ally's secret and hidden kinship with herself. She saw it as if through some medium, once troubled and now made suddenly transparent. It was because of that queer kinship that Ally had divined her. However awful she was, however tragically foredoomed and driven, Ally was decent. She knew what Gwenda was doing because it was what, if any sustained lucidity were ever given her, she might have done herself.

But in Ally no idea but the one idea was very deeply rooted. Sustained lucidity never had been hers. It would be easy to delude her.

"I'm going," Gwenda said, "because I want to. If I stayed I wouldn't marry Steven Rowcliffe, and Steven Rowcliffe wouldn't marry me."

"But—I thought—I thought——"

"What did you think?"

"That there was something between you. Papa said so."

"If Papa said so you might have known there was nothing in it."

"And isn't there?"

"Of course there isn't. You can put that idea out of your head forever."

"All the same I believe that's why you're going."

"I'm going because I can't stand this place any longer. You said I'd be sick of it in three months."

"You're not sick of it. You love it. It's me you can't stand."

"No, Ally—no."

She plunged for another argument and found it.

"What I can't stand is living with Papa."

Ally agreed that this was rather more than plausible.

XXXVIII

THE next person to be told was Rowcliffe.

It was known in the village through the telegrams that Gwenda was going away. The postmistress told Mrs. Gale, who told Mrs. Blenkiron. These two persons and four or five others had known ever since Sunday that the Vicar's daughter was going away; and the Vicar did not know it yet.

And Mrs. Blenkiron told Rowcliffe on the Wednesday before Alice told him.

For it was Alice who told him, and not Gwenda. Gwenda was not at home when he called at the Vicarage at three o'clock. But he heard from Alice that she would be back at four.

And it was Alice who told Mrs. Gale that when the doctor called again he was to be shown into the study.

He had waited there thirteen minutes before Gwenda came to him.

He looked at her and was struck by a difference he found in her, a difference that recalled some look in her face that he had seen before. It was dead white, and in its whiteness her blue eyes, dark and dilated, quivered with defiance and a sort of fear. She looked older and at the same time younger, as young as Alice and as helpless in her fear. Then he remembered that she had looked like that the night she had passed him in the doorway of the house at Upthorne.

"How cold your hands are," he said.

She hid them behind her back as if they had betrayed her.

"Do you want to see me about Ally?"

"No, I don't want to see you about Ally. I want to see you about yourself."

Her eyes quivered again.

"Won't you come into the drawing-room, then?"

"I'd rather stay here if you don't mind. I say, how much time have I?"

"Till when?"

"Well—till your father comes back?"

"He won't be back for another hour. But——"

"I hear you're going away on Friday; and that you're going for good."

"Did Mary tell you?"

"No. It was Alice. She said I was to try and stop you."

"You can't stop me if I want to go."

"I'll do my best."

They stood, as they talked, in rigid attitudes that suggested that neither was going to yield an inch.

"Why didn't you tell me yourself, Gwenda?"

She closed her eyes. It was as if she had forgotten why.

"Was it because you knew I wouldn't let you? Did you want to go as much as all that?"

"It looks like it, doesn't it?"

"Yes. But you don't want to go a bit."

"Would I go if I didn't?"

"Yes. It's just the sort of thing you would do, if you thought it would annoy me. It's only what you've been doing for the last three months—getting away from me."

"Three months——"

"Oh, I cared for you before that. It's only the last three months I've been trying to tell you."

"You never told me anything."

"Because you never gave me a chance. You kept on putting me off."

"And if I did, didn't that show that I didn't want you to tell me? I don't want you to tell me now."

He made an impatient movement.

"But you knew without telling. You knew then."

"I didn't. I didn't."

"Well, then, you know now. Will you marry me or will you not? I want it straight."

"No. No."

"And—why not?"

He was horribly cool and calm.

"Because I don't want to marry you. I don't want to marry anybody."

"Good God! What *do* you want, then?"

"I want to go away and earn my own living as other women do."

The absurdity of it melted him. He could have gone down on his knees at her feet and kissed her cold hands. He wondered afterward why on earth he hadn't. Then he remembered that all the time she had kept her hands locked behind her.

"You poor child, you don't want to earn your own living. I'll tell you what you *do* want. You want to get away from home."

"And what if I do? You've seen what it's like. Would *you* stay in it a day longer than you could help if you were me?"

"Of course I wouldn't. Of course I've seen what it's like. I saw it the first time I saw you here in this detestable house. I want to take you away out of it. I think I wanted to take you away then."

"Oh, no. Not then. Not so long ago as that."

It was as if she had said, "Not that. That makes it too hard. Any cruelty you like but that, or I can't go through with it."

"Yes," he said, "as long ago as that."

"You can't take me away."

"Can't I? I can take you anywhere. And I will. Anywhere you like. You've only got to say. I *know* I can make you happy."

"How do you know?"

"Because I know you."

"That's what you're always saying. And you know nothing about me. Nothing. Nothing."

She said to herself: "He doesn't. He doesn't even know why I'm going."

"I know a lot more than you think. And a lot more than you know yourself. I know that you're not happy as you are, and I know that you can't *live* without happiness. If you're not happy you'll be ill; more horribly ill, perhaps, than Alice. Look at Alice."

"I'm not like Alice."

"Not now. Not next year. Not for ten years, perhaps, or twenty. But you don't know what you may be."

She raised her head.

"I shall never be like that. Never."

Rowcliffe laughed.

It struck her then that that was what she ought never to have said if she wanted to carry out her purpose.

"When I say I'm not like Ally I mean that I'm not so dependent on people. I'm not gentle like Ally. I'm not as loving and I'm not as womanly. In fact, I'm not womanly at all."

"My dear child, do you suppose it matters to me what you're not, as long as I love you as you are?"

"No," she said, "you don't love me really. You only think you do."

She clung to that.

"Why do you say that, Gwenda?"

"Because, if you did, I should have known it before now."

"Well, considering that you *do* know it now——"

"I mean, you'd have said so before."

"I say! I like that. I'd have said so about five times if you'd ever given me a chance."

"Oh, no. You had your chance."

"When did I have it? When?"

"The other day. Up at Bar Hill."

"You thought so then?"

"I didn't say I thought so then. I think so now."

"That's rather clever of you. Because, you see, if you thought so then that shows——"

"What does it show?"

"Why, that you knew all the time—and that you were thinking of me. You *did* know. You *did* think——"

"No. No. It's only that I've got to—that you're *making* me think of you now. But I'm not thinking of you the way you want."

"If you're not—if you haven't thought of me—*the way I want*—then I can't make you out. You're beyond me."

They sat down, tired out with the struggle, as if they had reached the same point of exhaustion at the same instant.

"Why not leave it at that?" she said.

He rallied.

"Because I can't leave it at that. You knew I cared.

You must have seen. I could have sworn you saw. I could have sworn——"

She knew what he was going to swear and she stopped him.

"I *did* see that you thought you cared for me. If you'd been quite sure you'd have told me. You wouldn't have waited. You're not quite sure now. You're only telling me now because I'm going away. If I hadn't said I was going away you'd never have told me. You'd just have gone on waiting till you were quite sure."

She had irritated him now beyond endurance.

"Gwenda," he said savagely, "you're enough to drive a man mad."

"You've told me *that* before, anyhow. Don't you see that I should go on driving you mad? Don't you see how unhappy you'd be with me, how impossible it all is?"

She laughed. It was marvelous to her how she achieved that laugh. It was as if she had just thought of it and it came.

"I can see," he said, "that *you* don't care for me."

He had given himself into her hands—hands that seemed to him diabolic in their play.

"Did I ever *say* I cared?"

"Well—of all the women—you *are*——! No, you didn't *say* it."

"Did I ever show it?"

"Good God, how do *I* know what you showed? If it had been any other woman—yes, I could have sworn."

"You can't swear to any woman—I'm afraid—till you've married her. Perhaps—not then."

"You shouldn't say things like that; they sound——"

"How do they sound?"

"As if you knew too much."

She smiled.

"Well, then—there's another reason."

He softened suddenly.

"I didn't mean that, Gwenda. You don't know what you're saying. You don't know anything. It's only that you're so beastly clever."

"That's a better reason still. You don't want to marry a beastly clever woman. You really don't."

"I'd risk it. That sort of cleverness doesn't last long."

"It would last your time," she said.

She rose. It was as much as giving him his dismissal.

He stood a moment watching her. She and all her movements still seemed to him incredible.

"Do you mind telling me where you're going *to?*"

"I'm going to Mummy." She explained to his blankness: "My stepmother."

He remembered. Mummy was the lady who was "the very one," the lady of remarkable resources.

It seemed to him then that he saw it all. He knew what she was going for.

"I see. Instead of your sister," he sneered.

"Papa wouldn't let Ally go to her. But he can't stop *me.*"

"Oh, no. Nobody could stop *you.*"

She smiled softly. She had missed the brutality of his emphasis.

He said to himself that Gwenda was impossible. She was obstinate and conceited and wrong-headed. She was utterly selfish, a cold mass of egoism.

"Cold?" He was not so sure. She might be. But she was capable, he suspected, of adventures. Instead of taking her sister away to have her chance, she was rushing off to secure it herself. And the irony of the thing was that it was he who had put it into her head.

Well—she was no worse, and no better—than the rest of them. Only unlike them in the queerness of her fascination. He wondered how long it would have lasted?

You couldn't go on caring for a woman like that, who had never cared a rap about you.

And yet—he could have sworn—— Oh, *that* was nothing. She had only thought of him because he had been her only chance.

He made himself think these things of her because they gave him unspeakable consolation.

All the way back to Morfe he thought them, while on his right hand Karva rose and receded and rose again, and changed at every turn its aspect and its form. He thought them to an accompaniment of an interior, persistent voice, the voice of his romantic youth, that said to him, "That is her hill, her hill—do you remember? That's where you met her first. That's where you saw her jumping. That's her hill—her hill—her hill."

XXXIX

THE Vicar had been fidgeting in his study, getting up and sitting down, and looking at the clock every two minutes. Gwenda had told him that she wanted to speak to him, and he had stipulated that the interview should be after prayer time, for he knew that he was going to be upset. He never allowed family disturbances, if he could help it, to interfere with the attitude he kept up before his Maker.

He knew perfectly well she was going to tell him of her engagement to young Rowcliffe; and though he had been prepared for the news any time for the last three months he had to pull himself together to receive it. He would have to pretend that he was pleased about it when he wasn't pleased at all. He was, in fact, intensely sorry for himself. It had dawned on him that, with Alice left a permanent invalid on his hands, he couldn't really afford to part with Gwenda. She might be terrible in the house, but in her way—a way he didn't altogether approve of—she was useful in the parish. She would cover more of it in an afternoon than Mary could in a month of Sundays.

But, though the idea of Gwenda's marrying was disagreeable to him for so many reasons, he was not going to forbid it absolutely. He was only going to insist that she should wait. It was only reasonable and decent that she should wait until Alice got either better or bad enough to be put under restraint.

The Vicar's pity for himself reached its climax when he considered that awful alternative. He had been considering it ever since Rowcliffe had spoken to him about Alice.

It was just like Gwenda to go and get engaged at such a moment, when he was beside himself.

But he smoothed his face into a smile when she appeared.

"Well, what is it? What is this great thing you've come to tell me?"

It struck him that for the first time in her life Gwenda looked embarrassed; as well she might be.

"Oh—it isn't very great, Papa. It's only that I'm going away."

"Going—*away?*"

"I don't mean out of the country. Only to London."

"Ha! Going to London——" He rolled it ruminatingly on his tongue.

"Well, if that's all you've come to say, it's very simple. You can't go."

He bent his knees with the little self-liberating gesture that he had when he put his foot down.

"But," said Gwenda, "I'm going."

He raised his eyebrows.

"And why is this the first time I've heard of it?"

"Because I want to go without any bother, since I'm going to go."

"Oh—consideration for me, I suppose?"

"For both of us. I don't want you to worry."

"That's why you've chosen a time when I'm worried out of my wits already."

"I know, Papa. That's why I'm going."

He was arrested both by the astounding statement and

by something unusually placable in her tone. He stared at her as his way was.

Then, suddenly, he had a light on it.

"Gwenda, there must be something behind all this. You'd better tell me straight out what's happened."

"Nothing has happened."

"You know what I mean. We've spoken about this before. Is there anything between you and young Rowcliffe."

"Nothing. Nothing whatever of the sort you mean."

"You're sure there hasn't been"—he paused discreetly for his word—"some misunderstanding?"

"Quite sure. There isn't anything to misunderstand. I'm going because I want to go. There are too many of us at home."

"Too many of you—in the state your sister's in?"

"That's exactly why I'm going. I'm trying to tell you. Ally'll go on being ill as long as there are three of us knocking about the house. You'll find she'll buck up like anything when I'm gone. There's nothing the matter with her, really."

"That may be your opinion. It isn't Rowcliffe's."

"I know it isn't. But it soon will be. It was your own idea a little while ago."

"Ye—es; before this last attack, perhaps. D'you know what Rowcliffe thinks of her?"

"Yes. But I know a lot more about Ally than he does. So do you."

"Well——"

They were sitting down to it now.

"But I can't afford to keep you if you go away."

"Of course you can't. You won't have to keep me. I'm going to keep myself."

Again he stared. This was preposterous.

"It's all right, Papa. It's all settled."

"By whom?"

"By me."

"You've found something to do in London?"

"Not yet. I'm going to look——"

"And what," inquired the Vicar with an even suaver irony, *"can* you do?"

"I can be somebody's secretary."

"Whose?"

"Oh," said Gwenda airily, "anybody's."

"And—if I may ask—what will you do, and where do you propose to stay, while you're looking for him?" (He felt that he expressed himself with perspicacity.)

"That's all arranged. I'm going to Mummy."

The Vicar was silent with the shock of it.

"I'm sorry, Papa," said Gwenda; "but there's nowhere else to go to."

"If you go there," said Mr. Cartaret, "you will certainly not come back here."

All that had passed till now had been mere skirmishing. The real battle had begun.

Gwenda set her face to it.

"I shall not be coming back in any case," she said.

"That question can stand over till you've gone."

"I shall be gone on Friday by the three train."

"I shall not allow you to go—by any train."

"How are you going to stop me?"

He had not considered it.

"You don't suppose I'm going to give you any money to go with?"

"You needn't. I've got heaps."

"And how are you going to get your luggage to the station?"

"Oh—the usual way."

"There'll be no way if I forbid Peacock to carry it—or you."

"Can you forbid Jim Greatorex? *He*'ll take me like a shot."

"I can put your luggage under lock and key."

He was still stern, though he was aware that the discussion was descending to sheer foolishness.

"I'll go without it. I can carry a toothbrush and a comb, and Mummy will have heaps of nightgowns."

The Vicar leaned forward and hid his face in his hands before that poignant evocation of Robina.

Gwenda saw that she had gone too far. She had a queer longing to go down on her knees before him and drag his hands from his poor face and ask him to forgive her. She struggled with and overcame the morbid impulse.

The Vicar lifted his face, and for a moment they looked at each other while he measured, visibly, his forces against hers.

She shook her head at him almost tenderly. He was purely pathetic to her now.

"It's no use, Papa. You'd far better give it up. You know you can't do it. You can't stop me. You can't stop Jim Greatorex. You can't even stop Peacock. You don't want *another* scandal in the parish."

He didn't.

"Oh, go your own way," he said, "and take the consequences."

"I *have* taken them," said Gwenda.

She thought, "I wonder what he'd have said if I'd told him the truth? But, if I had, he'd never have believed it."

The truth indeed was far beyond the Vicar's power of belief. He only supposed (after some reflection) that Gwenda was going off in a huff, because young Rowcliffe had failed to come to the scratch. He knew what this running up to London and earning her own living meant—she! He would have trusted Ally sooner. Gwenda was capable of anything.

And as he thought of what she might be capable of in London, he sighed, "God help her!"

XL

IT was May, five weeks since Gwenda had left Garth-dale.

Five Wednesdays came and went and Rowcliffe had not been seen or heard of at the Vicarage. It struck even the Vicar that considerably more had passed between his daughter and the doctor than Gwenda had been willing to admit. Whatever had passed, it had been something that had made Rowcliffe desire not to be seen or heard of.

All the same, the Vicar and his daughter Alice were both so profoundly aware of Rowcliffe that for five weeks they had not mentioned his name to each other. When Mary mentioned it on Friday, in the evening of that disgraceful day, he said that he had had enough of Rowcliffe and he didn't want to hear any more about the fellow.

Mr. Cartaret had signified that his second daughter's name was not to be mentioned, either. But, becoming as his attitude was, he had not been able to keep it up. In the sixth week after Gwenda's departure, he was obliged to hear (it was Alice, amazed out of all reticence, who told him) that Gwenda had got a berth as companion secretary to Lady Frances Gilbey, at a salary of a hundred a year.

Mummy had got it for her.

"You may well stare, Molly, but it's what she says."

The Vicar, as if he had believed Ally capable of fabricating this intelligence, observed that he would like to see that letter.

His face darkened as he read it.   He handed it back
without a word.

The thing was not so incredible to the Vicar as it was
to Mary.

He had always known that Robina could pull wires.   It
was, in fact, through her ability to pull wires that Robina
had so successfully held him up.   She had her hands on
the connections of an entire social system.   Her superior
ramifications were among those whom Mr. Cartaret habit-
ually spoke and thought of as "the best people."   And
when it came to connections, Robina's were of the very
best.   Lady Frances was her second cousin.   In the days
when he was trying to find excuses for marrying Robina,
it was in considering her connections that he found his
finest.   The Vicar had informed his conscience that he
was marrying Robina because of what she could do for
his three motherless daughters—and himself.

Preferment even lay (through the Gilbeys) within Robina's scope.

But to have planted Gwenda on Lady Frances Robina
must have pulled all the wires she knew.   Lady Frances
was a distinguished philanthropist and a rigid Evangelical, so rigid and so distinguished that, in the eyes of poor
parsons waiting for preferment, she constituted a pillar
of the Church.

To the Vicar, as he brooded over it, Robina's act was
more than mere protection of his daughter Gwenda.   Not
only was it carrying the war into the enemy's camp with
a vengeance, it was an act of hostility subtler and more
malignant than overt defiance.

Ever since she left him, Robina had been trying to get
hold of the girls, regarding them as the finest instruments
in her relentless game.   For it never occurred to Mr. Cartaret that his third wife's movements could by any pos-

sibility refer to anybody but himself. Robina, according
to Mr. Cartaret, was perpetually thinking of him and of
how she could annoy him. She had shown a fiendish cleverness in placing Gwenda with Lady Frances. She
couldn't have done anything that could have annoyed him
more. More than anything that Robina had yet done, it
put him in the wrong. It put him in the wrong not only
with Lady Frances and the best people, but it put him
in the wrong with Gwenda and kept him there. Against
Gwenda, with Lady Frances and a salary of a hundred a
year at her back, he hadn't the appearance of a leg to
stand on. The thing had the air of justifying Gwenda's
behavior by its consequences.

That was what Robina had been reckoning on. For,
if it had been Gwenda she had been thinking of, she would
have kept her instead of handing her over to Lady Frances.
The companion secretaries of that distinguished philanthropist had no sinecure even at a hundred a year.

As for Gwenda's accepting such a post, that proved
nothing as against his view of her. It only proved, what
he had always known, that you could never tell what
Gwenda would do next.

And because nothing could be said with any dignity,
the Vicar had said nothing as he rose and went into his
study.

It was there, hidden from his daughters' scrutiny, that
he pondered these things.

They waited till the door had closed on him before they
spoke.

"Well, after all, that'll be very jolly for her," said
Mary.

"It isn't half as jolly as it looks," said Ally. "It means
that she'll have to live at Tunbridge Wells."

"Oh," said Mary, "it won't be all Tunbridge Wells."
She couldn't bear to think that it would be all Tunbridge
Wells. Not that she did think it for a moment. It
couldn't be all Tunbridge Wells for a girl like Gwenda.
Mummy could never have contemplated that. Gwenda
couldn't have contemplated it. And Mary refused to con-
template it either. She persuaded herself that what had
happened to her sister was simply a piece of the most
amazing luck. She even judged it probable that Gwenda
had known very well what she was doing when she went
away.

Besides she had always wanted to do something. She
had learned shorthand and typewriting at Westbourne,
as if, long ago, she had decided that, if home became insupportable, she would leave it. And there had always
been that agreement between her and Mummy.

When Mary put these things together, she saw that
nothing could be more certain than that, sooner or later,
Ally or no Ally, Gwenda would have gone away.

But this was after it had occurred to her that Rowcliffe ought to know what had happened and that she had
got to tell him. And that was on the day after Gwenda's
letter came, when Mrs. Gale, having brought in the tea-
things, paused in her going to say, " 'Ave yo' seen Dr.
Rawcliffe, Miss Mary? Ey—but 'e's lookin' baad."

"Everybody," said Mary, "is looking bad this muggy
weather. That reminds me, how's the baby?"

" 'E's woorse again, Miss. I tall Assy she'll navver
rear 'im."

"Has the doctor seen him to-day?"

"Naw, naw, nat yat. But 'e'll look in, 'e saays, afore
'e goas."

Mary looked at the clock. Rowcliffe left the surgery at
four-thirty. It was now five minutes past.

She wondered: Did he know, then, or did he not know? Would Gwenda have written to him? Was it because she had not written that he was looking bad, or was it because she had written and he knew?

She thought and thought it over; and under all her thinking there lurked the desire to know whether Rowcliffe knew and how he was taking it, and under her desire the longing, imperious and irresistible, to see him.

She would have to ask him to the house. She had not forgotten that she had to ask him, that she was pledged to ask him on Ally's account if, as Gwenda had put it, she was to play the game.

But she had had more than one motive for her delay. It would look better if she were not in too great a hurry. (She said to herself it would look better on Ally's account.) The longer he was kept away (she said to herself, that he was kept away from Ally) the more he would be likely to want to come. Sufficient time must elapse to allow of his forgetting Gwenda. It was not well that he should be thinking all the time of Gwenda when he came. (She said to herself it was not well on Ally's account.)

And it was well that their father should have forgotten Rowcliffe.

(This on Ally's account, too.)

For of course it was only on Ally's account that she was asking Rowcliffe, really.

Not that there seemed to be any such awful need.

For Ally, in those five weeks, had got gradually better. And now, in the first week of May, which had always been one of her bad months, she was marvelously well. It looked as if Gwenda had known what she was talking about when she said Ally would be all right when she was gone.

And of course it was just as well (on Ally's account)

that Rowcliffe should not have seen her until she was absolutely well.

Nobody could say that she, Mary, was not doing it beautifully. Nobody could say she was not discreet, since she had let five weeks pass before she asked him.

And in order that her asking him should have the air of happy chance, she must somehow contrive to see him first.

Her seeing him could be managed any Wednesday in the village. It was bound, in fact, to occur. The wonder was that it had not occurred before.

Well, that showed how hard, all these weeks, she had been trying not to see him. If she had had an uneasy conscience in the matter (and she said to herself that there was no occasion for one), it would have acquitted her.

Nobody could say she wasn't playing the game.

And then it struck her that she had better go down at once and see Essy's baby.

It was only five and twenty past four.

XLI

THE Vicar was right. Rowcliffe did not want to be
seen or heard of at the Vicarage. He did not want to
see or hear of the Vicarage or of Gwenda Cartaret again.
Twice a week or more in those five weeks he had to pass
the little gray house above the churchyard; twice a week
or more the small shy window in its gable end looked
sidelong at him as he went by. But he always pretended
not to see it. And if anybody in the village spoke to him
of Gwenda Cartaret he pretended not to hear, so that
presently they left off speaking.

He had sighted Mary Cartaret two or three times in
the village, and once, on the moor below Upthorne, a
figure that he recognised as Alice; he had also overtaken
Mary on her bicycle, and once he had seen her at a shop
door on Morfe Green. And each time Mary (absorbed
in what she was doing) had made it possible for him not
to see her. He was grateful to her for her absorption
while he saw through it. He had always known that Mary
was a person of tact.

He also knew that this preposterous avoidance could not
go on forever. It was only that Mary gave him a blessed
respite week by week. Presently one or other of the two
would have to end it, and he didn't yet know which of
them it would be. He rather thought it would be Mary.

And it *was* Mary.

He met her that first Wednesday in May, as he was
leaving Mrs. Gale's cottage.

215

She was coming along the narrow path by the beck and there was no avoiding her.

She came toward him smiling. He had always rather liked her smile. It was quiet. It never broke up, as it were, her brooding face. He had noticed that it didn't even part her lips or make them thinner. If anything it made them thicker, it curved still more the crushed bow of the upper lip and the pensive sweep of the lower. But it opened doors; it lit lights. It broadened quite curiously the rather too broad nostrils; it set the wide eyes wider; it brought a sudden blue into their thick gray. In her cheeks it caused a sudden leaping and spreading of their flame. Her rather high and rather prominent cheekbones gave character and a curious charm to Mary's face; they had the effect of lifting her bloom directly under the pure and candid gray of her eyes, leaving her red mouth alone in its dominion. That mouth with its rather too long upper lip and its almost perpetual brooding was saved from immobility by its alliance with her nostrils.

Such was Mary's face. Rowcliffe had often watched it, acknowledging its charm, while he said to himself that for him it could never have any meaning or fascination, any more than Mary could. There wasn't much in Mary's face, and there wasn't much in Mary. She was too ruminant, too tranquil. He sometimes wondered how much it would take to trouble her.

And yet there were times when that tranquillity was soothing. She had always, even when Ally was at her worst, smiled at him as if nothing had happened or could happen, and she smiled at him as if nothing had happened now. And it struck Rowcliffe, as it had frequently struck him before, how good her face was.

She held out her hand to him and looked at him.

And as if only then she had seen in his face the signs

of a suffering she had been unaware of, her eyes rounded in a sudden wonder of distress. They said in their goodness and their candor, "Oh, I see how horribly you've suffered. I didn't know and I'm so sorry." Then they looked away, and it was like the quiet withdrawal of a hand that feared lest in touching it should hurt him.

Mary began to talk of the weather and of Essy and of Essy's baby, as if her eyes had never seen anything at all. Then, just as they parted, she said, "When are you coming to see us again?" as if he had been to see them only the other day.

He said he *would* come as soon as he was asked.

And Mary reflected, as one arranging a multitude of engagements.

"Well, then—let me see—can you come to tea on Friday? Or Monday? Father'll be at home both days."

And Rowcliffe said thanks, he'd come on Friday.

Mary went on to the cottage and Rowcliffe to his surgery.

He wondered why she hadn't said a word about Gwenda. He supposed it was because she knew that there was nothing she could say that would not hurt him.

And he said to himself, "What a nice girl she is. What a thoroughly nice girl."

But what he wanted, though he dreaded it, was news of Gwenda. He didn't know whether he could bring himself to ask for it, but he rather thought that Mary would know what he wanted and give it him without his asking.

That was precisely what Mary knew and did.

She was ready for him, alone in the gray and amber drawing-room, and she did it almost at once, before Alice or her father could come in. Alice was out walking, she said, and her father was in the study. They would be in soon. She thus made Rowcliffe realise that if she was going to be abrupt it was because she had to be; they had both of them such a short time.

With admirable tact she assumed Rowcliffe's interest in Ally and the Vicar. It made it easier to begin about Gwenda. And before she began it seemed to her that she had better first find out if he knew. So she asked him point-blank if he had heard from Gwenda?

"No," he said.

At her name he had winced visibly. But there was hope even in his hurt eyes. It sprang from Mary's taking it for granted that he would be likely to hear from her sister.

"We only heard—really," said Mary, "the other day."

"Is that so?"

"Of course she wrote; but she didn't say much, because, at first, I'm afraid, there wasn't very much to say."

"And is there?"

Rowcliffe's hands were trembling slightly. Mary looked down at them and away.

"Well, yes."

And she told him that Gwenda had got a secretaryship to Lady Frances Gilbey.

It would have been too gross to have told him about Gwenda's salary. But it might have been the salary she was thinking of when she added that it was of course an awfully good thing for Gwenda.

"And who," said Rowcliffe, "is Lady Frances Gilbey?"

"She's a cousin of my stepmother's."

He considered it.

"And Mrs.—er—Cartaret lives in London, doesn't she?"

"Oh, yes."

Mary's tone implied that you couldn't expect that brilliant lady to live anywhere else.

There was a moment in which Rowcliffe again evoked the image of the third Mrs. Cartaret who was "the very one." If anything could have depressed him more, that did.

But he pulled himself together. There were things he had to know.

"And does your sister like living in London?"

Mary smiled. "I imagine she does very much indeed."

"Somehow," said Rowcliffe, "I can't see her there. I thought she liked the country."

"Oh, you never can tell whether Gwenda really likes anything. She may have liked it. She may have liked it awfully. But she couldn't go on liking it forever."

And to Rowcliffe it was as if Mary had said that wasn't Gwenda's way.

"There's no doubt she's done the best thing. For herself, I mean."

Rowcliffe assented. "Perhaps she has."

And Mary, as if doubt had only just occurred to her, made a sudden little tremulous appeal.

"You don't really think Garth was the place for her?"

"I don't really think anything about it," Rowcliffe said.

Mary was pensive. Her brooding look said that she laid a secret fear to rest.

"Garth couldn't satisfy a girl like Gwenda."

Rowcliffe said no, he supposed it couldn't satisfy her. His dejection was by this time terrible. It cast a visible, a palpable gloom.

"She's a restless creature," said Mary, smiling.

She threw it out as if by way of lightening his oppression, almost as if she put it to him that if Gwenda was restless (by which Rowcliffe might understand, if he liked, capricious) she couldn't help it. There was no reason why he should be so horribly hurt. It was not as if there was anything personal in Gwenda's changing attitudes.

And Rowcliffe did indeed say to himself, Restless—restless. Yes. That was the word for her; and he supposed she couldn't help it.

The study door opened and shut. Mary's eyes made a sign to him that said, "We can't talk about this before my father. He won't like it."

But Mr. Cartaret had gone upstairs. They could hear him moving in the room overhead.

"How is your other sister getting on?" said Rowcliffe abruptly.

"Alice? She's all right. You wouldn't know her. She can walk for miles."

"You don't say so?"

He was really astonished.

"She's off now somewhere, goodness knows where."

"Ha!" Rowcliffe laughed softly.

"It's really wonderful," said Mary. "She's generally so tired in the spring."

It *was* wonderful. The more he thought of it the more wonderful it was.

"Oh, well——" he said, "she mustn't overdo it."

It was Mary he suspected of overdoing it. On Ally's account, of course. It wasn't likely that she would give the poor child away.

At that point Mrs. Gale came in with the tea-things. And presently the Vicar came down to tea.

He was more than courteous this time. He was affable. He too greeted Rowcliffe as if nothing had happened, and he abstained from any reference to Gwenda.

But he showed a certain serenity in his restraint. Leaning back in his armchair, his legs crossed, his hands joined lightly at the finger-tips, his forehead smoothed, conversing affably, Mr. Cartaret had the air of a man who might indeed have suffered through his outrageous family, but for whom suffering was passed, a man without any trouble or anxiety. And serenity without the memory of suffering was in Mary's good and happy face.

The house was very still, it seemed the stillness of life that ran evenly and with no sound. And it was borne in upon Rowcliffe as he sat there and talked to them that this quiet and tranquillity had come to them with Gwenda's going. She was a restless creature, and she had infected them with her unrest. They had peace from her now.

Only for him there could be no peace from Gwenda. He could feel her in the room. Through the open door she came and went—restless, restless!

He put the thought of her from him.

After tea the Vicar took him into his study. If Rowcliffe had a moment to spare, he would like, he said, to talk to him.

Rowcliffe looked at his watch. The idea of being talked to frightened him.

The Vicar observed his nervousness.

"It's about my daughter Alice," he said.

And it was.

The Vicar wanted him to know and he had brought him into his study in order to tell him that Alice had completely recovered. He went into it. The girl was fit. She was happy. She ate well. She slept well (he had kept her under very careful supervision) and she could walk for miles. She was, in fact, leading the healthy natural life he had hoped she would lead when he brought her into a more bracing climate.

Rowcliffe expressed his wonder. It was, he said, *very* wonderful.

But the Vicar would not admit that it was wonderful at all. It was exactly what he had expected. He had never thought for a moment that there was anything seriously wrong with Alice—anything indeed in the least the matter with her.

Rowcliffe was silent. But he looked at the Vicar, and the Vicar did not even pretend not to understand his look.

"I know," he said, "the very serious view you took of her. But I think, my dear fellow, when you've seen her you'll admit that you were mistaken."

Rowcliffe said there was nothing he desired more than to have been mistaken, but he was afraid he couldn't admit it. Miss Cartaret's state, when he last saw her, had been distinctly serious.

"You will perhaps admit that whatever danger there may have been then is over?"

"I haven't seen her yet," said Rowcliffe. "But"—he looked at him—"I told you the thing was curable."

"That's my point. What is there—what can there have been to cure her?"

Rowcliffe ignored the Vicar's point.

"Can you date it—this recovery?"

"I date it," said the Vicar, "from the time her sister left. She seemed to pull herself together after that."

Rowcliffe said nothing. He was reviewing all his knowledge of the case. He considered Ally's disastrous infatuation for himself. In the light of his knowledge her recovery was not only wonderful, it was incomprehensible. So incomprehensible that he was inclined to suspect her father of lying for some reason of his own. Family pride, no doubt. He had known instances.

The Vicar went on. He gave himself a long innings.

"But that does not account for it altogether, though it may have started it. I really put it down to other things —the pure air—the quiet life—the absence of excitement —the regular *work* that *takes* her *out* of herself——" Here the Vicar fell into that solemn rhythm that marked the periods of his sermons.

He perorated. "The *simple* following *out* of *my* prescription. You will remember" (he became suddenly cheery and conversational) "that it *was* mine."

"It certainly wasn't mine," said Rowcliffe.

He saw it all. *That* was why the Vicar was so affable. That was why he was so serene.

And he wasn't lying. His state of mind was obviously much too simple. He was serenely certain of his facts.

By courteous movement of his hand the Vicar condoned Rowcliffe's rudeness, which he attributed to professional pique very natural in the circumstances.

With admirable tact he changed the subject.

"I also wished to consult you about another matter. Nothing" (he again reassured the doctor's nervousness) "to do with my family."

Rowcliffe was all attention.

"It's about—it's about that poor girl, Essy Gale."

"Essy," said Rowcliffe, "is very well and very happy."

The Vicar's sudden rigidity implied that Essy had no business to be happy.

"If she is, it isn't your friend Greatorex's fault."

"I'm not so sure of that," said Rowcliffe.

"I suppose you know he has refused to marry her?"

"I understood as much. But who asked him to?"

"I did."

"My dear sir, if you don't mind my saying so, I think

you made a mistake—if you *want* him to marry her. You know what he is."

"I do indeed. But a certain responsibility rests with the parson of the parish."

"You can't be responsible for everything that goes on."

"Perhaps not—when the place is packed with nonconformists. Greatorex comes of bad dissenting stock. I can't hope to have any influence with him."

He paused.

"But I'm told that *you* have."

"Influence? Not I. I've a sneaking regard for Greatorex. He isn't half a bad fellow if you take him the right way."

"Well, then, can't you take him? Can't you say a judicious word?"

"If it's to ask him to marry Essy, that wouldn't be very judicious, I'm afraid. He'll marry her if he wants to, and if he doesn't, he won't."

"But, my dear Dr. Rowcliffe, think of the gross injustice to that poor girl."

"It might be a worse injustice if he married her. Why *should* he marry her if he doesn't want to, and if she doesn't want it? There she is, perfectly content and happy with her baby. It's been a little seedy lately, but it's absolutely sound. A very fine baby indeed, and Essy knows it. There's nothing wrong with the baby."

Rowcliffe continued, regardless of the Vicar's stare: "She's better off as she is than tied to a chap who isn't a bit too sober. Especially if he doesn't care for her."

The Vicar rose and took up his usual defensive position on the hearth.

"Well, Dr. Rowcliffe, if those are your ideas of morality——"

"They are not my ideas of morality, only my judgment of the individual case."

"Well—if that's your judgment, after all, I think that the less you meddle with it the better."

"I never meddle," said Rowcliffe.

But the Vicar did not leave him. He had caught the sound of the opening and shutting of the gate. He listened.

His manner changed again to a complete affability.

"I think that's Alice. I should like you to see her. If you——"

Rowcliffe gathered that the entrance of Alice had better coincide with his departure. He followed the Vicar as he went to open the front door.

Alice stood on the doorstep.

She was not at first aware of him where he lingered in the half-darkness at the end of the passage.

"Alice," said the Vicar, "Dr. Rowcliffe is here. You're just in time to say good-bye to him."

"It's a pity if it's good-bye," said Alice.

Her voice might have been the voice of a young woman who is sanely and innocently gay, but to Rowcliffe's ear there was a sound of exaltation in it.

He could see her now clearly in the light of the open door. The Vicar had not lied. Alice had all the appearances of health. Something had almost cured her.

But not quite. As she stood there with him in the doorway, chattering, Rowcliffe was struck again with the excitement of her voice and manner, imperfectly restrained, and with the quivering glitter of her eyes. By these signs he gathered that if Alice was happy her happiness was not complete. It was not happiness in his sense of the word. But Alice's face was unmistakably the face of hope.

Whatever it was, it had nothing to do with him.   He
saw that Alice's eyes faced him now with the light, un-
seeing look of indifference, and that they turned every
second toward the wall at the bottom of the garden.   She
was listening to something.

He was then aware of footsteps on the road.   They came
down the hill, passing close under the Vicarage wall and
turning where it turned to skirt the little lane at the bottom between the garden and the churchyard.   The lane
led to the pastures, and the pastures to the Manor.   And
from the Manor grounds a field track trailed to a small
wicket gate on the north side of the churchyard wall.   A
flagged path went from the wicket to the door of the north
transept.   It was a short cut for the lord of the Manor
to his seat in the chancel, but it was not the nearest way
for anybody approaching the church from the high road.

Now, the slope of the Vicarage garden followed the slope
of the road in such wise that a person entering the churchyard from the high road could be seen from the windows
of the Vicarage.   If that person desired to remain unseen
his only chance was to go round by the lane to the wicket
gate, keeping close under the garden wall.

Rowcliffe heard the wicket gate click softly as it was
softly opened and shut.

And he could have sworn that Alice heard it too.

He waited twenty minutes or so in his surgery.   Then,
instead of sending at once to the Red Lion for his trap,
he walked back to the church.

Standing in the churchyard, he could hear the sound of
the organ and of a man's voice singing.

He opened the big west door softly and went softly in.

XLII

There is no rood-screen in Garth church. The one aisle down the middle of the nave goes straight from the west door to the chancel-rails.

Standing by the west door, behind the font, Rowcliffe had an uninterrupted view of the chancel.

The organ was behind the choir stalls on the north side. Alice was seated at the organ. Jim Greatorex stood behind her and so that his face was turned slantwise toward Rowcliffe. Alice's face was in pure profile. Her head was tilted slightly backward, as if the music lifted it.

Rowcliffe moved softly to the sexton's bench in the left hand corner. Sitting there he could see her better and ran less risk of being seen.

The dull stained glass of the east window dimmed the light at that end of the church. The organ candles were lit. Their jointed brackets, brought forward on each side, threw light on the music book and the keys, also on the faces of Alice and Greatorex. He stood so close to her as almost to touch her. She had taken off her hat and her hair showed gold against the drab of his waistcoat.

On both faces there was a look of ecstasy.

It was essentially the same ecstasy; only, on Alice's face it was more luminous, more conscious, and at the same time more abandoned, as if all subterfuge had ceased in her and she gave herself up, willing and exulting, to the unspiritual sense that flooded her.

On the man's face this look was more confused. It was also more tender and more poignant, as if in soaring Jim's rapture gave him pain. You would have said that he had not given himself to it, but that he was driven by it, and that yet, with all its sensuous trouble, there ran through it, secret and profoundly pure, some strain of spiritual longing.

And in his thick, his poignant and tender half-barytone, half-tenor, Greatorex sang:

> " 'At e-ee-vening e-er the soon was set,
>   The sick, oh Lo-ord, arou-ound thee laay—
>   Oh, with what divers pains they met,
>   And with what joy they went a-waay——' "

But Alice stopped playing and Rowcliffe heard her say, "Don't let's have that one, Jim, I don't like it."

It might have passed—even the name—but that Rowcliffe saw Greatorex put his hand on Alice's head and stroke her hair.

Then he heard him say, "Let's 'ave mine," and he saw that his hand was on Alice's shoulders as he leaned over her to find the hymn.

"Good God!" said Rowcliffe to himself. "That explains it."

He got up softly. Now that he knew, he felt that it was horrible to spy on her.

But Greatorex had begun singing again, and the sheer beauty of the voice held Rowcliffe there to listen.

> " 'Lead—Kindly Light—amidst th' encircling gloo-oom,
>   Lead Thou me o-on.
>   Keep—Thou—my—feet—I do not aa-aassk too-oo see-ee-ee
>   Ther di-is-ta-aant scene, woon step enoo-oof for mee-eea.' "

Greatorex was singing like an angel. And as he sang it was as if two passions, two longings, the earthly and the heavenly, met and mingled in him, so that through all its emotion his face remained incongruously mystic, queerly visionary.

    " 'O'er moor and fen—o'er crag and torrent ti-ill——' "

The evocation was intolerable to Rowcliffe.
He turned away and Greatorex's voice went after him.

" 'And—with—the—morn tho-ose angel fa-a-ce-es smile
   Which I-i—a-ave looved—long since—and lo-ost awhi-ile.' "

Again Rowcliffe turned; but not before he had seen that Greatorex had his hand on Alice's shoulder a second time, and that Alice's hand had gone up and found it there.
The latch of the west door jerked under Rowcliffe's hand with a loud clashing. Alice and Greatorex looked round and saw him as he went out.
Alice got up in terror. The two stood apart on either side of the organ bench, staring into each other's faces.
Then Alice went round to the back of the organ and addressed the small organ-blower.
"Go," she said, "and tell the choir we're waiting for them. It's five minutes past time."
Johnny ran.
Alice went back to the chancel where Greatorex stood turning over the hymn books of the choir.
"Jim," she said, "that was Dr. Rowcliffe. Do you think he saw us?"
"It doesn't matter if he did," said Greatorex. "He'll not talk."

"He might tell Father."

Jim turned to her.

"And if he doos, Ally, yo' knaw what to saay."

"That's no good, Jim. I've told you so. You mustn't think of it."

"I shall think of it. I shall think of noothing else," said Greatorex.

The choir came in, aggrieved, and explaining that it wasn't six yet. Not by the church clock.

XLIII

As Rowcliffe went back to his surgery he recalled two
things he had forgotten.   One was a little gray figure he
had seen once or twice lately wandering through the fields
about Upthorne Farm.   The other was a certain interview he had had with Alice when she had come to ask
him to get Greatorex to sing.   That was in November, not
long before the concert.   He remembered the suggestion
he had then made that Alice should turn her attention
to reclaiming Greatorex.   And, though he had no morbid
sense of responsibility in the matter, it struck him with
something like compunction that he had put Greatorex
into Alice's head chiefly to distract her from throwing
herself at his.

And then, he had gone and forgotten all about it.

He told himself now that he had been a fool not to
think of it.   And if he was a fool, what was to be said
of the Vicar, under whose nose this singular form of
choir practice had been going on for goodness knew how
long?

It did not occur to the doctor that if his surgery day
had been a Friday, which was choir practice day, he would
have been certain to have thought of it.   Neither was he
aware that what he had observed this evening was only
the unforeseen result of a perfectly innocent parochial ar-
rangement.   It had begun at Christmas and again at
Easter, when it was understood that Greatorex, who was
nervous about his voice, should turn up for practice ten

minutes before the rest of the choir to try over his part
in an anthem or cantata, so that, as Alice said, he might
do himself justice.

Since Easter the ten minutes had grown to fifteen or
even twenty. And twice in the last three weeks Greatorex, by collusion with Alice, had arrived a whole hour
before his time. Still, there was nothing in this circumstance itself to alarm the Vicar. Choir practice was choir
practice, a mysterious thing he never interfered with,
knowing himself to be unmusical.

Rowcliffe had had good reason for refusing to urge
Greatorex to marry Essy Gale. But what he had seen in
Garth church made him determined to say something to
Greatorex, after all.

He went on his northerly round the very next Sunday
and timed it so that he overtook his man on his way home
from church. He gave Greatorex a lift with the result
(which he had calculated) that Greatorex gave him dinner,
as he had done once or twice before. The after-dinner
pipe made Jim peculiarly approachable, and Rowcliffe
approached him suddenly and directly. "I say, Greatorex, why don't you marry? Not a bad thing for you,
you know."

"Ay. Saw they tall me," said Greatorex amicably.

Rowcliffe went on to advise his marrying Essy, not on
the grounds of morality or of justice to the girl (he was a
tactful person), but on Greatorex's account, as the best
thing Greatorex could do for himself.

"Yo mane," said Greatorex, "I ought to marry her?"

Rowcliffe said no, he wasn't going into that.

Greatorex was profoundly thoughtful.

Presently he said that he would speak to Essy.

He spoke to her that afternoon.

In the cottage down by the beck Essy sat by the hearth, nursing her baby. He had recovered from his ailment and lay in her lap, gurgling and squinting at the fire. He wore the robe that Mrs. Gale had brought to Essy five months ago. Essy had turned it up above his knees, and smiling softly she watched his little pink feet curling and uncurling as she held them to the fire. Essy's back and the back of the baby's head were toward the door, which stood open, the day being still warm.

Greatorex stood there a moment looking at them before he tapped on the door.

He felt no tenderness for either of them, only a sullen pity that was half resentment.

As if she had heard his footsteps and known them, Essy spoke without looking round.

"Yo' can coom in ef yo' want," she said.

"Thank yo'," he said stiffly and came in.

"I caan't get oop wi' t' baaby. But there's a chair soomwhere."

He found it and sat down.

"Are yo' woondering why I've coom, Essy?"

"Naw, Jim. I wasn't woondering about yo' at all."

Her voice was sweet and placable. She followed the direction of his eyes.

" 'E's better. Ef thot's what yo've coom for."

"It isn' what I've coom for. I've soomthing to saay to yo', Essy."

"There's nat mooch good yo're saayin' anything, Jim. I knaw all yo' 'ave t' saay."

"Yo'll 'ave t' 'ear it, Essy, whether yo' knaw it or not. They're tallin' mae I ought to marry yo'."

Essy's eyes flashed.

"Who's tallin' yo'?"

"T' Vicar, for woon."

"T' Vicar! 'E's a nice woon t' taalk o' marryin', whan 'is awn wife caan't live wi' 'im, nor 'is awn daughter, neither. And 'oo also talled yo'? 'Twasn' Moother?"

"Naw. It wasn' yore moother."

"An' 'twasn' mae, Jim, and navver will bae."

"'Twas Dr. Rawcliffe."

"'E? 'E's anoother. 'Ooo's 'e married? Miss Gwanda? Nat 'e!"

"Yo' let t' doctor bae, Essy. 'E's right enoof. Saw I ought t' marry yo'. But I'm nat goain' to."

"'Ave yo' coom t' tall mae thot? 'S ef I didn' knaw it. 'Ave I avver aassked yo' t' marry mae?"

"Naw, Essy."

"Yo' *can* aassk mae; yo'll bae saafe enoof. Fer I wawn't 'ave yo'. Woonce I med 'a' been maad enoof. I med 'a' said yes t' yo'. But I'd saay naw to-day."

At that he smiled.

"Yo' wouldn' 'ave a good-fer-noothin' falla like mae, would yo', laass? Look yo'—it's nat that I couldn' 'ave married yo'. I could 'ave married yo' right enoof. An' it's nat thot I dawn' think yo' pretty. Yo're pretty enoof fer me. It's—it's—I caan't rightly tall whot it is."

"Dawn' tall mae. I dawn' want t' knaw."

He looked hard at her.

"I might marry yo' yat," he said. "But yo' knaw you wouldn' bae happy wi' mae. I sud bae crool t' yo'. Nat because I wanted t' bae crool, but because I couldn' halp mysel. Theer'd bae soomthin' alse I sud bae thinkin' on and wantin' all t' while."

"I knaw. I knaw. I wouldn' lat yo', Jim. I wouldn' lat yo'."

"I knaw there's t' baaby an' all. It's hard on yo', Essy. But—I dawn' knaw—I ned bae crool to t' baaby, too."

Then she looked up at him, but with more incredulity than reproach.

"Yo' wudn'," she said. "Yo' cudn' bae crool t' lil Jimmy."

He scowled.

"Yo've called 'im thot, Essy?"

"An' why sudn' I call 'im? 'E's a right to thot naame, annyhow. Yo' caann't taake thot awaay from 'im."

"I dawn' want t' taake it away from 'im. But I wish yo' 'adn'. I wish you 'adn', Essy."

"Why 'alf t' lads in t' village is called Jimmy. Yo're called Jimmy yourself, coom t' thot."

He considered it. "Well—it's nat as ef they didn' knaw—all of 'em."

"Oh—they knaws!"

"D'yo' mind them, Essy? They dawn't maake yo' feel baad about it, do they?"

She shook her head and smiled her dreamy smile.

He rose and looked down at her with his grieved, resentful eyes.

"Yo' moosn' suppawse I dawn feel baad, Essy. I've laaid awaake manny a night, thinkin' what I've doon t' yo'."

"What *'ave* yo' doon, Jimmy? Yo' maade mae 'appy fer sex moonths. An' there's t' baaby. I didn' want 'im before 'e coom—seemed like I'd 'ave t' 'ave 'im stead o' yo'. But yo' can goa right awaay, Jimmy, an' I sudn' keer ef I navver saw yo' again, so long's I 'ad 'im."

"Is thot truth, Essy?"

"It's Gawd's truth."

He put out his hand and caressed the child's downy head as if it was the head of some young animal.

"I wish I could do more fer 'im, Essy. I will, maaybe, soom daay."

"I wouldn' lat yo'. I wouldn' tooch yo're mooney now ef I could goa out t' wark an' look affter 'im too. I wouldn' tooch a panny of it, I wouldn'."

"Dawn' yo' saay thot, Essy. Yo' dawn' want to spite mae, do yo'?"

"I didn' saay it t' spite yo', Jimmy. I said it saw 's yo' sudn' feel saw baad."

He smiled mournfully.

"Poor Essy," he said.

She gave him a queer look. "Yo' needn' pity *mae*," she said.

He went away considerably relieved in his mind, but still suffering that sullen uneasiness in his soul.

XLIV

It was the last week in June.

Mary Cartaret sat in the door of the cottage by the beck. And in her lap she held Essy's baby. Essy had run in to the last cottage in the row to look after her great aunt, the Widow Gale, who had fallen out of bed in the night.

The Widow Gale, in her solitude, had formed the habit of falling out of bed. But this time she had hurt her head, and Essy had gone for the doctor and had met Miss Mary in the village and Mary had come with her to help.

For by good luck—better luck than the Widow Gale deserved—it was a Wednesday. Rowcliffe had sent word that he would come at three.

It was three now.

And as he passed along the narrow path he saw Mary Cartaret in the doorway with the baby in her lap.

She smiled at him as he went by.

"I'm making myself useful," she said.

"Oh, more than that!"

His impression was that Mary had made herself beautiful. He looked back over his shoulder and laughed as he hurried on.

Up till now it hadn't occurred to him that Mary could be beautiful. But it didn't puzzle him. He knew how she had achieved that momentary effect.

He knew and he was to remember. For the effect repeated itself.

As he came back Mary was standing in the path, hold-

ing the baby in her arms. She was looking, she said, for
Essy. Would Essy be coming soon?

Rowcliffe did not answer all at once. He stood contemplating the picture. It wasn't all Mary. The baby
did his part. He had been "short-coated" that month,
and his thighs, crushed and delicately creased, showed rose
red against the white rose of Mary's arm. She leaned her
head, brooding tenderly, to his, and his head (he was a
dark baby) was dusk to her flame.

Rowcliffe smiled. "Why?" he said. "Do you want to
get rid of him?"

As if unconsciously she pressed the child closer to her.
As if unconsciously she held his head against her breast.
And when his fingers worked there, in their way, she
covered them with her hand.

"No," she said. "He's a nice baby. (Aren't you a nice
baby? There!) Essy's unhappy because he's going to
have blue eyes and dark hair. But I think they're the
prettiest, don't you?"

"Yes," said Rowcliffe.

He was grave and curt.

And Mary remembered that that was what Gwenda had
—blue eyes and dark hair.

It was what Gwenda's children might have had, too.
She felt that she had made him think of Gwenda.

Then Essy came and took the baby from her.

"'E's too 'eavy fer yo', Miss," she said. She laughed
as she took him; she gazed at him with pride and affection unabashed. His one fault, for Essy, was that, though
he had got Greatorex's eyes, he had not got Greatorex's
hair.

Mary and Rowcliffe went back together.

"You're coming in to tea, aren't you?" she said.

"Rather." He had got into the habit again of looking

in at the Vicarage for tea every Wednesday. They were
having tea in the orchard now. And in June the Vicarage
orchard was a pleasanter place than the surgery.

It was in fact a very pleasant place. Pleasanter than
the gray and amber drawing-room.

When Rowcliffe came to think of it, he owed the Cartarets many pleasant things. So he had formed another
habit of asking them back to tea in his orchard. He had
had no idea what a pleasant place his orchard could be too.

Now, though Rowcliffe nearly always had tea alone
with Mary at the Vicarage, Mary never came to tea at
Rowcliffe's house alone. She always brought Alice with
her. And Rowcliffe found that a nuisance. For one
thing, Alice had the air of being dragged there against
her will, so completely had she recovered from him. For
another, he couldn't talk to Mary quite so well. He didn't
know that he wanted to talk to Mary. He didn't know
that he particularly wanted to be alone with her, but
somehow Alice's being there made him want it.

He was to be alone with Mary to-day, in the orchard.

The window of the Vicar's study raked the orchard.
But that didn't matter, for the Vicar was not at home
this Wednesday.

The orchard waited for them. Two wicker-work armchairs and the little round tea-table were set out under
the trees. Mary's knitting lay in one of the chairs. She
had the habit of knitting while she talked, or while Rowcliffe talked and she listened. The act of knitting disposed her to long silences. It also occupied her, so that
Rowcliffe, when he liked, could be silent too.

But generally he talked and Mary listened.

They hadn't many subjects. But Mary made the most
of what they had. And she always knew the precise

moment when Rowcliffe had ceased to be interested in any one of them. She knew, as if by instinct, all his moments.

They were talking now, at tea-time, about the Widow Gale. Mary wanted to know ·how the poor thing was getting on. The Widow Gale had been rather badly shaken and she had bruised her poor old head and one hip. But she wouldn't fall out of bed again to-night. Rowcliffe had barricaded the bed with a chest of drawers. Afterward there must be a rail or something.

Mary was interested in the Widow Gale as long as Rowcliffe liked to talk about her. But the Widow Gale didn't carry them very far.

What would have carried them far was Rowcliffe himself. But Rowcliffe never wanted to talk about himself to Mary. When Mary tried to lead gently up to him, Rowcliffe shied. He wouldn't talk about himself any more than he would talk about Gwenda.

But Mary didn't want to talk about Gwenda either now. So that her face showed the faintest flicker of dismay when Rowcliffe suddenly began to talk about her.

"Have you any idea," he said, "when your sister's coming back?"

"She won't be long," said Mary. "She's only gone to Upthorne village."

"I meant your other sister."

"Oh, Gwenda——"

Mary brooded. And the impression her brooding made on Rowcliffe was that Mary knew something about Gwenda she did not want to tell.

"I don't think," said Mary gravely, "that Gwenda ever will come back again. At least not if she can help it. I thought you knew that."

"I suppose I must have known."

He left it there.

Mary took up her knitting. She was making a little vest for Essy's baby. Rowcliffe watched it growing under her hands.

"As I can't knit, do you mind my smoking?"

She didn't.

"If more women knitted," he said, "it would be a good thing. They wouldn't be bothered so much with nerves."

"I don't do it for nerves. I haven't any," said Mary.

He laughed. "No, I don't think you have."

She fell into one of her gentle silences. A silence not of her own brooding, he judged. It had no dreams behind it and no imagination that carried her away. A silence, rather, that brought her nearer to him, that waited on his mood.

His eyes watched under half-closed lids the movements of her hands and the pretty droop of her head. And he said to himself, "How sweet she is. And how innocent. And good."

Their chairs were set near together in the small plot of grass. The little trees of the orchard shut them in. He began to notice things about her that he had not noticed before, the shape and color of her finger nails, the modeling of her supple wrists, the way her ears were curved and laid close to her rather broad head. He saw that her skin was milk-white at the throat, and honey-white at her ears, and green-white, the white of an elder flower, at the roots of her red hair.

And as she unwound her ball of wool it rolled out of her lap and fell between her feet.

She stooped suddenly, bringing under Rowcliffe's eyes the nape of her neck, shining with golden down, and her shoulders, sun-warmed and rosy under the thin muslin of her blouse.

They dived at the same moment, and as their heads came up again their faces would have touched but that Rowcliffe suddenly drew back his own.

"I say, I *do* beg your pardon!"

It was odd, but in the moment of his recoil from that imminent contact Rowcliffe remembered the little red-haired nurse. Not that there was much resemblance; for, though the little nurse was sweet, she was not altogether innocent, neither was she what good people like Mary Cartaret would call good. And Mary, leaning back in her chair with the recovered ball in her lap, was smiling at his confusion with an innocence and goodness of which he could have no doubt.

When he tried to account to himself for the remembrance he supposed it must have been the red hair that did it.

And up to the end and to the end of the end Rowcliffe never knew that, though he had been made subject to a sequence of relentless inhibitions and of suggestions overpowering in their nature and persistently sustained, it was ultimately by aid of that one incongruous and irresistible association that Mary Cartaret had cast her spell.

He had never really come under it until that moment.

July passed. It was the end of August. To the west Karva and Morfe High Moor were purple. To the east the bare hillsides with their limestone ramparts smouldered in mist and sun, or shimmered, burning like any hillside of the south. The light even soaked into the gray walls of Garth in its pastures. The little plum-trees in the Vicarage orchard might have been olive trees twinkling in the sun.

Mary was in the Vicar's bedroom, looking now at the door, and now at her own image in the wardrobe glass. It was seven o'clock in the evening and she had chosen a perilous moment for the glass. She wore a childlike frock of rough green silk; it had no collar but was cut square at the neck showing her white throat. The square was bordered with an embroidered design of peacock's eyes. The parted waves of her red hair were burnished with hard brushing; its coils lay close, and smooth as a thick round cap. It needed neither comb nor any ornament.

Mary had dressed, for Rowcliffe was coming to dinner. Such a thing had never been heard of at the Vicarage; but it had come to pass. And as Mary thought of how she had accomplished it, she wondered what Alice could possibly have meant when she said to her "There are moments when I hate you," as she hooked her up the back.

For it never could have happened if she had not persuaded the Vicar (and herself as well) that she was asking Rowcliffe on Alice's account.

The Vicar had come gradually to see that if Alice must be married she had better marry Rowcliffe and have done with it. He had got used to Rowcliffe and he rather liked him; so he had only held out against the idea for a fortnight or so. He had even found a certain austere satisfaction in the thought that he, the doctor, who had tried to terrify him about Ally's insanity, having thrown that bomb into the peaceful Vicarage, should be blown up, as it were, with his own explosion.

The Vicar never doubted that it was Ally that Rowcliffe wanted. For the idea of his wanting Gwenda was so unpleasant to him that he had dismissed it as preposterous; as for Mary, he had made up his mind that Mary would never dream of marrying and leaving him, and that, if she did, he would put his foot down.

There had been changes in the Vicarage in the last two

months.   The shabby gray and amber drawing-room was
not all shabbiness and not all gray and amber now.   There
were new cretonne covers on the chairs and sofa, and pure
white muslin curtains at the windows, and the lamp had
a new frilled petticoat.   Every afternoon Mrs. Gale was
arrayed in a tight black gown and irreproachable cap and
apron.

All day long Mary and Mrs. Gale had worked like gal-
ley slaves over the preparations for dinner, and between
them they had achieved perfection.   What was more they
had produced an effect of achieving it every day, clear
soup, mayonnaise salad and cheese straws and all.

And the black coffee made by Mary and served in the
orchard afterward was perfection too.

And the impression made on Rowcliffe by the Vicarage
was that of a house and a household rehabilitated after a
long period of devastation, by the untiring, selfless labor
of a woman who was good and sweet.

After they had drunk Mary's coffee the Vicar strolled
away to his study so as to leave Rowcliffe alone with Mary,
and Alice strolled away heaven knew where so as to leave
Mary alone with Rowcliffe.   And the Vicar said to himself, "Mary is really doing it very well.   Ally ought to
be grateful to her."

But Ally wasn't a bit grateful.   She said to herself,
"I've half a mind to tell him; only Gwenda would hate
me."   And she called over her shoulder as she strolled
away, "You'd better not stay out too long, you two.   It's
going to rain."

Morfe High Moor hangs over Garth and a hot and
swollen cloud was hanging over Morfe High Moor.   Above
the gray ramparts the very east was sultry.   In the orchard under the low plum-trees it was as airless as in a
tent.

Rowcliffe didn't want to stay out too long in the orchard. He knew that the window of the Vicar's study raked it. So he asked Mary if she would come with him for a stroll. (His only criticism of Mary was that she didn't walk enough.)

Mary thought, "My nice frock will be ruined if the rain comes." But she went.

"Shall it be the moor or the fields?" he said.

Mary thought again, and said, "The fields."

He was glad she hadn't said "The moor."

They strolled past the village and turned into the pasture that lay between the high road and the beck. The narrow paths led up a slope from field to field through the gaps in the stone walls. The fields turned with the turning of the dale and with that turning of the road that Rowcliffe knew, under Karva. Instinctively, with a hand on her arm he steered her, away from the high road and its turning, toward the beck, so that they had their backs to the thunder storm as it came up over Karva and the High Moor.

It was when they were down in the bottom that it burst.

There was shelter on the further side of the last field. They ran to it, climbed, and crouched together under the stone wall.

Rowcliffe took off the light overcoat he wore and tried to put it on her. But Mary wouldn't let him. She looked at his clothes, at the round dinner jacket with its silk collar and at the beautiful evening trousers with their braided seams. He insisted. She refused. He insisted still, and compromised by laying the overcoat round both of them.

And they crouched together under the wall, sitting closer so that the coat might cover them.

It thundered and lightened. The rain pelted them

from the high batteries of Karva. And Rowcliffe drew Mary closer. She laughed like a happy child.

Rowcliffe sighed.

It was after he had sighed that he kissed her under the cover of the coat.

They sat there for half an hour; three-quarters; till the storm ceased with the rising of the moon.

"I'm afraid the pretty frock's spoiled," he said.

"That doesn't matter. Your poor suit's ruined."

He laughed.

"Whatever's been ruined," he said, "it was worth it."

Hand in hand they went back together through the drenched fields.

At the first gap he stopped.

"It's settled?" he said. "You won't go back on it? You *do* care for me? And you *will* marry me?"

"Yes."

"Soon?"

"Yes; soon."

At the last gap he stopped again.

"Mary," he said, "I suppose you knew about Gwenda?"

"I knew there was something. What was it?"

He had said to himself, "I shall have to tell her. I shall have to say I cared for her."

What he did say was, "There was nothing in it. It's all over. It was all over long ago."

"I knew," she said, "it was all over."

And the solemn white moon came up, the moon that Gwenda loved; it came up over Greffington Edge and looked at them.

XLV

It was Sunday afternoon, the last Sunday of August, the first since that evening (it was a Thursday) when Steven Rowcliffe had dined at the Vicarage. Mary had announced her engagement the next day.

The news had an extraordinary effect on Alice and the Vicar.

Mary had come to her father in his study on Friday evening after Prayers. She informed him of the bare fact in the curtest manner, without preface or apology or explanation. A terrible scene had followed; at least the Vicar's part in it had been terrible. Nothing he had ever said to Gwenda could compare with what he then said to Mary. Alice's behavior he had been prepared for. He had expected anything from Gwenda; but from Mary he had not expected this. It was her treachery he resented, the treachery of a creature he had depended on and trusted. He absolutely forbade the engagement. He said it was unheard of. He spoke of her "conduct" as if it had been disgraceful or improper. He declared that "that fellow" Rowcliffe should never come inside his house again. He bullied and threatened and bullied again. And through it all Mary sat calm and quiet and submissive. The expression of the qualities he had relied on, her sweetness and goodness, never left her face. She replied to his violence, "Yes, Papa. Very well, Papa, I see." But, as Gwenda had warned him, bully as he would, Mary beat him in the end.

She looked meekly down at the hearth-rug and said, "I know how you feel about it, Papa dear. I understand all you've got to say and I'm sorry. But it isn't any good. You know it isn't just as well as I do."

It might have been Gwenda who spoke to him, only that Gwenda could never have looked meek.

The Vicar had not recovered from the shock. He was convinced that he never would recover from it. But on that Sunday he had found a temporary oblivion, dozing in his study between two services.

There had been no scene like that with Alice. But what had passed between the sisters had been even worse.

Mary had gone straight from the study to Ally's room. Ally was undressing.

Ally received the news in a cruel silence. She looked coldly, sternly almost, and steadily at Mary.

"You needn't have told me that," she said at last. "I could see what you were doing the other night."

"What *I* was doing?"

"Yes, you. I don't imagine Steven Rowcliffe did it."

"Really Ally—what do you suppose I did?"

"I don't know what it was. But I know you did something and I know that—whatever it was—*I* wouldn't have done it."

And Mary answered quietly. "If I were you, Ally, I wouldn't show my feelings quite so plainly."

And Ally looked at her again.

"It's not *my* feelings——" she said.

Mary reddened. "I don't know what you mean."

"You'll know, some day," Ally said and turned her back on her.

Mary went out, closing the door softly, as if she spared her sick sister's unreasonably irritated nerves. She felt

rather miserable as she undressed alone in her bedroom.
She was wounded in her sweetness and her goodness, and
she was also a little afraid of what Ally might take it into
her head to say or do.   She didn't try to think what Ally
had meant.   Her sweetness and goodness, with their instinct of self-preservation, told her that it might be better
not.

The August night was warm and tender, and, when
Mary had got into bed and lay stretched out in content-
ment under the white sheet, she began to think of Rowcliffe to the exclusion of all other interests; and presently,
between a dream and a dream, she fell asleep.

But Ally could not sleep.
She lay till dawn thinking and thinking, and turning
from side to side between her thoughts.   They were not
concerned with Gwenda or with Rowcliffe.   After her
little spurt of indignation she had ceased to think about
Gwenda or Rowcliffe either.   Mary's news had made her
think about herself, and her thoughts were miserable.
Ally was so far like her father the Vicar, that the idea of
Mary's marrying was intolerable to her and for precisely
the same reason, because she saw no prospect of marrying
herself.   Her father had begun by forbidding Mary's engagement but he would end by sanctioning it.   He would
never sanction *her* marriage to Jim Greatorex.

Even if she defied her father and married Jim Greatorex in spite of him there would be almost as much shame
in it as if, like Essy, she had never married him at all.

And she couldn't live without him.

Ally had suffered profoundly from the shock that had
struck her down under the arcades on the road to Upthorne.   It had left her more than ever helpless, more
than ever subject to infatuation, more than ever morally

inert. Ally's social self had grown rigid in the traditions of her class, and she was still aware of the unsuitability of her intimacy with Jim Greatorex; but disaster had numbed her once poignant sense of it. She had yielded to his fascination partly through weakness, partly in defiance, partly in the sheer, healthy self-assertion of her suffering will and her frustrated senses. But she had not will enough to defy her father. She credited him with an infinite capacity to crush and wound. And for a day and a half the sight of Mary's happiness—a spectacle which Mary did not spare her—had made Ally restless. Under the incessant sting of it her longing for Greatorex became insupportable.

On Sunday the Vicar was still too deeply afflicted by the same circumstance to notice Ally's movements, and Ally took advantage of his apathy to excuse herself from Sunday school that afternoon. And about three o'clock she was at Upthorne Farm. She and Greatorex had found a moment after morning service to arrange the hour.

And now they were standing together in the doorway of the Farmhouse.   .

In the house behind them, in the mistal and the orchard, in the long marshes of the uplands and on the brooding hills there was stillness and solitude.

Maggie had gone up to her aunt at Bar Hill. The farm servants were scattered in their villages.

Alice had just told Greatorex of Mary's engagement and the Vicar's opposition.

"Eh, I was lookin' for it," he said. "But I maade sure it was your oother sister."

"So did I, Jim. So it was. So it would have been, only——"

She stopped herself. She wasn't going to give Mary away to Jim.

He looked at her.

"Wall, it's nowt t' yo, is it?"

"No. It's nothing to me—now. How did you know I cared for him?"

"I knew because I looved yo. Because I was always thinkin' of yo. Because I watched yo with him."

"Oh Jim—would other people know?"

"Naw. Nat they. They didn't look at yo the saame as I did."

He became thoughtful.

"Wall—this here sattles it," he said presently. "Yo caann't be laft all aloan in t' Vicarage. Yo'll 'ave t' marry mae."

"No," she said. "It won't be like that. It won't, really. If my father won't let my sister marry Dr. Row-cliffe, you don't suppose he'll let me marry you? It makes it more impossible than ever. That's what I came to tell you."

"It's naw use yo're tallin' mae. I won't hear it."

He bent to her.

"Ally—d'yo knaw we're aloan here?"

"Yes, Jim."

"We're saafe till Naddy cooms back for t' milkin'. We've three hours."

She shook her head. "Only an hour and a half, Jim. I must be back for tea."

"Yo'll 'ave tae here. Yo've had it before. I'll maake it for yo."

"I daren't, Jim. They'll expect me. They'll wonder."

"Ay, 'tis thot waay always. Yo're no sooner coom than yo've got to be back for this, thot and toother. I'm fair sick of it."

"So am I."

She sighed.

"Wall then—yo must end it."

"How can I end it?"

"Yo knaw how."

"Oh Jim—darling—haven't I told you?"

"Yo've toald mae noothin' that makes a hap'orth o' difference to mae.   Yo've coom to mae.   Thot's all I keer for."

He put his hand on her shoulder and turned her toward the house-place.

"Let me shaw yo t' house—now you've coom."

His voice pleaded and persuaded.   In spite of its north-country accent Ally loved his voice.   It sounded musical and mournful, like the voices of the mountain sheep coming from far across the moor and purified by distance.

He took her through the kitchen and the little parlor at the end of the house.

As he looked round it, trying to see it with her eyes, doubt came to him.   But Ally, standing there, looked toward the kitchen.

"Will Maggie be there?" she said.

"Ay, Maaggie'll be there, ready when yo want her."

"But," she said, "I don't want her."

He followed her look.

"I'll 'ave it all claned oop and paapered and paainted. Look yo—I could have a hole knocked through t' back wall o' t' kitchen and a winder put there—and roon oop a wooden partition and make a passage for yo t' goa to yore awn plaace, soa's Maaggie'll not bae in yore road."

"You needn't.   I like it best as it is."

"Do yo?   D'yo mind thot Soonda yo caame laasst year?   Yo've aassked mae whan it was I started thinkin' of yo.   It was than.   Thot daay whan yo sot there in thot

chair by t' fire, taalkin' t' mae and drinkin' yore tae so
pretty."

She drew closer to him.

"Did you really love me then?"

"Ay—I looved yo than."

She pondered it.

"Jim—what would you have done if I hadn't loved
you?"

He choked back something in his throat before he answered her. "What sud I have doon? I sud have goan
on looving yo joost the saame.

"We'll goa oopstairs now."

He took her back and out through the kitchen and up
the stone stairs that turned sharply in their narrow place
in the wall. He opened the door at the head of the
landing.

"This would bae our room. 'Tis t' best."

He took her into the room where John Greatorex had
died. It was the marriage chamber, the birth-chamber,
and the death-chamber of all the Greatorexes. The low
ceiling still bulged above the big double bed John Greatorex had died in.

The room was tidy and spotlessly clean. The walls had
been whitewashed. Fresh dimity curtains hung at the
window. The bed was made, a clean white counterpane
was spread on it.

The death room had been made ready for the living.
The death-bed waited for the bride.

Ally stood there, under the eyes of her lover, looking at
those things. She shivered slightly.

She said to herself, "It's the room his father died in."

And there came on her a horror of the room and of all
that had happened in it, a horror of death and of the
dead.

She turned away to the window and looked out. The long marshland stretched below, white under the August sun. Beyond it the green hills with their steep gray cliffs rose and receded, like a coast line, head after head.

To Ally the scene was desolate beyond all bearing and the house was terrible.

Her eyelids pricked. Her mouth trembled. She kept her back turned to Greatorex while she stifled a sob with her handkerchief pressed tight to her lips.

He saw and came to her and put his arm round her.

"What is it, Ally? What is it, loove?"

She looked up at him.

"I don't know, Jim. But—I think—I'm afraid."

"What are you afraid of?"

She thought a moment. "I'm afraid of father."

"Yo med bae ef yo staayed with him. Thot's why I want yo t' coom to mae."

He looked at her.

"'Tisn' thot yo're afraid of. 'Tis soomthin' alse thot yo wawn't tall mae."

"Well—I think—I'm a little bit afraid of this house. It's—it's so horribly lonely."

He couldn't deny it.

"A'y; it's rackoned t' bae loanly. But I sall navver leaave yo. I'm goain' t' buy a new trap for yo, soa's yo can coom with mae and Daaisy. Would yo like thot, Ally?"

"Yes, Jim, I'd love it. But——"

"It'll not bae soa baad. Whan I'm out in t' mistal and in t' fields and thot, yo'll have Maaggie with yo."

She whispered. "Jim—I can't bear Maggie. I'm afraid of her."

"Afraid o' pore Maaggie?"

He took it in. He wondered. He thought he understood.

"Maaggie sall goa. I'll 'ave anoother. An' yo sall 'ave a yooung laass t' waait on yo. Ef it's Maaggie, shea sall nat stand in yore road."

"It isn't Maggie—altogether."

"Than—for Gawd's saake, loove, what is it?"

She sobbed. "It's everything. It's something in this house—in this room."

He looked at her gravely now.

"Naw," he said slowly, " 'tis noon o' thawse things. It's mae. It's mae yo're afraid of. Yo think I med bae too roough with yo."

But at that she cried out with a little tender cry and pressed close to him.

"No—no—no—it isn't you. It isn't. It couldn't be."

He crushed her in his arms. His mouth clung to her face and passed over it and covered it with kisses.

"Am I too roough? Tall mae—tall mae."

"No," she whispered.

He pushed back her hat from her forehead, kissing her hair. She took off her hat and flung it on the floor.

His voice came fast and thick.

"Kiss mae back ef yo loove mae."

She kissed him. She stiffened and leaned back in the crook of his arm that held her.

His senses swam. He grasped her as if he would have lifted her bodily from the floor. She was light in his arms as a child. He had turned her from the window.

He looked fiercely round the room that shut them in. His eyes lowered; they fixed themselves on the bed with its white counterpane. They saw under the white counterpane the dead body of his father stretched there, and the stain on the grim beard tilted to the ceiling.

He loosed her and pushed her from him.

"We moost coom out o' this," he muttered.

He pushed her from the room, gently, with a hand on her shoulder, and made her go before him down the stairs.

He went back into the room to pick up her hat.

He found her waiting for him, looking back, at the turn of the stair where John Greatorex's coffin had stuck in the corner of the wall.

"Jim—I'm so frightened," she said.

"Ay. Yo'll bae all right downstairs."

They stood in the kitchen, each looking at the other, each panting, she in her terror and he in his agony.

"Take me away," she said. "Out of the house. That room frightened me. There's something there."

"Ay;" he assented. "There med bae soomthing. Sall we goa oop t' fealds?"

The Three Fields looked over the back of Upthorne Farm. Naked and gray, the great stone barn looked over the Three Fields. A narrow track led to it, through the gaps, slantwise, from the gate of the mistal.

Above the fields the barren, ruined hillside ended and the moor began. It rolled away southward and westward, in dusk and purple and silver green, utterly untamed, uncaught by the network of the stone walls.

The barn stood high and alone on the slope of the last field, a long, broad-built nave without its tower. A single thorn-tree crouched beside it.

Alice Cartaret and Greatorex went slowly up the Three Fields. There was neither thought nor purpose in their going.

The quivering air was like a sheet of glass let down between plain and hill.

Slowly, with mournful cries, a flock of mountain sheep came down over the shoulder of the moor. Behind them a solitary figure topped the rise as Alice and Greatorex came up the field-track.

Alice stopped in the track and turned.

"Somebody's coming over the moor. He'll see us."

Greatorex stood scanning the hill.

" 'Tis Nad, wi' t' dawg, drivin' t' sheep."

"Oh, Jim, he'll see us."

"Nat he!"

But he drew her behind the shelter of the barn.

"He'll come down the fields. He'll be sure to see us."

"Ef he doos, caann't I walk in my awn fealds wi' my awn sweetheart?"

"I don't want to be seen," she moaned.

"Wall——" he pushed open the door of the barn. "Wae'll creep in here than, tall he's paassed."

A gray light slid through the half-shut door and through the long, narrow slits in the walls. From the open floor of the loft there came the sweet, heavy scent of hay.

"He'll see the door open. He'll come in. He'll find us here."

"He wawn't."

But Jim shut the door.

"We're saafe enoof. But 'tis naw plaace for yo. Yo'll mook yore lil feet. Staay there—where yo are—tell I tall yo."

He groped his way in the half darkness up the hay loft stair. She heard his foot going heavily on the floor over her head.

He drew back the bolt and pushed open the door in the high wall. The sunlight flooded the loft; it streamed down the stair. The dust danced in it.

Jim stood on the stair. He smiled down at Alice where she waited below.

"Coom oop into t' haay loft, Ally."

He stooped. He held out his hand and she climbed to him up the stair.

They sat there on the floor of the loft, silent, in the attitude of children who crouch hiding in their play. He had strewn for her a carpet of the soft, sweet hay and piled it into cushions.

"Oh, Jim," she said at last. "I'm so frightened. I'm so horribly frightened."

She stretched out her arm and slid her hand into his.

Jim's hand pressed hers and let it go. He leaned forward, his elbows propped on his knees, his hands clutching his forehead. And in his thick, mournful voice he spoke.

"Yo wouldn't bae freetened ef yo married mae. There'd bae an and of these scares, an' wae sudn't 'ave t' roon these awful risks."

"I can't marry you, darling. I can't."

"Yo caann't, because yo're freetened o' mae. I coom back to thot. Yo think I'm joost a roough man thot caann't understand yo. But I do. I couldn't bae roough with yo, Ally, anny more than Nad, oop yon, could bae roough wi' t' lil laambs."

He was lying flat on his back now, with his arms stretched out above his head. He stared up at the rafters as he went on.

"Yo wouldn't bae freetened o' mae ef yo looved mae as I loove yo."

That brought her to his side with her soft cry.

For a moment he lay rigid and still.

Then he turned and put his arm round her. The light streamed on them where they lay. Through the open

doorway of the loft they heard the cry of the sheep coming down into the pasture.

Greatorex got up and slid the door softly to.

XLVI

MORFE FAIR was over and the farmers were going home.

A broken, straggling traffic was on the roads from dale to dale. There were men who went gaily in spring carts and in wagons. There were men on horseback and on foot who drove their sheep and their cattle before them.

A train of three were going slowly up Garthdale, with much lingering to gather together and rally the weary and bewildered flocks.

Into this train there burst, rocking at full gallop, a trap drawn by Greatorex's terrified and indignant mare. Daisy was not driven by Greatorex, for the reins were slack in his dropped hands, she was urged, whipped up, and maddened to her relentless speed. Her open nostrils drank the wind of her going.

Greatorex's face flamed and his eyes were brilliant. They declared a furious ecstasy. Ever and again he rose and struggled to stand upright and recover his grip of the reins. Ever and again he was pitched backward on to the seat where he swayed, perilously, with the swaying of the trap.

Behind him, in the bottom of the trap, two young calves, netted in, pushed up their melancholy eyes and innocent noses through the mesh. Hurled against each other, flung rhythmically from side to side, they shared the blind trouble of the man and the torment of the mare.

For the first two miles out of Morfe the trap charged, scattering men and beasts before it and taking the curves of the road at a tangent. With the third mile the pace slackened. The mare had slaked her thirst for the wind of her going and Greatorex's fury was appeased. At the risk of pitching forward over the step he succeeded in gathering up the reins as they neared the dangerous descent to Garthdale.

He had now dropped from the violence of his ecstasy into a dream-like state in which he was borne swaying on a vague, interminable road that overhung, giddily, the bottomless pit and was flanked by hills that loomed and reeled, that oppressed him with their horrible immensity.

He passed the bridge, the church, the Vicarage, the schoolhouse with its beckoning tree, and by the mercy of heaven he was unaware of them.

At the turn of the road, on Upthorne hill, the mare, utterly sobered by the gradient, bowed her head and went with slow, wise feet, taking care of the trap and of her master.

As for Greatorex, he had ceased to struggle. And at the door of his house his servant Maggie received him in her arms.

He stayed in bed the whole of the next day, bearing his sickness, while Maggie waited on him. And in the evening when he lay under her hand, weak, but clear-headed, she delivered herself of what was in her mind.

"Wall—yo may thank Gawd yo're laayin' saafe in yore bed, Jim Greatorex. It'd sarve yo right ef Daaisy 'd lat yo coom hoam oopside down wi yore 'ead draggin' in t' road. Soom daay yo'll bae laayin' there with yore nack brawken.

"Ay, yo may well scootle oonder t' sheets, though there's nawbody but mae t' look at yo. Yo'd navver tooch anoother drap o' thot felthy stoof, Jimmy, ef yo could sea yoreself what a sight yo bae. Naw woonder Assy Gaale wouldn't 'ave yo, for all yo've laft her wi' t' lil baaby."

"Who toald yo she wouldn't 'ave mae?"

"Naybody toald mae. But I knaw. I knaw. I wouldn't 'ave yo myself ef yo aassked mae. I want naw droonkards to marry mae."

Greatorex became pensive.

"Yo'd bae freetened o' mae, Maaggie?" he asked.

And Maggie, seeing her advantage, drove it home.

"There's more than mae and Assy thot's freetened t' marry yo," she said.

He darkened. "Yo 'oald yore tongue. Yo dawn't knaw what yo're saayin', my laass."

"Dawn't I? There's more than mae thot knaws, Mr. Greatorex. Assy isn't t' awnly woon yo've maade talk o' t' plaace."

"What do yo mane? Speaak oop. What d'yo mane—— Yo knaw?"

"Yo'd best aassk Naddy. He med tall ye 'oo was with yo laasst Soonda oop t' feald in t' girt byre."

"Naddy couldn't sae 'oo 't was. Med a been Assy. Med a been yo."

"'T wasn' mae, Mr. Greatorex, an' 't was n' Assy. Look yo 'ere. I tall yo Assy's freetened o' yo."

"'Oo says she's freetened?"

"I saays it. She's thot freetened thot she'd wash yore sweet'eart's dirty cleathes sooner 'n marry yo."

"She doesn't wash them?"

"Shea does. T' kape yore baaby, Jim Greatorex."

With that she left him.

For the next three months Greatorex was more than ever uneasy in his soul. The Sunday after Maggie's outburst he had sat all morning and afternoon in his parlor

with his father's Bible. He had not even tried to see
Alice Cartaret.

For three months, off and on, in the intervals of seeing
Alice, he longed, with an intense and painful longing, for
his God. He longed for him just because he felt that he
was utterly separated from him by his sin. He wanted
the thing he couldn't have and wasn't fit to have. He
wanted it, just as he wanted Alice Cartaret.

And by his sin he did not mean his getting drunk.
Greatorex did not think of God as likely to take his getting drunk very seriously, any more than he had seemed
to take Maggie and Essy seriously. For Greatorex measured God's reprobation by his own repentance.

His real offense against God was his offense against
Alice Cartaret. He had got drunk in order to forget it.

But that resource would henceforth be denied him. He
was not going to get drunk any more, because he knew
that if he did Alice Cartaret wouldn't marry him.

Meanwhile he nourished his soul on its own longing, on
the Psalms of David and on the Book of Job.

Greatorex would have made a happy saint. But he
was a most lugubrious sinner.

XLVII

THE train from Durlingham rolled slowly into Reyburn station.

Gwenda Cartaret leaned from the window of a third class carriage and looked up and down the platform. She got out, handing her suit-case to a friendly porter. Nobody had come to meet her. They were much too busy up at the Vicarage.

From the next compartment there alighted a group of six persons, a lady in widow's weeds, an elderly lady and gentleman who addressed her affectionately as "Fanny, dear," and (obviously belonging to the pair) a very young man and a still younger woman.

There was also a much older man, closely attached to them, but not quite so obviously related.

These six people also looked up and down the platform, expecting to be met. They were interested in Gwenda Cartaret. They gazed at her as they had already glanced, surreptitiously and kindly, on the platform at Durlingham. Now they seemed to be saying to themselves that they were sure it must be she.

Gwenda walked quickly away from them and disappeared through the booking-office into the station yard.

And then Rowcliffe, who had apparently been hiding in the general waiting-room, came out on to the platform.

The six fell upon him with cries of joy and affection.

They were his mother, his paternal uncle and aunt, his two youngest cousins, and Dr. Harker, his best friend

and colleague who had taken his place in January when
he had been ill.

They had all come down from Leeds for Rowcliffe's
wedding.

Rowcliffe's trap and Peacock's from Garthdale stood
side by side in the station-yard.

Gwenda in Peacock's trap had left the town before she
heard behind her the clanking hoofs of Rowcliffe's little
brown horse.

She thought, "He will pass in another minute. I shall
see him."

But she did not see him. All the way up Rathdale to
Morfe the sound of the wheels and of the clanking hoofs
pursued her, and Rowcliffe still hung back. He did not
want to pass her.

"Well," said Peacock, "thot beats mae. I sud navver
a thought thot t' owd maare could a got away from t'
doctor's horse. Nat ef 'e'd a mind t' paass 'er."

"No," said Gwenda. She was thinking, "It's Mary.
It's Mary. How could she, when she *knew*, when she was
on her honor not to think of him?"

And she remembered a conversation she had had with
her stepmother two months ago, when the news came.
(Robina had seized the situation at a glance and she had
probed it to its core.)

"You wanted him to marry Ally, did you? It wasn't
much good you're going away if you left him with Mary."

"But," she had said, "Mary knew."

And Robina had answered, marvelously. "You should
never have let her. It was her knowing that did it. You
were three women to one man, and Mary was the one
without a scruple. Do you suppose she'd think of Ally
or of you, either?"

And she had tried to be loyal to Mary and to Rowcliffe. She had said, "If we *were* three, we all had our innings, and he made his choice."

And Robina, "It was Mary did the choosing."

She had added that Gwenda was a little fool, and that she ought to have known that though Mary was as meek as Moses she was that sort.

She went on, thinking, to the steady clanking of the hoofs.

"I suppose," she said to herself, "she couldn't help it."

The lights of Morfe shone through the November darkness. The little slow mare crawled up the winding hill to the top of the Green; Rowcliffe's horse was slower. But no sooner had Peacock's trap passed the doctor's house on its way out of the village square, than the clanking hoofs went fast.

Rowcliffe was free to go his own pace now.

"Which of you two is going to hook me up?" said Mary.

She was in the Vicar's room, putting on her wedding-gown before the wardrobe glass. Her two sisters were dressing her.

"I will," said Gwenda.

"You'd better let me," said Alice. "I know where the eyes are."

Gwenda lifted up the wedding-veil and held it ready. And while Alice pulled and fumbled Mary gazed at her own reflection and at Alice's.

"You should have done as Mummy said and had your frock made in London, like Gwenda. They'd have given you a decent cut. You look as if you couldn't breathe."

"My frock's all right," said Alice.

Her fingers trembled as she strained at the hooks and eyes.

And in the end it was Gwenda who hooked Mary up while Alice held the veil. She held it in front of her. The long streaming net shivered with the trembling of her hands.

The wedding was at two o'clock. The church was crowded, so were the churchyard and the road beside the Vicarage and the bridge over the beck. Morfe and Greffington had emptied themselves into Garthdale. (Greffington had lent its organist.)

It was only when it was all over that somebody noticed that Jim Greatorex was not there with the village choir. "Celebrating a bit too early," somebody said.

And it was only when it was all over that Rowcliffe found Gwenda.

He found her in the long, flat pause, the half-hour of profoundest realisation that comes when the bride disappears to put off her wedding-gown for the gown she will go away in. She had come out to the wedding-party gathered at the door, to tell them that the bride would soon be ready. Rowcliffe and Harker were standing apart, at the end of the path, by the door that led from the garden to the orchard.

He came toward her. Harker drew back into the orchard. They followed him and found themselves alone.

For ten minutes they paced the narrow flagged path under the orchard wall. And they talked, quickly, like two who have but a short time.

"Well—so you've come back at last?"

"At last? I haven't been gone six months."

"You see, time feels longer to us down here."

"That's odd. It goes faster."

"Anyhow, you're not tired of London?"

She stared at him for a second and then looked away.

"Oh no, I'm not tired of it yet."

They turned.

"Shall you stop long here?"

"I'm going back to-morrow."

"To-morrow? You're so glad to get back then?"

"So glad to get back. I only came down for Mary's wedding."

He smiled.

"You won't come for anything but a wedding?"

"A funeral might fetch me."

"Well, Gwenda, I can't say you look as if London agreed with you particularly."

"I can't say you look as if Garthdale agreed very well with you."

"I'm only tired—tired to death."

"I'm sorry."

"I want a holiday. And I'm going to get one—for a month. *You* look as if you'd been burning the candle at both ends, if you'll forgive my saying so."

"Oh—for all the candles I burn! It isn't such awfully hard work, you know."

"What isn't?"

"What I'm doing."

He stopped straight in the narrow path and looked at her.

"I say, what *are* you doing?"

She told him.

His face expressed surprise and resentment and a curious wonder and bewilderment.

"But I thought—I thought—— They told me you were having no end of a time."

"Tunbridge Wells isn't very amusing. No more is Lady Frances."

Again he stopped dead and stared at her.

"But they told me—I mean I thought you were in London with Mrs. Cartaret, all the time."

She laughed.

"Did Papa tell you that?"

"No. I don't know who told me. I—I got the impression." He almost stammered. "I must have misunderstood."

She meditated.

"It sounds awfully like Papa. He simply can't believe, poor thing, that I'd stick to anything so respectable."

"Hah!" He laughed out his contempt for the Vicar. He had forgotten that he too had wondered.

"Chuck it, Gwenda," he said, "chuck it."

"I can't," she said. "Not yet. It's too lucrative."

"But if it makes you seedy?"

"It doesn't. It won't. It isn't hard work. Only——"
She broke off. "It's time for you to go."

"Steve! Steve!"

Rowcliffe's youngest cousin was calling from the study window.

"Come along. Mary's ready."

"All right," he shouted. "I'm coming."

But he stood still there at the end of the orchard under the gray wall.

"Good-bye, Steven."

Gwenda put out her hand.

He held her with his troubled eyes. He did not see her hand. He saw her eyes only that troubled his.

"I say, is it very beastly?"

"No. Not a bit. You must go, Steven, you must go."

"If I'd only known," he persisted.

They were going down the path now toward the house.

"I wouldn't have let you——"

"You couldn't have stopped me."

(It was what she had always said to all of them.)

She smiled. "You didn't stop me going, you know."

"If you'd only told me——"

She smiled again, a smile as of infinite wisdom. "Dear Steven, there was nothing to tell."

They had come to the door in the wall. It led into the garden. He opened to let her pass through.

The wedding-party was gathered together on the flagged path before the house. It greeted them with laughter and cries, cheerfully ironic.

The bride in her traveling dress stood on the threshold. Outside the carriage waited at the open gate.

Rowcliffe took Mary's hand in his and they ran down the path.

"He can sprint fast enough now," said Rowcliffe's uncle.

But his youngest cousin and Harker, his best friend, had gone faster. They were waiting together on the bridge, and the girl had a slipper in her hand.

"Were you ever," she said, "at such an awful wedding?"

Harker saw nothing wrong about the wedding but he admitted that his experience was small.

The youngest cousin was not appeased by his confession. She went on.

"Why on earth didn't Steven *try* to marry Gwenda?"

"Not much good trying," said the doctor, "if she wouldn't have him."

"You believe that silly story? I don't. Did you see her face?"

Harker admitted that he had seen her face.

And then, as the carriage passed, Rowcliffe's youngest

cousin did an odd thing. She tossed the slipper over the bridge into the beck.

Harker had not time to comment on her action. They were coming for him from the house.

Rowcliffe's youngest sister-in-law had fainted away on the top landing.

Everybody remembered then that it was she who had been in love with him.

XLVIII

ALICE had sent for Gwenda.

Three months had gone by since her sister's wedding, and all her fears were gathered together in the fear of her father and of what was about to happen to her.

And before Gwenda could come to her, Rowcliffe and Mary had come to the Vicar in his study. They had been a long time with him, and then Rowcliffe had gone out. They had sent him to Upthorne. And the two had gone into the dining-room and they had her before them there.

It was early in a dull evening in February. The lamps were lit and in their yellow light Ally's face showed a pale and quivering exaltation. It was the face of a hunted and terrified thing that has gathered courage in desperation to turn and stand. She defended herself with sullen defiance and denial.

It had come to that. For Ned, the shepherd at Upthorne, had told what he had seen. He had told it to Maggie, who told it to Mrs. Gale. He had told it to the head-gamekeeper at Garthdale Manor, who had a tale of his own that he too had told. And Dr. Harker had a tale. Harker had taken his friend's practice when Rowcliffe was away on his honeymoon. He had seen Alice and Greatorex on the moors at night as he had driven home from Upthorne. And he had told Rowcliffe what he had seen. And Rowcliffe had told Mary and the Vicar.

And at the cottage down by the beck Essy Gale and her mother had spoken together, but what they had spoken and what they had heard they had kept secret.

"I haven't been with him," said Alice for the third time. "I don't know what you're talking about."

"Ally—there's no use your saying that when you've been seen with him."

It was Mary who spoke.

"I ha—haven't."

"Don't lie," said the Vicar.

"I'm not. They're l-l-lying," said Ally, shaken into stammering now.

"Who do you suppose would lie about it?" Mary said.

"Essy would."

"Well—I may tell you, Ally, that you're wrong. Essy's kept your secret. So has Mrs. Gale. You ought to go down on your knees and thank the poor girl—after what you did to her."

"It *was* Essy. I know. She's mad to marry him herself, so she goes lying about *me*."

"Nobody's lying about her," said the Vicar, "but herself. And she's condemning herself with every word she says. You'd better have left Essy out of it, my girl."

"I tell you that she's lying if she says she's seen me with him. She's never seen me."

"It wasn't Essy who saw you," Mary said.

"Somebody else is lying then. Who was it?"

"If you *must* know who saw you," the Vicar said, "it was Dr. Harker. You were seen a month ago hanging about Upthorne alone with that fellow."

"Only once," Ally murmured.

"You own to 'once'? You—you——" he stifled with his fury. "Once is enough with a low blackguard like Greatorex. And you were seen more than once. You've been seen with him after dark." He boomed. "There isn't a poor drunken slut in the village who's disgraced herself like you."

Mary intervened. "Sh—sh—Papa. They'll hear you in the kitchen."

"They'll hear *her*. (Ally was moaning.) "Stop that whimpering and whining."

"She can't help it."

"She can help it if she likes. Come, Ally, we're all here—— Poor Mary's come up and Steven. There are things we've got to know and I insist on knowing them. You've brought the most awful trouble and shame on me and your sister and brother-in-law, and the least you can do is to answer truthfully. I can't stand any more of this distressing altercation. I'm not going to extort any painful confession. You've only got to answer a simple Yes or No. Were you anywhere with Jim Greatorex before Dr. Harker saw you in December? Think before you speak. Yes or No.

She thought.

"N-no."

"Remember, Ally," said Mary, "he saw you in November."

"He didn't. Where?"

The Vicar answered her. "At your sister's wedding."

She recovered. "Of course he did. Jim Greatorex wasn't there, anyhow."

"He was *not*."

The stress had no significance for Ally. Her brain was utterly bewildered.

"Well. You say you were never anywhere with Greatorex before December. You were not with him in— when was it, Mary?"

"August," said Mary. "The end of August."

Ally simply stared at him in her white bewilderment.
Dates had no meaning as yet for her cowed brain.

He helped her.

"In the Three Fields. On a Sunday afternoon. Did
you or did you not go into the barn?"

At that she cried out with a voice of anguish. "No—
No—No!"

But Mary had her knife ready and she drove it home.
"Ally—Ned Langstaff *saw* you."

When Rowcliffe came back from Upthorne he found
Alice cowering in a corner of the couch and crying out to
her tormentors.

"You brutes—you brutes—if Gwenda was here she
wouldn't let you bully me!"

Mary turned to her husband.

"Steven—will you speak to her? She won't tell us
anything. We've been at it more than half an hour."

Rowcliffe stared at her and the Vicar with strong
displeasure.

"I should think you had by the look of her. Why can't
you leave the poor child alone?"

At the sound of his voice, the first voice of compassion
that had yet spoken to her, Alice cried to him.

"Steven! Steven! They've been saying awful things
to me. Tell them it isn't true. Tell them you don't believe it."

"There—there——" His voice stuck in his throat.

He put his hand on her shoulder, standing between
her and her father.

"Tell them——" She looked up at him with her piteous eyes.

"She's worried to death," said Rowcliffe. "You might
have left it for to-night at any rate."

"We couldn't, Steven, when you've sent for Greatorex. We *must* get at the truth before he comes."

Rowcliffe shrugged his shoulders.

"Have you brought him?" said the Vicar.

"No, I haven't. He's in Morfe. I've sent word for him to come on here."

Alice looked sharply at him.

"What have you sent for *him* for? Do you suppose *he'd* give me away?"

She began to weep softly.

"All this," said Rowcliffe, "is awfully bad for her."

"You don't seem to consider what it is for us."

Rowcliffe took no notice of the Vicar.

"Look here, Mary—you'd better take her upstairs before he comes. Put her to bed. Try and get her to sleep."

"Very well. Come, Ally." Mary was gentler now.

Then Ally became wonderful.

She stood up and faced them all.

"I won't go," she said. "I'll stay till he comes if I sit up all night. How do I know what you're going to do to him? Do you suppose I'm going to leave him with you? If anybody touches him I'll *kill* them."

"Ally, dear——"

Mary put her hand gently on her sister's arm to lead her from the room.

Ally shook off the hand and turned on her in hysteric fury.

"Stop pawing me—you! How dare you touch me after what you've said. Steven—she says I took Essy's lover from her."

"I didn't, Ally. She doesn't know what she's saying."

"You *did* say it. She did, Steven. She said I ought to thank Essy for not splitting on me when I took her lover from her. As if *she* could talk when *she* took Steven from Gwenda."

"Oh—Steven!"

Rowcliffe shook his head at Mary, frowning, as a sign to her not to mind what Alice said.

"You treat me as if I was dirt, but I'd have died rather than have done what she did."

"Come, Alice, come. You know you don't mean it," said Rowcliffe, utterly gentle.

"I do mean it! She sneaked you from behind Gwenda's back and lied to you to make you think she didn't care for you——"

"Be quiet, you shameful girl!"

"Be quiet yourself, Papa. I'm not as shameful as Molly is. I'm not as shameful as you are yourself. You killed Mother."

"Oh—my—God——" The words were almost inaudible in the Vicar's shuddering groan.

He advanced on her to turn her from the room. Ally sank on her sofa as she saw him come.

Rowcliffe stepped between them.

"For God's sake, sir——"

Ally was struggling in hysterics now, choking between her piteous and savage cries.

Rowcliffe laid her on the sofa and put a cushion under her head. When he tried to loosen her gown at her throat she screamed.

"It's all right, Ally, it's all right."

"*Is* it? *Is* it?" The Vicar hissed at him.

"It won't be unless you leave her to me. If you go on bullying her much longer I won't answer for the consequences. You surely don't want——

"It's all right, Ally. Lie quiet, there—like that.

That's a good girl. Nobody's going to worry you any more."

He was kneeling by the sofa, pressing his hand to her forehead. Ally still sobbed convulsively, but she lay quiet. She closed her eyes under Rowcliffe's soothing hand.

"You might go and see if you can find some salvolatile, Mary," he said.

Mary went.

The Vicar, who had turned his back on this scene, went, also, into his study.

Ally still kept her eyes shut.

"Has Mary gone?"

"Yes."

"And Papa?"

"Yes. Lie still."

She lay still.

There was the sound of wheels on the road. It brought Mary and the Vicar back into the room. The wheels stopped. The gate clanged.

Rowcliffe rose.

"That's Greatorex. I'll go to him."

Ally lay very still now, still as a corpse, with closed eyes.

The house door opened.

Rowcliffe·drew back into the room.

"It isn't Greatorex," he said. "It's Gwenda."

"Who sent for her?" said the Vicar.

"I did," said Ally.

She had opened her eyes.

"Thank God for that, anyhow," said Rowcliffe.

Mary and her father looked at each other. Neither of

them seemed to want to go out to Gwenda. It struck Rowcliffe that the Vicar was afraid.

They waited while Gwenda paid her driver and dismissed him. They could hear her speaking out there in the passage.

The house door shut and she came to them. She paused in the doorway, looking at the three who stood facing her, embarrassed and expectant. She seemed to be thinking that it was odd that they should stand there. The door, thrown back, hid Alice, who lay behind it on her sofa.

"Come in, Gwenda," said the Vicar with exaggerated suavity.

She came in and closed the door. Then she saw Alice.

She took the hand that Rowcliffe held out to her without looking at him. She was looking at Alice.

Alice gave a low cry and struggled to her feet.

"I thought you were never coming," she said.

Gwenda held her in her arms. She faced them.

"What have you been doing to her—all of you?"

Rowcliffe answered. Though he was the innocent one of the three he looked the guiltiest. He looked utterly ashamed.

"We've had rather a scene, and it's been a bit too much for her," he said.

"So I see," said Gwenda. She had not greeted Mary or her father.

"If you could persuade her to go upstairs to bed——"

"I've told you I won't go till he comes," said Ally.

She sat down on the sofa as a sign that she was going to wait.

"Till who comes?" Gwenda asked.

She stared at the three with a fierce amazement. And they were abashed.

"She doesn't know, Steve," said Mary.

"I certainly don't," said Gwenda.

She sat down beside Ally.

"Has anybody been bullying you, Ally?"

"They've all been bullying me except Steven. Steven's been an angel. He doesn't believe what they say. Papa says I'm a shameful girl, and Mary says I took Jim Greatorex from Essy. And they think——"

"Never mind what they think, darling."

"I must protest——"

The Vicar would have burst out again but that his son-in-law restrained him.

"Better leave her to Gwenda," he said.

He opened the door of the study. "Really, sir, I think you'd better. And you, too, Mary."

And with her husband's compelling hand on her shoulder Mary went into the study.

The Vicar followed them.

As the door closed on them Alice looked furtively around.

"What is it, Ally?" Gwenda said.

"Don't you know?" she whispered.

"No. You haven't told me anything."

"You don't know why I sent for you? Can't you think?"

Gwenda was silent.

"Gwenda—I'm in the most awful trouble——" She looked around again. Then she spoke rapidly and low with a fearful hoarse intensity.

"I won't tell them, but I'll tell you. They've been trying to get it out of me by bullying, but I wasn't going to let them. Gwenda—they wanted to make me tell straight out, there—before Steven. And I wouldn't—I wouldn't. They haven't got a word out of me. But it's true, what they say."

She paused.

"About me."

"My lamb, I don't know what they say about you."

"They say that I'm going to——"

Crouching where she sat, bent forward, staring with her stare, she whispered.

"Oh—Ally—darling——"

"I'm not ashamed, not the least little bit ashamed. And I don't care what they think of me. But I'm not going to tell them. I've told *you* because I know you won't hate me, you won't think me awful. But I won't tell Mary, and I won't tell Papa. Or Steven. If I do they'll make me marry him."

"Was it—was it——"

Ally's instinct heard the name that her sister spared her.

"Yes—Yes—Yes. It is."

She added, "I don't care."

"Ally—what made you do it?"

"I don't—know."

"Was it because of Steven?"

Ally raised her head.

"No. It was *not*. Steven isn't fit to black his boots. I know that——"

"But—you don't care for him?"

"I did—I did. I do. I care awfully——"

"Well——"

"Oh, Gwenda, can they *make* me marry him?"

"You don't want to marry him?"

Ally shook her head, slowly, forlornly.

"I see. You're ashamed of him."

"I'm *not* ashamed. I told you I wasn't. It isn't that——"

"What is it?"

"I'm afraid."

"Afraid——"

"It isn't his fault. He wants to marry me. He wanted to all the time. He never meant that it should be like this. He asked me to marry him. Before it happened. Over and over again he asked me and I wouldn't have him."

"Why wouldn't you?"

"I've told you. Because I'm afraid."

"Why are you afraid?"

"I don't know. I'm not really afraid of *him*. I think I'm afraid of what he might do to me if I married him."

"*Do* to you?"

"Yes. He might beat me. They always do, you know, those sort of men, when you marry them. I couldn't bear to be beaten."

"Oh——" Gwenda drew in her breath.

"He wouldn't do it, Gwenda, if he knew what he was about. But he might if he didn't. You see, they say he drinks. That's what frightens me. That's why I daren't tell Papa. Papa wouldn't care if he did beat me. He'd say it was my punishment."

"If you feel like that about it you mustn't marry him."

"They'll make me."

"They shan't make you. I won't let them. It'll be all right, darling. I'll take you away with me to-morrow, and look after you, and keep you safe."

"But—they'll have to know."

"Yes. They'll have to know. *I*'ll tell them."

She rose.

"Stay here," she said. "And keep quiet. I'm **going** to tell them now."

"Not now—please, not now."

"Yes. Now. It'll be all over. And you'll sleep."

She went in to where they waited for her.

Her father and her sister lifted their eyes to her as she came in. Rowcliffe had turned away.

"Has she said anything?"

(Mary spoke.)

"Yes."

The Vicar looked sternly at his second daughter.

"She denies it?"

"No, Papa. She doesn't deny it."

He drove it home. "Has—she—confessed?"

"She's told me it's true—what you think."

In the silence that fell on the four Rowcliffe stayed where he stood, downcast and averted. It was as if he felt that Gwenda could have charged him with betrayal of a trust.

The Vicar looked at his watch. He turned to Rowcliffe.

"Is that fellow coming, or is he not?"

"He won't funk it," said Rowcliffe.

He turned. His eyes met Gwenda's. "I think I can answer for his coming."

"Do you mean Jim Greatorex?" she said.

"Yes."

"What is it that he won't funk?"

She looked from one to the other. Nobody answered her. It was as if they were, all three, afraid of her.

"I see," she said. "If you ask me I think he'd much better not come."

"My dear Gwenda——" The Vicar was deferent to the power that had dragged Ally's confession from her.

"We *must* get through with this. The sooner the better. It's what we're all here for."

"I know. Still—I think you'll have to leave it."

"Leave it?"

"Yes, Papa."

"We can't leave it," said Rowcliffe. "Something's got to be done."

The Vicar groaned and Rowcliffe had pity on him.

"If you'd like me to do it—I can interview him."

'I wish you would."

"Very well." He moved uneasily. "I'd better see him here, hadn't I?"

"You'd better not see him anywhere," said Gwenda. "He can't marry her."

She held them all three by the sheer shock of it.

The Vicar spoke first. "What do you mean, 'he can't'? He *must*."

"He must not. Ally doesn't want to marry him. He asked her long ago and she wouldn't have him."

"Do you mean," said Rowcliffe, surprised out of his reticence, "before this happened?"

"Yes."

"And she wouldn't have him?"

"No. She was afraid of him."

"She was afraid of him—and yet——" It was Mary who spoke now.

"Yes, Mary. And yet—she cared for him."

The Vicar turned on her.

"You're as bad as she is. How can you bring yourself to speak of it, if you're a modest girl? You've just told us that your sister's shameless. Are we to suppose that you're defending her?"

"I am defending her. There's nobody else to do it. You've all set on her and tortured her——"

"Not *all,* Gwenda," said Rowcliffe. But she did not heed him.

"She'd have told you everything if you hadn't frightened her. You haven't had an atom of pity for her. You've never thought of *her* for a minute. You've been thinking of yourselves. You might have killed her. And you didn't care."

The Vicar looked at her.

"It's you, Gwenda, who don't care."

"About what she's done, you mean? I don't. *You* ought to be gentle with her, Papa. You drove her to it."

Rowcliffe answered.

"We'll not say what drove her, Gwenda."

"She was driven," she said.

"'Let no man say he is tempted of God when he is driven by his own lusts and enticed,'" said the Vicar.

He had risen, and the movement brought him face to face with Gwenda. And as she looked at him it was as if she saw vividly and for the first time the profound unspirituality of her father's face. She knew from what source his eyes drew their darkness. She understood the meaning of the gross red mouth that showed itself in the fierce lifting of the ascetic, grim moustache. And she conceived a horror of his fatherhood.

"No man ought to say that of his own daughter. How does he know what's her own and what's his?" she said.

Rowcliffe stared at her in a sort of awful admiration. She was terrible; she was fierce; she was mad. But it was the fierceness and the madness of pity and of compassion.

She went on.

"You've no business to be hard on her. You must have known."

"I knew nothing," said the Vicar.

He appealed to her with a helpless gesture of his hands.

"You did know. You were warned. You were told not to shut her up. And you did shut her up. You can't blame her if she got away. You flung her to Jim Greatorex. There wasn't anybody who cared for her but him."

"Cared for her!" He snarled his disgust.

"Yes. Cared for her. You think that's horrible of her —that she should have gone to him—and yet you want to tie her to him when she's afraid of him. And I think it's horrible of you."

"She must marry him." Mary spoke again. "She's brought it on herself, Gwenda."

"She hasn't brought it on herself. And she shan't marry him."

"I'm afraid she'll have to," Rowcliffe said.

"She won't have to if I take her away somewhere and look after her. I mean to do it. I'll work for her. I'll take care of the child."

"Oh, you—*you*——!" The Vicar waved her away with a frantic flapping of his hands.

He turned to his son-in-law.

"Rowcliffe—I beg you—will you use your influence?"

"I have none."

That drew her. "Steven—help me—can't you see how terrible it is if she's afraid of him?"

"But *is* she?"

He looked at her with his miserable eyes, then turned them from her, considering gravely what she had said.

It was then, while Rowcliffe was considering it, that the garden gate opened violently and fell to.

They waited for the sound of the front door bell.

Instead of it they heard two doors open and Ally's voice calling to Greatorex in the hall.

As the Vicar flung himself from his study into the other room he saw Alice standing close to Greatorex by the shut door. Her lover's arms were round her.

He laid his hands on them as if to tear them apart.

"You shall not touch my daughter—until you've married her."

The young man's right arm threw him off; his left arm remained round Alice.

"It's yo' s'all nat tooch her, Mr. Cartaret," he said. "Ef yo' coom between her an' mae I s'all 'ave t' kill yo'. I'd think nowt of it. Dawn't yo' bae freetened, my laass," he murmured tenderly.

The next instant he was fierce again.

"An' look yo' 'erc, Mr. Cartaret. It was yo' who aassked mae t' marry Assy. Do yo' aassk mae t' marry Assy now? Naw! Assy may rot for all yo' care. (It's all right, my sweet'eart. It's all right.) I'd a married Assy right enoof ef I'd 'a' looved her. But do yo' suppawss I'd 'a' doon it fer yore meddlin'? Naw! An' yo' need n' aassk mae t' marry yore daughter—— (There—there—my awn laass)——"

"You are not going to be asked," said Gwenda. "You are not going to marry her."

"Gwenda," said the Vicar, "you will be good enough to leave this to me."

"It can't be left to anybody but Ally."

"It s'all be laft to her," said Greatorex.

He had loosened his hold of Alice, but he still stood between her and her father.

"It's for her t' saay ef she'll 'aave mae."

"She has said she won't, Mr. Greatorex."

"Ay, she's said it to mae, woonce. But I rackon she'll 'ave mae now."

"Not even now."

"She's toald yo'?"

He did not meet her eyes.

"Yes."

"She's toald yo' she's afraid o' mae?"

"Yes. And you know why."

"Ay. I knaw. Yo're afraid o' mae, Ally, because yo've 'eard I haven't always been as sober as I might bae; but yo're nat 'aalf as afraid o' mae, droonk or sober, as yo' are of yore awn faather. Yo' dawn't think I s'all bae 'aalf as 'ard an' crooil to yo' as yore faather is. She doosn't, Mr. Cartaret, an' thot's Gawd's truth."

"I protest," said the Vicar.

"Yo' stond baack, sir. It's for 'er t' saay."

He turned to her, infinitely reverent, infinitely tender.

"Will yo' staay with 'im? Or will yo' coom with mae?"

"I'll come with you."

With one shoulder turned to her father, she cowered to her lover's breast.

"Ay, an' yo' need n' be afraaid I'll not bae sober. I'll bae sober enoof now. D'ye 'ear, Mr. Cartaret? Yo' need n' bae afraaid, either. I'll kape sober. I'd kape sober all my life ef it was awnly t' spite yo'. An' I'll maake 'er 'appy. For I rackon theer's noothin' I could think on would spite yo' moor. Yo' want mae t' marry 'er t' poonish 'er. *I* knaw."

"That'll do, Greatorex," said Rowcliffe.

"Ay. It'll do," said Greatorex with a grin of satisfaction.

He turned to Alice, the triumph still flaming in his face. "Yo're *nat* afraaid of mae?"

"No," she said gently. "Not now."

"Yo navver were," said Greatorex; and he laughed.

That laugh was more than Mr. Cartaret could bear.
He thrust out his face toward Greatorex.

Rowcliffe, watching them, saw that he trembled and
that the thrust-out, furious face was flushed deeply on
the left side.

The Vicar boomed.

"You will leave my house this instant, Mr. Greatorex.
And you will never come into it again."

But Greatorex was already looking for his cap.

"I'll navver coom into et again," he assented placably.

There were no prayers at the Vicarage that night.

It was nearly eleven o'clock. Greatorex was gone.
Gwenda was upstairs helping Alice to undress. Mary
sat alone in the dining-room, crying steadily. The Vicar
and Rowcliffe were in the study.

In all this terrible business of Alice, the Vicar felt that
his son-in-law had been a comfort to him.

"Rowcliffe," he said suddenly, "I feel very queer."

"I don't wonder, sir. I should go to bed if I were you."

"I shall. Presently."

The one-sided flush deepened and darkened as he
brooded. It fascinated Rowcliffe.

"I think it would be better," said the Vicar slowly, "if
I left the parish. It's the only solution I can see."

He meant to the problem of his respectability.

Rowcliffe said yes, perhaps it would be better.

He was thinking that it would solve his problem too.

For he knew that there would be a problem if Gwenda
came back to her father.

The Vicar rose heavily and went to his roll-top desk.
He opened it and began fumbling about in it, looking for
things.

He was doing this, it seemed to his son-in-law, for quite a long time.

But it was only eleven o'clock when Mary heard sounds in the study that terrified her, of a chair overturned and of a heavy body falling to the floor. And then Steven called to her.

She found him kneeling on the floor beside her father, loosening his clothes. The Vicar's face, which she discerned half hidden between the bending head of Rowcliffe and his arms, was purple and horribly distorted.

Rowcliffe did not look at her.

"He's in a fit," he said. "Go upstairs and fetch Gwenda. And for God's sake don't let Ally see him."

XLIX

The village knew all about Jim Greatorex and Alice Cartaret now. Where their names had been whispered by two or three in the bar of the Red Lion, over the post-office counter, in the schoolhouse, in the smithy, and on the open road, the loud scandal of them burst with horror.

For the first time in his life Jim Greatorex was made aware that public opinion was against him. Wherever he showed himself the men slunk from him and the women stared. He set his teeth and held his chin up and passed them as if he had not seen them. He was determined to defy public opinion.

Standing in the door of his kinsman's smithy, he defied it.

It was the day before his wedding. He had been riding home from Morfe Market and his mare Daisy had cast a shoe coming down the hill. He rode her up to the smithy and called for Blenkiron, shouting his need.

Blenkiron came out and looked at him sulkily.

"I'll shoe t' maare," he said, "but yo'll stand outside t' smithy, Jim Greatorex."

For answer Jim rode the mare into the smithy and dismounted there.

Then Blenkiron spoke.

"You'd best 'ave staayed where yo' were. But yo've coom in an' yo' s'all 'ave a bit o' my toongue. To-morra's yore weddin' day, I 'ear?"

Jim intimated that if it was his wedding day it was no business of Blenkiron's.

"Wall," said the blacksmith, "ef they dawn't gie yo' soom roough music to-morra night, it'll bae better loock than yo' desarve—t' two o' yo'."

Greatorex scowled at his kinsman.

"Look yo' 'ere, John Blenkiron, I warn yo'. Any man in t' Daale thot speaaks woon word agen my wife 'e s'all 'ave 'is nack wroong."

"An' 'ow 'bout t' women, Jimmy? There'll bae a sight o' nacks fer yo' t' wring, I rackon. They'll 'ave soomat t' saay to 'er, yore laady."

"T' women? T' women? Domned sight she'll keer for what they saay. There is n' woon o' they bitches as is fit t' kneel in t' mood to 'er t' tooch t' sawle of 'er boots."

Blenkiron peered up at him from the crook of the mare's hind leg.

"Nat Assy Gaale?" he said.

"Assy Gaale? 'Oo's she to mook 'er naame with 'er dirty toongue?"

"Yo'll not goa far thot road, Jimmy. 'Tis wi' t' womenfawlk yo'll 'aave t' racken."

He knew it.

The first he had to reckon with was Maggie.

Maggie, being given notice, had refused to take it.

"Yo' can please yoresel, Mr. Greatorex. I can goa. I can goa. But ef I goa yo'll nat find anoother woman as'll coom to yo'. There's nat woon as'll keer mooch t' work for *yore* laady."

"Wull yo' wark for 'er, Maaggie?" he had said.

And Maggie, with a sullen look and hitching her coarse apron, had replied remarkably:

"Ef Assy Gaale can wash fer er I rackon *I* can shift to baake an' clane."

"Wull yo' waait on 'er?" he had persisted.

Maggie had turned away her face from him.

"Ay, I'll waait on 'er," she said.

And Maggie had stayed to bake and clean. Rough and sullen, without a smile, she had waited on young Mrs. Greatorex.

But Alice was not afraid of Maggie. She was not going to admit for a moment that she was afraid of her. She was not going to admit that she was afraid of anything but one thing—that her father would die.

If he died she would have killed him.

Or, rather, she and Greatorex would have killed him between them.

This statement Ally held to and reiterated and refused to qualify.

For Alice at Upthorne had become a creature matchless in cunning and of subtle and marvelous resource. She had been terrified and tortured, shamed and cowed. She had been hounded to her marriage and conveyed with an appalling suddenness to Upthorne, that place of sinister and terrible suggestion, and the bed in which John Greatorex had died had been her marriage bed. Her mind, like a thing pursued and in deadly peril, took instantaneously a line. It doubled and dodged; it hid itself; its instinct was expert in disguises, in subterfuges and shifts.

In her soul she knew that she was done for if she once admitted and gave in to her fear of Upthorne and of her husband's house, or if she were ever to feel again her fear of Greatorex, which was the most intolerable of all her fears. It was as if Nature itself were aware that, if Ally were not dispossessed of that terror before Greatorex's child was born her own purpose would be insecure; as if the unborn child, the flesh and blood of the Greatorexes that had entered into her, protested against her disastrous cowardice.

So, without Ally being in the least aware of it, Ally's mind, struggling toward sanity, fabricated one enormous fear, the fear of her father's death, a fear that she could own and face, and set it up in place of that secret and dangerous thing which was the fear of life itself.

Ally, insisting a dozen times a day that she had killed poor Papa, was completely taken in by this play of her surreptitiously self-preserving soul. Even Rowcliffe was taken in by it. He called it a morbid obsession. And he began to wonder whether he had not been mistaken about Ally after all, whether her nature was not more subtle and sensitive than he had guessed, more intricately and dangerously mixed.

For the sadness of the desolate land, of the naked hillsides, of the moor marshes with their ghostly mists; the brooding of the watchful, solitary house, the horror of haunted twilights, of nightfall and of midnights now and then when Greatorex was abroad looking after his cattle and she lay alone under the white ceiling that sagged above her bed and heard the weak wind picking at the pane; her fear of Maggie and of what Maggie had been to Greatorex and might be again; her fear of the savage, violent and repulsive elements in the man who was her god; her fear of her own repulsion; the tremor of her recoiling nerves; premonitions of her alien blood, the vague melancholy of her secret motherhood; they were all mingled together and hidden from her in the vast gloom of her one fear.

And once the dominant terror was set up, her instinct found a thousand ways of strengthening it. Through her adoration of her lover her mind had become saturated with his mournful consciousness of sin. In their moments of contrition they were both convinced that they would be punished. But Ally had borne her sin superbly; she had declared that it was hers and hers only, and that she and not Greatorex would be punished. And now the punishment had come. She persuaded herself that her father's death was the retribution Heaven required.

And all the time, through the perilous months, Nature, mindful of her own, tightened her hold on Ally through Ally's fear. Ally was afraid to be left alone with it. Therefore she never let Greatorex out of her sight if she could help it. She followed him from room to room of the sad house where he was painting and papering and whitewashing to make it fine for her. Where he was she had to be. Stowed away in some swept corner, she would sit with her sweet and sorrowful eyes fixed on him as he labored. She trotted after him through the house and out into the mistal and up the Three Fields. She would crouch on a heap of corn-sacks, wrapped in a fur coat, and watch him at his work in the stable and the cow-byre. In her need to immortalise this passion she could not have done better. Her utter dependence on him flattered and softened the distrustful, violent and headstrong man. Her one chance, and Ally knew it, was to cling. If she had once shamed him by her fastidious shrinking she would have lost him; for, as Mrs. Gale had told her long ago, you could do nothing with Jimmy when he was shamed. Maggie, for all her coarseness, had contrived to shame him; so had Essy in her freedom and her pride. Ally's clinging, so far from irritating or obstructing him, drew out the infinite pity and tenderness he had for all sick and helpless things. He could no more have pushed little Ally from him than he could have kicked a mothering ewe, or stamped on a new dropped

lamb. He would call to her if she failed to come. He
would hold out his big hand to her as he would have held
it to a child. Her smallness, her fineness and fragility
enchanted him. The palms of her hands had the smooth-
ness and softness of silk, and they made a sound like silk
as they withdrew themselves with a lingering, stroking
touch from his. He still felt, with a fearful and admir-
ing wonder, the difference of her flesh from his.

To be sure Jim's tenderness was partly penitential.
Only it was Ally alone who had moved him to a perfect
and unbearable contrition. For the two women whom
he had loved and left Greatorex had felt nothing but a
passing pang. For the woman he had made his wife he
would go always with a wound in his soul.

And with Ally, too, the supernatural came to Nature's
aid. Her fear had a profound strain of the uncanny in
it, and Jim's bodily presence was her shelter from her
fear. And as it bound them flesh to flesh, closer and
closer, it wedded them in one memory, one consolation
and one soul.

One day she had followed him into the stable, and on
the window-sill, among all the cobwebs where it had been
put away and forgotten, she found the little bottle of
chlorodyne.

She took it up, and Jim scolded her gently as if she
had been a child.

"Yore lil haands is always maddlin'. Yo' put thot
down."

"What is it?"

"It's poison, is thot. There's enoof there t' kili a
maan. Yo' put it down whan I tall yo'."

She put it down obediently in its place on the window-
sill among the cobwebs.

He made a nest for her of clean hay, where she sat and watched him as he gave Daisy her feed of corn. She watched every movement of him, every gesture, thoughtful and intent.

"I can't think, Jim, why I ever was afraid of you. *Was* I afraid of you?"

Greatorex grinned.

"Yo' used t' saay yo' were."

"How silly of me. And I used to be afraid of Maggie."

"*I*'ve been afraaid of Maaggie afore now. She's got a roough side t' 'er toongue and she can use it. But she'll nat use it on yo'. Yo've naw call to be afraaid ef annybody. There isn't woon would hoort a lil thing like yo'."

"They say things about me. I know they do."

"And yo' dawn't keer what they saay, do yo'?"

"I don't care a rap. But I think it's cruel of them, all the same."

"But yo're happy enoof, aren't yo'—all the same?"

"I'm very happy. At least I would be if it wasn't for poor Papa. It wouldn't have happened if it hadn't been for what we did."

Wherever they started, whatever round they fetched, it was to this that they returned.

And always Jim met it with the same answer:

"'Tisn' what we doon; 'tis what 'e doon. An' annyhow it had to bae."

Every week Rowcliffe came to see her and every week Jim said to him: "She's at it still and I caan't move 'er."

And every week Rowcliffe said: "Wait. She'll be better before long."

And Jim waited.

He waited till one afternoon in February, when they

were again in the stable together.   He had turned his back on her for a moment.

When he looked round she was gone from her seat on the cornsacks.   She was standing by the window-sill with the bottle of chlorodyne in her hand and at her lips.   He thought she was smelling it.

She tilted her head back.   Her eyes slewed sidelong toward him.   They quivered as he leaped to her.

She had not drunk a drop and he knew it, but she clutched her bottle with a febrile obstinacy.   He had to loosen her little fingers one by one.

He poured the liquid into the stable gutter and flung the bottle on to the dung heap in the mistal.

"What were you doing wi' thot stoof?" he said.

"I don't know.   I was thinking of Papa."

After that he never left her until Rowcliffe came.

Rowcliffe said: "She's got it into her head he's going to die, and she thinks she's killed him.   You'd better let me take her to see him."

L

THE Vicar had solved his problem by his stroke, but not quite as he had anticipated.

Nothing had ever turned out as he had planned or thought or willed. He had planned to leave the parish. He had thought that in his wisdom he had saved Alice by shutting her up in Garthdale. He had thought that she was safe at choir-practice with Jim Greatorex. He had thought that Mary was devoted to him and that Gwenda was capable of all disobedience and all iniquity. She had gone away and he had forbidden her to come back again. He had also forbidden Greatorex to enter his house.

And Greatorex was entering it every day, for news of him to take to Alice at Upthorne. Gwenda had come back and would never go again, and it was she and not Mary who had proved herself devoted. And it was not his wisdom but Greatorex's scandalous passion for her that had saved Alice. As for leaving the parish because of the scandal, the Vicar would never leave it now. He was tied there in his Vicarage by his stroke.

It left him with a paralysis of the right side and an utter confusion and enfeeblement of intellect.

In three months he recovered partially from the paralysis. But the flooding of his brain had submerged or carried away whole tracts of recent memory, and the last vivid, violent impression—Alice's affair—was wiped out.

There was no reason why he should not stay on. What

was left of his memory told him that Alice was at the Vicarage, and he was worried because he never saw her about.

He did not know that the small gray house above the churchyard had become a place of sinister and scandalous tragedy; that his name and his youngest daughter's name were bywords in three parishes; and that Alice had been married in conspicuous haste by the horrified Vicar of Greffington to a man whom only charitable people regarded as her seducer.

And the order of time had ceased for him with this breach in the sequence of events. He had a dim but enduring impression that it was always prayer time. No hours marked the long stretches of blank darkness and of confused and crowded twilight. Only, now and then, a little light pulsed feebly in his brain, a flash that renewed itself day by day; and day by day, in a fresh experience, he was aware that he was ill.

It was as if the world stood still and his mind moved. It "wandered," as they said. And in its wanderings it came upon strange gaps and hollows and fantastic dislocations, landslips where a whole foreground had given way. It looked at these things with a serene and dream-like wonder and passed on.

And in the background, on some half-lit, isolated tract of memory, raised above ruin, and infinitely remote, he saw the figure of his youngest daughter. It was a girlish, innocent figure, and though, because of the whiteness of its face, he confused it now and then with the figure of Alice's dead mother, his first wife, he was aware that it was really Alice.

This figure of Alice moved him with a vague and tender yearning.

What puzzled and worried him was that in his flashes of luminous experience he didn't see her there. And it was then that the Vicar would make himself wonderful and piteous by asking, a dozen times a day, "Where's Ally?"

For by the stroke that made him wonderful and piteous the Vicar's character and his temperament were changed. Nothing was left of Ally's tyrant and Robina's victim, the middle-aged celibate, filled with the fury of frustration and profoundly sorry for himself. His place was taken by a gentle old man, an old man of an appealing and childlike innocence, pure from all lust, from all self-pity, enjoying, actually enjoying, the consideration that his stroke had brought him.

He was changed no less remarkably in his affections. He was utterly indifferent to Mary, whom he had been fond of. He yearned for Alice, whom he had hated. And he clung incessantly to Gwenda, whom he had feared.

When he looked round in his strange and awful gentleness and said, "Where's Ally?" his voice was the voice of a mother calling for her child. And when he said, "Where's Gwenda?" it was the voice of a child calling for its mother.

And as he continually thought that Alice was at the Vicarage when she was at Upthorne, so he was convinced that Gwenda had left him when she was there.

Rowcliffe judged that this confusion of the Vicar's would be favorable to his experiment.

And it was.

When Mr. Cartaret saw his youngest daughter for the first time since their violent rupture he gazed at her tranquilly and said, "And where have *you* been all this time?"

"Not very far, Papa."

He smiled sweetly.

"I thought you'd run away from your poor old father. Let me see—was it Ally? My memory's going. No. It was Gwenda who ran away. Wasn't it Gwenda?"

"Yes, Papa."

"Well—she must come back again. I can't do without Gwenda."

"She has come back, Papa."

"She's always coming back. But she'll go away again. Where is she?"

"I'm here, Papa dear."

"Here one minute," said the Vicar, "and gone the next."

"No—no. I'm not going. I shall never go away and leave you."

"So you say," said the Vicar. "So you say."

He looked round uneasily.

"It's time for Ally to go to bed. Has Essy brought her milk?"

His head bowed to his breast. He fell into a doze. Ally watched.

And in the outer room Gwenda and Steven Rowcliffe talked together.

"Steven—he's always going on like that. It breaks my heart."

"I know, dear, I know."

"Do you think he'll ever remember?"

"I don't know. I don't think so."

Then they sat together without speaking. She was thinking: "How good he is. Surely I may love him for his goodness?" And he that the old man in there had solved *his* problem, but that his own had been taken out of his hands.

And he saw no solution.

If the Vicar had gone away and taken Gwenda with
him, that would have solved it. God knew he had been
willing enough to solve it that way.

But here they were, flung together, thrust toward each
other when they should have torn themselves apart; tied,
both of them, to a place they could not leave. Week in,
week out, he would be obliged to see her whether he would
or no. And when her tired face rebuked his senses, she
drew him by her tenderness; she held him by her goodness. There was only one thing for him to do—to clear
out. It was his plain and simple duty. If it hadn't
been for Alice and for that old man he would have done
it. But, because of them, it was his still plainer and
simpler duty to stay where he was, to stick to her and
see her through.

He couldn't help it if his problem was taken out of
his hands.

They started. They looked at each other and smiled
their strained and tragic smile.

In the inner room the Vicar was calling for Gwenda.
It was prayer time, he said.

Rowcliffe had to drive Alice back that night to Upthorne.

"Well," he said, as they left the Vicarage behind them,
"you see he isn't going to die."

"No," said Alice. "But he's out of his mind. I
haven't killed him. I've done worse. I've driven him
mad."

And she stuck to it. She couldn't afford to part with
her fear—yet.

Rowcliffe was distressed at the failure of his experiment. He told Greatorex that there was nothing to be

done but to wait patiently till June. Then—perhaps—they would see.

In his own mind he had very little hope. He said to himself that he didn't like the turn Ally's obsession had taken. It was *too* morbid.

But when May came Alice lay in the big bed under the sagging ceiling with a lamentably small baby in her arms, and Greatorex sat beside her by the hour together, with his eyes fixed on her white face. Rowcliffe had told him to be on the lookout for some new thing or for some more violent sign of the old obsession. But nine days had passed and he had seen no sign. Her eyes looked at him and at her child with the same lucid, drowsy ecstasy.

And in nine days she had only asked him once if he knew how poor Papa was?

Her fear had left her. It had served its purpose.

LI

THERE was no prayer time at the Vicarage any more.

There was no more time at all there as the world counts
time.

The hours no longer passed in a procession marked by
distinguishable days. They rolled round and round in an
interminable circle, monotonously renewed, monotonously
returning upon itself. The Vicar was the center of the
circle. The hours were sounded and measured by his
monotonously recurring needs. But the days were neither
measured nor marked. They were all of one shade.
There was no difference between Sunday and Monday in
the Vicarage now. They talked of the Vicar's good days
and his bad days, that was all.

For in this house where time had ceased they talked
incessantly of time. But it was always *his* time; the
time for his early morning cup of tea; the time for his
medicine; the time for his breakfast; the time for reading
his chapter to him while he dozed; the time for washing
him, for dressing him, for taking him out (he went out
now, in a wheel-chair drawn by Peacock's pony); the
time for his medicine again; his dinner time; the time
for his afternoon sleep; his tea-time; the time for his last
dose of medicine; his supper time and his time for being
undressed and put to bed. And there were several times
during the night which were his times also.

The Vicar had desired supremacy in his Vicarage and

he was at last supreme. He was supreme over his daughter Gwenda. The stubborn, intractable creature was at his feet. She was his to bend or break or utterly destroy. She who was capable of anything was capable of an indestructible devotion. His times, the relentless, the monotonously recurring, were her times too.

If it had not been for Steven Rowcliffe she would have had none to call her own (except night time, when the Vicar slept). But Rowcliffe had kept to his days for visiting the Vicarage. He came twice or thrice a week; not counting Wednesdays. Only, though Mary did not know it, he came as often as not in the evenings at dusk, just after the Vicar had been put to bed. When it was wet he sat in the dining-room with Gwenda. When it was fine he took her out on to the moor under Karva.

They always went the same way, up the green sheep-track that they knew; they always turned back at the same place, where the stream he had seen her jumping ran from the hill; and they always took the same time to go and turn. They never stopped and never lingered; but went always at the same sharp pace, and kept the same distance from each other. It was as if by saying to themselves, "Never any further than the stream; never any longer than thirty-five minutes; never any nearer than we are now," they defined the limits of their whole relation. Sometimes they hardly spoke as they walked. They parted with casual words and with no touching of their hands and with the same thought unspoken—"Till the next time."

But these times which were theirs only did not count as time. They belonged to another scale of feeling and another order of reality. Their moments had another pulse, another rhythm and vibration. They burned as they beat. While they lasted Gwenda's life was lived with

an intensity that left time outside its measure. Through
this intensity she drew the strength to go on, to endure
the unendurable with joy.

But Rowcliffe could not endure the unendurable at all.
He was savage when he thought of it. That was her life
and she would never get away from it. She, who was
born for the wild open air and for youth and strength
and freedom, would be shut up in that house and tied
to that half-paralyzed, half-imbecile old man forever. It
was damnable. And he, Rowcliffe, could have prevented
it if he had only known. And if Mary had not lied to
him.

And when his common sense warned him of their danger, and his conscience reproached him with leading her
into it, he said to himself, "I can't help it if it is dangerous. It's been taken out of my hands. If somebody
doesn't drag her out of doors, she'll get ill. If somebody doesn't talk to her she'll grow morbid. And there's
nobody but me."

He sheltered himself in the immensity of her tragedy.
Its darkness covered them. Her sadness and her isolation sanctified them. Alice had her husband and her
child. Mary had—all she wanted. Gwenda had nobody
but him.

She had never had anybody but him. For in the beginning the Vicar and his daughters had failed to make
friends among their own sort. Up in the Dale there had
been few to make, and those few Mr. Cartaret had contrived to alienate one after another by his deplorable
legend and by the austere unpleasantness of his person-
ality. People had not been prepared for intimacy with
a Vicar separated so outrageously from his third wife.

Nobody knew whether it was he or his third wife who
had been outrageous, but the Vicar's manner was not
such as to procure for him the benefit of any doubt. The
fact remained that the poor man was handicapped by an
outrageous daughter, and Alice's behavior was obviously
as much the Vicar's fault as his misfortune. And it had
been felt that Gwenda had not done anything to redeem
her father's and her sister's eccentricities, and that Mary,
though she was a nice girl, had hardly done enough. For
the last eighteen months visits at the Vicarage had been
perfunctory and very brief, month by month they had
diminished, and before Mary's marriage they had almost
ceased.

Still, Mary's marriage had appeased the parish. Mrs.
Steven Rowcliffe had atoned for the third Mrs. Cartaret's
suspicious absence and for Gwenda Cartaret's flight. Lady
Frances Gilbey's large wing had further protected Gwenda.

Then, suddenly, the tale of Alice Cartaret and
Greatorex went round, and it was as if the Vicarage had
opened and given up its secret.

At first, the sheer extremity of his disaster had sheltered
the Vicar from his own scandal. Through all Garthdale
and Rathdale, in the Manors and the Lodges and the
Granges, in the farmhouses and the cottages, in the inns
and little shops, there was a stir of pity and compassion.
The people who had left off calling at the Vicarage called
again with sympathy and kind inquiries. They were inclined to forget how impossible the Cartarets had been.
They were sorry for Gwenda. But they had been checked
in their advances by Gwenda's palpable recoil. She had
no time to give to callers. Her father had taken all her
time. The callers considered themselves absolved from
calling.

Slowly, month by month, the Vicarage was drawn back

into its silence and its loneliness. It assumed, more and more, its aspect of half-sinister, half-sordid tragedy. The Vicar's calamity no longer sheltered him. It took its place in the order of accepted and irremediable events.

Only the village preserved its sympathy alive. The village, that obscure congregated soul, long-suffering to calamity, welded together by saner instincts and profound in memory, the soul that inhabited the small huddled, humble houses, divided from the Vicarage by no more than the graveyard of its dead, the village remembered and it knew.

It remembered how the Vicar had come and gone over its thresholds, how no rain nor snow nor storm had stayed him in his obstinate and punctual visiting. And whereas it had once looked grimly on its Vicar, it looked kindly on him now. It endured him for his daughter Gwenda's sake, in spite of what it knew.

For it knew why the Vicar's third wife had left him. It knew why Alice Cartaret had gone wrong with Great-orex. It knew what Gwenda Cartaret had gone for when she went away. It knew why and how Dr. Rowcliffe had married Mary Cartaret. And it knew why, night after night, he was to be seen coming and going on the Garthdale road.

The village knew more about Rowcliffe and Gwenda Cartaret than Rowcliffe's wife knew.

For Rowcliffe's wife's mind was closed to this knowledge by a certain sensual assurance. When all was said and done, it was she and not Gwenda who was Rowcliffe's wife. And she had other grounds for complacency. Her sister, a solitary Miss Cartaret, stowed away in Garth Vicarage, was of no account. She didn't matter. And as Mary Cartaret Mary would have mattered even less. But Steven Rowcliffe's professional reputation served him well. He counted. People who had begun by trusting him had ended by liking him, and in two years' time his social value had become apparent. And as Mrs. Steven Rowcliffe Mary had a social value too.

But while Steven, who had always had it, took it for granted and never thought about it, Mary could think of nothing else. Her social value, obscured by the terrible two years in Garthdale, had come to her as a discovery and an acquisition. For all her complacency, she could not regard it as a secure thing. She was sensitive to every breath that threatened it; she was unable to forget that, if she was Steven Rowcliffe's wife, she was Alice Greatorex's sister.

Even as Mary Cartaret she had been sensitive to Alice. But in those days of obscurity and isolation it was not in her to cast Alice off. She had felt bound to Alice, not as Gwenda was bound, but pitiably, irrevocably, for better, for worse. The solidarity of the family had held.

She had not had anything to lose by sticking to her sister. Now it seemed to her that she had everything to lose. The thought of Alice was a perpetual annoyance to her.

For the neighborhood that had received Mrs. Steven Rowcliffe had barred her sister.

As long as Alice Greatorex lived at Upthorne Mary went in fear.

This fear was so intolerable to her that at last she spoke of it to Rowcliffe.

They were sitting together in his study after dinner. The two armchairs were always facing now, one on each side of the hearth.

"I wish I knew what to do about Alice," she said.

"What to *do* about her?"

"Yes. Am I to have her at the house or not?"

He stared.

"Of course you're to have her at the house."

"I mean when we've got people here. I can't ask her to meet them."

"You must ask her. It's the very least you can do for her."

"People aren't going to like it, Steven."

"People have got to stick a great many things they aren't going to like. I'm continually meeting people I'd rather not meet. Aren't you?"

"I'm afraid poor Alice is——"

"Is what?"

"Well, dear, a little impossible, to say the least of it. Isn't she?"

He shrugged his shoulders.

"I don't see anything impossible about 'poor Alice.' I never did."

"It's nice of you to say so."

He maintained himself in silence under her long gaze.

"Steven," she said, "you are awfully good to my people."

She saw that she could hardly have said anything that would have annoyed him more.

He positively writhed with irritation.

"I'm not in the least good to your people."

The words stung her like a blow. She flushed, and he softened.

"Can't you see, Molly, that I hate the infernal humbug and the cruelty of it all? That poor child had a dog's life before she married. She did the only sane thing that was open to her. You've only got to look at her now to see that she couldn't have done much better for herself

even if she hadn't been driven to it. What's more, she's
done the best thing for Greatorex. There isn't another
woman in the world who could have made that chap chuck
drinking. You mayn't like the connection. I don't suppose any of us like it."

"My dear Steven, it isn't only the connection. I could
get over that. It's—the other thing."

His blank stare compelled her to precision.

"I mean what happened."

"Well—if Gwenda can get over 'the other thing,' I
should think *you* might. She has to see more of her."

"It's different for Gwenda."

"How is it different for Gwenda?"

She hesitated. She had meant that Gwenda hadn't
anything to lose. What she said was, "Gwenda hasn't
anybody but herself to think of. She hasn't let you in
for Alice."

"No more have you."

He smiled. Mary did not understand either his answer
or his smile.

He was saying to himself, "Oh, hasn't she? It was
Gwenda all the time who let me in."

Mary had a little rush of affection.

"My dear—I think I've let you in for everything. I
wouldn't mind—I wouldn't really—if it wasn't for you."

"You needn't bother about me," he said. "I'd rather
you bothered about your sister."

"Which sister?"

For the life of her she could not tell what had made
her say that. The words seemed to leap out suddenly
from her mind to her tongue.

"Alice," he said.

"Was it Alice we were talking about?"

"It was Alice I was thinking about."

"Was it?"

Again her mind took its insane possession of her tongue.

The evening dragged on. The two chairs still faced each other, pushed forward in their attitude of polite attention and expectancy.

But the persons in the chairs leaned back as if each withdrew as far as possible from the other. They made themselves stiff and upright as if they braced themselves, each against the other in the unconscious tension of hostility. And they were silent, each thinking an intolerable thought.

Rowcliffe had taken up a book and was pretending to read it. Mary's hands were busy with her knitting. Her needles went with a rapid jerk, driven by the vibration of her irritated nerves. From time to time she glanced at Rowcliffe under her bent brows. She saw the same blocks of print, a deep block at the top, a short line under it, then a narrower block. She saw them as vague, meaningless blurs of gray stippled on white. She saw that Rowcliffe's eyes never moved from the deep top paragraph on the left-hand page. She noted the light pressure of his thumbs on the margins.

He wasn't reading at all; he was only pretending to read. He had set up his book as a barrier between them, and he was holding on to it for dear life.

Rowcliffe moved irritably under Mary's eyes. She lowered them and waited for the silken sound that should have told her that he had turned a page.

And all the time she kept on saying to herself, "He *was* thinking about Gwenda. He's sorry for Alice because of Gwenda, not because of me. It isn't *my* people that he's good to."

The thought went round and round in Mary's mind, troubling its tranquillity.

She knew that something followed from it, but she refused to see it. Her mind thrust from it the conclusion. "Then it's Gwenda that he cares for." She said to herself, "After all I'm married to him." And as she said it she thrust up her chin in a gesture of assurance and defiance.

In the chair that faced her Rowcliffe shifted his position. He crossed his legs and the tilted foot kicked out, urged by a hidden savagery. The clicking of Mary's needles maddened him.

He glanced at her. She was knitting a silk tie for his birthday.

She saw the glance. The fierceness of the small fingers slackened; they knitted off a row or two, then ceased. Her hands lay quiet in her lap.

She leaned her head against the back of the chair. Her grieved eyes let down their lids before the smouldering hostility in his.

Her stillness and her shut eyes moved him to compunction. They appeased him with reminiscence, with suggestion of her smooth and innocent sleep.

He had been thinking of what she had done to him; of how she had lied to him about Gwenda; of the abominable thing that Alice had cried out to him in her agony. The thought of Mary's turpitude had consoled him mysteriously. Instead of putting it from him he had dwelt on it, he had wallowed in it; he had let it soak into him till he was poisoned with it.

For the sting of it and the violence of his own resentment were more tolerable to Rowcliffe than the stale, dull realisation of the fact that Mary bored him. It had come to that. He had nothing to say to Mary now that he had married her. His romantic youth still moved uneasily within him; it found no peace in an armchair, facing Mary. He dreaded these evenings that he was compelled to spend with her. He dreaded her speech. He dreaded her silences ten times more. They no longer soothed him. They were pervading, menacing, significant.

He thought that Mary's turpitude accounted for and justified the exasperation of his nerves.

Now as he looked at her, lying back in the limp pose reminiscent of her sleep, he thought, "Poor thing. Poor Molly." He put down his book. He stood over her a moment, sighed a long sigh like a yawn, turned from her and went to bed.

Mary opened her eyes, sighed, stretched herself, put out the light, and followed him.

LII

NOT long after that night it struck Mary that Steven was run down. He worked too hard. That was how she accounted to herself for his fits of exhaustion, of irritability and depression.

But secretly, for all her complacence, she had divined the cause.

She watched him now; she inquired into his goings out and comings in. Sometimes she knew that he had been to Garthdale, and, though he went there many more times than she knew, she had noticed that these moods of his followed invariably on his going. It was as if Gwenda left her mark on him. So much was certain, and by that certainty she went on to infer his going from his mood.

One day she taxed him with it.

Rowcliffe had tried to excuse his early morning temper on the plea that he was "beastly tired."

"Tired?" she had said. "Of course you're tired if you went up to Garthdale last night."

She added, "It isn't necessary."

He was silent and she knew that she was on his trail.

Two evenings later she caught him as he was leaving the house.

"Where are you going?" she said.

"I'm going up to Garthdale to see your father."

Her eyes flinched.

"You saw him yesterday."

"I did."

"Is he worse?"

He hesitated. Lying had not as yet come lightly to him.

"I'm not easy about him," he said.

She was not satisfied. She had caught the hesitation.

"Can't you tell me," she persisted, "if he's worse?"

He looked at her calmly.

"I can't tell you till I've seen him."

That roused her. She bit her lip. She knew that whatever she did she must not show temper.

"Did Gwenda send for you?"

Her voice was quiet.

"She did not."

He strode out of the house.

After that he never told her when he was going up to Garthdale toward nightfall. He was sometimes driven to lie. It was up Rathdale he was going, or to Greffington, or to smoke a pipe with Ned Alderson, or to turn in for a game of billiards at the village club.

And whenever he lied to her she saw through him. She was prepared for the lie. She said to herself, "He is going to see Gwenda. He can't keep away from her."

And then she remembered what Alice had said to her. "You'll know some day."

She knew.

LIII

AND with her knowledge there came a curious calm.

She no longer watched and worried Rowcliffe. She knew that no wife ever kept her husband by watching and worrying him.

She was aware of danger and she faced it with restored complacency.

For Mary was a fount of sensual wisdom. Rowcliffe was ill. And from his illness she inferred his misery, and from his misery his innocence.

She told herself that nothing had happened, that she knew nothing that she had not known before. She saw that her mistake had been in showing that she knew it. That was to admit it, and to admit it was to give it a substance, a shape and color it had never had and was not likely to have.

And Mary, having perceived her blunder, set herself to repair it.

She knew how. Under all his energy she had discerned in her husband a love of bodily ease, and a capacity for laziness, undeveloped because perpetually frustrated. Insidiously she had set herself to undermine his energy while she devised continual opportunities for ease.

Rowcliffe remained incurably energetic. His profession demanded energy.

Still, there were ways by which he could be captured. He was not so deeply absorbed in his profession as to be indifferent to the arrangements of his home. He liked.

and he showed very plainly that he liked, good food and silent service, the shining of glass and silver, white table linen and fragrant sheets for his bed.

With all these things Mary had provided him.

And she had her own magic and her way.

Her way, the way she had caught him, was the way she would keep him. She had always known her power, even unpracticed. She had always known by instinct how she could enthrall him when her moment came. Gwenda had put back the hour; but she had done (and Mary argued that therefore she could do) no more.

Here Mary's complacency betrayed her. She had fallen into the error of all innocent and tranquil sensualists. She trusted to the present. She had reckoned without Rowcliffe's future or his past.

And she had done even worse. By habituating Rowcliffe's senses to her way, she had produced in him, through sheer satisfaction, that sense of security which is the most dangerous sense of all.

LIV

ONE week in June Rowcliffe went up to Garthdale
two nights running. He had never done this before and
he had had to lie badly about it both to himself and Mary.

He had told himself that the first evening didn't count.

For he had quarreled with Gwenda the first evening.
Neither of them knew how it had happened or what it
was about. But he had hardly come before he had left
her in his anger.

The actual outburst moved her only to laughter, but
the memory of it was violent in her nerves, it shook and
shattered her. She had not slept all night and in the
morning she woke tired and ill. And, as if he had known
what he had done to her, he came to see her the next
evening, to make up.

That night they stayed out later than they had meant.

As they touched the moor the lambs stirred at their
mothers' sides and the pewits rose and followed the white
road to lure them from their secret places; they wheeled
and wheeled round them, sending out their bored and
weary cry. In June the young broods kept the moor
and the two were forced to the white road.

And at the turn they came in sight of Greffington Edge.
She stood still. "Oh—Steven—look," she said.

He stood with her and looked.

The moon was hidden in the haze where the gray day
and the white night were mixed. Across the bottom on
the dim, watery green of the eastern slope, the thorn

trees were in flower. The hot air held them like still
water. It quivered invisibly, loosening their scent and
scattering it. And of a sudden she saw them as if thrown
back to a distance where they stood enchanted in a great
stillness and clearness and a piercing beauty.

There went through her a sudden deep excitement, a
subtle and mysterious joy. This passion was as distant
and as pure as ecstasy. It swept her, while the white
glamour lasted, into the stillness where the flowering thorn
trees stood.

She wondered whether Steven had seen the vision of
the flowering thorn trees. She longed for him to see it.
They stood a little apart and her hand moved toward him
without touching him, as if she would draw him to the
magic.

"Steven——" she said.

He came to her. Her hand hung limply by her side
again. She felt his hand close on it and press it.

She knew that he had seen the vision and felt the
subtle and mysterious joy.

She wanted nothing more.

"Say good-night now," she said.

"Not yet. I'm going to walk back with you."

They walked back in a silence that guarded the memory of the mystic thing.

They lingered a moment by the half-open door; she on
the threshold, he on the garden path; the width of a flag-
stone separated them.

"In another minute," she thought, "he will be gone."

It seemed to her that he wanted to be gone and that it
was she who held him there against his will and her own.

She drew the door to.

"Don't shut it, Gwenda."

It was as if he said, "Don't let's stand together out here like this any longer."

She opened the door again, leaning a little toward it across the threshold with her hand on the latch.

She smiled, raising her chin in the distant gesture that was their signal of withdrawal.

But Steven did not go.

"May I come in?" he said.

Something in her said, "Don't let him come in." But she did not heed it. The voice was thin and small and utterly insignificant, as if one little brain cell had waked up and started speaking on its own account. And something seized on her tongue and made it say "Yes," and the full tide of her blood surged into her throat and choked it, and neither the one voice nor the other seemed to be her own.

He followed her into the little dining-room where the lamp was. The Vicar was in bed. The whole house was still.

Rowcliffe looked at her in the lamplight.

"We've walked a bit too far," he said.

He made her lean back on the couch. He put a pillow at her head and a footstool at her feet.

"Just rest," he said, and she rested.

But Rowcliffe did not rest. He moved uneasily about the room.

A sudden tiredness came over her.

She thought, "Yes. We walked too far." She leaned her head back on the cushion. Her thin arms lay stretched out on either side of her, supported by the couch.

Rowcliffe ceased to wander. He drew up with his back against the chimney-piece, where he faced her.

"Close your eyes," he said.

She did not close them. But the tired lids drooped.
The lifted bow of her mouth drooped. The small, sharp-
pointed breasts drooped.

And as he watched her he remembered how he had
quarreled with her in that room last night. And the
thought of his brutality was intolerable to him.

His heart ached with tenderness, and his tenderness
was intolerable too.

The small white face with its suffering eyes and drooping eyelids, the drooping breasts, the thin white arms
slackened along the couch, the childlike helplessness of
the tired body moved him with a vehement desire. And
his strength that had withstood her in her swift, defiant
beauty melted away.

"Steven——"

"Don't speak," he said.

She was quiet for a moment.

"But I want to, Steven. I want to say something."

He sighed.

"Well—say it."

"It's something I want to ask you."

"Don't ask impossibilities."

"I don't think it's impossible. At least it wouldn't be
if you really knew. I want you to be more careful with
me."

She paused.

He turned from her abruptly.

His turning made it easier for her. She went on.

"It's only a little thing—a silly little thing. I want
you, when you're angry with me, not to show it quite so
much."

He had turned again to her suddenly. The look on his
face stopped her.

"I'm never angry with you," he said.

"I know you aren't—really. I know. I know. But you make me think you are; and it hurts so terribly."

"I didn't know you minded."

"I don't always mind. But sometimes, when I'm stupid, I simply can't bear it. It makes me feel as if I'd done something. Last night I got it into my head——"

"What did you get into your head? Tell me——"

"I thought I'd made you hate me. I thought you thought I was awful—like poor Ally."

"*You?*"

He drew a long breath and sent it out again.

"You know what I think of you."

He looked at her, threw up his head suddenly and went to her.

His words came fast now and thick.

"You know I love you. That's why I've been such a brute to you—because I couldn't have you in my arms and it made me mad. And you know it. That's what you mean when you say it hurts you. You shan't be hurt any more. I'm going to end it."

He stooped over her suddenly, steadying himself by his two hands laid on the back of her chair. She put out her arms and pushed with her hands against his shoulders, as if she would have beaten him off. He sank to her knees and there caught her hands in his and kissed them. He held them together helpless with his left arm and his right arm gathered her to him violently and close.

His mouth came crushing upon her parted lips and her shut eyes.

Her small thin hands struggled piteously in his and for pity he released them. He felt them pushing with their silk-soft palms against his face. Their struggle and their resistance were pain to him and exquisite pleasure,

"Not that, Steven! Not that! Oh, I didn't think—I didn't think you would."

"Don't send me away, Gwenda. It's all right. We've suffered enough. We've got to end it this way."

"No. Not this way."

"Yes—yes. It's all right, darling. We've struggled till we can't struggle any more. You must. Why not? When you love me."

He pressed her closer in his arms. She lay quiet there. When she was quiet he let her speak.

"I can't," she said. "It's Molly. Poor little Molly."

"Don't talk to me of Molly. She lied about you."

"Whatever she did she couldn't help it."

"Whatever we do now we can't help it."

"We can. We're different. Oh—don't! Don't hold me like that. I can't bear it."

His arms tightened. His mouth found hers again as if he had not heard her.

She gave a faint cry that pierced him.

He looked at her. The lips he had kissed were a purplish white in her thin bloodless face. "I say, are you ill?"

She saw her advantage and took it.

"No. But I can't stand things very well. They make me ill. That's what I meant when I asked you to be careful."

Her helplessness stilled his passion as it had roused it. He released her suddenly.

He took the thin arm surrendered to his gentleness, turned back her sleeve and felt the tense jerking pulse.

He saw what she had meant.

"Do you mind my sitting beside you if I keep quiet?" She shook her head.

"Can you stand my talking about it?"

"Yes. If you don't touch me."

"I won't touch you. We've got to face the thing. It's making you ill."

"It isn't."

"What is, then?"

"Living with Papa."

He smiled through his agony. "That's only another name for it.

"It can't go on. Why shouldn't we be happy?

"Why shouldn't we?" he insisted. "It's not as if we hadn't tried."

"I—can't."

"You're afraid?"

"Oh, no, I'm not afraid. It's simply that I can't."

"You think it's a sin? It isn't. It's we who are sinned against.

"If you're afraid of deceiving Mary—I don't care if I do. She deceived me first. Besides we can't. She knows and she doesn't mind. She can't suffer as you suffer. She can't feel as you feel. She can't care."

"She does care. She must have cared horribly or she wouldn't have done it."

"She didn't. Anybody would have done for her as well as me. I tell you I don't want to talk about Mary or to think about her."

"Then I must."

"No. You must think of me. You don't owe anything to Mary. It's me you're sinning against. You think a lot about sinning against Mary, but you think nothing about sinning against me."

"When did I ever sin against you?"

"Last year. When you went away. That was the

beginning of it all. Why *did* you go, Gwenda? You knew. We should have been all right if you hadn't."

"I went because of Ally. She had to be married. I thought—perhaps—if I wasn't there——"

"That I'd marry her? Good God! Ally! What on earth made you think I'd do that? I wouldn't have married her if there hadn't been another woman in the world."

"I couldn't be sure. But after what you said about her I had to give her a chance."

"What *did* I say?"

"That she'd die or go mad if somebody didn't marry her."

"I never said that. I wouldn't be likely to."

"But you did, dear. You frightened me. So I went away to see if that would make it any better."

"Any better for whom?"

"For Ally."

"Oh—Ally. I see."

"I thought if it didn't—if you didn't marry her—I could come back again. And when I did come back you'd married Mary."

"And Mary knew that?"

"There's no good bothering about Mary now."

Utterly weary of their strife, she lay back and closed her eyes.

"Poor Gwenda."

Again he had compassion on her. He waited.

"You see how it was," she said.

"It doesn't help us much, dear. What are we going to do?"

"Not what you want, Steven, I'm afraid."

"Not now. But some day. You'll see it differently when you've thought of it."

"Never. Never any day. I've had all these months to think of it and I can't see it differently yet."

"You *have* thought of it?"

"Not like that."

"But you did think. You knew it would come to this."

"I tried not to make it come. Do you know why I tried? I don't think it was for Molly. It was for myself. It was because I wanted to keep you. That's why I shall never do what you want."

"But that's how you *would* keep me. There's no other way."

She rose with a sudden gesture of her shoulders as if she shook off the obsession of him.

She stood leaning against the chimney-piece in the attitude he knew, an attitude of long-limbed, insolent, adolescent grace that gave her the advantage. Her eyes disdained their pathos. They looked at him with laughter under their dropped lids.

"How funny we are," she said, "when we know all the time we couldn't really do a caddish thing like that."

He smiled queerly.

"I suppose we couldn't."

He too rose and faced her.

"Do you know what this means?" he said. "It means that I've got to clear out of this."

"Oh, Steven——" The brave light in her face went out.

"You wouldn't go away and leave me?"

"God knows I don't want to leave you, Gwenda. But we can't go on like this. How can we?"

"I could."

"Well, I can't. That's what it means to me. That's

what it means to a man. If we're going to be straight we simply mustn't see each other."

"Do you mean for always? That we're never to see each other again?"

"Yes, if it's to be any good."

"Steven, I can bear anything but that. It *can't* mean that."

"I tell you it's what it means for me. There's no good talking about it. You've seen what I've been like to-night."

"This? This is nothing. You'll get over this. But think what it would mean to me."

"It would be hard, I know."

"Hard?"

"Not half so hard as this."

"But I can bear this. We've been so happy. We can be happy still."

"This isn't happiness."

"It's *my* happiness. It's all I've got. It's all I've ever had."

"What is?"

"Seeing you. Or not even seeing you. Knowing you're there."

"Poor child. Does that make you happy?"

"Utterly happy. Always."

"I didn't know."

He stooped forward, hiding his face in his hands.

"You don't realise it. You've no idea what it'll mean to be boxed up in this place together, all our lives, with this between us."

"It's always been between us. We shall be no worse off. It may have been bad now and then, but conceive what it'll be like when you go."

"I suppose it would be pretty beastly for you if I did go."

"Would it be too awful for you if you stayed?"

He was a long time before he answered.

"Not if it really made you happier."

"Happier?"

She smiled her pitiful, strained smile. It said, "Don't you see that it would kill me if you went?"

And again it was by her difference, her helplessness, that she had him.

He too smiled drearily.

"You don't suppose I really could have left you?"

He saw that it was impossible, unthinkable, that he should leave her.

He rose. She went with him to the door. She thought of something there.

"Steven," she said, "don't worry about to-night. It was all my fault."

"You—you," he murmured. "You're adorable."

"It was really," she said. "I made you come in."

She gave him her cold hand. He raised it and brushed it with his lips and put it from him.

"Your little conscience was always too tender."

LV

Two years passed.

Life stirred again in the Vicarage, feebly and slowly, with the slow and feeble stirring of the Vicar's brain.

Ten o'clock was prayer time again.

Twice every Sunday the Vicar appeared in his seat in the chancel. Twice he pronounced the Absolution. Twice he tottered to the altar rails, turned, shifted his stick from his left hand to his right, and, with his one good arm raised, he gave the Benediction. These were the supreme moments of his life.

Once a month, kneeling at the same altar rails, he received the bread and wine from the hands of his ritualistic curate, Mr. Grierson.

It was his uttermost abasement.

But, whether he was abased or exalted, the parish was proud of its Vicar. He had shown grit. His parishioners respected the indestructible instinct that had made him hold on.

For Mr. Cartaret was better, incredibly better. He could creep about the house and the village without any help but his stick. He could wash and feed and dress himself. He had no longer any use for his wheel-chair. Once a week, on a Wednesday, he was driven over his parish in an ancient pony carriage of Peacock's. It was low enough for him to haul himself in and out.

And he had recovered large tracts of memory, all, apparently, but the one spot submerged in the catastrophe that had brought about his stroke. He was aware of events and of their couplings and of their sequences in time, though the origin of some things was not clear to him. Thus he knew that Alice was married and living at Upthorne, though he had forgotten why. That she should have married Greatorex was a strange thing, and he couldn't think how it had happened. He supposed it must have happened when he was laid aside, for he would never have permitted it if he had known. Mary's marriage also puzzled him, for he had a most distinct idea that it was Gwenda who was to have married Rowcliffe, and he said so. But he would own humbly that he might be mistaken, his memory not being what it was.

He had settled more or less into his state of gentleness and submission, broken from time to time by fits of violent irritation and relieved by pride, pride in his feats of independence, his comings and goings, his washing, his dressing and undressing of himself. Sometimes this pride was stubborn and insistent; sometimes it was sweet and joyous as a child's. His mouth, relaxed forever by his stroke, had acquired a smile of piteous and appealing innocence. It smiled upon the just and upon the unjust. It smiled even on Greatorex, whom socially he disapproved of (he took care to let it be known that he disapproved of Greatorex socially), though he tolerated him.

He tolerated all persons except one. And that one was the ritualistic curate, Mr. Grierson.

He had every reason for not tolerating him. Not only was Mr. Grierson a ritualist, which was only less abominable than being a non-conformist, but he had been foisted on him without his knowledge or will. The Vicar had simply waked up one day out of his confused twilight to a state of fearful lucidity and found the young man there.

Worse than all it was through the third Mrs. Cartaret that he had got there.

For the Vicar of Greffington had applied to the Additional Curates Aid Society for a grant on behalf of his afflicted brother, the Vicar of Garthdale, and he had applied in vain. There was a prejudice against the Vicar of Garthdale. But the Vicar of Greffington did not relax his efforts. He applied to young Mrs. Rowcliffe, and young Mrs. Rowcliffe applied to her step-mother, and not in vain. Robina, answering by return of post, offered to pay half the curate's salary. Rowcliffe made himself responsible for the other half.

Robina, in her compact little house in St. John's Wood, had become the prey of remorse. Her conscience had begun to bother her by suggesting that she ought to go back to her husband now that he was helpless and utterly inoffensive. She ought not to leave him on poor Gwenda's hands. She ought, at any rate, to take her turn.

But Robina couldn't face it. She couldn't leave her compact little house and go back to her husband. She couldn't even take her turn. Flesh and blood shrank from the awful sacrifice. It would be a living death. Your conscience has no business to send you to a living death.

Robina's heart ached for poor Gwenda. She wrote and said so. She said she knew she was a brute for not going back to Gwenda's father. She would do it if she could, but she simply couldn't. She hadn't got the nerve.

And Robina did more. She pulled wires and found the curate. That he was a ritualist was no drawback in Robina's eyes. In fact, she declared it was a positive advantage. Mr. Grierson's practices would wake them up in Garthdale. They needed waking. She had added that Mr. Grierson was well connected, well behaved and extremely good-looking.

Even charity couldn't subdue the merry devil in Robina.

"I can't see," said Mary reading Robina's letter, "what Mr. Grierson's good looks have got to do with it."

Rowcliffe's face darkened. He thought he could see.

But Mr. Grierson did not wake Garthdale up. It opened one astonished eye on his practices and turned over in its sleep again. Mr. Grierson was young, and the village regarded all he did as the folly of his youth. It saw no harm in Mr. Grierson; not even when he conceived a Platonic passion for Mrs. Steven Rowcliffe, and spent all his spare time in her drawing-room and on his way to and from it.

The curate lodged in the village at the Blenkirons' over Rowcliffe's surgery, and from that vantage ground he lay in wait for Rowcliffe. He watched his movements. He was ready at any moment to fling open his door and spring upon Rowcliffe with ardor and enthusiasm. It was as if he wanted to prove to him how heartily he forgave him for being Mrs. Rowcliffe's husband. There was a robust innocence about him that ignored the doctor's irony.

Mary had her own use for Mr. Grierson. His handsome figure, assiduous but restrained, the perfect image of integrity in adoration, was the very thing she wanted for her drawing-room. She knew that its presence there had the effect of heightening her own sensual attraction. It served as a reminder to Rowcliffe that his wife was a woman of charm, a fact which for some time he appeared to have forgotten. She could play off her adorer against her husband, while the candid purity of young Grierson's homage renewed her exquisite sense of her own goodness.

And then the Curate really was a cousin of Lord
Northfleet's and Mrs. Rowcliffe had calculated that to
have him in her pocket would increase prodigiously her
social value. And it did. And Mrs. Rowcliffe's social
value, when observed by Grierson, increased his adoration.

And when Rowcliffe told her that young Grierson's
Platonic friendship wasn't good for him, she made wide
eyes at him and said, "Poor boy! He must have *some*
amusement."

She didn't suppose the curate could be much amused
by calling at the Vicarage. Young Grierson had confided
to her that he couldn't "make her sister out."

"I never knew anybody who could," she said, and gave
him a subtle look that disturbed him horribly.

"I only meant——" He stammered and stopped, for
he wasn't quite sure what he did mean. His fair, fresh
face was strained with the effort to express himself.

He meditated.

"You know, she's really rather fascinating. You can't
help looking at her. Only—she doesn't seem to see that
you're there. I suppose that's what puts you off."

"I know. It does, dreadfully," said Mary.

She summoned a flash and let him have it. "But she's
magnificent."

"Magnificent!" he echoed with his robust enthusiasm.

But what he thought was that it was magnificent of
Mrs. Rowcliffe to praise her sister.

And Rowcliffe smiled grimly at young Grierson and
his Platonic passion. He said to himself, "If I'd only
known. If I'd only had the sense to wait six months.
Grierson would have done just as well for Molly."

Still, though Grierson had come too late, he welcomed
him and his Platonic passion. It wasn't good for Grierson but it was good for Molly. At least, he supposed it

was better for her than nothing. And for him it was
infinitely better. It kept Grierson off Gwenda.

Young Grierson was right when he said that Gwenda
didn't see that he was there. He had been two years in
Garthdale and she was as far from seeing it as ever. He
didn't mind; he was even amused by her indifference,
only he couldn't help thinking that it was rather odd of
her, considering that he *was* there.

The village, as simple in its thinking as young Grierson, shared his view. It thought that it was something
more than odd. And it had a suspicion that Mrs. Rowcliffe was at the bottom of it. She wouldn't be happy if
she didn't get that young man away from her sister. The
village hinted that it wouldn't be for the first time.

But in two years, with the gradual lifting of the pressure that had numbed her, Gwenda had become aware.
Not of young Grierson, but of her own tragedy, of the
slow life that dragged her, of its relentless motion and its
mass. Now that her father's need of her was intermittent, she was alive to the tightness of the tie. It had been
less intolerable when it had bound her tighter; when she
hadn't had a moment; when it had dragged her all the
time. Its slackening was torture. She pulled then, and
was jerked on her chain.

It was not only that Rowcliffe's outburst had waked
her and made her cruelly aware. He had timed it badly,
in her moment of revived lucidity, the moment when she
had become vulnerable again. She was the more sensitive because of her previous apathy, as if she had died and
was new-born to suffering and virgin to pain.

What hurt her most was her father's gentleness. She
could stand his fits of irritation and obstinacy; they

braced her, they called forth her will.   But she was defenseless against his pathos, and he knew it.   He had
phrases that wrung her heart.   "You're a good girl,
Gwenda."   "I'm only an irritable old man, my dear.
You mustn't mind what I say."   She suffered from the
incessant drain on her pity; for she wanted all her will
if she was to stand against Rowcliffe.   Pity was a dangerous solvent in which her will sank and was melted
away.

There were moments when she saw herself as two
women.   One had still the passion and the memory of
freedom.   The other was a cowed and captive creature
who had forgotten; whose cramped motions guided her;
whose instinct of submission she abhorred.

Her isolation was now extreme.   She had had nothing
to give to any friends she might have made.   Rowcliffe
had taken all that was left of her.   And now, when in-
tercourse was possible, it was they who had withdrawn.
They shared Mr. Grierson's inability to make her out.
They had heard rumors; they imagined things; they remembered also.   She was the girl who had raced all over
the country with Dr. Rowcliffe, the girl whom Dr. Rowcliffe, for all their racing, had not cared to marry.   She
was the girl who had run away from home to live with a
dubious step-mother; and she was the sister of that awful
Mrs. Greatorex, who—well, everybody knew what Mrs.
Greatorex was.

Gwenda Cartaret, like her younger sister, had been
talked about.   Not so much in the big houses of the Dale.
The queer facts had been tossed up and down a smoke-
room for one season and then dropped.   In the big houses
they didn't remember Gwenda Cartaret.   They only remembered to forget her.

But in the little shops and in the little houses in Morfe there had been continual whispering. They said that even after Dr. Rowcliffe's marriage to that nice wife of his, who was her own sister, the two had been carrying on. If there wasn't any actual harm done, and maybe there wasn't, the doctor had been running into danger. He was up at Garthdale more than he need be now that the old Vicar was about again. And they had been seen together. The head gamekeeper at Garthdale had caught them more than once out on the moor, and after dark too. It was said in the little houses that it wasn't the doctor's fault. (In the big houses judgment had been more impartial, but Morfe was loyal to its doctor.) It was hers, every bit, you might depend on it. Of Rowcliffe it was said that maybe he'd been tempted, but he was a good man, was Dr. Rowcliffe, and he'd stopped in time. Because they didn't know what Gwenda Cartaret was capable of, they believed, like the Vicar, that she was capable of anything.

It was only in her own village that they knew. The head gamekeeper had never told his tale in Garth. It would have made him too unpopular.

Gwenda Cartaret remained unaware of what was said. Rumor protected her by cutting her off from its own sources.

And she had other consolations besides her ignorance. So long as she knew that Rowcliffe cared for her and always had cared, it did not seem to matter to her so much that he had married Mary. She actually considered that, of the two, Mary was the one to be pitied; it was so infinitely worse to be married to a man who didn't care for you than not to be married to a man who did.

Of course, there was the tie. Her sister had outward

and visible possession of him. But she said to herself "I wouldn't give what I have for *that,* if I can't have both."

And of course there was Steven, and Steven's misery which was more unbearable to her than her own. At least she thought it was more unbearable. She didn't ask herself how bearable it would have been if Steven's marriage had brought him a satisfaction that denied her and cast her out.

For she was persuaded that Steven also had his consolation. He knew that she cared for him. She conceived this knowledge of theirs as constituting an immaterial and immutable possession of each other. And it did not strike her that this knowledge might be less richly compensating to Steven than to her.

Her woman's passion, forced inward, sustained her with an inward peace, an inward exaltation. And in this peace, this exaltation, it became one with her passion for the place.

She was unaware of what was happening in her. She did not know that her soul had joined the two beyond its own power to put asunder. She still looked on her joy in the earth as a solitary emotion untouched by any other. She still said to herself "Nothing can take this away from me."

For she had hours, now and again, when she shook off the slave-woman who held her down. In those hours her inner life moved with the large rhythm of the seasons and was soaked in the dyes of the visible world; and the visible world, passing into her inner life, took on its radiance and intensity. Everything that happened and that was great and significant in its happening, happened there.

Outside nothing happened; nothing stood out; nothing

moved.   No procession of events trod down or blurred
her perfect impressions of the earth and sky.   They eter-
nalised themselves in memory.   They became her memory.

The days were carved for her in the lines of the hills
and painted for her in their colors; days that were dim
green and gray, when the dreaming land was withdrawn
under a veil so fine that it had the transparency of water,
or when the stone walls, the humble houses and the high
ramparts, drenched with mist and with secret sunlight,
became insubstantial; days when all the hills were hewn
out of one opal; days that had the form of Karva under
snow, and the thin blues and violets of the snow.   She
remembered purely, without thinking, "It was in April
that I went away from Steven," or, "It was in November
that he married Mary," or "It was in February that we
knew about Ally, and Father had his stroke."

Her nature was sound and sane; it refused to brood
over suffering.   She was not like Alice and in her unlikeness she lacked some of Alice's resources.   She
couldn't fling herself on to a Polonaise of a Sonata any
more than she could lie on a couch all day and look at her
own white hands and dream.   Her passion found no outlet in creating violent and voluptuous sounds.   It was
passive, rather, and attentive.   Cut off from all contacts
of the flesh, it turned to the distant and the undreamed.
Its very senses became infinitely subtle; they discerned
the hidden soul of the land that had entranced her.

There were no words for this experience.   She had no
sense of self in it and needed none.   It seemed to her
that she *was* what she contemplated, as if all her senses
were fused together in the sense of seeing and what her
eyes saw they heard and touched and felt.

But when she came to and saw herself seeing, she said,

"At least this is mine. Nobody, not even Steven, can take it away from me."

She also reminded herself that she had Alice.

She meant Alice Greatorex. Alice Cartaret, oppressed by her own "awfulness," had loved her with a sullen selfish love, the love of a frustrated and unhappy child. But there was no awfulness in Alice Greatorex. In the fine sanity of happiness she showed herself as good as gold.

Marriage, that had made Mary hard, made Alice tender. Mary was wrapped up in her husband and her house, and in her social relations and young Grierson's Platonic passion, so tightly wrapped that these things formed round her an impenetrable shell. They hid a secret and inaccessible Mary.

Alice was wrapped up in her husband and children, in the boy of three who was so like Gwenda, and in the baby girl who was so like Greatorex. But through them she had become approachable. She had the ways of some happy household animal, its quick rushes of affection, and its gaze, the long, spiritual gaze of its maternity, mysterious and appealing. She loved Gwenda with a sad-eyed, remorseful love. She said to herself, "If I hadn't been so awful, Gwenda might have married Steven." She saw the appalling extent of Gwenda's sacrifice. She saw it as it was, monstrous, absurd, altogether futile.

It was the futility of it that troubled Alice most. Even if Gwenda had been capable of sacrificing herself for Mary, which had been by no means her intention, that would have been futile too. Alice was of Rowcliffe's opinion that young Grierson would have done every bit as well for Mary.

Better, for Mary had no children.

"And how," said Alice, "could she expect to have them?"

She saw in Mary's childlessness not only God's but Nature's justice.

There were moments when Mary saw it too. But she left God out of it and called it Nature's cruelty.

If it was not really Gwenda. For in flashes of extreme lucidity Mary put it down to Rowcliffe's coldness.

And she had come to know that Gwenda was responsible for that.

LVI

But one day in April, in the fourth year of her marriage, Mary sent for Gwenda.

Rowcliffe was out on his rounds. She had thought of that. She was fond of having Gwenda with her in Rowcliffe's absence, when she could talk to her about him in a way that assumed his complete indifference to Gwenda and utter devotion to herself. Gwenda was used to this habit of Mary's and thought nothing of it.

She found her in Rowcliffe's study, the room that she knew better than any other in his house. The window was closed. The panes cut up the colors of the orchard and framed them in small squares.

Mary received her with a gentle voice and a show of tenderness. She said very little. They had tea together, and when Gwenda would have gone Mary kept her.

She still said very little. She seemed to brood over some happy secret.

Presently she spoke. She told her secret.

And when she had told it she turned her eyes to Gwenda with a look of subtle penetration and of triumph.

"At last," she said,—"After three years."

And she added, "I knew you would be glad."

"I *am* glad," said Gwenda.

She *was* glad. She was determined to be glad. She looked glad. And she kissed Mary and said again that she was very glad.

But as she walked back the four miles up Garthdale

343

under Karva, she felt an aching at her heart which was odd considering how glad she was.

She said to herself, "I *will* be glad. I want Mary to be happy. Why shouldn't I be glad? It's not as if it could make any difference."

LVII

In September Mary sent for her again.

Mary was very ill. She lay on her bed, and Rowcliffe and her sister stood on either side of her. She gazed from one to the other with eyes of terror and entreaty. It was as if she cried out to them—the two who were so strong—to help her. She stretched out her arms on the counterpane, one arm toward each of them; her little hands, palm-upward, implored them.

Each of them laid a hand in Mary's hand that closed on it with a clutch of agony.

Rowcliffe had sat up all night with her His face was white and haggard and there was fear and misery in his eyes. They never looked at Gwenda's lest they should see the same fear and the same misery there. It was as if they had no love for each other, only a profound and secret pity that sprang in both of them from their fear.

Only once they found each other, outside on the landing, when they had left Mary alone with Hyslop, the old doctor from Reyburn, and the nurse. Each spoke once.

"Steven, is there really any danger?"

"Yes. I wish to God I'd had Harker. Do you mind sending him a wire? I must go and see what that fool Hyslop's doing."

He turned back again into the room.

Gwenda went out and sent the wire.

But at noon, before Harker could come to them, it was over. Mary lay as Alice had lain, weak and happy, with

345

her child tucked in the crook of her arm. And she smiled at it dreamily.

The old doctor and the nurse smiled at Rowcliffe.

It couldn't, they said, have gone off more easily. There hadn't been any danger, nor any earthly reason to have sent for Harker. Though, of course, if it had made Rowcliffe happier——!

The old doctor added that if it had been anybody else's wife Rowcliffe would have known that it was going all right.

And in the evening, when her sister stood again at her bedside, as Mary lifted the edge of the flannel that hid her baby's face, she looked at Gwenda and smiled, not dreamily but subtly in a triumph that was almost malign.

That night Gwenda dreamed that she saw Mary lying dead and with a dead child in the crook of her arm.

She woke in anguish and terror.

LVIII

THREE years passed and six months. The Cartarets had been in Garthdale nine years.

Gwenda Cartaret sat in the dining-room at the Vicarage alone with her father.

It was nearly ten o'clock of the March evening. They waited for the striking of the clock. It would be prayer time then, and after prayers the Vicar would drag himself upstairs to bed, and in the peace that slid into the room when he left it Gwenda would go on with her reading.

She had her sewing in her lap and her book, Bergson's *Évolution créatrice* propped open before her on the table. She sewed as she read. For the Vicar considered that sewing was an occupation and that reading was not. He was silent as long as his daughter sewed and when she read he talked. Toward ten his silence would be broken by a continual sighing and yearning. The Vicar longed for prayer time to come and end his day. But he had decreed that prayer time was ten o'clock and he would not have permitted it to come a minute sooner.

He nursed a book on his knees, but he made no pretence of reading it. He had taken off his glasses and sat with his hands folded, in an attitude of utter resignation to his own will.

In the kitchen Essy Gale sat by the dying fire and waited for the stroke of ten. And as she waited she stitched at the torn breeches of her little son.

347

Essy had come back to the house where she had been turned away. For her mother was wanted by Mrs. Greatorex at Upthorne and what Mrs. Greatorex wanted she got. There were two more children now at the Farm and work enough for three women in the house. And Essy, with all her pride, had not been too proud to come back. She had no feeling but pity for the old man, her master, who had bullied her and put her to shame. If it pleased God to afflict him that was God's affair, and, even as a devout Wesleyan, Essy considered that God had about done enough.

As Essy sat and stitched, she smiled, thinking of Greatorex's son who lay in her bed in the little room over the kitchen. Miss Gwenda let her have him with her on the nights when Mrs. Gale slept up at the Farm.

It was quiet in the Vicarage kitchen. The door into the back yard was shut, the door that Essy used to keep open when she listened for a footstep and a whisper. That door had betrayed her many a time when the wind slammed it to.

Essy's heart was quiet as the heart of her sleeping child. She had forgotten how madly it had leaped to her lover's footsteps, how it had staggered at the slamming of the door. She had forgotten the tears that she had shed when Alice's wild music had rocked the house, and what the Vicar had said to her that night when she spilled the glass of water in the study.

But she remembered that Gwenda had given her son his first little Sunday suit; and that, before Jimmy came, when Essy was in bed, crying with the face-ache, she had knocked at her door and said, "What is it, Essy? Can I do anything for you?" She could hear her saying it now.

Essy's memory was like that.

She had thought of Gwenda just then because she heard the sound of Dr. Rowcliffe's motor car tearing up the Dale.

The woman in the other room heard it too. She had heard its horn hooting on the moor road nearly a mile away.

She raised her hand and listened. It hooted again, once, twice, placably, at the turning of the road, under Karva. She shivered at the sound.

It hooted irritably, furiously, as the car tore through the village. Its lamps swung a shaft of light over the low garden wall.

At the garden gate the car made a shuddering pause.

Gwenda's face and all her body listened. A little unborn, undying hope quivered in her heart always at that pausing of the car at her gate.

It hardly gave her time for one heart-beat before she heard the grinding of the gear as the car took the steep hill to Upthorne.

But she was always taken in by it. She had always that insane hope that the course of things had changed and that Steven had really stopped at the gate and was coming to her.

It *was* insanity, for she knew that Rowcliffe would never come to see her in the evening now. After his outburst, more than five years ago, there was no use pretending to each other that they were safe. He had told her plainly that, if she wanted him to hold out, he must never be long alone with her at any time, and he must give up coming to see her late at night. It was much too risky.

"When I can come and see you *that* way," he had said,

"it'll mean that I've left off caring. But I'll look in every Wednesday if I can. Every Wednesday as long as I live."

He *had* come now and then, not on a Wednesday, but "that way." He had not been able to help it. But he had left longer and longer intervals between. And he had never come ("that way") since last year, when his second child was born.

Nothing but life or death would bring Rowcliffe out in his car after nightfall. Yet the thing had her every time. And it was as if her heart was ground with the grinding and torn with the tearing of the car.

Then she said to herself, "I must end it somehow. It's horrible to go on caring like this. He was right. It would be better not to see him at all."

And she began counting the days and the hours till Wednesday when she would see him.

LIX

WEDNESDAY was still the Vicar's day for visiting his
parish. It was also Rowcliffe's day for visiting his
daughter. But the Vicar was not going to change it on
that account. On Wednesday, if it was a fine afternoon,
she was always sure of having Rowcliffe to herself.

Rowcliffe himself had become the creature of unalter-
able habit.

She was conscious now of the normal pulse of time, a
steady pulse that beat with a large rhythm, a measure
of seven days, from Wednesday to Wednesday.

She filled the days between with reading and walking
and parish work.

There had been changes in Garthdale. Mr. Grierson
had got married in one of his bursts of enthusiasm and
had gone away. His place had been taken by Mr. Macey,
the strenuous son of a Durlingham grocer. Mr. Macey
had got into the Church by sheer strenuousness and had
married, strenuously, a sharp and sallow wife. Between
them they left very little parish work for Gwenda.

She had become a furious reader. She liked hard stuff
that her brain could bite on. It fell on a book and gutted
it, throwing away the trash. She read all the modern
poets and novelists she cared about, English and foreign.
They left her stimulated but unsatisfied. There were
not enough good ones to keep her going. She worked
through the Elizabethan dramatists and all the Vicar's
Tudor Classics, and came on Jowett's Translations of the

351

Platonic Dialogues by the way, and was lured on the quest of Ultimate Reality, and found that there was nothing like Thought to keep you from thinking. She took to metaphysics as you take to dram-drinking. She must have strong, heavy stuff that drugged her brain. And when she found that she could trust her intellect she set it deliberately to fight her passion.

At first it was an even match, for Gwenda's intellect, like her body, was robust. It generally held its ground from Thursday morning till Tuesday night. But the night that followed Wednesday afternoon would see its overthrow.

This Wednesday it fought gallantly till the very moment of Steven's arrival. She was still reading Bergson, and her brain struggled to make out the sense and rhythm of the sentences across the beating of her heart.

After seven years her heart still beat at Steven's coming.

It remained an excitement and adventure, for she never knew how he would be. Sometimes he hadn't a word to say to her and left her miserable. Sometimes, after a hard day's work, he would be tired and heavy; she saw him middle-aged and her heart would ache for him. Sometimes he would be young almost as he used to be. She knew that he was only young for her. He was young because he loved her. She had never seen him so with Mary. Simetimes he would be formal and frigid. He talked to her as a man talks to a woman he is determined to keep at a distance. She hated Steven then, as passion hates. He had come before now in a downright bad temper and was the old, irritable Steven who found fault with everything she said and did. And she had loved him for it as she had loved the old Steven. It was his queer way of showing that he loved her.

But he had not been like that for a very long time. He had grown gentler as he had grown older.

To-day he showed her more than one of his familiar moods. She took them gladly as so many signs of his unchanging nature.

He still kept up his way of coming in, the careful closing of the door, the slight pause there by the threshold, the look that sought her and that held her for an instant before their hands met.

She saw it still as the look that pleaded with her while it caressed her, that said, "I know we oughtn't to be so pleased to see each other, but we can't help it, can we?"

It was the look of his romantic youth.

As long as she saw it there it was nothing to her that Rowcliffe had changed physically, that he moved more heavily, that his keenness and his slenderness were going, that she saw also a slight thickening of his fine nose, a perceptible slackening of the taut muscles of his mouth, and a decided fulness about his jaw and chin. She saw all these things; but she did not see that his romantic youth lay dying in the pathos of his eyes and that if it pleaded still it pleaded forgiveness for the sin of dying.

His hand fell slackly from hers as she took it.

It was as if they were still on their guard, still afraid of each other's touch.

As he sat in the chair that faced hers he held his hands clasped loosely in front of him, and looked at them with a curious attention, as if he wondered what kind of hands they were that could resist holding her.

When he saw that she was looking at him they fell apart with a nervous gesture.

They picked up the book she had laid down and turned it. His eyes examined the title page. Their pathos lightened and softened: it became compassion; they

smiled at her with a little pitiful smile, half tender, half
ironic, as if they said, "Poor Gwenda, is that what you're
driven to?"

He opened the book and turned the pages, reading a
little here and there.

He scowled. His look changed. It darkened. It was
angry, resentful, inimical. The dying youth in it came
a little nearer to death.

Rowcliffe had found that he could not understand what
he had read.

"Huh! What do you addle your brains with that stuff
for?" he said.

"It amuses me."

"Oh—so long as you're amused."

He pushed away the book that had offended him.

They talked—about the Vicar, about Alice, about
Rowcliffe's children, about the changes in the Dale, the
coming of the Maceys and the going of young Grierson.

"He wasn't a bad chap, Grierson."

He softened, remembering Grierson.

"I can't think why you didn't care about him."

And at the thought of how Gwenda might have cared
for Grierson and hadn't cared his youth revived; it came
back into his eyes and lit them; it passed into his scowling face and caressed and smoothed it to the perfect look
of reminiscent satisfaction. Rowcliffe did not know,
neither did she, how his egoism hung upon her passion,
how it drew from it food and fire.

He raised his head and squared his shoulders with the
unconscious gesture of his male pride.

It was then that she saw for the first time that he wore
the black tie and had the black band of mourning on his
sleeve.

"Oh Steven—what do you wear that for?"

"This? My poor old uncle died last week."

"Not the one I saw?"

"When?"

"At Mary's wedding."

"No. Another one. My father's brother."

He paused.

"It's made a great difference to me and Mary."

He said it gravely, mournfully almost. She looked at him with tender eyes.

"I'm sorry, Steven."

He smiled faintly.

"Sorry, are you?"

"Yes. If you cared for him."

"I'm afraid I didn't very much. It's not as if I'd seen a lot of him."

"You said it's made a difference."

"So it has. He's left me a good four hundred a year."

"Oh—*that* sort of difference."

"My dear girl, four hundred a year makes all the difference; it's no use pretending that it doesn't."

"I'm not pretending. You sounded sorry and I was sorry for you. That was all."

At that his egoism winced. It was as if she had accused him of pretending to be sorry.

He looked at her sharply. His romantic youth died in that look.

Silence fell between them. But she was used to that. She even welcomed it. Steven's silences brought him nearer to her than his speech.

Essy came in with the tea-tray.

He lingered uneasily after the meal, glancing now and then at the clock. She was used to that, too. She also had her eyes on the clock, measuring the priceless moments.

"Is anything worrying you, Steven?" she said presently.

"Why? Do I look worried?"

"Not exactly, but you don't look well."

"I'm getting a bit rusty. That's what's the matter with me. I want some hard work to rub me up and put a polish on me and I can't get it here. I've never had enough to do since I left Leeds. Harker was a wise chap to stick to it. It would do me all the good in the world if I went back."

"Then," she said, "you'll *have* to go, Steven."

She did not know, in her isolation, that Rowcliffe had been going about saying that sort of thing for the last seven years. She thought it was the formidable discovery of time.

"You ought to go if you feel like that about it. Why don't you?"

"I don't know."

"You *do* know."

She did not look at him as she spoke, so she missed his bewilderment.

"You know why you stayed, Steven."

He understood. He remembered. The dull red of his face flushed with the shock of the memory.

"Do I?" he said.

"I made you."

His flush darkened. But he gave no other sign of having heard her.

"I don't know why I'm staying now."

He rose and looked at his watch.

"I must be going home," he said.

He turned at the threshold.

"I forgot to give you Mary's message. She sent her love and she wants to know when you're coming again to see the babies."

"Oh—some day soon."

"You must make it very soon or they won't be babies any more. She's dying to show them to you."

"She showed them to me the other day."

"She says it's ages since you've been. And if she says it is she thinks it is."

Gwenda was silent.

"I'm coming all right, tell her."

"Well, but what day? We'd better fix it. Don't come on a Tuesday or a Friday, I'll be out."

"I must come when I can."

LX

SHE went on a Tuesday.

She had had tea with her father first. Meal-time had become sacred to the Vicar and he hated her to be away for any one of them.

She walked the four miles, going across the moor under Karva and loitering by the way, and it was past six before she reached Morfe.

She was shown into the room that was once Rowcliffe's study. It had been Mary's drawing-room ever since last year when the second child was born and they turned the big room over the dining-room into a day nursery. Mary had made it snug and gay with cushions and shining, florid chintzes. There were a great many things in rose-wood and brass; a piano took the place of Rowcliffe's writing table; a bureau and a cabinet stood against the wall where his bookcases had been; and a tall palm-tree in a pot filled the little window that looked on to the orchard.

She had only to close her eyes and shut out these objects and she saw the room as it used to be. She closed them now and instantly she opened them again, for the vision hurt her.

She went restlessly about the room, picking up things and looking at them without seeing them.

In the room upstairs she heard the cries of Rowcliffe's children, bumping and the scampering of feet. She stood still then and clenched her hands. The pain at her heart

358

was like no other pain. It was as if she hated Rowcliffe's children.

Presently she would have to go up and see them.

She waited. Mary was taking her own time.

Upstairs the doors opened and shut on the sharp grief
of little children carried unwillingly to bed.

Gwenda's heart melted and grew tender at the sound.
But its tenderness was more unbearable to her than its
pain.

The maid-servant came to the door.

"Mrs. Rowcliffe says will you please go upstairs to the
night nursery, Miss Gwenda. She can't leave the children."

That was the message Mary invariably sent. She left
the children for hours together when other visitors were
there. She could never leave them for a minute when
her sister came. Unless Steven happened to be in.
Then Mary would abandon whatever she was doing and
hurry to the two. In the last year Gwenda had never
found herself alone with Steven for ten minutes in his
house. If Mary couldn't come at once she sent the nurse
in with the children.

Upstairs in the night nursery Mary sat in the nurse's
low chair. Her year-old baby sprawled naked in her
lap. The elder infant stood whining under the nurse's
hands.

Mary had changed a little in three and a half years.
She was broader and stouter; the tender rose had hardened over her high cheek bones. Her face still kept its
tranquil brooding, but her slow gray eyes had a secret
tremor, they were almost alert, as if she were on the
watch.

And Mary's mouth, with its wide, turned back lips, had

lost its subtlety, it had coarsened slightly and loosened, under her senses' continual content.

Gwenda brushed Mary's mouth lightly with the winged arch of her upper lip. Mary laughed.

"You don't know how to kiss," she said. "If you're going to treat Baby that way, and Molly too——"

Gwenda stooped over the soft red down of the baby's head. To Gwenda it was as if her heart kept her hands off Rowcliffe's children, as if her flesh shrank from their flesh while her lips brushed theirs in tenderness and repulsion.

But seeing them was always worse in anticipation than reality.

For there was no trace of Rowcliffe in his children. The little red-haired, white-faced things were all Cartaret. Molly, the elder, had a look of Ally, sullen and sickly, as if some innermost reluctance had held back the impulse that had given it being. Even the younger child showed fragile as if implacable memory had come between it and perfect life.

Gwenda did not know why her fierceness was appeased by this unlikeness, nor why she wanted to see Mary and nothing but Mary in Rowcliffe's children, nor why she refused to think of them as his; she only knew that to see Rowcliffe in Mary's children would have been more than her flesh and blood could bear.

"You've come just in time to see Baby in her bath," said Mary.

"I seem to be always in time for that."

"Well, you're not in time to see Steven. He won't be home till nine at least."

"I didn't expect to see him. He told me he'd be out."

She saw the hidden watcher in Mary's eyes looking out at her.

"When did he tell you that?"

"Last Wednesday."

The watcher hid again, suddenly appeased.

Mary busied herself with the washing of her babies. She did it thoroughly and efficiently, with no sentimental tendernesses, but with soft, sensual pattings and strokings of the white, satin-smooth skins.

And when they were tucked into their cots and disposed of for the night Mary turned to Gwenda.

"Come into my room a minute," she said.

Mary's joy was to take her sister into her room and watch her to see if she would flinch before the signs of Steven's occupation. She drew her attention to these if Gwenda seemed likely to miss any of them.

"We've had the beds turned," she said. "The light hurt Steven's eyes. I can't say I like sleeping with my head out in the middle of the room."

"Why don't you lie the other way then?"

"My dear, Steven wouldn't like that. Oh, what a mess my hair's in!"

She turned to the glass and smoothed her disordered waves and coils, while she kept her eyes fixed on Gwenda's image there, appraising her clothes, her slenderness and straightness, the set of her head on her shoulders, the air that she kept up of almost insolent adolescence. She noted the delicate lines on her forehead and at the corners of her eyes; she saw that her small defiant face was still white and firm, and that her eyes looked violet blue with the dark shadows under them.

Time was the only power that had been good to Gwenda.

"She ought to look more battered," Mary thought. "She *does* carry it off well. And she's only two years younger than I am.

"It's her figure, really, not her face. She's got more lines than I have. But if I wore that long straight coat I should look awful in it."

"It's all very well for you," she said. "You haven't had two children."

"No. I haven't. But what's all very well?"

"The good looks you contrive to keep, my dear. Nobody would know you were thirty-three."

"*I* shouldn't, Molly, if you didn't remind me every time."

Mary flushed.

"You'll say next that's why you don't come."

"Why—I—don't come?"

"Yes. It's ages since you've been here."

That was always Mary's cry.

"I haven't much time, Molly, for coming on the offchance."

"The off chance! As if I'd never asked you! You can go to Alice."

"Poor Ally wouldn't have anybody to show the baby to if I didn't. You haven't seen one of Ally's babies."

"I can't, Gwenda. I must think of the children. I can't let them grow up with little Greatorexes. There are three of them, aren't there?"

"Didn't you know there's been another?"

"Steven *did* tell me. She had rather a bad time, hadn't she?"

"She had. Molly—it wouldn't do you any harm now to go and see her. I think it's horrid of you not to. It's such rotten humbug. Why, you used to say *I* was ten times more awful than poor little Ally."

"There are moments, Gwenda, when I think you are."

"Moments? You always did think it. You think it still. And yet you'll have me here but you won't have

her. Just because she's gone a technical howler and I
haven't."

"You haven't. But you'd have gone a worse one if
you'd had the chance."

Gwenda raised her head.

"You know, Molly, that that isn't true."

"I said if. I suppose you think you had your chance,
then?"

"I don't think anything. Except that I've got to go."

"You haven't. You're going to stay for dinner now
you're here."

"I can't, really, Mary."

But Mary was obstinate. Whether her sister stayed or
went she made it hard for her. She kept it up on the
stairs and at the door and at the garden gate.

"Perhaps you'll come some night when Steven's here.
You know he's always glad to see you."

The sting of it was in Mary's watching eyes. For,
when you came to think of it, there was nothing else she
could very well have said.

LXI

THAT year, when spring warmed into summer, Gwenda's strength went from her.

She was always tired. She fought with her fatigue and got the better of it, but in a week or two it returned. Rowcliffe told her to rest and she rested, for a day or two, lying on the couch in the dining-room where Ally used to lie, and when she felt better she crawled out on to the moor and lay there.

One day she said to herself, "There's Ally. I'll go and see how she's getting on."

She dragged herself up the hill to Upthorne.

It was a day of heat and hidden sunlight. The moor and the marshes were drenched in the gray June mist. The hillside wore soft vapor like a cloak hiding its nakedness.

At the top of the Three Fields the nave of the old barn showed as if lifted up and withdrawn into the distance. But it was no longer solitary. The thorn-tree beside it had burst into white flower; it shimmered far-off under the mist in the dim green field, like a magic thing, half-hidden and about to disappear, remaining only for the hour of its enchantment.

It gave her the same subtle and mysterious joy that she had had on the night she and Rowcliffe walked together and saw the thorn-trees on Greffington Edge white under the hidden moon.

The gray Farm-house was changed, for Jim Greatorex had got on. He had built himself another granary on the

364

north side of the mistal. He built it long and low, of
hewn stone, with a corrugated iron roof. And he had
made himself two fine new rooms, a dining-room and a
nursery, one above the other, within the blind walls of the
house where the old granary had been. The walls were
blind no longer, for he had knocked four large windows
out of them. And it was as if one-half of the house were
awake and staring while the other half, in its old and
alien beauty, dozed and dreamed under its scowling
mullions.

As Gwenda came to it she wondered how the Farm
could ever have seemed sinister and ghost-haunted; it
had become so entirely the place of happy life.

Loud noises came from the open windows of the dining-
room where the family were at tea; the barking of dogs,
the competitive laughter of small children, a gurgling
and crowing and spluttering; with now and then the sudden delicate laughter of Ally and the bellowing of Jim.

"Oh—there's Gwenda!" said Ally.

Jim stopped between a bellowing and a choking, for his
mouth was full.

"Ay—it's 'er."

He washed down his mouthful. "Coom, Ally, and
open door t' 'er."

But Ally did not come. She had her year-old baby on
her knees and was feeding him.

At the door of the old kitchen Jim grasped his sister-
in-law by the hand.

"Thot's right," he said. "Yo've joost coom in time
for a cup o' tae. T' misses is in there wi' t' lil uns."

He jerked his thumb toward his dining-room and led
the way there.

Jim was not quite so alert and slender as he had been.
He had lost his savage grace. But he moved with his old

directness and dignity, and he still looked at you with his pathetic, mystic gaze.

Ally was contrite; she raised her face to her sister to be kissed. "I can't get up," she said, "I'm feeding Baby. He'd howl if I left off."

"I'd let 'im howl. I'd spank him ef 'twas me," said Jim.

"He wouldn't, Gwenda."

"Ay, thot I would. An' 'e knows it, doos Johnny, t' yoong rascal."

Gwenda kissed the four children; Jimmy, and Gwendolen Alice, and little Steven and the baby John. They lifted little sticky faces and wiped them on Gwenda's face, and the happy din went on.

Ally didn't seem to mind it. She had grown plump and pink and rather like Mary without her subtlety. She sat smiling, tranquil among the cries of her offspring.

Jim turned three dogs out into the yard by way of discipline. He and Ally tried to talk to each other across the tumult that remained. Now and then Ally and the children talked to Gwenda. They told her that the black and white cow had calved, and that the blue lupins had come up in the garden, that the old sow had died, that Jenny, the chintz cat, had kittened and that the lop-eared rabbit had a litter.

"And Baby's got another tooth," said Ally.

"I'm breaakin' in t' yoong chestnut," said Jim. "Poor Daasy's gettin' paasst 'er work."

All these happenings were exciting and wonderful to Ally.

"But you're not interested, Gwenda."

"I am, darling, I am."

She was. Ally knew it but she wanted perpetual reassurance.

"But you never tell us anything."

"There's nothing to tell. Nothing happens."

"Oh, come," said Ally, "how's Papa?"

"Much the same except that he drove into Morfe yesterday to see Molly."

"Yes, darling, of course you may."

Ally was abstracted, for Gwenny had slipped from her chair and was whispering in her ear.

It never occurred to Ally to ask what Gwenda had been doing, or what she had been thinking of, or what she felt, or to listen to anything she had to say.

Her sister might just as well not have existed for all the interest Ally showed in her. She hadn't really forgotten what Gwenda had done for her, but she couldn't go on thinking about it forever. It was the sort of thing that wasn't easy or agreeable to think about and Ally's instinct of self-preservation urged her to turn from it. She tended to forget it, as she tended to forget all dreadful things, such as her own terrors and her father's illness and the noises Greatorex made when he was eating.

Gwenda was used to this apathy of Ally's and it had never hurt her till to-day. To-day she wanted something from Ally. She didn't know what it was exactly, but it was something Ally hadn't got.

She only said, "Have you seen the thorn-trees on Greffington Edge?"

And Ally never answered. She was heading off a stream of jam that was creeping down Stevey's chin to plunge into his neck.

"Gwenda's aasskin' yo 'ave yo seen t' thorn-trees on Greffington Edge," said Greatorex. He spoke to Ally as if she were deaf.

She made a desperate effort to detach herself from Stevey.

"The thorn-trees? Has anybody set fire to them?"

"Tha silly laass!——"

"What about the thorn-trees, Gwenda?"

"Only that they're all in flower," Gwenda said.

She didn't know where it had come from, the sudden impulse to tell Ally about the beauty of the thorn-trees.

But the impulse had gone. She thought sadly, "They want me. But they don't want me for myself. They don't want to talk to me. They don't know what to say. They don't know anything about me. They don't care—really. Jim likes me because I've stuck to Ally. Ally loves me because I would have given Steven to her. They love what I was, not what I am now, nor what I shall be.

"They have nothing for me."

It was Jim who answered her. "I knaw," he said, "I knaw."

"Oh! You little, little—lamb!"

Baby John had his fingers in his mother's hair.

Greatorex rose. "You'll not get mooch out o' Ally as long as t' kids are about. Yo'd best coom wi' mae into t' garden and see t' loopins."

She went with him.

He was silent as they threaded the garden path together. She thought, "I know why I like him."

They came to a standstill at the south wall where the tall blue lupins rose between them, vivid in the tender air and very still.

Greatorex also was still. His eyes looked away over the blue spires of the lupins to the naked hillside. They saw neither the hillside nor anything between.

When he spoke his voice was thick, almost as though he were in love or intoxicated.

"I knaw what yo mane about those thorn-trees. 'Tisn' no earthly beauty what yo see in 'em."

"Jim," she said, "shall I always see it?"

"I dawn—knaw. It cooms and it goas, doos sech-like."

"What makes it come?"

"What maakes it coom? Yo knaw better than I can tall yo."

"If I only did know. I'm afraid it's going."

"I can tell yo this for your coomfort. Ef yo soofer enoof mebbe it'll coom t' yo again. Ef yo're snoog and 'appy sure's death it'll goa."

He paused.

"It 'assn't coom t' mae sence I married Ally."

She was wrong about Jim. He had not forgotten her. He was not saying these things for himself; he was saying them for her, getting them out of himself with pain and difficulty. It was odd to think that nobody but she understood Jim, and that nobody but Jim had ever really understood her. Steven didn't understand her, any more than Ally understood her husband. And it made no difference to her, and it made no difference to Jim.

"I'll tell yo anoother quare thing. 'T' assn't got mooch t' do wi' good and baad. T' drink 'll nat drive it from yo, an' sin'll nat drive it from yo. Saw I raakon 't is mooch t' saame thing as t' graace o' Gawd."

"Did the grace of God go away from you when you married, Jim?"

"Mebbe t' would 'aave ef I'd roon aaffter it. 'Tis a tricky thing is Gawd's graace."

"But *it's* gone," she said. "You gave your *soul* for Ally when you married her."

He smiled. "I toald 'er I'd give my sawl t' marry 'er," he said.

LXII

As she went home she tried to recapture the magic of the flowering thorn-trees. But it had gone and she could not be persuaded that it would come again. She was still too young to draw joy from the memory of joy, and what Greatorex had told her seemed incredible.

She said to herself, "Is it going to be taken from me like everything else?"

And a dreadful duologue went on in her.

"It looks like it."

"But it *was* mine. It was mine like nothing else."

"It never had anything for you but what you gave it."

"Am I to go on giving the whole blessed time? Am I never to have anything for myself?"

"There never is anything for anybody but what they give. Or what they take from somebody else. You should have taken. You had your chance."

"I'd have died, rather."

"Do you call this living?"

"I *have* lived."

"He hasn't. Why did you sacrifice him?"

"For Mary."

"It wasn't for Mary. It was for yourself. For your own wretched soul."

"For *his* soul."

"How much do you suppose Mary cares about his soul? It would have had a chance with you. Its one chance."

The unconsoling voice had the last word. For it was

370

not in answer to it that a certain phrase came into her brooding mind.

"I couldn't do a caddish thing like that."

It puzzled her. She had said it to Steven that night. But it came to her now attached to an older memory. Somebody had said it to her before then. Years before.

She remembered. It was Ally.

LXIII

A YEAR passed. It was June again.

For more than a year there had been rumors of changes in Morfe. The doctor talked of going. He was always talking of going and nobody had yet believed that he would go. This time, they said, he was serious, it had been a toss-up whether he stayed or went. But in the end he stayed. Things had happened in Rowcliffe's family. His mother had died and his wife had had a son.

Rowcliffe's son was the image of Rowcliffe.

The doctor had no brothers or sisters, and by his mother's death he came into possession both of his father's income and of hers. He had now more than a thousand a year over and above what he earned.

On an unearned thousand a year you can live like a rich man in Rathdale.

Not that Rowcliffe had any idea of giving up. He was well under forty and as soon as old Hyslop at Reyburn died or retired he would step into his practice. He hadn't half enough to do in Morfe and he wanted more.

Meanwhile he had bought the house that joined on to his own and thrown the two and their gardens into one. They had been one twenty years ago, when the wide-fronted building, with its long rows of windows, was the dominating house in Morfe village. Rowcliffe was now the dominating man in it. He had given the old place back its own.

And he had spent any amount of money on it. He

had had all the woodwork painted white, and the whole house repapered and redecorated. He had laid down parquet flooring in the big square hall that he had made and in the new drawing-room upstairs; and he had bought a great deal of beautiful and expensive furniture.

And now he was building a garage and laying out a croquet ground and tennis lawns at the back.

He and Mary had been superintending these works all afternoon till a shower sent them indoors. And now they were sitting together in the drawing-room, in the breathing-space that came between the children's hour and dinner.

Mary had sent the children back to the nursery a little earlier than usual. Rowcliffe had complained of headache.

He was always complaining of headaches. They dated from his marriage, and more particularly from one night in June eight years ago.

But Rowcliffe ignored the evidence of dates. He ignored everything that made him feel uncomfortable. He had put Gwenda from him. He had said plainly to Mary (in one poignant moment not long before the birth of their third child), "If you're worrying about me and Gwenda, you needn't. She was never anything to me."

That was not saying there had never been anything between them, but Mary knew what he had meant.

He said to himself, and Mary said that he had got over it. But he hadn't got over it. He might say to himself and Mary, "She was never anything to me"; he might put her and the thought of her away from him, but she had left her mark on him. He hadn't put her away. She was there, in his heavy eyes and in the irritable gestures of his hands, in his nerves and in his wounded memory. She had knitted herself into his secret being.

Mary was unaware of the cause of his malady. If it had been suggested to her that he had got into this state because of Gwenda she would have dismissed the idea with contempt. She didn't worry about Rowcliffe's state. On the contrary, Rowcliffe's state was a consolation and a satisfaction to her for all that she had endured through Gwenda. She would have thought you mad if you had told her so, for she was sorry for Steven and tender to him when he was nervous or depressed. But to Mary her sorrow and her tenderness were a voluptuous joy. She even encouraged Rowcliffe in his state. She liked to make it out worse than it really was, so that he might be more dependent on her.

And she had found that it could be induced in him by suggestion. She had only to say to him, "Steven, you're thoroughly worn out," and he *was* thoroughly worn out. She had more pleasure, because she had more confidence, in this lethargic, middle-aged Rowcliffe than in Rowcliffe young and energetic. His youth had attracted him to Gwenda and his energy had driven him out of doors. And Mary had set herself, secretly, insidiously, to destroy them.

It had taken her seven years.

For the first five years it had been hard work for Mary. It had meant, for her body, an ignominious waiting and watching for the moment when its appeal would be irresistible, for her soul a complete subservience to her husband's moods, and for her mind perpetual attention to his comfort, a thousand cares that had seemed to go unnoticed. But in the sixth year they had begun to tell. Once Rowcliffe had made up his mind that Gwenda couldn't be anything to him he had let go and through sheer exhaustion had fallen more and more into his wife's

hands, and for the last two years her labor had been easy
and its end sure.

She had him, bound to her bed and to her fireside.

He said and thought that he was happy. He meant
that he was extremely comfortable.

"Is your head very bad, Steven?"

He shook his head. It wasn't very bad, but he was
worried. He was worried about himself.

From time to time his old self rose against this new
self that was the slave of comfort. It made desperate
efforts to shake off the strangling lethargy. When he
went about saying that he was getting rusty, that he ought
never to have left Leeds, and that it would do him all the
good in the world to go back there, he was saying what
he knew to be the truth. The life he was leading was
playing the devil with his nerves and brain. His brain
had nothing to do. Hard work might not be the cure for
every kind of nervous trouble, but it was the one cure for
the kind that he had got.

He ought to have gone away seven years ago. It was
Gwenda's fault that he hadn't gone. He felt a dull anger
against her as against a woman who had wrecked his
chance.

He had a chance of going now if he cared to take it.

He had had a letter that morning from Dr. Harker
asking if he had meant what he had said a year ago, and
if he'd care to exchange his Rathdale practice for his old
practice in Leeds. Harker's wife was threatened with
lung trouble, and they would have to live in the country
somewhere, and Harker himself wouldn't be sorry for the
exchange. His present practice was worth twice what it
had been ten years ago and it was growing. There were

all sorts of interesting things to be done in Leeds by a man of Rowcliffe's keenness and energy.

"Do you know, Steven, you're getting quite stout?"

"I do know," he said almost with bitterness.

"I don't mean horridly stout, dear, just nicely and comfortably stout."

"I'm *too* comfortable," he said. "I don't do enough work to keep me fit."

"Is that what's bothering you?"

He frowned. It was Harker's letter that was bothering him. He said so.

For one instant Mary looked impatient.

"I thought we'd settled that," she said.

Rowcliffe sighed.

"What on earth makes you want to go and leave this place when you've spent hundreds on it?"

"I should make pots of money in Leeds."

"But we couldn't live there."

"Why not?"

"It would be too awful. My dear, if it were a big London practice I shouldn't say no. That might be worth while. But whatever should we have in Leeds?"

"We haven't much here."

"We've got the county. You might think of the children."

"I do," he said mournfully. "I do. I think of nothing else but the children—and you. If you wouldn't like it there's an end of it."

"You might think of yourself, dear. You really are *not* strong enough for it."

He felt that he really was not.

He changed the subject.

"I saw Gwenda the other day."

"Looking as young as ever, I suppose?"

"No. Not quite so young. I thought she was looking rather ill."

He meditated.

"I wonder why she never comes."

He really did wonder.

"It's a quarter past seven, Steven."

He rose and stretched himself. They went together to the night nursery where the three children lay in their cots, the little red-haired girls awake and restless, and the dark-haired baby in his first sleep. They bent over them together. Mary's lips touched the red hair and the dark where Steven's lips had been.

They spent the evening sitting by the fire in Rowcliffe's study. The doctor dozed. Mary, silent over her sewing, was the perfect image of tranquillity. From time to time she looked at her husband and smiled as his chin dropped to his breast and recovered itself with a start.

At the stroke of ten she murmured, "Steven, are you ready for bed?"

He rose, stumbling for drowsiness.

As they passed into the square hall he paused and looked round him before putting out the lights.

"Yes" (he yawned). "Ye-hes. I think we shall do very comfortably here for the next seven years."

He was thinking of old Hyslop. He had given him seven years.

LXIV

The next day (it was a Friday), when Mary came home to tea after a round of ineffectual calling she was told that Miss Gwenda was in the drawing-room.

Mary inquired whether the doctor was in.

Dr. Rowcliffe was in but he was engaged in the surgery.

Mary thought she knew why Gwenda had come to-day.

For the last two or three Wednesdays Rowcliffe had left Garthdale without calling at the Vicarage.

He had not meant to break his habit, but it happened so. For, this year, Mary had decided to have a day, from May to October. And her day was Wednesday.

Her sister had ignored her day, and Mary was offended.

She had every reason. Mary believed in keeping up appearances, and the appearance she most desired to keep up was that of behaving beautifully to her sister. This required her sister's co-operation. It couldn't appear if Gwenda didn't. And Gwenda hadn't given it a chance. She meant to have it out with her.

She greeted her therefore with a certain challenge.

"What are you keeping away for? Do you suppose we aren't glad to see you?"

"I'm not keeping away," said Gwenda.

"It looks uncommonly like it. Do you know it's two months since you've been here?"

"Is it? I've lost count."

"I should think you did lose count!"

"I'm sorry, Molly. I couldn't come."

"You talk as if you had engagements every day in Garthdale."

"If it comes to that, it's months since you've been to us."

"It's different for me. I *have* engagements. And I've my husband and children too. Steven hates it if I'm out when he comes home."

"And Papa hates it if *I'm* out."

"It's no use minding what Papa hates. What's making you so sensitive?"

"Living with him."

"Then for goodness sake get away from him when you can. One afternoon here can't matter to him."

Gwenda said nothing, neither did she look at her. But she answered her in her heart. "It matters to *me*. It matters to *me*. How stupid you are if you don't see how it matters. Yet I'd die rather than you should see."

Mary went on, exasperated by her sister's silence.

"We may as well have it out while we're about it. Why can't you look me straight in the face and say plump out what I've done?"

"You've done nothing."

"Well, is it Steven, then? Has he done anything?"

"Of course he hasn't. What *could* he do?"

"Poor Steven, goodness knows! I'm sure I don't. No more does he. Unless——"

She stopped. Her sister was looking her straight in the face now.

"Unless what?"

"My dear Gwenda, don't glare at me like that. I'm not saying things and I'm not thinking them. I don't know what *you're* thinking. If you weren't so nervy you'd own that I've always been decent to you. I'm sure I *have* been. I've always stood up for you. I've **always** wanted to have you here——"

"And why shouldn't you?"

Mary blinked. She had seen her blunder.

"I never said you weren't decent to me, Molly."

"You behave as if I weren't."

"How am I to behave?"

"I know it's difficult," said Mary. The memory of her blunder rankled.

"Are you offended because Steven hasn't been to see you?"

"My *dear* Molly——"

Mary ignored her look of weary tolerance.

"Because you can't expect him to keep on running up to Garthdale when Papa's all right."

"I don't expect him."

"Well then——!" said Mary with the air of having exhausted all plausible interpretations.

"If I were offended," said Gwenda, "should I be here?"

The appearance of the tea-tray and the parlormaid absolved Mary from the embarrassing compulsion to reply. She addressed herself to the parlormaid.

"Tell Dr. Rowcliffe that tea is ready and that Miss Gwendolen is here."

She really wanted Steven to come and deliver her from the situation she had created. But Rowcliffe delayed his coming.

"Is it true that Steven's going to give up his practice?" Gwenda said presently.

"Well no—whatever he does he won't do that," said Mary.

She thought, "So that's what she came for. Steven hasn't told her anything."

"What put that idea into your head?" she asked.

"Somebody told me so."

"He *has* had an offer of Dr. Harker's practice in Leeds, and he'd some idea of taking it. He seemed to think it might be a good thing."

There was a flicker in the whiteness of Gwenda's face. It arrested Mary.

It was not excitement nor dismay nor eagerness, nor even interest. It was a sort of illumination, the movement of some inner light, the shining passage of some idea. And in Gwenda's attitude, as it now presented itself to Mary, there was a curious still withdrawal and detachment. She seemed hardly to listen but to be preoccupied with her idea.

"He thought it would be a good thing," she said.

"I think I've convinced him," said Mary, "that it wouldn't."

Gwenda was stiller and more withdrawn than ever, guarding her idea.

"Can I see Steven before I go?" she said presently.

"Of course. He'll be up in a second——"

"I can't—here."

Mary stared. She understood.

"You're ill. Poor dear, you shall see him this minute." She rang the bell.

LXV

FIVE minutes passed before Rowcliffe came to Gwenda in the study.

"Forgive me," he said. "I had a troublesome patient."

"Don't be afraid. You're not going to have another."

"Come, *you* haven't troubled me much, anyhow. This is the first time, isn't it?"

Yes, she thought, it was the first time. And it would be the last. There had not been many ways of seeing Steven, but this way had always been open to her if she had cared to take it. But it had been of all ways the most repugnant to her, and she had never taken it till now when she was driven to it.

"Mary tells me you're not feeling very fit."

He was utterly gentle, as he was with all sick and suffering things.

"I'm all right. That's not why I want to see you."

He was faintly surprised. "What is it, then? Sit down and tell me."

She sat down. They had Steven's table as a barrier between them.

"You've been thinking of leaving Rathdale, haven't you?" she said.

"I've been thinking of leaving it for the last seven years. But I haven't left it yet. I don't suppose I shall leave it now."

"Even when you've got the chance?"

"Even when I've got the chance."

382

"You said you wanted to go, and you do, don't you?"

"Well, yes—for some things."

"Would you think me an awful brute if I said I wanted you to go?"

He gave her a little queer, puzzled look.

"I wouldn't think you a brute whatever you wanted. Do you mind my smoking a cigarette?"

"No."

She waited.

"Steven——

"I wish I hadn't made you stay."

"You're not making me stay."

"I mean—that time. Do you remember?"

He smiled a little smile of reminiscent tenderness.

"Yes, yes. I remember."

"I didn't understand, Steven."

"Well, well. There's no need to go back on that now. It's done, Gwenda."

"Yes. And I did it. I wouldn't have done it if I'd known what it meant. I didn't think it would have been like this."

"Like what?"

Rowcliffe's smile that had been reminiscent was now vague and obscurely speculative.

"I ought to have let you go when you wanted to," she said.

Rowcliffe looked down at the table. She sat leaning sideways against it; one thin arm was stretched out on it. The hand gripped the paper weight that he had pushed away. It was this hand, so tense and yet so helpless, that he was looking at. He laid his own over it gently. Its grip slackened then. It lay lax under the sheltering hand.

"Don't worry about that, my dear," he said. "It's been all right——"

"It hasn't. It hasn't."

Rowcliffe's nerves winced before her fierce intensity. He withdrew his sheltering hand.

"Just at first," she said, "it was all right. But you see—it's broken down. You said it would."

"You mustn't keep on bothering about what I said."

"It isn't what you said. It's what is. It's this place. We're all tied up together in it, tight. We can't get away from each other. It isn't as if I could leave. I'm stuck here with Papa."

"My dear Gwenda, did I ever say you ought to leave?"

"No. You said *you* ought. It's the same thing."

"It isn't. And I don't say it now. What is the earthly use of going back on things? That's what makes you ill. Put it straight out of your mind. You know I can't help you if you go on like this."

"You can."

"My dear, I wish I knew how. You asked me to stay and I stayed. I can understand *that*."

"If I asked you to go, would you go, Steven? Would you understand that too?"

"My dear child, what good would that do you?"

"I want you to go, Steven."

"You want me to go?"

He screwed up his eyes as if he were trying to see the thing clearly.

"Yes," she said.

He shook his head. He had given it up.

"No, my dear, you don't want me to go. You only think you do. You don't know what you want."

"I shouldn't say it if I didn't."

"Wouldn't you! It's exactly what you would say. Do you suppose I don't know you?"

She had both her arms stretched before him on the table now. The hands were clasped. The little thin hands implored him. Her eyes implored him. In the tense clasp and in the gaze there was the passion of entreaty that she kept out of her voice.

But Rowcliffe did not see it. He had shifted his position, sinking a little lower into his chair, and his head was bowed before her. His eyes, somberly reflective, looked straight in front of him under their bent brows.

He seemed to be really considering whether he would go or stay.

"No," he said presently. "No, I'm not going."

But he was dubious and deliberate. It was as if he still weighed it, still watched for the turning of the scale.

The clock across the market-place struck eight. He gathered himself together. And it was then as if the strokes, falling on his ear, set free some blocked movement in his brain.

"No," he said, "I don't see how I can go, as things are. Besides—it isn't necessary."

"I see," she said.

She rose. She gave him a long look. A look that was still incredulous of what it saw.

His eyes refused to meet it as he rose also.

They stood so for a moment without any speech but that of eyes lifted and eyes lowered.

Still without a word, she turned from him to the door. He sprang to open it.

Five minutes later he was aware that his wife had come into the room.

"Has Gwenda gone?" he said.

"Yes. Steven——" There was a small, fluttering fright in Mary's eyes. "Is there anything the matter with her?"

"No," he said. "Nothing. Except living with your father."

LXVI

GWENDA had no feeling in her as she left Rowcliffe's house. Her heart hid in her breast. It was so mortally wounded as to be unaware that it was hurt.

But at the turn of the white road her heart stirred in its hiding-place. It stirred at the sight of Karva and with the wind that brought her the smell of the flowering thorn-trees.

It discerned in these things a power that would before long make her suffer.

She had no other sense of them.

She came to the drop of the road under Karva where she had seen Rowcliffe for the first time.

She thought, "I shall never get away from it."

Far off in the bottom the village waited for her.

It had always waited for her; but she was afraid of it now, afraid of what it might have in store for her. It shared her fear as it crouched there, like a beaten thing, with its huddled houses, naked and blackened as if fire had passed over them.

And Essy Gale stood at the Vicarage gate and waited. She had her child at her side. The two were looking for Gwenda.

"I thought mebbe something had 'appened t' yo," she said.

As if she had seen what had happened to her she hurried the child in out of her sight.

Ten minutes to ten.

In the small dull room Gwenda waited for the hour of her deliverance. She had taken up her sewing and her book.

The Vicar sat silent, waiting, he too, with his hands folded on his lap.

And, loud through the quiet house, she heard the sound of crying and Essy's voice scolding her little son, avenging on him the cruelty of life.

On Greffington Edge, under the risen moon, the white thorn-trees flowered in their glory.

THE END.

was born in Liverpool in 1863, the only daughter and youngest child of the six children of Amelia and William Sinclair. In the 1870s her father's shipowning business went bankrupt and the family moved first to Essex, then to Gloucester, later to Devon. Her parents lived apart, due in part to her father's intermittent alcoholism. Her brothers suffered from inherited heart disease, four dying before their fifties, most of them nursed by their sister. May Sinclair had no formal education until her eighteenth year, which she spent at Cheltenham Ladies' College taught by the great educator Dorothea Beale. Under her influence, she began to read philosophy, psychology and Greek literature, and to write, first poetry, then fiction. She published her first novel, *Audrey Craven,* in 1897 and with its publication moved to London where she continued to live with her mother until her death in 1901.

From 1908 she was active in the fight for the vote, working with writers such as Violet Hunt and Cicely Hamilton for the Suffragist cause. Critically acclaimed in both Britain and America as one of the great writers of the Georgian Age, she was the friend and contemporary of Wells, James, Hardy, Galsworthy, Ford Madox Ford, and of Dorothy Richardson, about whose work she first coined the famous phrase 'stream of consciousness'. She was one of the earliest English novelists to be influenced by the work of Freud and Jung, and was influenced too by her friendships with the Imagists Richard Aldington, Ezra Pound and Hilda Doolittle. She wrote poetry, criticism, philosophical works, short stories, and twenty-four novels in all, the best known of which are *The Divine Fire* (1904); *The Tree of Heaven* (1917); *Mary Olivier: A Life* (1919) — also published as a Virago Modern Classic — and *Life and Death of Harriett Frean* (1922). For the last fifteen years of her life May Sinclair was incapacitated by Parkinson's disease. In 1932 she retired to Buckinghamshire, where she died in 1946.